The Devil

Taylor K Scott

This is a work of fiction. Names, characters, places and incidents are either the product of the author's imagination or are used fictitiously. Any resemblance to actual persons, living or dead, business establishments, events, or locales is entirely coincidental.

Copyright ©2023 Taylor K. Scott

All rights reserved. No part of this publication may be reproduced, stored in or introduced into a retrieval system, or transmitted, in any form, or by any means (electronic, mechanical, photocopying, recording, or otherwise) without prior written permission of the author.

Warning: The following work of fiction describes content of a sexual nature. It also discusses sensitive themes including violence and mental health issues. See Author's Note for more information.

DEDICATION

To my fellow cygnet inkers, a special group of authors, readers and reviewers, set up by the amazing TL Swan, whose books got me hooked on this wonderful journey.

MUSICAL INFLUENCES

No Air – Jordin Sparks

Kissing You – Des'ree

Iris – Goo Goo Dolls

Say Something – A Great Big World and Christina Aquilera

I Wanna Dance With Somebody – Marian Hill

Numb – Linkin Park

Dangerous Woman – Ariana Grande

Breathin – Ariana Grande

Stronger – Sugababes

I Fell in Love with the Devil – Avril Lavigne (The Devil-Book 3)

Into Your Arms – Witt Lowry

Apologize – Timbaland (feat. One Republic)

Here With Me - Dido

Keeping Your Head Up - Birdy

ACKNOWLEDGMENTS

Thank you to the community of writers and readers out there who have answered questions, read my work, given me advice, and shared my work. Thank you to all of you!

To my beta readers, Liz Rogers, Freya Martin, Charlotte Mieu, Phoebe Black, and Mama Sue, who all took the time to read this book during the early stages. Just to have someone read my work and offer their opinion is always so empowering for me. I sincerely appreciate you offering me your time, support, and advice.

I must also thank my poor, suffering husband for supporting me through my obsession with writing. Not only has he had to live with my reading habit, which is becoming more and more consuming, but also has the added bonus of losing me to my own works of fiction. Know that I love you dearly, as well as our two beautiful girls, and appreciate all the encouragement you have given me.

Finally, but most importantly, thanks to everyone who has taken a chance on my novel. I hope it hasn't disappointed, and that you might take a chance to read some of my upcoming releases. Thank you so much again.

Author's Note
(Trigger warnings)

I write books that encompass more than a central romance plot. Experience with mental health, living with PTSD, and working with people from different backgrounds have all helped me to shape my characters and their storylines. A lot of what I've included in my books is based on real people and real situations, or at least, a version of them. This includes my own experiences. I write stories that are sometimes hard to read; I don't shy away from trauma. I also don't write flawless characters because real people are never without fault. My characters might act irrationally or choose an option that an objective person might question, but they do, based on what I've seen and lived, behave realistically.

This series contains scenes that may be hard to read and may trigger some people. They include sexual, physical, and emotional abuse. This series has a major theme of mental health running through it, including attempted suicide, depression, abuse, bullying, anxiety, and PTSD.

Part I – The Devil's Plaything

"Be careful, the devil can hear your prayers too. He doesn't always come with horns and a pitchfork, sometimes he comes dressed up like everything you wanted."

-UNKNOWN

Prologue

Let us begin with a party.

An innocent night of care-free fun amongst teenagers.

Nate Carter, the popular boy with a heart, was throwing one of his infamous bashes that aimed to let the kids of Westlake Prep let down their hair and give into their urges within the safe confines of the Carter household.

Everyone knew who the Carters were, but none more so than me. After all, I grew up with them, lived with them day in, day out, right up until just over a year ago. I was their big sister, their little sister, and their best friend. ***Was*** being the operative word. Now, we barely talk.

I never attended Nate's party. In fact, I wasn't anywhere near my parents' house that night. I was lying on the kitchen floor of my two-bedroom cottage, far away from anyone, knocked out cold. While I lay there oblivious to the world around me, together with the mess of another dinner thrown across the floor in a fit of rage, my daughter was sleeping soundly upstairs. And for that, I am thankful. My Jessica is everything to me.

Conversely, my husband, Evan, was nowhere to be seen. But he would return; he always does. I might not have been at that party, but I felt the repercussions of what happened that night. I lost a little bit more of myself, brushed away another few bruises for another day, and pushed back more bad memories for my future self to deal with. So long as Jessica needs me, I will absorb the pain, become that little bit more numb, and plaster on my fake smile for all of them.

And it works; no one sees and no one asks. So long as I am what they expect me to be, they are happy with me tied up inside of their little, neat box. My brothers have always been forgiven for stepping outside the boundaries, but as the girl, I was destined to fulfill a role of subservience, obedience, and a contentedness to be what I essentially am – a function. A wife, a mother, and a daughter who always does as she's told. A girl who never steps outside the lines, never answers back, and never complains. And perhaps I could have lived in this role without question or the need for more. But then I met ***him***.

To tell my story, I have to go back much further in time. In fact, I need to start with someone else's history. Someone who is as damaged as I am. Someone who is feared. Someone who has a reputation so bad, I was warned by my entire family to keep away from him. Someone who demanded that I be his. Someone who won my heart. Someone I lost.

This is not just my story, it's also his. This is the story of how the little mouse fell in love with ***The Devil***.

Chapter 1

Past

Lucius

Have you ever wondered what it feels like to have everything you thought you knew to wither away and die in a matter of moments? Alas, the day my mother died was not the first time I was forced into feeling like this. Being only thirteen when she passed, you would think this was my first introduction to heartbreak, especially when I tell you she killed herself with a piece of rope and an old tree in the backyard. To be fair to her, she had at least chosen to wait until I was at school before carrying out her task that day; I suppose I should be grateful for that small mercy. Magda, my nanny and housekeeper, was the first to discover her lifeless body, however, it had taken both the gardener and her husband to cut her down. Everything was nicely cleaned up before I returned home from school and with my tea already waiting for me – spaghetti meatballs; it was Tuesday after all. Meatballs were always served up on a Tuesday, even when your mother decides to take a premature exit from the world. I still refuse to touch my once-upon-a-time favorite meal.

I had already had a thoroughly frustrating day, all because Tommy Slater had decided to start a fight with my best friend, Eric. Being the brains of the friendship, I had had to get involved, if only to prevent them from killing one another. Of course, all the thuggery got the better of me, resulting in Eric and I having to participate in a week's worth of after-school detention. The truly sad part of all this was the fact that it was all over hurt pride during a football match, a game I could care less about. However, I couldn't stand by and let Tommy-the-gorilla-Slater pummel Eric into a bloody mess. Our counterattack was extremely simple and not at all sophisticated; I held the lump of a boy from behind while Eric kicked him in an area that would be sure to keep him hobbling along for the next few days.

Had I simply returned home to normality, I might have brushed aside my anger and seen the funny side. However, this wasn't ever going to happen after my father sat me down to inform me that the woman who had given birth to me had decided to end her own life. No, after that little chat, I had had about enough of this particular Tuesday. Life was, forgive my crassness, a shitshow, and you only had yourself to rely on.

"Lucius," Paul had begun, sounding suitably grave as he sat down next to me, depressing the sofa cushions under his large frame. "I guess now is a pretty God-awful time to tell you the truth, but after what's happened today, I think this conversation is long overdue."

He then paused for breath while I waited with a disinterested expression on my pubescent face. Do not judge my obnoxious reaction just yet, for truth be known, I already knew what he was going to tell me. His 'big reveal' was going to be thoroughly anticlimactic, for me at least.

"Now, this doesn't change anything between us," he

reassured me before he'd even ventured to tell me the actual bad news. "But I'm not your biological father, son."

I remember smirking over his choice of words. You see, the bitterness of it had begun to seep in years ago, when I had first found this out.

"But in every other sense of the word, I am still your dad."

Looking pale and grief-stricken, he finally sat back and sighed with a hint of relief. He remained staring at me as if he was giving me the time and space to let that revelation sink in.

"Ok," I replied with an arrogant shrug of my shoulders. My cold reaction to such news had caused him to lurch forward with a look of shock and hurt written all over his puffy, red face. I don't remember feeling angry at Paul, just knew that I was angry. I had already been an angry child for so long, I had forgotten what it felt like to not feel such an emotion in my everyday life. I knew he loved me, and I knew he had loved her, but it still didn't make up for the fact that she hadn't loved me. My.Mother.Did.Not.Love.Me.

"*Ok*?! Is that all?" he eventually gasped, to which I merely nodded before asking if I could go outside and kick the ball around. My laidback reaction to everything that had come to pass that day was enough to silence him for a good five minutes or so, all the while I stared back at him with an expression that only spoke of my desire to go outside and play.

"Lucius, you've just lost your mom, I'm not the man you thought I was, have you nothing to say? Nothing to ask me?"

I pretended, for his sake, to at least think about it, but eventually settled on a shake of my head.

"Ok, son, yeah, go ahead."

What my poor father didn't know was that when I was nine, I had blown up in an almighty tantrum that was all aimed at my mother. She wouldn't let me go to Eric's birthday party because she didn't approve of him. So, I kicked and screamed and threw things all over the place.

When I had eventually expelled all my energy, I was, quite rightly, sent to my room and told to keep my ass there until I could show her more respect. I remained brooding up in my room until I heard Paul return home from work because I was just that stubborn; I still am. In fact, it was another two hours before I ventured out, finally ready to apologize for my deplorable behavior.

On my very first step outside of my room, it was as though I had walked inside of a Stephen King novel. The house had been eerily quiet, dark, and atmospheric. I recall sensing the presence of something nightmarish, an intangible fog that's only purpose was to suck the living soul out of unsuspecting pre-teen boys. In the back of my mind, I knew I was being foolish, allowing my immature fears to take over the rational part of my brain. However, the back of my mind was wrong, for something was about to reveal itself to me, something that would diminish my soul, rendering its owner dark and unforgiving.

My mother sounded exasperated when I finally heard her tired, somewhat frantic voice. Paul and Mom always took to the living room after dinner, so I came to the logical conclusion that I had missed the evening meal in my attempts to punish her by sulkily remaining inside of my room for hours. Though that didn't bother me nearly as much as the obvious disdain lacing every word that was coming out through my mother's lips. Lips that smiled at me, lips that uttered placations - 'I love you baby', 'I'm proud of you, son', and 'whatever you want, mio topolino' – lips that kissed me goodnight. However, the words escaping through those lips now were anything but affectionate and reaffirming. Now, I got to hear what she really thought of her 'topolino'.

"Oh, come on, Elenore, you love Lucius," I heard Paul practically begging her. "He's a nine-year-old boy being a nine-year-old boy. That's all!"

"Do I, Paul? Do I love him?" Her words hit me like a sledgehammer covered in torturous spikes that were ready to pierce through every crevice of my heart. "How can I love someone that reminds me of *him*? He has those same eyes, that same smirk, even that same cruel laugh. He is an exact replica of his biological father!"

"You can't think like that, Elenore." Paul's shoes shuffled across the room before coming to a dead-end stop, presumably closing the gap between him and the woman who can't even bear to look at me. "He knows nothing of his birth father, and besides, it's not Lucius' fault. That boy idolizes you, adores you, how can you say these things?"

"I can't help it; I see the same evil in him," she replied, sounding desperate, as though a monster was about to unleash itself from her son's human casing any day now. "I didn't at first, he was just a little kid, but today, I saw it. I can't ignore it anymore, Paul. How can I love someone who has that in him? My poor boy is going to end up alone. No one can love him, he's the product of a monster, can't you see that?" Her words began to spill out in a jumbled mess of contradictions before she finally cried out the words that could never be taken back, could never be forgiven, and would never allow me to trust another woman again. "I should have terminated him!"

"I don't know how you can talk like this! Have you been drinking?" Paul gasped at the same time as his shoes took a few steps back over the parquet flooring. "Elenore, darling, I love you, but I'm worried about you. Lucius can never hear you talking like this."

"Maybe," she mumbled, more to herself than to anyone else. "Maybe you're right; maybe I need to go to bed."

Her rational brain might well have been starting to take over at this moment, however, my head was anything but rational. Paul was not my blood, and my mother, my unconditional love and protector, had just wished I never existed. She'd condemned me to loneliness and a lifetime of therapy I would stubbornly refuse to go to. So, ask yourself, what would a nine-year-old boy do in my position? I cannot speak for any other kid who has found himself questioning everything in a life that had been built on lies, but as for me, I got the hell out of there and enclosed my heart in an icy case, vowing to never let anyone near it again. Self-preservation turned me into the devil of an asshole I would become.

Years on and now with a dead mother, my mind is clearer, harder, and lacks the capacity to suffer fools like Tommy Slater. The imbecile shouldn't have tried to jump me on the day after my mother had ended her life. He should have left me well alone. But being one brain cell away from an amoeba, he ignored my warning and tried to attack me anyway. I was forced to teach Tommy a hard lesson by gifting him with a broken nose and a black eye. It was not only worth it to see his pain, but to also show the gathered crowd what would happen if they tried to replicate Tommy's blunt course of action. People soon came to realize that I had absolutely no qualms about beating someone to a bloody pulp if I so chose to. I had no qualms about telling anyone exactly what I thought of them, even when it led to a parent-teacher meeting that would have Paul reaching for the top-shelf whiskey bottle afterward. I had no qualms about destroying anything or anyone if I felt it was necessary for my own amusement.

THE DEVIL

I don't want their pity or their understanding, I want them to realize that if you come after me, I will destroy you. If you try and get close to me, I will burn you. If you try and hurt me, I will not break, I will make you crumble.

Fortunately for most, if they leave me well alone, I usually lack the inclination to bother with them. Unfortunately, for my little mouse, she ignited a passion for more, as well as emotions I had wished to repress. She never intentionally set out to cross me, but cross me she did, and in the cruelest way possible. She brought my heart back to life; she made me fall in love with her.

Chapter 2

Helena

My favorite film of all time is *The Sound of Music*. Cam used to jibe me about it, telling me I was the real-life version of Maria, the nun who fell in love with Captain Von Trapp, the uptight, grumpy, but oh, so handsome hero who melted over Maria's gentle heart and nurturing nature. I never took his words as an insult, for I could fully relate to Maria. Like me, she hid herself away in a house that taught her subservience, obedience, and virtue. It wasn't wholly my daddy's fault for being as old-fashioned as he was, he was merely a product of his time and his parents' stern upbringing. And my childhood, though less adventurous than what my brothers were allowed to get away with, was a good and happy one. But perhaps that's because children know no different from their own experiences. When I reached puberty and attended high school, I saw the stark differences between me and other girls my age. They had so much freedom, so much confidence, so much of what my brothers had, and of what I did not.

I remember watching them with curiosity, studying the way the boys would flirt with them, and how they would flirt back without fear. Sure, I had seen it with Cameron and his friends, but this was different; these people were my age; they were who I was supposed to make friends with. Not that I did. I lacked the confidence to engage in any sort of conversation with them. If they tried to talk to me, I would have to run through what I might say before I uttered the words out loud, by which time, they had given up and moved on.

Now, at seventeen years old, I still haven't spoken to a boy in any real depth other than with my brothers. Cam and Nate always tell people it's because I am shy, which I am. So painfully so, I'm amazed I've made it this far, standing in front of my cousin's house that is miles away from my hometown. Worse still, I'm about to spend the entire summer here. I say 'house', but it looks more like a five-star resort, something that wouldn't be out of place in a centerfold in a property guide for the rich and famous. I literally have to crane my neck to see the terracotta tiles decorating the roof of this fancy villa. It makes our five-bed detached home look like a hovel in the middle of a dystopian slum city.

The first thing I notice, when I get close enough, is a huge set of wooden double doors that stand between me and the interior of this ridiculously lavish abode. My eyes soon travel along the fancy tiled brickwork, all the while I struggle to get over the countless intricately designed windows lining the equally numerous sets of walls closing it all in. Just over the back, there is a circular centerpiece that adorns a set of skylights. It must be pretty spectacular to be up in that room at night; I could quite happily live in that part of the building all on its own.

This excessive piece of real estate is way out of my comfort zone and makes me more nervous than mixed-sex swimming lessons at school. I feel exactly like Maria when she arrives at the Von Trapp grand estate, feeling small and nervous. I can do academia, I can do exams, and I can do pop quizzes, all in my sleep. I can write an essay with precision, facts, and flair and hand it over with a smugness my brothers usually reserve for when they look at themselves in the mirror. I know I will ace it and can predict my A plus before the teacher has even read it. But this? Staying with unfamiliar people, even those to who I am related, is like my own version of Dante's seven circles of hell.

So, why am I here, you may well ask. Why have I traveled over seven hours in a hot, stuffy metal tube of a train, with no air conditioning, sat between a man who smelled of stale sweat and a screaming toddler whose mother chose to wear headphones and listen to techno on repeat? I almost felt sorry for the little guy, right up until he kicked me in the shin and yelled in my ear with a cocktail of spit and snot spraying all over my face. I should have seen this as a sign that I had made the wrong choice. Because believe it or not, this was my choice and my choice alone.

The other option available was to attend some cheesy camp in the middle of the woods with a bunch of counselors who are probably only about a year or two older than me. The very thought of staying in a hut filled with a bitchy group of kids from a fucked-up version of the Brady Bunch appealed to me about as much as spending the summer in a nudist's colony. Fortunately, my parents had only subjected me to summer camp a handful of times, all pre-puberty, but that was more than enough for an introvert like me.

After having stayed at one of these godforsaken places, I knew I wouldn't survive another summer crocheting friendship blankets, canoeing across murky, freezing cold lakes, or preparing for an end-of-camp production. Not to mention the enforced attendance at weekly discos where, apparently, reading is not encouraged. Keep us young, dumb, and buying into the belief that wearing make-up to gain the attention of some horny boy is what every girl should strive for in life. No thank you, not going to happen. I'm too damn old for that kind of torture.

Cam is already at college, so opted to stay there for the summer, working part-time by day and on his computer projects by night. Nate, being the party boy that he is, thrived in places like camp, so it took him less than a minute to make his choice. He was guaranteed a prime position of popularity among the masses, as well as getting plenty of action with over-sexed teenage girls.

So, what was a girl with limited options to do? Mom and Dad were going to be travelling across Europe for a second honeymoon, aka, time away from their kids, and for some unknown reason, they didn't deem it appropriate for me to stay alone at home. If I were Cam or Nate, I would have fully agreed with their over cautious decision to not let me stay. They were a nightmare waiting to happen without proper adult supervision. But me? People joked that I was even more responsible than my folks.

Though it took me several hours of working up the courage to confront them, I eventually approached my father with an indignant stance and an expression that was meant to say confident, but most likely only revealed how nervous I was.

Mom had smiled with affection and encouragement while trying to explain that it was for my own good. She wanted me to get out there, make friends and enjoy my youth, whereas Dad spouted out his usual spiel about fearing for my safety, that it wasn't a good idea for a vulnerable young girl like me to be staying all by herself. My point-blank refusal to go to camp with the added threat of me trying to canoe away but probably drowning in the process, had Mom suggesting that I stay with Merial, my cousin of the same age. Her mom, my aunt, had recently married some ridiculously rich guy, her very own Mr Von Trapp, who was widowed a good few years ago.

Merial and I had always got on well enough, but I can't pretend that we would have been friends if it wasn't for the fact that we were related. Merial is an 'It' girl who uses text language in everyday speech. She collects boyfriends like they're stickers to go in the latest collect-them-all book. Shakespeare's plays only exist in the form of the latest movie version, while her reading material consists of 'Just Seventeen' and other such useless information.

That being said, as much as I can sit here and judge her superficial lifestyle, I can't deny that I live vicariously through her. She's like my very own soap opera, gifting me stories of groping on a first date and sneaking out to college parties. I listen with as much fascination as I do with the girls at school. Now that her mother has married Mr Big Balls lawyer with a hefty income to supplement her every whim, her exploits seem to have gotten even more exciting.

Back to the here and now, trying to process all of the exuberance exhibited in this one mansion, I find myself in front of the gates of Mordor, or at least that's what it feels like. My balled fist hardly makes a pop when I throw it against the wooden door. My sporting abilities have never really impressed anyone, unlike Nate and Cam who both made it big on the football field during their high school careers. On the rare occasions I've been in contact with a ball, I always found myself putting in a lot of effort only to fall flat on my face.

Muttering a curse, I draw back my hand and contemplate calling Merial to let her know I'm outside, apparently incapable of doing something as simple as knocking on a door. However, someone must be watching all this from above and has decided to throw me a pity gift because when I look to the side, there's a small button with which to ring the doorbell.

THE DEVIL

Disney's theme tune begins ringing from inside and I have to stifle a laugh, knowing that this will be an Aunty Jen fixture. If nothing else, she is a straight-up Disney nut. She even married her first husband at the iconic castle in Florida, much to Merial's embarrassment. Too bad the marriage wasn't the stuff of fairy tales and shiny, cartoon dreams. Dear old Uncle Vince had a little gambling problem, exacerbated by alcohol and drugs. When Meriel was only five years old, he cleared out their accounts and hasn't been seen since. Another reason I'm rooting for her recent marriage to San Fran's millionaire lawyer of the century.

I don't know Paul very well due to only having met him at their wedding. He seemed nice enough - polite, friendly, smart, and attractive for an older guy. You could see how smitten Jen was, though this only made my father feel all the more anxious for his little sister. She has a pattern of falling hard for men, giving them all she has, only to have them throw it back in her face in a spectacular fashion.

It turns out they had met each other on a skiing holiday after she and Merial had won a little sum on scratch cards. Jen's motto has always been 'spend it, don't save it', which she has successfully passed onto her daughter. Dad has had to bail her out on more than one occasion, but he's never complained, not even once. Mom chooses not to interfere but secretly resents the fact that Jen has never been forced to learn from her mistakes; she merely runs to her big brother when she needs saving from them.

Just as the chirpy doorbell comes to an end, the door is thrust open by the spawn of the devil himself - Lucius Hastings. The boy is either going to be a serial killer or a villainous mastermind one day. From what little I've seen of him, and what Meriel has told me, he is the ultimate predator - cold, calculating, intimidating as hell, and all wrapped up in a couldn't-give-shit attitude. At Paul and Jen's wedding, he was broody and aloof; he never uttered a word until we walked in on him and my brother's date exploring one another's tonsils in one of the reception rooms. Suffice it to say, the scene wasn't taken at all well by my brother, Cam, who decided to lunge at the one guy who has a bigger ego than my siblings combined. I remember his smug, self-satisfied grin when my father had had to pull him and Cameron apart. He taunted Cam with a raise of his brow and a wipe of his mouth with his thumb pad, all thrown in with a sardonic smile. Believe me when I say, it was an incredibly uncomfortable ride back home that evening.

Now, lucky me gets to come face-to-face with Lucius Hastings once again, only this time, there're no parental figures to hide behind, just me, myself, and I. I guess his satanic attitude rubs off on me because as soon as he opens the door, snarling at the overly happy ending to the Disney theme tune, I feel the need to press it again. *'For you, brother,'* I think inside of my head. His towering figure fills up the door frame with a sneer and a mutter of "Shut the fuck up," for the inanimate object that is still telling us all to *'wish upon a star'*. His murderous expression almost makes me regret my little rebellion, particularly when he looks me over from top to bottom with what I can only describe as disgust in his darkened eyes.

I don't usually like to cast aspersions on people I barely know, but Lucius Hastings has to be the rudest, moodiest, and most arrogant man I've ever met. He is a whole new level of bad guy, which, of course, makes him practically God-like to the opposite sex. The fallen angel himself come to reap his own source of amusement. Girls and women drop their panties for him, even though he promises them nothing more than his own gratification and an immediate case of memory loss after he's had you and tossed you aside. Fortunately, Dad has schooled me over the years to avoid boys like Lucius, warning me of what would happen once

I had given into his charms.

"You know, Helena, it's not the same for you as it is for your brothers. Unfair as it may seem, girls are judged more harshly than boys. And I know you, Helena, you would fall apart if you fell for someone who didn't love you back. You are beautiful, intelligent, and so important to me. I don't want you to follow in my little sister's footsteps, I always want to feel proud of you. Save yourself for a good man, a man with a bright future and nothing but love for you. Will you do that for me, honey?"

"Ok, Daddy."

The day after this conversation with my father, I was given Cameron's input:

"Look, Helena, you can date whoever the hell you like. Personally, I think Dad is way too old-fashioned when it comes to you; it actually pisses me off most of the time. However, when it comes to Lucius Hastings, I have to agree with him. Some of the guys at college used to go to his school, and let's just say, he didn't have the nicest reputation. Normally, I would say let the guy prove himself before listening to gossip, but after Jen's wedding, I think we both know he's as shitty as they come. I wouldn't trust the motherfucker as far as I could throw him. So, though it pains me to do the overbearing big brother bit, I need you to promise you'll stay away from him."

His maniacal pacing up and down had made me smile, but after his speech, I simply scoffed before reassuring him with the fact that I didn't think Lucius would be a problem. Fortunately, guys like that don't come near girls like me. In fact, there're very few guys who do come near me, and if I'm honest, that suits me just fine.

"Fuck," Lucius mutters, shaking his head with a look of

pure derision, one that makes him appear both bored and humored all at the same time. Looking up at the sky, he lets out a heavy sigh, and I half wonder if he's going to slam the door in my face. However, then he looks right at me, scanning me from head to toe with a confused frown.

"If I have had any kind of sexual encounter with you in the last three months, I wouldn't remember. Jase has been giving out bad batches of weed, so I was most likely out of it. Plus…" he trails off with a smirk and a study of my outfit, "…I don't ever return for seconds, so take the wholly innocent, country Laura-fucking-Ingles look and crawl back to wherever the hell you came from. It's a waste of time."

The door begins to close as he swings it effortlessly with one of his large hands. I have to put both of mine up to actually stop it from hitting back in my face. My self-defense obviously pisses him off, given that he's now glaring at me with a clenched jaw and a *'how dare you'* scowl written across his dark features. Normally, I would be shrinking back, heeding my father's words of warning to have as little to do with this man as possible, however, something tells me to fight back, and not be silenced. It's the weirdest sensation, for I've never had it before, especially not with a man who is also virtually a stranger.

"Lucius Hastings, ever the charmer I see," I say politely with a fake, sugary smile. "I'm sure if I had slept with you, I would have remembered it by the visit to the GUM clinic I would have forced myself to attend." I sigh as I drop my heavy bag to the ground, feeling good about getting a hold of myself and my pride. "Not to mention the abrasive scrubbing I would have needed to remove you from crawling all over my skin."

Lucius rubs his freshly shaven chin with a contemplative expression before slowly lifting the corners of his mouth into a wicked smile, laughing at me for his own personal enjoyment. I can't make out what he's thinking about exactly, but whatever it is, it's probably vile and enough to make me vomit.

"Well, hell, perhaps you should stick around. I have a few buddies who wouldn't mind putting that smart mouth to good use."

There it is, that vomit-inducing mind that's enough to make me shudder over his vile suggestion.

"Is Merial home?" I ask, sounding completely exasperated by his need to be a complete ass at any given opportunity. Though, if I'm being honest, I can't help feeling a little excited over my newfound confidence away from my father's old-fashioned judgment. "I'm her cousin, Helena. We met at your father's wedding. You groped my brother's date."

He looks to the ground and scratches his head as if trying to remember, but I know he recalls pawing at someone else's date all too well. He's cocky, just like my brothers, though in a completely disrespectful way.

"Don't worry, sweetheart," he says with a grin, "I know who you are."

Surprised he did remember who *I* was, I drop my mouth open, but can't think of a single thing to say. Amused by my speechlessness, he takes the opportunity to move in close, with his lips only a mere inch or two away from my cheek.

"I just wanted to see that sexy little blush of yours." I feel my face screw up at the same time as I gasp over his audacity. "I'm also betting that if you'd have slept with *any* guy, you would have written it in a 'Dear Diary' moment. But you and I both know that's never happened. Not. Even. Close."

He withdraws and begins to chew on a piece of gum,

enjoying the angry expression he's managed to put on my face.

"Hels!" Merial shouts out from the stairwell behind. She's all smiles and perfect, white teeth coming at me, and with way too much enthusiasm for a post-meeting with her stepbrother. "I can't believe you're here!"

"Laters, virgin!"

Lucius slips away quietly, but not before a quick insult and a lazy wave as he walks back into his grand house. Guess I have a new nickname, as sophisticated and original as it is, I don't really care at this moment in time. Being a virgin is hardly a cause for a mental breakdown, so why not let him have it.

Merial frowns at me at first, but then rolls her eyes in an irritated fashion when she seems to remember that we're dealing with her evil stepbrother. Donning a pair of high wedges and a pair of Daisy Dukes, she still bends down to pick up my bag. It's hardly surprising that she's exceptionally more polite than Lucius, but it still doesn't make me judge him any less for it.

Chapter 3

Helena

I won't lie; I don't act anywhere near indifferent when I eventually set foot inside the incredible interior of this beautiful house. It's clean and modern, but also homey at the same time. There are white marble and wooden lines with delicate fabric throws and cushions to soften their hardness. It reflects Lucius and Merial to a tee. Though, with the lifeless pieces, it works incredibly well together, blending all the sharp edges with the smooth, soft ones, and is one delicious feast for the eyes.

From the technology on show, I can see it's all top-of-the-line and arranged to subtly blend in with the surroundings. If the house wasn't enough to scream money, then the appliances sure do. However, I'm a simple girl who rarely watches TV and always chooses a paperback over a screen version. I quickly move past the electrical stuff and instead, marvel at the photography on display. I can't paint, draw, sing, or dance, but I do have a passion for photography. I used to own an old manual camera, but after Cam showed me what I could do with a digital print, I reluctantly conceded to buying a more up-to-date version.

There are a few black and white prints dotted around the otherwise blank, white walls, but no personal pictures, only shots of landscapes and inanimate objects. It's a little disappointing because I love taking pictures of people who don't realize you're there; the personal moments and candid shots are my favorites. I had taken some at Jen's wedding but didn't have the confidence to share them with anyone other than my mother. I can picture them now, hidden under my bed like a shameful secret. The photographs hanging here are all artistically shot but give off a cold and detached vibe. They remind me of Lucius, impressive to look at but completely cold in every other way.

Being in danger of losing track of my host, I run up the wooden staircase to catch up with Merial, pausing every few moments to take stock of the modern, dark, square steps with a clean, glass banister. They're the type you wouldn't dare dream of having if you had children or anyone else who needs sturdy support. When we reach the top landing, I fall into line behind Merial, pacing along the corridor with plain, wooden doors running along both sides of the walls. It's like a freaking hotel and I half expect Merial to give me a key card to get into my room. At the end of the corridor, it turns again to go down another, shorter corridor.

This corridor is missing a wall to the left, revealing a small lounge on the floor below, complete with couches, a state-of-the-art music system, a bookcase, a flat screen TV, and a coffee table. Behind the larger sofa, there is a set of expensive bi-fold doors overlooking a swimming pool and decking area. Merial catches me looking around in awe and dons a smug smile across her face.

"There's also a small kitchen and bar beneath us. Mom thought it would be a good idea to put you here so you can feel a bit more self-contained."

It's only then that I notice she has dyed her naturally chestnut-colored hair platinum blonde and has set it poker straight.

She's also perfected her make-up artistry skills; the last time I had seen her, she wore one color of eyeshadow, usually bright blue, and sugar pink lipstick. Today, it looks immaculate, along with her professionally manicured nails that have a layer of thick gloss and tiny gems stuck on them. And to top it all off, I notice her phone fixed firmly inside her tight back pocket, looking ready to be drawn like a cowboy from an old Western movie. Suddenly feeling self-conscious, I glance down at my skinny but ill-fitting jeans, and loose black t-shirt, complete with a pair of flip-flops that have lasted me at least two summers already. My hair is swept back into a French braid, and I already know the small amount of foundation I had put on has now worn off. I could never pull off the flawless look that Merial seems to manage so easily, so I don't even try.

"Make-up tells boys you're up for anything they want," Grandma, on my father's side, whispered when she caught me looking at some lipsticks in the drug store. *"It screams 'cheap'."*

"So, here is your room," she says, leading me into a spacious bedroom that overlooks a garage, no doubt filled with expensive cars, which I hear Paul is passionate about. There's a double bed with clean, crisp white sheets and a small bathroom to the side. It lacks any personality and looks remarkably like a generic hotel suite. It's clean, neat, and probably bigger than my room back home, but it surprises me when I get a sudden pang of homesickness.

"Thank you, it's great," I utter, smiling awkwardly her way. "Where's your room?"

"Oh, I'm on the other side of the house," she informs me, then takes a step closer, as though getting ready to reveal some juicy intel. "You may want to move in with me on the weekends, it can get pretty loud over this way. Lucius likes to use this place when he throws parties, aka, a body, drinking, and dodgy weed fest!"

"He's allowed to throw parties? Frequently?"

"Yeah, Paul and Mom are often away at the weekends. Lucius and I are not invited, if you know what I mean," she says, grinning with a wink, just in case I didn't get the subtle memo.

"If it is what I think you mean, then eww!" I laugh at her as she sits back on the bed with a wicked smile on her face. "So, if he's throwing parties, what do you do?"

"I sometimes go to them," she replies, lowering her voice; I'm not sure who she thinks is listening in, but her secretive behavior is making me want to search the room for hidden bugs. "He may be an ass, but his friends are hot!"

"I see you're still very deep, Meri," I tease. "Can I lock the door during these parties?"

"Sure, here's your key." She walks over to the mechanism on the door and shows me how it works. "It's sometimes a bit stiff but if you lift it up a bit, it usually works."

"Right, I'll keep my phone charged in case I get stuck." I then walk over to practice locking and unlocking the 'sticky' door. "I'll be fine if I can lock it all out. I wouldn't want to interrupt anything going on inside your room, especially if you have eyes on all his 'hot' friends."

Safe in the knowledge that the lock works without too much trouble, I begin to text Mom to let her know I got here ok.

"Good point, Hels," she says, "you always have been the brains. Let's unpack your essentials and I'll take you out. We can do one of the cheesy sightseeing tours of San Fran. If nothing else, it will keep us out of Lucius' way."

Chapter 4

Helena

    I rather enjoyed sightseeing, even with Meri being glued to her phone; embarrassingly, it seemed to know the most inappropriate times in which to beep on the loudest setting possible. And being Meri, it didn't faze her at all when it frequently interrupted the tour guide's talks. Me, on the other hand, I sank so low in my seat, I was almost sitting on the floor with the dried-out chewing gum and stale crumbs. The tuts from the other tourists, together with the tour guide's evil glaring caused my cheeks to burn and my self-esteem to hit rock bottom.

    Meri's driving on the way home isn't at all reassuring either, particularly when she prioritizes catching up with people from her social clique over safety. She frequently violates traffic laws while simultaneously making my heart stop every time she veers too close to an oncoming vehicle. The only thing to make up for it, is listening to her put on a fake voice for all her friends; it's fascinating and a little bit reassuring to know I'm not the only one hiding away my true self around others. In between calls, I get a running commentary of gossip; she dishes the dirt on each of her friends with delicious glee written all over her face. Listening to all of them, however, I don't doubt they all do it to each other. I remind myself that this is exactly why I lead a solitary existence at school.

"Meri!" a voice cries out over the speakers with a sense of urgency. "Crisis call! David has just broken up with Scarlet and she is talking about throwing herself off the Golden Gate Bridge. She's such a fucking drama queen. Can you come?"

"Wait a minute, babes, I have my cousin with me, just hold the line." She presses a button to hold the call while glancing my way, choosing to ignore the fact that my hands are now clutching hold of the seatbelt with white knuckle force. "You wanna come, Hels? Or do you wanna take my key and I can drop you off? Scarlet will probably bitch on and on about David, who is way better off without her," she begins, but then pauses and looks at me with a mild look of guilt, or perhaps sympathy, probably both. "I know this isn't really your scene."

"Oh, hey, you go, I'll be fine." I flap my hand in front of me to signal it's no big deal, only to bring it straight back to grab hold of my seatbelt again. "I need to unpack anyway."

She smiles and air kisses me, a gesture I cannot bring myself to reciprocate.

"Be there in ten, babes," she beams as soon as she presses the button to take the call off hold.

Helena

Back at Hasting's Villa, a nickname for my home away from home, for I've decided this is my very own version of the Von Trapp villa, I quietly open the door and hope no one is home to hear the squeaky hinges that are trying their best to give me away. Silence greets me and I let out a sigh of relief, feeling beyond glad that the place appears to be empty while I don't have

Meri to hide behind. It also gives me the perfect opportunity to wander about and have a good nose around the natural habitat of the uber-rich. This time I avoid the staircase and walk through into a large, airy kitchen. It's incredibly white, almost clinical in appearance, but the wall of glass doors allows the warm sunshine to seep through. It's late afternoon, so there's a hint of orange touching every surface, which only has me feeling homesick again. The glow gives off a feeling of nostalgia, of Sunday afternoons in my father's study, stealing time to be alone with a library of old books.

The greenness that is practically radiating outside pulls me straight over to the glass doors so I can take a better look at the gardens behind Hasting's Villa. An azure blue, large swimming pool sits just beyond the decking and is standing still with sunlight dancing on top of the surface. There are deck chairs and sunbeds dotted around the perimeter, each with matching cushions of navy and white stripes. Standing to the side, there is another bar area, fully stocked with enough booze to serve a post-prom party, and still have some left over for fun. I can only imagine the parties Lucius throws and feel instantly relieved to know I can lock it all out. My room will serve as a haven in which I can hide. If only it had the same collection of books I could find at home, then I could pretend I was still there.

Beyond the pool, there is a manicured lawn of perfectly green grass, mowed in neat, methodical straight lines. It's so immaculate, I doubt anyone ever sets foot on it. To the left of the lawn, there are tennis courts and a wooden barn, a gym maybe. Behind the lawn, there is a garden area with colors gushing out from an array of plants, herbs, and flowers. Even further behind, there is a tall bush marking the boundary of the property.

The garden intrigues me the most, almost calling me to go and explore, but when I try the door handle, I find that it's locked.

Instinctively, I look around for a key but there doesn't seem to be one.

"Looking for something?" a low, velvety voice asks from behind me, making me jump over the sudden intrusion.

I already know it's him without looking, his voice is so distinctive, being that it usually sounds so unconcerned by anything. When I do finally turn to face Lucius, I bite the corner of my mouth to stop a nervous grin from spreading across my face. The last thing I want to do is let him know how much he intimidates me.

Smirking to himself, he saunters over to where I'm standing with his hands in his pockets, looking beyond confident in his own skin; I wonder how that feels. I wonder what it's like to not worry about anything or anyone because you've learned to only satisfy yourself. No one else's opinion matters, just your own. How *does* that feel?

Taking that information on board, I quickly conclude that Lucius can only be here to play with me for his own amusement, so I make an executive decision to say as little as possible. He pulls the small silver key from his jeans' pocket and places it inside the lock of the bi-fold doors, unlocking it with virtually no effort whatsoever as soon as it hits the metal.

"Thank you," I say as quietly as possible while still sounding polite. "Do you usually carry that key around in your pocket?"

What the hell, Helena? I thought we agreed to stay tight-lipped!

Lucius merely offers a shrug before about turning and wandering off into the kitchen to get a glass of water.

"Ok," I whisper to myself, feeling relieved to have gotten away with opening my mouth.

As quickly as I can, I open the door to get away from him. The moment the light breeze hits me, it feels as though I've reached the surface and can breathe again.

With my sights set on the garden ahead, I make my way over, the lawn taking longer to cross than I had first anticipated. As I approach the stunning colorful display before me, I instinctively take in the amazing scents that invade my nostrils. Whoever planted it all included fragrant herbs, roses, jasmine, lilac, and honeysuckle, plus many more I should imagine. It's a bee's personal heaven and I smile as they buzz around collecting their early evening nectar. Butterflies rest on nearby petals, and some early summer seeds are floating around in the breeze. I indulge myself by walking around touching, smelling, and looking; it has me feeling at home.

A clatter of buckets hit the gravel, causing me to jump around to face a tall man who is wearing gardening attire. Standing up straight, he sees me and looks equally surprised by my presence. He's in his mid-forties, I would hazard a guess, and is very handsome. So much so, he could easily pass for a model or an actor. In fact, as I take in his tall, fair, and rough-around-the-edges appearance, he strikes me that he could easily pass for a Viking. Tattoos lace around his incredibly thick arms and he has a few piercings in his left ear. His smile is friendly but with a hint of deviousness behind it, the type that makes you want to spend the afternoon listening to him tell you all about how he got each and every one of those tattoos.

"Sorry to startle you," he says in a friendly manner, his voice croaky and with a hint of what I believe to be an Irish accent. "I'm not used to seeing people out here. You lose your way?"

"No, I'm Merial's cousin," I explain, "just staying here for the summer. Did you do all this?" I ask, gesturing to the garden that hums and flourishes all around us. He nods with obvious pride over his little oasis. "Wow, it's gorgeous," I tell him with a genuine smile. "I love the way you've incorporated wildflowers too; great for the bees."

"Thank you," he says, looking almost shocked that I'd noticed. "I don't usually have any of the inhabitants come and take note of this garden. I'm just left to do whatever I want with it. Kind of lucky, I guess."

"I love being outside," I mutter, almost to myself, "and it smells amazing out here."

"Well, I started with the herbs, then slowly added different flowers. Get a lot of weeds though," he says as he gestures to the full buckets. "You like to garden?"

"I'm ashamed to say I've never really done it. Must be quite therapeutic and rewarding," I reply shyly. Talking to strangers, especially older, rugged, and attractive male ones, is usually about as appealing as a trip to the dentist, but this man surprisingly puts me at ease.

"I can give you your own little plot if you like?" he offers at the same time as peeling off his gardening gloves and chucking them into the bucket of weeds. He then wipes his sweaty brow with the back of his thick, inked arms, and I can't help but stare with a sense of awe. "I'll show you where the potting shed is and tell you which plants would be best to grow at this time of year," he tells me, snapping me out of my ogling. I cannot remember having ever ogled anyone before; it's a strange sensation. "Only if that appeals to you though?"

"I'd love that," I answer rather too enthusiastically, so try to rein it in a little without being too obvious. "Got a whole summer to kill here. I don't exactly fit in with the rest of them. Shocking, huh?"

I laugh softly with my cheeks beginning to burn through embarrassment.

"Me neither," he says, returning my laughter with his own, "but I can't fault them really. Paul and Lucius have been very good to me. Top blokes, both of them." His words instantly cause me to frown, for I've never heard Lucius being described as anything other than wicked. He smiles at me, as though he knows exactly what I'm thinking. "Come by here tomorrow, about ten, and I'll show you everything."

"Thanks, I will."

I smile as I watch him pick up the buckets to take them behind a small wooden shed, feeling strangely pleased with myself for making a friend of sorts.

"Consorting with the help, I see?" Lucius' voice surprises me yet again, but I don't flinch this time. "We can get you your own employee benefits if you like."

He takes a drag on what I can only assume is weed, given the smell which is now cutting through the beautiful fragrances of the garden and invading my senses.

"Can I help you with something, Lucius?" I ask with a sigh of frustration over his lurking around me like a dark shadow. "You seem to be following me about."

He shrugs his shoulders nonchalantly while puffing out some smoke into a thin stream that billows away until it can no longer be seen. I watch it evaporate into nothing while he stares at me without expression.

"Guess I'm just bored," he eventually replies before taking another inhale.

With little else to go on, I smile momentarily, then begin walking through the garden again. He falls into following me around like a figurative and literal bad smell. I can't help but feel a little intimidated in his presence, so find myself talking to cut through the awkward silence.

"Besides, the 'help' as you so eloquently put it, seems to think you treat him well," I level with him, "so you can cut the act with me."

Lucius gives me his trademark smirk, the one I bet a lot of girls think they can fix into something more genuine. I'm sure their efforts only end up with them being just as broken as his smile. He takes his time to respond. However, having two brothers, his procrastinating doesn't faze me.

"It doesn't mean I'll treat *you* well. I rather enjoy my 'act' with certain people."

He remains walking behind me, and I feel the long puff of his smoke float over the back of my neck, causing me to cough when the foul-smelling substance reaches my nose. Ignoring my spluttering, he continues in his quest to engage in this weird conversation with me.

"In answer to your original question, you're a strange one, Carter, you act as though you were born into the wrong century; you've piqued my interest. I wonder how far I can push you before I have you dangling on a string like all the other girls around here."

"Really?" I feign laughter to try and fend off the terrifying thought of him trying to seduce me. "Your life must be very dull if trying to coerce me into liking you is all you have for entertainment."

"Trust me, it wouldn't take much effort, Carter. I'm sure I wouldn't bother if it weren't for the fact that there aren't a lot of other virgins around here your age. Perhaps I can help you to blend in where that area is concerned."

"Oh, how cliché of you. A man lusting after me because my hymen is still intact." He laughs with what sounds like genuine amusement, a sound that has me secretly smiling to myself too.

"Shall I go the whole way and call you 'virgin' from now on?" he teases.

"No, Lucius, my sexual experience or orientation shouldn't be called out for all to hear, and if you have any decency about you, you will respect that."

I hear his footsteps stop behind me for a moment or two, but I just keep walking onward, hoping he'll tire of this conversation and leave me to it.

"You know, my mother used to call me something when I was little, she called me her topolino. It is the perfect name for you, Helena. Yes, my shy topolina."

"What does it mean?" I enquire, trying to sound indifferent, but also grateful that he isn't choosing to call me 'virgin'.

"You will find out," he begins when I turn to face him, to which he smiles.

His arrogance radiates from him, and unfortunately, it is the very thing that makes me finally see why a lot of girls are powerless to resist his lack of charm. He is achingly handsome, well-built, just like my brothers, tall and intoxicating to look at, but it is his condescension that makes him strangely and irritatingly irresistible. The perfect temptation you should resist at all costs.

"Orientation? Are you telling me you're gay?" he asks, snapping me out of my dangerous thoughts. "I can respect any woman choosing one of their own over the opposite sex, particularly when the male of the species often lacks any kind of sophistication. Though, I have to admit, to learn that I have nothing that might excite you would be extremely disappointing. So…are you?"

"Maybe," I reply with barely any breath left inside of me after hearing his admission. He notices, and it pleases him, so I turn around to continue walking.

He doesn't respond, just keeps walking behind me. There is no urgency in his movements, and for a long while, we walk in silence, right up until I reach the end of the path and turn around to come back again. He blocks my way with his tall and imposing figure, making no attempt to move. I look right into his eyes, blue like the Caribbean Sea, before politely asking him to let me through. For a moment or two, I worry he's not going to, that instead, he's going to keep me under his gaze until I submit to his temptation. But then he stands to the side and gestures for me to walk past. He, in turn, falls back into following behind me again.

"Are you going to do this all afternoon?" I ask him coolly. "Because I have two brothers who annoy me constantly, so you won't get a rise out of me."

"I don't know, haven't decided yet," he teases, and contrary to what I just said to him, he starts to make me feel hot with discomfort. "So, how come you, Topolina, are so much different from your cocky brothers?"

"Different?" I ask innocently and with a thick layer of

confusion. "What makes you say that?"

I'm glad he can't see the grin on my face because the differences between mine and my brothers' attitudes in life would take all night to itemize out loud.

"Please, do not insult my intelligence, nor yours, we both know you are a complete contrast to them. Both your brothers ooze confidence; they positively rule in popular crowds and no doubt kiss their own reflection every morning. You, on the other hand, intentionally dress to cover yourself, wear little make-up, tie your hair back like some kind of middle-aged librarian, and hang out in country gardens. Anything to remain invisible to others."

"Admittedly, hiding from others is my goal in life," I admit without any hint of sadness or shame.

"Hmm, perhaps there's a difference in bloodline between you and your brothers. Did mommy dearest play away from home?"

His suggestion makes me want to laugh out loud, but instead, I continue to show my indifference over his obvious attempts to get a rise out of me.

"Maybe." I shrug with a smile on my face, for my siblings and I look too much alike to have different parents. My father is fairer than my mother, so my lighter complexion comes from him. However, apart from our slightly different skin tones, we very much resemble my mother, who is of Italian descent. I guess we have that in common, for Meri told me that Lucius' mother was also from Italy.

"You know, I have to wonder, Lucius, does my indifference to the norms of what society deems I should be interested in bother you?" I suddenly round on him to ask while looking him in the eye. "In fact, do I make you uncomfortable generally? As you say, I'm not like Merial who describes you and your friends as 'hot', and I don't foam at the mouth when one of you offers a smile or a moment of your time. Does it bother you that I'd rather read a book than attend one of your weekend parties? Parties where the attendees dry hump, or actually fuck for all I know, in the pool, donned in their branded bikinis that most likely cost a normal person's weekly salary. Does it bother you that I choose not to smear crap all over my face in an attempt to attract a guy?"

"Maybe," he replies after keeping me hanging for a few beats of silence. What would you do if it did?"

He watches me intently but with a casual attitude written all over his body language, then takes another drag on his blunt.

"I'd smile," I tell him, so I do.

He laughs softly before dropping his blunt to the floor and stamping it out with his foot.

"Bad news, my topolina," he begins, "I'm having people over on Friday and I'd better not see you there; you wouldn't set the right vibe for all the dry humping and fucking."

"Oh, really?" I pout for theatrical purposes. "You not wanting me there is gonna keep me up all night in anguish. Mind you, I do still have a copy of the tour guide I went on today, so I'm sure that will keep me just as entertained as your little party."

Lucius quirks his lips at me for a while before leaning in close, so close I think he's going to touch me or something else as equally abhorrent. It makes me nervous, and I suddenly become aware of how hard I'm having to work to keep my breath steady and even. As he moves in closer, I lean back on the spot to try and avoid contact. My heart beats loudly between my ears as he lifts his hand and reaches toward my hair.

"What the hell are you doing?" I gasp, sounding strangely pitched.

With his smirk still in place, he pulls his hand back to reveal a single green leaf that had been nestled in amongst my straggly loose tendrils. I swallow down my pride as he places it inside my hand, before eventually turning to leave. As he walks away, I feel half relieved, but also half annoyed that he had the last word in our little exchange.

Chapter 5

Helena

In the last few days, I have kept myself busy in the garden with Owen, the gardener. In doing so, I've managed to avoid Lucius and having to hang out with Meri's irritating friends. I did the latter on the Wednesday just gone and it was an experience I decided I never wanted to repeat. If you've ever wondered what it would be like to be inside of a teenage chick flick, that was it; all drama and squealing over Scarlet's recent breakup with David. Even I found myself feeling sympathetic for the poor guy. To have put up with her narcissistic whining and gaslighting for as long as he did, the sad sap must need a good week or so on an exotic island just to re-cooperate and perhaps reassess his taste in women.

The story goes he found Scarlet kissing his best friend at one of their social gatherings. Her excuse for cheating was she had heard a rumor that he was cheating on her. She didn't want to look like the party who would be cheated on, so she convinced his best friend to kiss her. His friend's excuse was less dramatic – she's a good-looking girl who wanted him to kiss her. Who was he to say no?

David caught them, an argument ensued with accusation after accusation that I eventually lost track of, until he finally declared he never wanted to see either of them ever again. Her friends feigned sympathy, but then gossiped and bitched about her like crazy whenever she left the room, including Meri. Once I had managed to collect myself over Scarlet trying to convince all who would listen that she was the injured party and that somehow, David was the villain of the story, I tried to remain impartial. They weren't my friends and although I shouldn't judge others, I obviously do.

Lucius hasn't been seen around the house since I had him following me around like I was his pet poodle, waiting for me to poop so he could go back inside. I'm relieved for his absence seeing as he seems to make me feel even more awkward than I normally do. He challenges me in such a way I cannot ignore him; he forces me out of myself. Not many people outside of my family do that with me, especially not boys who look the way he does. It's intimidating and sets my heart to racing, though I can't work out if it's in a good way or an epically bad way. Dad would advise me to keep away at all costs and to not engage with a boy like him. If I am to think about a boy in that way, then I should stick to nice guys who will treat me the way he treats my mother. In other words, someone who will love me unconditionally and without any risk. And he's right…isn't he?

Boys aside, it is now the day after my glimpse into all things teenage and girly, and I've decided to stay well clear of them. I'm currently hiding out in the cooling shade of the garden. It's incredibly hot and I already have a sheen of sweat clinging to my body and it's only mid-morning. It looks attractive on Owen, but just plain gross on me, much like if I wore Meri's makeup, I would end up looking like a clown. Life has deemed me to only be comfortable in my own skin and seeing as I am more than content to hide in the shadows, I don't mind that at all.

Owen comes sauntering up to where I'm crouched before a bed of newly upturned soil and offers me a cold drink of something, which I'll take whether I like it or not. I'm parched and in danger of setting off one of my migraines, an affliction I've been prone to ever since I hit puberty. I smile with genuine thanks for the offering at the same time as he crouches down beside me. It would seem we're going to have a break together, something I'm not used to unless it's with Mom or Dad. I watch him pick up a poor, unsuspecting worm and throw it over the back to stop my trowel from cutting it in half. It makes me smile, for I feel a kinship with him; I'm forever rescuing snails, bees, and other creepy crawlies from coming to a tragic end beneath somebody's boot.

"So, how's your stay going?" he asks without looking at me, for he's too busy filtering through the soil for other bugs, stones, and weeds. "Feel like one of the natives yet?"

"Not really," I reply with a happy-go-lucky shrug of my shoulders. I'm used to being the outsider. "I haven't even seen Aunt Jen yet, or Paul for that matter. Do they even live here?"

Owen chuckles gently at my side as he straightens up and tilts his face toward the sun. His skin is weathered, looking as though he's never worn suncream in his life, but it only makes him look all the more rugged and manly.

"As far as I know, but they've not long been married and I guess the privacy of Paul's apartment in the city is rather appealing at the moment, if you know what I mean."

"I think the worms know what you mean, Owen," I reply with a theatrical shiver, to which he looks at me and laughs heartily. "Can't say I want to picture anyone doing what you mean, let alone my aunt."

"It's the most natural thing in the world you know," he says as he goes back to rooting for minibeasts that he can save. "Wouldn't be here without it."

"You could say the same thing about childbirth," I retort as I look out over the sunny lawn to where a guy of about Lucius' age is sauntering toward us with a casual walk that says he's been here before. "Can't say I want to see that either. Who's that?"

I point to the guy who is getting ever closer to us, grinning from ear to ear as we come into focus. Owen pauses in his mission to rescue worms so he can follow my line of sight. The man offers him a smile and a momentary wave of his hand. He looks the antithesis of Lucius, so much so, I wonder if they are friends; he appears much too affable for Lucius' tastes. Owen returns the welcoming gesture, then gets to his feet again. By the time the guy reaches us, I'm feeling a little inadequate on the ground, particularly with these two incredibly tall men looking down on top of my head. I make to stand, rather ungraciously, but still come up short next to them.

"Hey, Eric, Lucius isn't here at the moment, think he went to meet Paul in town," Owen says to the guy who nods in an 'oh well' kind of way. His eyes then dart to me, looking me up and down in my gardening gear and dirty skin.

Returning his attention to Owen, I think he expects some sort of introduction, but when one doesn't come, he holds his hand out for mine. Not wanting to appear rude, I take his hand and shake it. His grip is firm but warm and he's all smiles and politeness when he looks at me.

"It would seem Owen, here," he nods his head over to the

gardener who is smirking to himself, "has forgotten his manners. I'm Eric, a friend of Lucius from back when we were in high school."

"I'm Helena, Meri's cousin," I answer quietly, still shaking his hand rather uncomfortably. He smiles with acknowledgment and then breaks our contact. I immediately pull my hands into my back pockets and smile tightly. I know I'm already blushing, it's a curse of mine, to be embarrassed by every single man I come across. I think Owen's gotten used to it now, but this guy sees my crimson cheeks and appears to look a little smug about it.

"Just got back from college in New York, I was hoping to catch up with the asshole," he explains as he looks around and takes in the gardening that Owen and I are doing. "Mind if I hang out here till he gets back?"

Owen and I glance at one another, not being entirely sure of who he's asking; it's not like either of us owns the place. Eric's wide eyes and searching expression eventually have me answering just to stop the awkwardness of the situation.

"Sure," I reply, "we're just gardening but I guess it's ok. Not that it's really my place to answer for."

"Great," he grins, before taking off his shirt to reveal a dark red vest that seems to make his dirty blonde hair appear a little darker than before. "Tell me what I can do."

I don't make it easy on poor Eric because I have him helping Owen with the more physically challenging jobs for most of the morning. By lunchtime, he has the same coating of sweat that Owen often does and appears to be over the whole gardening thing. I can't hold it against him though; he *has* worked hard and clearly wasn't expecting to. However, he doesn't seem the least bit bothered by Lucius' non-appearance and makes no attempt to leave.

Feeling bad for making him work so hard, I offer to make everyone some lunch. Owen declines, having his usual lunchbox of last night's leftovers and a flask of herbal tea. Eric, on the other hand, jumps at the offer with an expression that reminds me of a golden retriever when being shown a big, juicy steak.

Eric suggests we eat out on the decking and with the parasol casting a decent amount of shade over the table, I nod in agreement. Kicking off my flip-flops and pacing over to the sink to wash my hands, I suddenly become overly aware of someone watching us. I can't see him, but I know he's there, like a gathering of thunderclouds before the storm actually hits; it's unnerving. Eric isn't fazed at all, but when his expression turns into a gradual smile, I know he feels it too.

"Hastings?" Eric utters, confirming my suspicions while washing his hands next to mine. He purposely brushes his skin against my fingers under the running water, still smiling to himself. "Thought you'd never show up."

I turn my head to see Lucius leaning up against the larder cupboard door, hands in pockets and with his signature pissed-off expression. His eyes are narrowed at the both of us and his smile is almost angry at the scene playing out before him. I wither a little under his gaze; he's making me feel like I've been caught sneaking out by my father on a school night. Something I've never done, by the way.

"Eric, Topolina," he utters, nodding to both of us before pushing off from his leaning stance and sauntering over to where we're standing. I manage to move in the nick of time under the guise of going to get a towel to dry my hands. "Have we been making...*friends*?"

He says 'friends' like it's a dirty word, one that he finds hard to push out through his lips. I make the decision not to answer, opting to get on with making some lunch so I can avoid both the question and his intense gaze. Eric, however, is not so quiet on the subject, but I get the feeling that this is the way these two communicate with one another - contempt and disdain, laced in mockery, but with a kind of mutual respect that others don't wholly understand.

"Sure, something like that," Eric replies in a highly suggestive manner. His inclusion of me in their sport makes me want to hit him square in the jaw, but instead, I audibly sigh before taking my collection of food out to the table on the decking, effectively leaving them alone to piss around the floor inside.

I have no choice but to listen to their lowered, dulcet voices talking from inside, but have no desire to try and make out their individual words. I have a feeling that if I did, my calm serenity would be smashed to pieces and an angry bull would take over my senses. Instead, I watch the hazy afternoon sunshine highlighting the numerous insects and plant seeds that are filling the air above the swimming pool, all while daydreaming about nothing in particular. My peace is soon shattered, however, when both Eric and Lucius saunter out through the bi-fold doors to join me. As soon as they take up their seats, my mouth freezes mid-chew and we all glance at one another with different expressions. Eric is enjoying the new development, aka me, Lucius appears to be angry about it and I'm feeling horribly uncomfortable by having these two for company.

"So, you kept this one quiet," Eric breaks the steely silence with his smug smile and theatrical nod over toward me, even though his eyes are on Lucius. I feel like I'm a lifeless mannequin, possessing neither the voice nor the ears to engage in any kind of communication between them. Lucius enjoys the scowl I plaster on my face, not least because I've been referred to as 'this one'. Not that he says anything, he lets his face do the talking for him.

"Is she gonna be here for tomorrow's event?" Eric asks Lucius, who is now staring at me with a quirk of his lips.

"No!" Lucius and I both cry out in unison.

"Helena is not into parties, are you, Topolina?" He pauses for a moment before linking his fingers together and resting the tops of his index pads on his closed lips. "She's more into books, far too intelligent for the likes of you, Eric."

"Intelligent enough to talk for myself," I say to both of them with a cold edge to my voice. "You realize women have voices nowadays? There's no need to pretend I can't use my own ears or my own mouth to communicate, right?"

Lucius laughs softly against his fingers at the same time as Eric raises his hands in a defensive stance, though still with amusement written all over his smug features.

"You're quite right," Eric says with enough charm to bed Cinderella *and* the step-sisters, most likely at the same time. "I was merely…*hoping* I would see you there, Helena. I didn't mean to offend you by talking over you."

I offer him a smile with an ounce of gratitude, choosing to not pick up on his obvious attempt to use me to get at Lucius by telling him he '*hoped*' I would be there.

"Matthews, if you're planning to get into this one's panties, I'm afraid you're going to be sorely disappointed." Lucius casually stretches his arms up into the air, causing the bottom of his shirt to lift and reveal his tightly packed abs under his mostly smooth, dark skin. "She's not going to drop them for you, plus…"

"Plus...?" Eric smiles, probing further with great delight.

"Plus, she's off limits to you," Lucius replies with a casual shrug.

It's enough to have me shoving back my chair before I set about stomping inside, feeling beyond furious with both of these assholes and their *my-dick's-bigger-than-your-dick* repertoire. If I could go back in time, I would have sent Eric packing when he first showed up. Hell, I might have even considered going to camp over this infuriating trip.

Chapter 6

Lucius

I enjoy the sound of my little mouse angrily slamming the door behind me and even allow myself a small smile over her angry outburst. Eric must do too because his laugh is offending my ears with its usual loud and obnoxious volume. He has always been brasher than me, though normally, I can forgive him for his lack of sophistication. At school, I was the dark, brooding asshole while he was the lighter, football-playing hero. He was widely known for being the angel to my devil. Ironic, given the guy is more fucked up than I am. I have had to clear up after his messes on more than one occasion. What little Helena doesn't realize is that I've just saved her neck by warning Eric away.

Helena Carter is an intriguing little mouse, especially in comparison to the rest of her family. Truth be known, I was initially only interested in sinking myself deep inside her virgin pussy. I'm sure I would have forgotten about her the next day; it's who I am and what I do. No mousey, little, shy girl was going to change that, least of all a Carter. It's not that I mind Paul's new wife, she's perfectly fuckable, but her daughter is somewhat more annoying. What's worse is she comes with a little pack of other irritating wannabe whores. Paul tells me to play nice and to let them come to my little social events, but I couldn't care less about any of them. But I find myself being irritatingly intrigued by Helena, being that what most girls pass for interesting, doesn't appeal to her at all. Apparently, it would seem I like this in a girl, and I especially like it in a girl who looks like she does.

My social gatherings are about three things for me - booze, hash, and pussy. Hardly original but it's the perfect combination of timewasters in which to lose myself, preferably into a state of mind where I don't need to think about anything or anyone for at least a few hours. Most of the attendees are likely here for the exact same reason. No one comes for meaningful conversation or to find their significant other, and it's definitely not the kind of scene for our little Helena to witness. I'd no doubt end up having to get her ass out of some compromising situation, which would not only piss me off but also get me into serious trouble with Paul and his new bride. I would rather ask one of Merial's mindless friends to come and discuss the theory of evolution than have to listen to Paul tell me what a disappointment I am. After so many times of hearing the same speech, it fast becomes tedious.

"So, she's off limits, is she?" Eric asks, interrupting my inner thoughts by trying to ascertain whether or not I'll let him try and fuck our new house guest. I won't of course, though something tells me the shy little mouse wouldn't touch him with a heavy articulated truck anyway. "I could do with a new bit of skirt to chase after. You know the last girl I slept with down this way claimed we'd already fucked each other before? I had no idea!" He proceeds to mimic an explosion going off inside of his brain. If only.

"Affirmative, my slut of a friend. I've decided Helena is strictly off limits to everyone, but especially to you." I look at him with an ounce of humor and a pound of warning. "If anyone is going to be darkening her virgin sheets, it will be me."

"Virgin too?" Eric gasps, blowing out a stream of air while pulling his brows together to form a deep crease, as though thinking how good it would be to dive inside of her for the very first time. For a moment, I remember what it felt like when I had beaten Tommy Slater to a pulp, when I had last felt something other than indifference or mild amusement. Only a moment, however, before I force the feeling away again. "I dunno, Hastings, I think I might need to sidestep your approval and go after that anyway."

"She's not a *that*, Matthews, and if you so much as kiss her on the cheek, I.Will.Bury.You!"

"Woah, Hastings!" He laughs loudly, being that he can only manage to do so at an insufferable volume. "Have you actually met a girl who you give a shit about?"

"Only the virgin part," I lie, shrugging my shoulders like he's so used to seeing me do, for I am fast growing bored of this conversation and have the urge to throw Eric out.

"She's not going to let you have that, trust me," he says, leaning in and winking in my direction before grabbing a handful of peanuts to throw into his mouth. I smile while conjuring up an image of him choking on one of them.

"Care to make it interesting, Matthews?" I look away to see Owen glancing our way, his expression is one of suspicion, and I half wonder if he's been listening in to our ridiculous banter. I've seen the way he looks at Helena, like a father protecting one of his own from the big, bad, wolf, which could be either one of us right now. Pity for him, we're both depraved when it comes to playing with others, particularly, I'm sad to say, with the fairer sex.

"Always," Eric replies, shrugging before leaning in even closer to hear what I have to say.

"If I pop her cherry by the end of summer, I get your sporty little motor out there." I refer to his new Lotus out front, both custom-made and his pride and joy. If I win, which I will, not only will he lose his beautiful car, but his father will no doubt cut his allowance, if not stop it altogether. "If I don't, which is highly unlikely, you can have my recently purchased Maserati."

Eric's eyes shoot up to the sky before a huge grin spreads across his arrogant face; I'm not proposing he risks anything I am not willing to lose myself.

"You're on, Hastings," he announces before shaking my hand from across the table. "But don't think I'm going to make it easy for you. The only rule is we don't mention the bet. That's all; anything else is all part of the fun!"

"You don't need to tell me the rules, Matthews," I utter. "Don't try to insult my intelligence when we all know I'm the brains of this outfit."

Helena

It's now Friday morning and I've only just let go of my anger from yesterday. It had stayed balled up inside of me like some sort of ugly virus, making me feel sick and exhausted all at the same time. Cam and Nate do a pretty good job of winding me up, but Lucius and Eric, the seemingly wholesome-looking guy who was anything but, are on another level when it comes to grating on my nerves. I've never felt so disrespected or humiliated in my entire life. Being ignored by the opposite sex is infinitely more appealing than being talked about like I'm a piece of meat for them to argue over, especially right in front of me. It was only after talking to Mom last night that I managed to wake up and throw it all away. She's always known how to calm me, even if she doesn't know she's needing to.

At midday, I begin potting up some tomatoes to go inside the greenhouse. I've grown fond of gardening, for it too, knows how to calm me. It appeals to my creative mind as well as keeps me busy in a place that still feels so alien. However, the sound of approaching footsteps suddenly fills me with a sense of dread. I can't bear the thought of having to face Lucius after I've only just let go of my temper. When I finally turn to face him head on, I am pleasantly surprised to find that the footsteps belong to my Aunt Jen. For a moment or two, I stand there gawking, not quite believing it's her. I've been here for over a week now and not seen her once. A fact I haven't told my parents because I know they'd be annoyed; I don't want to be that kid that tattles on their best friend just to get them into trouble.

When it does finally sink in, we both scream fondly at each other before I throw my arms around her and hug her tightly. My whacky Aunt Jen is dressed immaculately but still has a slight boho look leftover from her days before she married Paul. Her long, flowing red hair always looks stunning without any effort, and she fills her long maxi dress with all the right kinds of curves and edges. A wide-brimmed summer hat protects her freckled skin from the sun while her large sunglasses cover almost half of her face.

"How is my favorite niece?" she asks as she squeezes me to the point of not being able to breathe. "I'm so sorry I haven't been here to welcome you, but work has been crazy, and I knew Merial would take care of you."

Hmmm, well she sort of has, to begin with, maybe.

"I'm your *only* niece," I remind her. "Are you about for a bit now?"

She pouts at the same time as she looks to the ground with a sheepish expression. My heart automatically sinks with disappointment; I could do with someone other than Owen to talk to. Someone who isn't going to frustrate me to the point of screaming, like her evil stepson and Meri's ridiculous friends.

"Afraid not, darling, Paul and I are about to shoot off. We're away for the next week. He has business meetings in New York, and I've decided to go with him."

"Oh, that sounds fun," I say, unable to hide the distinct sadness from my voice. I suddenly feel like I need to spend time with someone who at least reminds me of my parents. She seems to feel even more guilty when she takes in my poor attempts to not look let down.

"I promise you, when I get back, we'll spend some time together," she says before hugging me again. "Apart from my lack of good aunty skills, are you ok here? Anything I can get for you before I go?"

"Actually, do you have any painkillers? I feel one of my heads coming on." I've been trying to ignore the tell-tale signs all morning, but now that my vision is starting to go on the fritz, I can no longer deny it's there, waiting to pounce on me with its full weight. "I've already had the flashes of light blocking my vision for the past half hour."

"Oh, Helena, perhaps I shouldn't go. Hang on..." She trails off as she reaches inside her bag to retrieve her phone, which she then starts scanning through. A really selfish part of me hopes she won't go, that she'll stay with me to be the Mom I can't have right now.

"No, no, I'm fine, honestly," I lie, beginning to flap my hands about in the air.

"I'm going to call our doctor," she explains, "I know you've needed stronger stuff in the past, so I'm going to explain the situation and leave you with his number. He's brilliant and Paul pays him enough, so don't worry about calling him if you need to. Now, go to bed and I'll drop the tablets in on the way out. No arguments. Get going!"

Still battling my emotions between relief, guilt, and disappointment, I eventually settle on saluting her way in defeat. At the end of the day, I know I'm only going to end up passing out anyway, so it's not like I'd be conscious if she did stay. She's probably right about heading to bed, though, it makes sense to try and stop it from progressing any further.

Once inside my room, I close all the curtains in an attempt to make it as dark as possible, then slide into bed. The flashes have already progressed to the point where I can see more sparkles of white light than anything else, and when my head finally hits the pillow, a sharp pain radiates around my forehead and deep into my eye sockets. All I can do is try and sleep it off before the nausea starts. Jen brings me two of her regular painkillers, which I manage to down before falling into an agitated sleep. It isn't at all restful; it's full of dreams and has me slipping in and out of consciousness.

When I finally wake, my head feels like someone has taken a hammer to it and I have to go and throw up in the bathroom. Once I feel like I've expelled everything I've consumed within the last few days, I only have enough energy to rest my forehead against the toilet seat. The coolness is soothing, and I no longer care about how unhygienic it is. All I can think about is how much I want to cut my head open and place my brain into a bucket of ice.

THE DEVIL

Every time I retch, it feels like a thousand knives are being pierced through my head, which only makes me want to throw up even more. I'm caught in a vicious cycle of pain and sickness. My vision is still blurry, and I feel extremely weak and exhausted.

From experience, I know normal painkillers aren't going to make a dent in a migraine as bad as this one; I need my stronger tablets, the ones that usually knock me out for a lot longer. I have a vague recollection of Aunt Jen telling me she would leave them in the kitchen downstairs. I agreed to this idea in a semi-conscious, just-let-me-die, state of mind, but now that my head is a little clearer, I could slap my earlier self. Aunt Jen is a bit scatty, and even though she thought leaving them next to the sink in the kitchen was a practical idea, it now means I have to get myself upright and down the stairs in order to take them. I might end up having to crawl on my hands and knees like a drunken idiot after kick-out time, but it's got to be worth it to stop the intense pain that refuses to go.

I feel down my body to check I'm at least wearing something. Thankfully, Jen must have helped me to put my camisole nightdress on before she left me to go to sleep. Just about able to get up onto my feet, I stagger out of the room, reaching my hand out to feel for any oncoming hazards. I still end up bumping into several pieces of furniture in the process, but so long as I can't see blood or bone, I'll keep going. Once I'm out the door, I hear a thudding beat coming from outside and lots of voices talking from down below. It dawns on me that this must be Lucius's little event in full swing, which means I've been out of it for hours. His warning to keep away repeats in my head, but it's not enough to make me stay in my room when blissful drugs await me downstairs.

I hold my forehead and breathe in deeply all the while reaching out for the blurry banister in front of me. My weak knees buckle, and I fall slightly, however, the wall beneath catches my legs and prevents me from full-on falling down. The impact of my knees hitting the ground feels like my brain has just slammed into my skull with full force and I groan as the pain radiates all through my body.

"Woah, this one's totally out of it!" a male voice calls out and a couple of people start to laugh. "How much has she had to drink? Or maybe she's had some of Eric's dodgy weed."

"Wait, is she in her underwear?" a girl's voice joins in.

Oh God, just what I need, an audience to my pain and humiliation. Actually, I'm in that much pain, I don't really care right now, I just need my pills.

"Where the fuck is Lucius?" the male voice calls out again…or is it the female? I can no longer tell for their voices sound echoey…tinny.

I move to my feet, then brace myself before attempting to walk again. Gripping hold of the banister, I begin to head down the stairs, praying I don't fall down and break my neck. The blurry figures below continue to watch me, making no actual attempts to help or ask me what's wrong. I must look like a complete drunk who only has herself to blame for her current predicament. I'm sure someone like me often appears at these sorts of gatherings.

When I eventually reach the bottom of the staircase, I put my hands out to steady myself, then try to move toward the blurry kitchen sink. The laughter around me continues; I must be looking more and more intoxicated. Fortunately, I manage to reach the sink unscathed. Unfortunately, I have to throw up again, which doesn't help with how drunk I must be looking right now.

"Fuck, she's bad," a guy helpfully observes. "Hey,

Matthews!"

"What?" another guy shouts back. It's a voice that sounds familiar; I'm almost certain that it's Eric, Lucius' obnoxious friend from yesterday. Things seem to be going from bad to worse. *Where the fuck are my tablets?*

"Check this chick out, think she needs help to a bed…like *immediately*!" the first guy says. "Isn't getting chicks to bed your area of expertise, Eric?"

Ignoring the unsubtle suggestion from whoever this creep is, I open the faucet and begin gulping at the running water. It's either going to make me feel a little better or have me throwing up again.

"Oh, shit, she does," he says with a somewhat concerned tone of voice. I can't make out if it's genuine or not, but then again, figuring that out isn't exactly at the top of my list of priorities right now. "Helena? Are you ok, beautiful?"

"Dude, her tits are loose," the first guy says and begins laughing again. I screw up my face, thinking how gross these guys are. I've just thrown up in the sink for fuck's sake. The state of my tits shouldn't really come into it, should it?

"Anyone touches her, and I will fucking end you!" a new, low growl of a voice warns the room. I think it belongs to Lucius, though I've never heard this level of emotion from him before. He's always so nonchalant, pissed-off, or silent even, but never animated like this. His footsteps come right up close to me as I fall in defeat against the sink. "Looking for these?" he asks me quietly as he places two tablets in the palm of my hand.

With no other choice but to trust him, I down them with a glass of water that Lucius has just given me. He then picks me up like he's carrying the helpless princess away, all the while muttering, "I told you not to come, there'll be payback for this, Topolina."

If I didn't feel so rough, I might laugh over the irony of him looking like the heroic knight coming in to save me. Lucius Hastings is anything but a knight in shining armor; he's more like the devil who endangered me in the first place. As it is, I don't even make a peep as we pass by all the blurry figures who have now fallen silent.

Lucius makes no apologies for kicking my door open as he carries me inside, slamming it back again with the very same boot he'd used to open it with. I moan a little when he places me back inside my bed, for I can't seem to form anything more coherent. It would seem he's feeling the same, seeing as he only offers me a grunt while he tucks me up tight. I lie completely motionless, feeling dazed like a deer in headlights.

After he's happy that I'm securely in bed, I fully expect him to stalk out the door again. Instead, he wanders over to the window and peeks through the curtains. He then crosses the room to check outside the door before turning to look at me again. We stare at each other as if trying to ascertain what to do or say next. I am completely vulnerable right now, and yet, I do not fear him at all. Not even with his reputation, not even with the intensity with which he is staring at me right now. I am perhaps the only person who completely trusts Lucius Hastings, which either makes me incredibly insightful, being able to see the man beyond the mask, or incredibly stupid.

"Thank you," I think I manage to mumble, but it's not long before blackness shrouds me, and I'm knocked out again. The last thing I see is his blurry figure lowering to sit on the window seat, staying with me but maintaining his distance.

THE DEVIL

Lucius

I leave my little lost mouse asleep in her room and make a move back into the living room downstairs. Eric is sprawled out against one of Meri's drunk friends, looking the epitome of smug. As I hit the bottom step, I'm suddenly accosted by another of her friends who slides her arm around my waist with a lustful glint in her eye. I don't even look at her properly before taking hold of her hand and spinning her away from me. Eric all but pisses himself laughing, but I offer nothing but a roll of my eyes when the girl pouts at me from across the room where she's just landed.

"Well, I never thought I'd see the day, fuck-face!" Eric laughs while continuing to fondle the tit of the girl who is lying across his lap. I sneer at the scene, quickly growing tired of Eric's loud and intrusive laughing. The whiskey bottle sitting on the kitchen counter calls to me so I waste no time in closing the gap to give into temptation. I pour three fingers of the stuff into a glass and proceed to polish it off within a few mouthfuls.

"You *like* the little virgin, don't you?" he asks with curiosity in his voice.

"Don't be so fucking ridiculous." I scowl as I pour another drink to try and zone him out. His laughter falls flat, but he's still wearing a punch-worthy grin on his face.

"Oh, well then," he eventually says as he pushes the girl off his lap to get to his feet. I watch as he heads to the bottom of the staircase that lead up to Helena's bedroom with angry anticipation. "You won't mind if I go and 'take care' of her then."

He waggles his brows about with a lascivious grin written all over his face, but before his foot even hits the first step, I throw my tumbler into the sink with such venom, it obliterates inside the basin. At least the bastard has the decency to look back at me, pausing in his mission to effectively go and sign his own death warrant.

"Don't you fucking dare!" I point at him, with my voice remaining steady and eerily quiet. "She is not for you and if you so much as look at her in a way I deem inappropriate, I will make you disappear." I then walk right up to his face, so we are almost nose to nose, just so I get my point across. "And you and I both know I can do that, Matthews!"

The room is silent apart from the background noise of music blasting away outside. Eric doesn't look too impressed by my threat, but other people's feelings rarely bother me. Besides, he's about as deep as a puddle of rat's piss, so he'll get over it soon enough.

Eventually, he moves aside to let me pass through because we all know who's won here. Eric has always been the subservient male in this outfit, so he knows when to call it quits. His compliance doesn't stop me from eyeballing him with warning when I shove past him. I also take my time walking up to Helena's bedroom, looking at everyone so they know whose fucking place this is and who has the final say.

Slowly, I open her door, moving inside so as not to wake her. The last thing I want to do is have her questioning me, given the mood I'm in, so I take small, careful steps to avoid such a scenario. As soon as I see her curled up in a small fetal position, hair sprawled out behind her, I know I'm safe. There's no way in hell she's waking up anytime soon. I push the door closed with my foot kicking out behind me, no longer worrying about the soft thud it makes when it hits the frame behind me. I then shove my hands inside my pockets as I walk to the bed, lean over her, and catch a glimpse of her face. She looks pale and sickly, but also peaceful in her unconscious state. The gentle rise and fall of the thin blanket on top tells me she's resting easily; her meds must have kicked in.

Not trusting any of the fuckers downstairs, I grab the superfluous amount of pillows and throws that Jen keeps inside these rooms, to construct a makeshift bed on the floor. It's still going to feel like sleeping on a slab of stone, and I know I'll feel like I've run a hundred miles tomorrow morning, but it will do for now.

Chapter 7

Helena

The room is lighter and the oppressive atmosphere I felt yesterday has finally lifted. So much so, I bask in the comfort of it a little while longer before consciously assessing the rest of me. My body feels cooler, and my previously throbbing head is now only somewhat muffled. Smiling to myself, I know the tablets have done their job and it feels euphoric. This is one of those moments when you are grateful to just feel normal instead of suffering in a world of pain.

Part of me doesn't want to move; there is every possibility this might set off another headache, but eventually, the need to use the bathroom forces me to. I am relieved when my head doesn't feel an ounce of discomfort as I turn toward the bathroom, and when I open my eyes, I can see normally again. The world is no longer a blur of colors; I can see clear outlines of everything in the room.

Lifting the cover, I swing my jelly-like legs over the mattress to begin walking over to the bathroom, but as soon as my foot hits the ground, I find myself stumbling over something warm and soft. The sensation is completely unexpected and causes me to yelp. The something moans on the floor beneath me, and I audibly gasp when I realize Lucius, the sullen boy who doesn't seem to give a shit about anyone, is lying flat out on my bedroom floor. My hand immediately flies to my mouth, as though trying to push the noise of surprise back inside my throat. I stare at him, still shocked, but then begin to study him; the way he's using his jacket as a pillow, the way his hands have small ink stains on them, the fact that he's fully clothed, and it hits me just how captivating he is on the eye. His jet-black hair is ruffled from sleep and the muscles in his biceps ripple under his tanned skin. For the first time ever, he looks peaceful. The sight of which snaps me back to my predicament. Thankfully, my foot was not enough to wake him, so I decide to step over his hulking great body and go to the bathroom.

As soon as I close the door on my six-foot-something devil of a problem, I mentally begin to think of some kind of plan. I decide on doing…nothing. I'll climb back into bed and pretend to be asleep. Knowing Lucius, he'll sneak out himself and we can avoid all the awkwardness. It's so simple, it can't go wrong. With that in mind, I quickly and quietly clean my teeth and splash my face. After all, I haven't done these most basic of hygienic activities in the last twenty-four hours or so.

The door does me a favor by opening without a single squeak or groan, and I walk out to find Lucius has rolled over into a fetal ball, making him look vaguely human, vulnerable almost. It's a weird sight to see someone like Lucius in this position so spoil myself by looking at him in this small, less intimidating state for a little longer. From here, I notice how classically Italian he looks. Meri has shown me pictures of his mother, so I know how beautiful she was. There is no mistaking that Lucius is her son and that he has been lucky enough to inherit her beauty.

Chastising myself for ogling my monster-in-shining-armor, I tiptoe around him and climb back into bed. However, as soon as my head hits the pillow, he jerks upright with a start.

"Topolina?" he calls out, staring at me with mild surprise. "Oh, fuck."

His eyes flutter closed, and he muffles a groan inside of his cupped hands. He shakes his head as though trying to clear his thoughts. I'm about to say something, but he suddenly jumps up and stretches.

"Do you know the last time I slept in a girl's room without fucking her?" He turns to face me, rubbing his eyes and reaching up high to stretch out his back. "I have never done such a thing."

"Well, there's a first for everything," I mutter. The use of my voice feels alien after my migraine, and I have to pause so I can cough and clear my throat. "But thank you, Lucius, last night was very chivalrous of you."

"Don't ever fucking say that again," he says, laughing as if to himself. "You're welcome." For a moment, I think he might actually be decent, deep down, but then he clears his throat to tell me, "But now you owe me."

"What?!" I take back the 'chivalrous' comment.

"You heard," he says with a wicked smile spreading across his face. "I told you to stay out of last night. I knew I'd have to come and save your hide if you showed up and that's exactly what happened. I just gotta decide what I want from you." He grabs his jacket from off the floor and makes a move toward the door. "Here're the rest of your pills," he says, placing them on my nightstand. "Your dress suits you by the way."

His comment makes me automatically lift the covers to my

neck to cover up any skin I have on show, not to mention the braless state of my chest. I realize he's already had a chance to see everything and more, but not covering myself at this point might make him think I am giving him permission to gawk. With this in mind, I look back at him with disbelief, only to find that wicked, tantalizing smirk still taunting me. I close my eyes as he walks out the door, softly closing it behind him.

*Do **not** fall for the devil, Helena!*

Half an hour after I've managed to dress myself, the whole time muttering obscenities about Lucius and his sleazy friends, I decide to face the world outside of my bedroom. I walk down the staircase to the sound of hungover teenagers moaning about their throbbing heads and bouts of nausea. When I eventually spy Meri, she's slumped in a chair, face down on the table, with her arms desperately trying to cover her head in an attempt to block out any light. Sitting to her left are two girls with deathly-looking complexions, and to her right, another girl is resting her head in the crook of her arm. I'm pretty sure she's asleep.

The remains of last night's party are still scattered all over the place, causing me to wonder who exactly cleans up all the mess. I can't imagine Lucius cleaning up after himself, or Meri for that matter. I find myself wincing for whoever it is; it looks like squatters have been in residence for the past ten years and have left all their shit behind.

Feeling much better, and ignoring all the detritus about the place, I skip down the stairs in a pair of cut-off denim shorts and an oversized red t-shirt. I've piled my hair up in a loose bun to avoid any pulling on my scalp. I'm currently in the danger zone of setting off another headache so will do whatever I can to make sure that doesn't happen. I make a beeline for the kitchen where I grab a pint glass from the cupboard and fill it with cold water. I seriously need to rehydrate myself.

"Someone's spritely; you feeling better, Hels?" Meri mumbles from her position at the table. Her eyes are still covered in makeup, and she has a bad case of panda eyes from a lack of sleep and far too much alcohol.

"Much, thank you," I reply as I lean against the sink behind me. "You don't look so good. Rough night?"

"Oh, you have no idea!" she says with a wicked grin spread across her face. She looks at me in such a way, I know there'll be more details later. Meri's terrible at keeping secrets, especially with me. She knows she never has to worry about me spilling them to anyone else.

"Or maybe she does?" The resting girl pops her head up, making me jump from the shock of it. Obviously, she wasn't asleep. "I saw you last night in your little black night-dress, minus underwear, being carried up to your room by none other than Lucius Hastings. That boy has a reputation don't you know. He does bad things but in such a good way."

The two other girls suddenly perk up and gasp over this piece of juicy information. Their staring has me shifting uncomfortably from one foot to the other because, to be fair, that did sound suspicious.

"Relax, idiot, Helena had a migraine," Meri chimes in, "it couldn't have been her."

"Actually, it kind of was," I reply shyly, even though what they saw was completely innocent.

"You slut!" one of the girls to Meri's left says to me with

real hatred in her eyes. Given that she looks like a streetside prostitute at the moment, I drop my mouth open over her unfounded insult. I think about trying to defend myself, to make her take it back, but in the end, I shrug my shoulders and choose to say nothing. After all, what's the point? I know these girls will believe whatever they want to, regardless of the facts.

"Lori!" Meri snaps on my behalf. "I'm sure there's a perfectly good explanation for it, isn't there, Hels?" She looks at me with worry in her eyes, as though she's got a hint of doubt about what happened between Lucius and me.

"When I get a migraine, I lose my vision and become very weak. Meri's mom had left my stronger painkillers down here and it was hard to find them. Lucius helped me take them and then put me to bed…alone!" I draw out the last word, just to make my point.

"So, why did I see him leaving your room about half an hour ago?" the one who I thought was asleep asks me. I think I'll call her stirrer, for a few obvious reasons.

"Why don't you ask him?" I shrug, becoming increasingly exasperated by this interrogation. I don't owe these people any explanation, apart from maybe Meri.

"I did," she replies, "he told me to ask you and then told me to fuck off and leave him alone," she huffs. "I can't believe you like that asshole, Lori!"

I try to hide my smile, imagining this little exchange between them. Lucius doesn't believe he owes anyone anything, so I can only imagine how insignificant he finds this little group of drama queens. Poor old Meri included.

"Oh, please, like you'd turn him down if he offered it to

you," the girl to the left of Lori laughs. "He's hotter than hell and has a devilishly wicked personality. Don't act like he doesn't get you wet between the legs."

I can no longer hold in my laughter, whereas Lori is becoming increasingly agitated over all this talk of girls gushing over the mere thought of her crush.

"Eww! Please don't be so crude, Lisa, it's too early and I'm too hungover," Meri grumbles. "Scarlet, stop interrogating my cousin, there's not a chance in hell she'd go near someone like Lucius. Right, Hels?"

I silently nod before walking toward the bi-fold doors so I can escape into the garden and continue potting plants, something that is much more my style. The girls settle back into silence while they nurse their pounding heads.

Chapter 8

Helena

Hasting's Villa remains quiet for the rest of the day and apart from a cleaning company coming in to clear up the mess, it remains empty. It's only when the light begins to fade that I realize I've been in the garden for most of the day. My little plot is beginning to take shape and I hope that what I've planted takes root. When I walk back to the kitchen, I leave my muddy flip-flops at the door. My hands are filthy and there's mud scraped up and down my arms, so I head straight to the sink to clean up before I go and change.

Once I turn off the faucet, I hear Lucius talking to someone on the phone. He sounds like his usual calm, almost bored-sounding self. I continue to listen as he wanders into the kitchen where I am still shaking my hands into the sink, only for him to stop when he sees me. I notice he has his ear glued to his phone and is continuing to talk to whoever is on the line. Seeing as he's making no attempt to acknowledge me, I carry on getting myself some water and a piece of toast. I don't want to eat it but if it means the headaches stay away, I'll force it down. I bypass Lucius on the phone as I head to the table where I park my butt and begin nibbling, all the while trying not to eavesdrop on his conversation.

"Topolina," he eventually says in greeting, "are you better now?"

The air feels heavier when he comes to sit on the chair opposite me, stretching himself out to his full length.

"I'm good, thank you," I reply, then continue eating my toast slowly, albeit uncomfortably in front of him. "And you? Meri was quite the picture of sickness this morning."

"I'm well," he says with a shrug, "those girls drink beyond their body's means. I am smarter than that, therefore I am rarely hungover the next day. Tell me, Topolina, have you ever had a drink before?"

"Of course," I scoff.

"I mean a 'proper' drink," he clarifies, "and I don't mean a glass of wine with your parents. I'm talking about really letting yourself go, so much so, you let all your timid inhibitions fall away."

He cocks his head to the side with his sadistic smirk, one that makes me feel like I have zero life experience in anything.

"Then, no." I sigh in frustration, bracing myself for him to tease me over it. "To be honest, it's not exactly something that's on my bucket list."

"In that case, I know precisely what I want; what you owe me." His smile turns even more sinister than before, warning me that I should run far away from him and his 'wants'. "I want you to attend my party next Friday and I want you to get completely fucked with me."

"No," I reply bluntly.

"*No?*" He laughs as he flings his head back. "Now, come on, Topolina, you owe me for being some pansy knight in shining armor yesterday. Do you know the shit I got for doing that?"

"Sorry, but I'm not really interested. In fact, it's more of a reason to decline," I answer matter of factly. "I'm not letting my inhibitions down when your disgusting friends are around. They would have slept with me under the influence of migraine medication, even after having just thrown up in the kitchen sink. I can't imagine what they'd do to me under the influence of alcohol."

"That's not a problem, Topolina," he says with a more serious expression, "they know you're off limits."

"*Off limits?*" I question, arching my eyebrow over his strange choice of words. "And how do they know I am *off limits?*"

"I told them," he says with a shrug of his shoulders, then leans in closer, as if he's about to impart some secret intel. "I told them you're *my* toy to play with."

Although I physically shudder over his words, I force myself to quickly regain my composure, clear my throat, and look him right in the eye.

"I'm no toy, Lucius, and you will never 'play' with me. So again, thank you for the invitation but I must decline. Slut-fest parties are not my scene."

I get up to leave him still smiling at me; I need to get away from that intense gaze of his before I do something stupid, like submit to his every desire.

"I hear Meri's friend, Lori, would be up for anything with

you, so maybe give her a call."

"One drink, Topolina," he calls out without bothering to turn and face me.

"No," I reply, walking upstairs to my bedroom. I hear him laughing all the while I try to keep up my casual pace instead of running like I so want to.

Meri and I seem to have come to an unspoken understanding; we get together in the evenings, usually to eat and have a catch-up on her latest gossip and then we go our separate ways. She wants to hang out with her drama queens, and I don't. I'm not here to ruin her summer and I don't want her to think she has to hang out with me. After all, I am perfectly used to leading a mostly solitary existence. I'm actually happier in my own thoughts and I usually prefer the company of older people who have outgrown the need to cause issues where there are none.

Lucius was accurate in his assessment of me and the fact that I was born in the wrong era, but I work with what I've got. Dad is always telling me that I am lucky to be content with the simple things in life, unlike my brothers, who crave more than the everyday. Though, if I really think about it, he's the one that has brought me up to be so. I was never allowed to have the same experiences as them; it being explained that I was more likely to get hurt, and that he was protecting me. Protecting me or caging me, it matters not. I am what I am, you cannot undo a childhood of being treated differently merely because of my sex. I will always listen to him and take on board his advice because he trained me to do so.

THE DEVIL

It's Monday and after working in the garden all morning, I take a seat on one of the many wooden benches that are dotted around the lawn. Sitting cross-legged, I close my eyes against the peaked sunshine and let the warmth spread over my face. I'm actually managing to develop a little bit of a tan, especially now that I've given in to wearing shorts when I'm gardening. It's far too hot to wear anything else. I sigh softly as a breeze brushes over my face and I hear birds twittering in the background. I am the epitome of calm and relaxed

"Here you are, Helena," Owen's familiar croaky voice calls out from across the flowerbeds, "got you a tea. It's the least I can do for all the weeding you've done for me."

Owen and I have developed a friendship and it feels nice to have someone normal to talk to. I still wish for my aunt to come home early, and I take in my mom's phone calls for all their worth, but I appreciate having a familiar and friendly face about the place. After all, he's the only adult here. Lucius may well be the same age as my big brother, but I hardly count him as human, let alone a responsible adult.

"Thank you," I say as I accept the tea, which is almost black, but I don't mind. "How often do you work here?" I ask as he takes a seat on the bench next to me.

"Most mornings and then I pop back in the afternoon to water everything when the heat's died down. I'm not here at the weekends though. Those are reserved for my son, Billy."

"I didn't realize you had a son." I smile awkwardly, feeling a little guilty for not trying harder to find out more about him. "How old is he?"

"Ten, going on twenty," he replies with a smile, one that says he loves him no matter how hard he might be to parent at times. "I nearly lost him a few years ago."

"Oh, God, that's awful. He's well now I hope?" I ask, suddenly feeling worried and saddened over the poor little boy who I've only just learned about.

"Oh, he's not sick," he says with a smile that showcases his teeth. His front teeth slightly overlap one another but it only adds to his charm. "I haven't always had the best clean record if you know what I mean. His mother didn't want me to have contact. I can't say I blame her," he explains before sipping his drink sadly. "But Paul took me on when Billy turned two, cleaned me up, and convinced Kerry to give me another chance. We used to hang out in this yard, Billy and me, under Paul's supervision at first." The memory seems to perk him up a little, and he becomes animated as he continues to tell the story. "Lucius used to join us and helped me to keep Billy entertained. It's unusual for a fourteen-year-old rich boy to be helping a guy like me to play with a two-year-old. He was great though, couldn't have done it without him."

"Huh?" I blurt out, thinking about Lucius' oddities and how they don't fit this picture at all. "He's a bit of a peculiar one," I agree, "what happened to him? Why's he so…so…"

"Shitty?" he answers for me bluntly and laughs. I can't help my instant reaction to laugh with him. He's so easy to talk to and we're forming quite the brotherly, sisterly relationship. "I think it started with his mom passing away; not many people get over something like that. Plus, you can't deny he's another bored, rich kid, I suppose. It's lucky he did have his mother's influence for the first thirteen years of his life, or I don't think the guy would have any moral compass whatsoever."

"I guess," I reply as I nod along, almost feeling a little sorry for Lucius. "Do you think it's a bit of an act?"

"Who knows? Could be," he muses, "but he's always been a stand-up guy to Billy and me." For a moment or two, we both stare into the bottom of our empty mugs of tea to contemplate the enigma that is Lucius Hastings. "Well, enough gossiping like two old ladies, I need to get back to it before I go and see Billy for lunch."

"Ok, thanks for the tea and gossip," I grin, and he winks at me before walking off down the path.

When I walk inside, about twenty minutes later, there is a note waiting for me on the kitchen table. I'm taken aback, so I open it before I've even washed off the dirt from the garden.

One drink, Topolina!

This can only be from the lord of darkness himself, which causes me to smirk. I then quickly reply by using the pen that's been left next to it; he fully expected me to have a response to his proposition.

No thank you. I'm washing my hair.

The whereabouts of Lucius' room still eludes me so I decide to just put it back where I found it. He's bound to look and if he doesn't, it really does not matter. Funny though, I'm beginning to enjoy our little jibes at one another. I continue getting my lunch together and take it outside to eat on the decking. Placing my legs up onto the chair opposite, I lay back and enjoy the sun beating down on my naked skin. It must be at least half an hour before I go back inside. As soon as I step through the doors with my dirty dishes, I notice the note is already gone.

This pattern of life continues over the next few days, right up until the day of Lucius' party. He leaves me notes that request my presence for a drink, to which I always reply with ridiculous reasons for why I can't. My personal favorite was telling him I had to trim my toenails using a ruler for precision and would therefore take me the entire evening.

During the morning, I hang out in the garden, chat with Owen over mid-morning tea, and then return to the kitchen for lunch where a note is waiting for me. Always the same original message, written in the same cursive script as the one I had found on Monday. Today, I go against the grain and leave it blank before I go out to eat. Of course, when I return inside, the note has been taken.

When early evening strikes, I make my way up to my room so as not to bump into anyone who might be setting up for Lucius' soiree. I know Meri and her friends have congregated in her room down the hall, already beautifying themselves in the hopes of bagging one of his friends, or indeed, the man himself. I couldn't think of anything worse, so I put on my music and end up taking an unintentional nap. A mixture of digging and too much sun has me passing out before I can stop myself from falling under.

By the time I wake, feeling disorientated, I can hear thumping music playing out in the yard. My senses are obviously more alert this time so I can hear laughing and shouting in amongst the music and splashing from the pool. It's all so loud, I emit a frustrated groan. This is most likely going to go on all night and I'm starving. But after what happened last time, I'll be damned if I'm going out there.

With that in mind, I try to ignore my growling stomach and grab a book, one of my favorites, and try to block it all out. I remain engrossed in the story for the first ten minutes or so, but then the music becomes even louder. I sigh, put my book down, and grab my headphones in the hopes that I can block out most of the assault of noise coming from the party. However, the outside

THE DEVIL

music only gets turned up even louder, so much so, I can no longer make out where my music ends and their music begins. It occurs to me that someone is doing this on purpose, the same someone who has been leaving me notes all week.

Still donning my gardening gear and with my hair pulled into a high messy bun, I brace myself for what I'm about to face when I open my door. My senses are hit with a barrage of noise, lights, and a strong waft of weed and alcohol. As I look over the banister, I notice the party is mainly taking place outside, though there is a small group of people lounging about in the living area below.

While descending the staircase, I feel their eyes on me, watching as I stomp down the steps. I know what I look like compared to their scantily dressed bodies, donning bikinis and board shorts, but right now, I don't care what I look like. I've been coerced into this situation against my will, and I'm going to put an end to it.

Leaning against the sink, Lucius is wearing his trademark smirk like a war medal to be proud of. He's already got two drinks in his hands and is just waiting for this very moment when I'll give into his demands. It grates on me that he knew I would eventually give into his form of pressure. He's wearing navy board shorts with a fitted white t-shirt, making me scoff over how model-like he's looking, fitting right in with all the Barbies and Kens walking around us. Truthfully, I'm a little disappointed that he's betraying his normal style to fit in; I could at least respect him when he acted indifferent to it all. Still, I'm not about to prolong this moment by calling him out on it, so I continue walking right up to where he's still leaning, take my own glass out of a nearby cupboard and open up a new bottle of Jack Daniels that was sitting on the kitchen counter. I proceed to pour my own damn drink, then turn to face him so he can see me down it and slam the glass back on the side.

He smiles with a hint of pride just before I grimace over the liquid burning down my throat.

"Fuck, that's gross!" I cry out before forcing myself to face him again. "There, I had a drink with you. Can you stop turning the God-damn music up now?"

"That's not exactly a drink *with* me, Topolina," he says as he grabs the same bottle but with two new glasses. "Come with me, Topolina. I'm guessing you don't trust the drinks I've already poured," he says as he starts walking. With a long sigh, I reluctantly follow behind, being that I just want this to be over as soon as possible so I can be left alone. "Your suspicious nature impresses me, Topolina. I would have been disappointed if you *had* trusted me."

I can't see his face, only his back as we walk out of the kitchen, but I can easily picture the grin now spreading across his smug features. I don't think I'll ever be able to forget it.

"Just so you know, I'm not doing this all night so you can get me off my face," I grumble with a roll of my eyes. "I have this one drink *with* you, and then you turn the music down, deal?"

"Of course," he says ever so reasonably, "I wouldn't dream of getting you 'off your face'."

He leads me into the living room, which is empty and quiet, but close enough that if he tried anything, I could scream, and someone would hear. Not that I think he will, but I've had enough lectures from Dad about keeping myself safe and knowing that you don't open yourself up to vulnerable situations. Hence getting my own glass. He gestures to the three-seater couch where we sit with enough distance between us that I feel suitably comfortable. Lucius pours the drinks, making it obvious that he's not adding anything else to the tumblers, other than what he will also be drinking. I'm handed one of the glasses while he keeps the other one and leans into the back of the couch.

"Sip," he instructs, "don't gulp."

Obediently, I sip, and it is better, apart from the fact that his intense eyes are fixed on my own the entire time. When he drops his glass back down from his sip, his lower lip scrapes over his top one, and he sighs contently. His arm reaches toward me and retrieves something from my hair. Another green leaf from the garden, and for a moment, I smile. He doesn't return my friendly expression, but it doesn't surprise me.

"You're very intense," I voice my observation. "It's intimidating. Is that always your intention?"

"Maybe," he says with a half-hearted shrug. "Though, I wouldn't say I try to be anything for anyone."

"That's not true," I reply with a teasing grin. "Look at your board shorts, your muscular physique, your boyband hair. You're just as vain as they are."

At first, I'm offered nothing more than a devious smile, one that almost tells me he's proud of me for making such an observation. It's also one that warns me to brace myself for what is about to come out of his wicked mouth.

"My vanity is not for anyone other than myself. My parties are for my own amusement, much like this drink is." He lifts his glass in a 'cheers' gesture before sipping back more liquor, his eyes remaining on mine the entire time. They hold you captive without you even realizing it; those icy blues are hypnotic, the perfect weapon.

"Tell me then," I begin, the alcohol beginning to hit me as a fuzzy sensation takes over, "why do you want to drink with me? I can tell that I am *so* not the type of girl you usually spend time with."

"That is precisely why I want to drink with you, Topolina," he says in such a way, I feel heady and surprisingly lustful. "I like a challenge. But for your information, I do not usually spend much time drinking with girls in general. Do you really think someone like Lori would pique my interest?"

"Well…" I murmur, trying to make peace with the fact that I am seriously a target for him. "Hmm…as flattered as I am, I have had a drink now, so I am going back to my room. I am one 'challenge' you will not be conquering."

I get up and walk toward the staircase feeling angry, though I'm not entirely sure why. Did I really think he thought anything more of me?

I walk past the banister that overlooks the kitchen to see that it is completely empty, the party is now taking place entirely outside. Well, at least he kept to his side of the deal I suppose. However, as soon as I turn to open my door, I feel a presence behind me. I know it's him, for he always makes the air feel heavier around me, not to mention I can smell his aftershave. Like him, it's unique and dizzying.

When I finally turn to face him, the intensity of lust in his eyes almost scares me, though I cannot deny that it also has me feeling slightly thrilled at the same time. The recognition of such a feeling has me remembering Cam's words of warning, forcing me to freeze on the spot. Lucius gently lifts my wrist away from the door handle before opening the door himself. He pushes me inwards so we are standing in the dusky light of my room; the moon is shining through the window, but I can only make out the outline of bedroom furniture.

The thrill of it slips a little, turning into fear of what I have never done before. I also consider the fact that no one is here to hear me scream if I need to. He could be evil in a beautiful disguise, and I have left myself completely vulnerable to him. My breathing quickens as he slowly walks me back until he is pressing me against the bedroom wall. I tell myself to scream, to fight back, to say something, but I can't, his gaze is too hypnotic.

Lucius maintains a distance between us but keeps hold of my wrist and places his finger against my lips.

"Shh, Topolina, I am not going to do anything to hurt you; that's not my style." His words are enough to calm me. I don't know why, but I believe him. "Have you ever kissed a man, Helena? I mean *really* kissed a man?"

He takes a step closer toward me, so I am under no illusion as to what he wants. I shake my head slowly while the rest of my body stays completely frozen against the wall.

"I am not a challenge, Lucius," I utter in barely a whisper, trying to sound firm and sure of myself.

"Not anymore," he whispers back, then removes his finger and delivers a chaste kiss on my lips. It's more of a graze of his lips against mine, but it's enough to set the butterflies in motion, deep inside my stomach and chest. It scares me and after a moment, I jerk my head back to reveal my wrath.

"You are such an arrogant bastard, Lucius," I snap through clenched teeth. He laughs softly as he pushes back a strand of my hair behind my ear. I jerk my head away from his touch.

"You want to know what I want from you, Topolina?" he whispers, so close that it blows a stray hair away from my cheek. "Why don't you ask me?"

"No," I reply. He theatrically tuts over my stubbornness.

"Ask.Me!" he repeats in a low threatening voice, but when I don't, he tells me anyway. "I want…" he begins, pausing for a moment to take an inhale of my hair. "I want all of you. I want to destroy everything good and pure about you and claim you as mine. What's more, you will give it willingly to me, and you…" He stops and sighs as he looks me up and down with sheer desire in his eyes. "Mm…you will be mine. Even when you're with another man who promises you the fairy tale lifestyle that Daddy has always wanted for you, you will belong to me. I will always have you because deep down, I am what you really crave."

"You're fucked up, you know that?" I growl at him, even though I feel like I'm melting on the inside. Every part of me is telling me to submit, to give in and break free of my cage, my good girl persona.

"Maybe," he says as he cups hold of my cheek and leans in, so we are but an inch apart. "But tell me you haven't thought about my hands stroking over your arms," he says as he gently brushes his fingertips over my tanned skin, causing me to shudder. "Tell me you haven't wished for me to reach for your hips and pull you in closer to mine," he says as he acts out each of his words with expert precision.

My body submits to him completely, all the while I'm screaming at myself to push away.

"I bet you're wet right now. I'd even bet you're…soaking!"

He moves in even closer and suddenly, his overwhelming figure clouds my thoughts, making me feel dizzy and hot. I need him to go before I do something I'll regret, something that would mean I couldn't look my father in the eye without telling him I had given myself to the complete opposite of who he wants for me. It would mean admitting I've been dissatisfied with everything I have been brought up to want.

"Leave, Lucius...please," I whisper with a hint of urgency. He's right, I am wet, and now I'm cursing my own body's betrayal of my senses.

"I will, for a kiss, Topolina," he says in a low, hungry voice. "A proper, first kiss. At least give me that."

"What does 'topolina' even mean, Lucius?"

"I will tell you, once you kiss me," he says, now closing the gap between us so his chest is up against mine, and with my heart pounding inside of it. "Or at least...let me kiss you."

"Fine," I reply with an exhale, "but-"

I don't have the chance to finish my sentence before his lips move in to claim mine. He's more desperate than before, with his hands still resting on top of my hips, but now pulling them in against his own. I place my own hands over his muscular biceps in a half-defensive, half-incredibly turned-on position. His tongue sweeps through my lips and begins to stroke my own. He's gentle at first but as he deepens our kiss, he begins to explore every part of me, making good on his promise to claim me in any which way he can. I feel his erection hardening against my stomach and my eyes burst open. I stop moving my lips against his, so he opens his eyes to meet mine, smiling against my mouth because he knows full well what has caused me to freeze. Lucius makes no attempt to move, so after a moment or two, I push him away.

"Not bad, my little mouse," he says with a soft laugh, wiping the corner of his mouth with the back of his hand. "Feel something you like?"

I remain silent, for anything I say is only going to make him say something more aggravating. I'm guessing *topolina* means 'little mouse', which only makes me feel even more humiliated.

"Leave!" I order in a quiet voice, keeping my eyes on the ground, even though part of me desperately wants him to kiss me again. A part governed by primitive urges and hormones, a part I need to ignore.

Lucius laughs when he eventually moves toward the door, gripping the handle to leave.

"You taste good by the way, really good." His intense gaze moves south over my body. "Makes me wonder what the rest of you tastes like."

He looks back up into my eyes, only now he isn't smiling. Instead, I see nothing but a lustful urge emanating from his icy blue orbs; they taunt me, dare me, order me to just give in.

"Please, Lucius…please, just leave!"

To my surprise, he nods just once and opens the door.

"Only ever willingly," he says with a strange expression. "But you will. Lock the door when I go, Topolina. I am not the only one lusting after you, and I cannot stay in your room again, not after that kiss. Goodnight."

"Goodnight," I whisper back, and he leaves, thankfully closing the door behind him.

When I finally manage to convince my feet to work, I march right over and lock the door, all the while releasing a long breath that I didn't even know had been stuck in my chest. I close my eyes and lean my back against the door, before slumping slowly to the ground.

I should have gone to bloody summer camp; I'm not equipped to deal with this.

Chapter 9

Helena

The day after I had lost myself in a kiss with the devil, I decided to forget about it, or at least try to. If I ignore it ever happened, perhaps Lucius will do the same and we can pretend things are no different from the way they were before. No one would need to know, least of all the men in my family. I wouldn't need to see my father's disappointment in me for giving away my first kiss to a man he would deem unworthy. In my head, I can take it all back, convince myself that I am still saving my first kiss and my first love for a boy who is good, wholesome, and so polite he'd apologize for saying 'darn' or 'Jesus'. I would then marry that boy and have a brood of just as good and wholesome kids, while making it my life's mission to serve my husband, including agreeing with each and every thing he says. Just like I do with my father now. Just like Mom.

I shake away those thoughts, the ones that have me realizing just how empty my life is; the ones that tell me I need more. **Desire** *more, Helena, there's a difference. Be grateful for what you have, be grateful your mom and I are here to keep you safe. You're different from Cam and Nate, what you do and say* *will be held against you. People remember when a girl acts up, and they don't forgive so easily. Behave and you will have a good life with a good man who will look after you. Don't you want someone to look after you?*

I need to rehydrate again, the whiskey from last night is threatening to make my head ache as well as causing me to think negatively. I can almost feel a physical layer of depression wrapping itself around me. But it's not real, it's just leftover alcohol. My life **is** good. It might not be perfect, but nobody's life is, not even for boys like Cameron and Nate.

Stepping outside, I ignore the usual garbage that is strewn all over the place from last night's gathering of randy teenagers. Instead, I walk straight over to the potting shed, wishing Owen a good morning as I pass by him on the way. Once inside the shed, I find a familiar-looking note lying on the counter.

Willing and mine. X

As I breathe out long and slow, I afford myself a moment to close my eyes and sigh, before screwing it up and throwing it inside the incinerator. The thought of sleeping with Lucius makes me feel tingly and nauseated all at the same time. My head becomes light, but worse than that, my panties dampen from my own irritating and traitorous arousal. After a stern internal talking to myself, I shake it off and continue with what I came out here to do.

Fortunately, when I walk back into the kitchen for lunch, I am delighted to find Meri and my aunt sitting at the breakfast bar.

"There she is, little Miss Green Thumb!" My aunt hugs me with a kiss on my cheek. It feels like one of my own parents embracing me, which instantly makes me feel all warm and fuzzy inside. "Don't go getting ideas about him. He's far too old for you," she says in a theatrically stern voice, completely out of the blue.

I immediately blush and my mouth drops open in shock. Did she see his note? Has he said something? Maybe Meri saw him coming into my room last night.

"Too old? What do you mean? I thought…er…what?" I stutter uncomfortably before losing my breath altogether.

"Yes, Owen, the roguish gardener. He's in his mid-forties! Gorgeous but not for you, Hels," she says with a mischievous grin on her face. "Though, I must confess, I've had quite a few daydreams about him taking me roughly inside the potting shed!"

"Ew, gross! You're my mother and a married woman," Meri scolds with a disgusted expression on her face, which only has Jen laughing with wicked delight. "Anyway, I was just telling Mom about how awful Lucius was to you when you first arrived. I hope he's stopped calling you 'virgin' now."

"Oh, Hels, you must ignore our handsome little devil. Don't let his beautiful exterior fool you. He's completely wicked. I don't think we've ever seen him with the same girl twice and he only uses them for one thing," she says with a wink that makes me think she can see right through me and into my shameful thoughts. "I think he's even been with the baby bride down the road; you know the one don't you, Meri? The one who must be half her husband's age? Scandalous!"

She theatrically raises her brow before sipping more of her coffee. I try to let that information sink in while Meri thinks about who her mother must be talking about.

"Oh, yes! Well, if that is true, the husband obviously has no idea. They still act like love's young dream," Meri finally replies.

"I heard Lucius was caught banging one of the professors within the first few months of college this year. She left not long after."

"Wow, he has quite the reputation," I mutter, still deep in thought about it all. I won't ever admit it, but after last night, I can see why girls like Lori find Lucius such a turn-on. It's the masochistic part in all of us, the part that has you willingly falling in love with the villain, like Stockholm syndrome. "Don't worry, Cam has already warned me to stay away from him, and that was before I even got here. Your friend, Lori, is welcome to him."

My words are convincing enough, but I've just told a complete lie to them. The thought of him with any of those women, including Lori, makes me want to vomit. Not that Meri and Jen can see this inner turmoil for I am an expert at maintaining a passive and neutral expression.

"Oh, how are your brothers?" Jen asks with renewed enthusiasm. "Both handsome boys but with a much more amiable personality. I bet they break a few hearts too."

"More than likely, but I don't really like to get involved in their love lives. Nate has started young, from what I hear. I know for a fact that my dear big brother, Cam, puts it about though."

I grimace over the thought while my aunt and cousin both laugh over my obvious discomfort. Funnily enough, so does my father, usually with the odd comment of, *'boys will be boys'*, or *'best to let them have their fun now.'* It is ridiculously unfair. I have often thought about mentioning it to Jen, but I don't want to bring up painful memories of her having always been compared to her perfect big brother. She did the opposite to me; she rebelled. She seems happy enough but then she's so much braver than I am. Her mother didn't speak to her for months after she fell pregnant out of wedlock. Her father called her all manner of names, while my dad said nothing. I think that's why he's always been there for her; he feels guilty. Though, not guilty enough to act any differently when it comes to me.

"And they say romance is dead," a low voice utters as it enters the room. Knowing exactly who it belongs to, I suddenly feel hot, as though the temperature has been turned up a notch or ten. "Afternoon, ladies," Lucius says as he appears from around the corner and offers a polite nod to my aunt and Meri.

When his eyes fall on my own, I instantly know that he isn't going to forget about that kiss, especially when he glances at my lips for a moment or two. His tongue darts out from between his lips and I feel my cheeks reddening over the sight of it. My heart rate picks up and I hope against hope that no one can see how awkward his presence is making me feel.

"Tell me, did Cameron and his girlfriend ever make up after the wedding? They looked like such a sweet couple."

"Lucius," my aunt says in friendly warning, "be nice please."

"Oh, Helena knows I'm only messing around," he says as he moves around to the sink and begins washing his hands, which appear to be spotlessly clean. His back remains to Meri and Jen, but he leans back to look me in the eye. "Don't you, Topolina?"

Placing my mouth onto the mug of cold tea that I've already finished; I try to remain expressionless. But he continues to stare at me in such a way, I feel like I must say something, if only to dispense with the stifling atmosphere he's created between us.

"Actually, she came down with a bad case of herpes. Tell me, Lucius, do you get yourself checked regularly? Might be a good idea."

I manage to smile innocently at him as I place my mug inside the sink. Meri and Jen stifle their grins while Lucius looks deadpan at me, making me quiver a little. Though, he soon turns on his trademark smirk while I fold my arms in front of me with defiance.

"Touche, Topolina," he whispers, just loud enough for me to hear. In fact, Meri and Jen have already begun to gossip about other things, no longer paying any attention to Lucius and me. "I always make sure I am clean for any sexual partner," he says just as quietly as before, "just so *you* know."

He winks before walking out into the living room, cool as a cucumber, all the while I remain frozen on the spot.

"Well done, Helly Belly," Jen says, using a nickname I haven't been called since I was a child, "he needs a good dose of sass to pull him back down to Earth."

I smile awkwardly but I know it doesn't reach my eyes. So instead, I choose to change the subject. Fortunately for me, they let me without question.

I manage to evade Lucius over the next few days. In fact, he seems positively absent from Hastings Villa, and I find myself relaxing. I fall back into being the girl from before, the one that doesn't question anything about my life and who will always be her daddy's good girl. I am happy and content. Meri and her mother dip in and out of the house, always asking if I would like to join them, even though they know I am likely to politely decline. My troubling thoughts have caused me to fear the outside world even more than usual; here, I feel safe, especially with Lucius being decidedly missing. Even Owen has been encouraging me to go out into the real world, but I am more than happy to remain hidden away. I read, I garden, I explore the grounds, and I listen to music in my own little bubble where no one can get to me. It's blissfully uncomplicated, so much so, I have completely lost track of what day it is.

A week passes by before I hear Lucius again but it doesn't sound like his usual calm and indifferent tone of voice. He's angry with someone; he sounds low and menacing, and every now and then, I hear the slam of a fist against a hard surface. The intensity of the thump makes me glad I am not on the other end of that argument.

"I told you, there's no fucking way," he growls at the phone, "it's not up for discussion."

I can hear his expensive shoes pacing back and forth across the marble flooring in the living room. I know I should probably go somewhere else, anywhere far away from him, especially with the mood he's in, but I can't help but remain frozen on the spot. My breathing is erratic, even though I'm trying to hold it in to make myself as quiet as possible. As I spy through a crack in the doorway, I see him taking a long inhale on his blunt before he begins running his fingers through his ebony black hair. He must have only just got home because his aviators are still covering his icy blues, and he's just thrown his car keys onto the table with a loud clatter.

"That was not part of the deal, Eric, and if you come near said deal, I will break your fucking legs!"

My eyes bulge over the threat he's just made to his best friend, all the while waving his arms around in his black blazer. His dark denim jeans hang low around his hips and his feet rest in a pair of black boots, even though it's more than a little warm today. Me, on the other hand, I'm dressed in my usual denim shorts and a black tank top, hair all over the place and probably covered in leaves again. I've been pruning for Owen; my little plot is now complete and waiting to grow. If I'm not careful, I'm going to have to find something new to occupy my time here.

"It's a given, by the end of the summer," he says, his angry tone now turning into menacing laughter. "Have I ever failed before?" Within moments, he's returned to the indifferent man who has just thrown himself onto an armchair with an unapologetic slouch taking over his body language. "So?! Do me a favor and tell every other little fuck sniffing around that they've been warned. I will not hold anything back if they dare come near her; she's mine!"

What the actual fuck? He better not be talking about me. Surely not!

That's it, I'm confronting him on it. However, when I walk into the living room, the complete mess that I am, I find him staring right at me with an arrogant grin on his bastard face. His phone is resting on the arm of his chair, and his ankle is perched on top of his other knee. He removes his aviators and continues to stare right at me.

"Eavesdropping Topolina?" he asks calmly. "So unbecoming of you."

"Was that last bit for my benefit?" I ask coldly. I'm not sure if he really was talking to Eric about me or if he'd already ended the call and was merely trying to wind me up. Either way, I've had enough, so turn to leave.

"What if I was, mia topolina?" he calls after me, and I stop. "Are you going to call me up on it? Or are you wondering how many of my friends are wanting to fuck you as much as I am?"

"You're disgusting, Lucius, I can't believe I let you inside my mouth. Excuse me while I go and try and scrub the thought of it away." I begin walking again but he rushes up and stands in the door, blocking my way while annihilating my stormy and dramatic exit. "Oh, God, what now, Lucius?"

"Maybe I want to kiss you again; maybe touch you too," he says as though he's just suggested we go out for lunch. My horrified expression makes him laugh, still with his body blocking my way. "Tell me you haven't thought about it. Honestly. Even after your aunt warned you away from me. Actually, *especially* after your aunt warned you away from me."

"Oh, please, plenty of people have warned me away from you," I argue, now crossing my arms defensively. "You seem to leave a seedy trail wherever you go."

"And, of course, you listen to them, like the good little mouse that you are." He leans casually against the door frame, goading me into defying everyone to give him what he wants. "I bet you've never stood out as doing anything slightly out of the ordinary in your life. I bet when you actually venture outside you like to be invisible. I bet the thought of showing me your naked body makes you tremble with fear...or maybe something else?"

I refuse to answer any of his ridiculous statements, even though wanting to remain invisible is one of my main goals in life. He merely smiles, looking at me in such a way, I fear he can read my every thought.

"Give me your hand, Topolina," he whispers.

I shake my head, no, but he reaches out and takes hold anyway. I try to pull back, but he merely raises his brow and holds on even tighter. I sigh, knowing I cannot fight him on this all the while he brings my hand closer to his lips. I brace myself for when they will make contact with my skin, only they never do. Instead, he pulls it down toward his jeans and hovers the palm of my hand over the apex of his legs. I shoot my gaze up to his hypnotically beautiful blue eyes which remain staring into my own. I try to say something, to move away, but I can't. He smiles before pulling my hand to cover the hard bulge beneath his jeans. Warm, hard, thick.

"See what you do to a man? You're making me horny as fuck," he whispers as he moves his lips to the shell of my ear. "I can only imagine what it would feel like inside of your tight, untouched pussy."

He closes his eyes and clenches his teeth as he continues to stroke himself with my hand. I don't know why I don't bolt, or at least try to stop him. He grabs my other hand and pulls me against his chest, all the while staring at me intensely. His lips move to rest against my own before he finally makes contact, pushing his tongue between them and massaging it against me with a soft touch. I find myself returning his actions and pretty soon, we're exploring each other's mouths more hungrily. And still, he strokes himself, emitting a groan of pleasure every now and then. *Oh, heaven help me, he is the beautiful spawn of Satan, sent to trick me into thinking he's a demi-God.*

The sound of softer footfalls beginning to descend the staircase has me jumping back from him with extreme shame and embarrassment. Lucius, who had made no such attempt to stop, simply smiles before adjusting himself to make his arousal less obvious.

"Oh, hey, Hels," Meri chirrups, sounding surprised when she sees Lucius standing next to me. *God, I hope my blushing isn't too obvious.* "Wanna come to the mall with me?"

"Actually, yes! Yes, I would," I quickly blurt out, grabbing the opportunity to escape the stifling environment. I don't trust myself around Lucius anymore, especially with that devious grin of his. "Let me just clean up. Give me ten minutes."

She looks shocked over my sudden desire to go out with her when she's so used to me refusing. Thankfully, being Meri, she doesn't question it, just smiles sweetly and nods. I rush past Lucius and head upstairs.

"Topolina?" his unhurried voice travels up the stairs to me.

Knowing I should ignore him, I curse myself when I tentatively look over the banister to see what he's going to say.

"Mine!" he mouths.

My heart feels like it's pounding like a freight train as I step back and head into my room without a sound.

Courage, Helena, courage!

Chapter 10

Helena

After proving to be a "thoroughly useless shopping companion", Meri leads the way to the food court so we can grab lunch and a quick catch-up before her gaggle of friends arrives. During my tour of Meri's favorite stores and boutiques, I've remained quiet, purposefully avoiding her questions about what she saw between Lucius and me. I've also managed to avoid giving any kind of meaningful comments about the various outfits she's shown, for in all honesty, I have no idea what is considered fashionable. What I deem to be trendy back in my hometown, Meri considers drab. She found my cluelessness amusing, but my silence over Lucius is telling; she knows something is up. I can feel her staring at me all the while I play with my food.

"You ok, chick?" she eventually asks, trying to sound cool about it, but I can tell she's concerned about me. It's as clear as day in her voice. "Was Lucius being an ass again?"

"No…well…no," I reply, shaking my head over how to answer that question. "I'm sure he was just being him."

"Do you want me to ask Mom to talk to Paul about it? I'm worried about how much you stay in. It's not healthy, Hels. Then whenever I see you with him, you seem to fall into a funk; you look like you're overthinking more than usual." I stifle a smile over her description, for I cannot argue with it. "Please let me help you," she says, taking my hand and smiling back at me.

For all her cliché American teenage 'It' girl habits, no one can deny how caring she is, especially towards me, her dowdy cousin. It makes me feel suddenly guilty for dissing her lifestyle habits, even if only in my head.

"No, don't say anything. He's just playing with me; I'm sure he does it with lots of girls." I shrug as I slurp on my drink to try and make it appear less than it is.

"What do you mean?" she asks, ignoring my attempt to downplay it all. "What's he doing exactly?"

"It's kind of embarrassing, I'd really rather not." I blush, but from the look she's giving me, I'm not going to get away with keeping quiet about this one.

"Oh, come on, I'm your cousin, your closest female family member," she says with a cheeky grin, but I guess she's right. Mom, Jen, and my grandmother are parental figures, and my other cousin, Ellie, is even younger than Nate. Meri is the only relative who is the same age as me. "You have to tell me! You also need to gossip, eat junk, talk about boys, and generally be a teenager. It is what we are after all. I know you enjoy acting like a middle-aged recluse, but you're in the mall with me right now. When in Rome and all that."

I continue playing with my food while offering her a tight-lipped smile. I don't know how to do the whole girlfriend thing. Most of my friends are adults; I feel more at ease with them, always have done. When the toddlers at pre-school were playing house with each other, I was sitting with the teachers, asking them questions about their families and what they had done at the weekend. I was the weird little kid who no doubt got talked about after hours by the teachers who were all trying to figure me out with their colleagues.

"Ok," Meri says abruptly, thus interrupting my thoughts, "what if I tell you a little secret about me? Would that make you open up?" I look at her, appearing half-interested, which is enough to convince her to carry out her suggestion. "I slept with David the other night…at the party."

"David?" I ask, momentarily trying to work out who David is. "Do you mean your friend's ex-boyfriend?" She nods her head, wincing, though it is an unconvincing look of remorse if ever I saw one. My eyes bulge at the same time as I drop my mouth open in shock. "Meri! Wh-why would you do that?"

"Because I've loved him for, like, ever!" She slumps in her chair, obviously feeling a little bad, though perhaps not as much as she should. "Scarlet never liked him like I do, she was always messing around behind his back. But now he wants to be with me and out in the open. What the hell do I do?"

"Er…talk to Scarlet maybe?" I offer. "Course, you should have done that before you went to bed with him." She sheepishly drops her eyes to the floor while I think on it for a moment or two. "Actually, maybe leave out the part about sleeping with him. Just explain how you feel about him. What else can you do?"

She nods disappointedly but is quick to perk up, looking hungry with anticipation.

"Ok, now your turn!" she says with excitement in her voice and a toothy grin on her face.

At first, I sigh, wondering what to say, or indeed, where the hell to start. In fact, I open my mouth to start explaining several times before closing it again without having said anything at all. After a while, she rolls her eyes with impatience.

"Oh, come on! It can't be any worse than what I've just admitted to." That's debatable, it is Lucius after all.

"Lucius, well, he kind of told me he wants to sleep with me by the end of the summer. He thinks I'm going to come willingly, after which, I will be 'his' because I've given him my virginity… or something." I shrug it off like it's nothing weird when actually, it totally is.

"Erm…that's…that's…"

As she falters over her words, she looks into the distance as though she's really thinking deeply about it.

"Intense? Creepy? Possessive? Fucked up?" I offer.

"Hot!" She smiles like the Cheshire cat, looking both devilish and intrigued. *Oh, brother!* I roll my eyes at her in despair; so much for the women's liberation movement. "Think about it, Hels, he's the hottest property around and he's totally hooked on you. Trust me, he doesn't give any girl the time of day and now he's wanting to have you, own you, or some shit like that? That's sexy as fuck, if you ask me."

"Do you hear yourself, Meri? First of all, he is not 'hooked' on me, this is just a game to him. I am merely his prey. Secondly, just because he's pretty to look at doesn't, mean I should automatically drop my panties for him. And finally, you've been warning me away from him ever since I got here. Now you think I should give it up to him?"

"What can I say? I'm shallow and fickle," she says with a

theatrical bat of her eyelids before slurping down the pink, syrupy crap from her throw-away cup. Said cup comes complete with a fluorescent straw with rainbows printed all over it. Says it all, really. After I contemplate how very superficial her life is, we both giggle at one another. I think she's superficial whereas she considers me old and frumpy, but we kind of work together. After a while, she looks at me with a much more serious expression, so I brace myself for what she's about to say.

"Maybe you should live a little, Hels? Stop being a spinster and all that. It doesn't have to be with Lucius; I admit, he's heartbreak through and through, but maybe give someone a chance?"

I shrug non-committedly. I've never been remotely interested in anyone, which is why Lucius is particularly dangerous. I feel like he would break me, and I'd have to live with the pain of it for the rest of my life.

"And don't sleep with Owen!" she warns me so suddenly and sternly, I can't help but laugh out loud. "Mom's right, he's too old and he's close enough for Lucius to murder. In fact, you can't get it on with anyone he knows because he doesn't share too well."

"There'll be no 'sharing'!" I tsk.

Our bonding is instantly silenced once her friends arrive, when she falls back into gossiping and dramatizing their lives. I momentarily pity poor David and the storm that is sure to come his way, though the guy is obviously a glutton for punishment. Apart from a few icy stares from Lori, I am pretty much back to being invisible again. Though, at least it gives me the chance to make my excuses and slip away. Not knowing the transportation system in this place, I figure I can just walk back to *Hastings Villa*. I don't remember it being that far away when Meri drove us here.

Besides, it gives me a chance to stretch my legs and take in the sights of all the rich houses I'll pass by on the way.

Unfortunately, this turns out to be a pretty crap idea when the scorching sunshine ignites one of my migraines. It is not a short journey at all. It's at least an hour's walk, not to mention devoid of any shops. My water runs out halfway, and I didn't bring any kind of painkillers with me, let alone my migraine medication. Why would I? I never usually go out. The flashes begin first, followed by throbbing pain around my eyes and deep in the hollows. It travels up my forehead, over the top and into the base of my skull. I want to lie down and close my eyes to it all, however, I soon realize I have no other choice but to keep on walking the last mile in the burning heat.

By the time I reach the gates to *Hastings Villa*, I'm retching on the grass while trying to hide it amongst the bushes. I feel bad for soiling Owen's plants but there's nothing I can do but give into my nausea. Sometimes it makes me feel better, though not today it would seem. Instead, it makes me feel dizzy, and I have to drop to my knees to try and concentrate on my breathing. In the end, I fall to the grass completely, trying to cool myself on the shady blades and parched soil. I'm so hot, I just want to peel the sticky clothes away from my body and bask in the fraction of air that's blowing into my hair. When I venture to open my eyes again, the flashing lights are worse, and I can only see in one direction.

"Fuck me, Helena, what have you done to yourself?" Lucius' low voice sounds concerned, almost caring. I can only surmise how awful I must look, for if the devil himself is worried about me, it can't be good.

He doesn't wait for any kind of response, instead, he grabs hold of my arm and wraps it around his neck before scooping me up against his chest. I cling onto him, but I don't have a lot of strength. I feel so exhausted from the walk that I can barely grip onto his shirt. My weakness doesn't prevent him from walking me into the house and straight up to my bedroom, where he places me gently onto the bed.

"I need to...close the..." I point to the curtains that are letting in a painful amount of light into the room. He follows my line of sight and immediately closes them before pacing into my bathroom to find my tablets in the medicine cupboard. While he is in there, I strip down to my bra and panties to allow the cool breeze from the open window to fall over my hot sweating body. After that, I sit on the bed and lift my face up to the breeze, indulging in the coolness and freshness of it.

"And you're in your underwear because...?" Lucius asks as he returns to the room with a glass of water and two tablets.

"I'm hot...so hot," I try to explain as he hands me the glass and medication. "Thank you."

"Did you actually *walk* back from the mall?" he asks, sounding accusatory.

"I couldn't hack Meri's friends anymore," I tell him, pushing the words out like they're stuck to my tongue. "And the mall is ridiculously boring."

"That was fucking stupid, Topolina," he chastises me while grabbing for my bag. Usually, I'd call him out on it, but I can barely see him, let alone warn him away from my belongings. "I'm putting my number in your phone. You call me next time; do you hear me?" I nod, choosing to let the argument go. "Now, as much as it pains me to ask you to cover up your fucking gorgeous little body, get into bed."

He holds the cover up, then helps me to slide myself inside

of the cool, soft sheets. Once lying down, he leans over me, bringing his face just inches away from mine.

"How many times do I have to save you, mia topolina?" I think I manage to smile before closing my eyes to go to sleep. I feel him stroking my hair gently before breathing out a long, frustrated sigh. "I've gotta get out of here," he whispers.

I think how nice it felt to have him here, stroking my hair, and soothing away the pain under the palm of his hands. Though, as soon as I hear him leave the room, I sink into blissful sleep.

♆

My eyes open to the darkness in my room and thankfully, my head has cleared. After a quiet celebration of relief, I grab my phone to see what time it is. It takes a moment or two for my eyes to focus and see that it's one in the morning. I've been asleep since two in the afternoon, so I'm now awake and ready to do something. I throw back the cover and make my way to the bathroom so I can splash my face. It feels so good, I decide to have a cool shower to wash away any remnants of my headache and nausea. The water melts over me and I feel the agony of my migraine wash away. I'm lucky it was short-lived this time around, nothing like my last one. Stepping out, I'm still shaky, but soon manage to dry myself, scoop up my hair into a braid, and pop my black night dress over my head.

Everyone is probably tucked up in bed, so I am thankful for my self-contained kitchen and living area downstairs. Hopefully, I'll unlikely wake anyone when I go and grab a glass of water and take a peek outside. The moon is full and bright and touches the garden with a sparkling of silver. Opening the door, the gentle night air hits me like a blanket of calm. My flip-flops are already on the step waiting for me, so I slip them on and shuffle over to the bench that sits next to the herb garden. I inhale the burst of basil, rosemary, and lavender all at once, then tuck up my legs to rest upon the bench. My eyes are closed but I am far from sleeping; I just feel blissful and appreciative for the feeling of normalcy.

After a few moments, something different infiltrates my senses while sitting here, still blinded by my closed eyelids. A smell of familiar cologne wafts up my nose, and a subtle rise in temperature seems to close in all around me. When I open my eyes in response to it, a tall, broad, darkened figure is sitting beside me. His skin, in contrast to mine, doesn't show up in the light so obviously, and I end up screaming. Lord knows why because I know exactly who it is. If all the other clues weren't enough to convince me that it's him, the low chuckle that falls from his mouth leaves me in no doubt as to who it is.

"Jesus fucking Christ, Lucius!" I gasp as I push at him, not that it moves him, not even a little bit.

"Sorry, Topolina," he says while continuing to laugh at me. I've never seen him looking so animated; it's a nice sight, even if it is at my expense. "I saw you squirreling away outside and couldn't resist."

For the first time ever, I find myself laughing along *with* him.

"I'm getting over a migraine, you jerk," I grumble before sipping at my water as if to highlight the point. "If it comes back, it will be all your fault!"

"Maybe I'm just after the chance to put you back to bed in your underwear again," he teases, with a devious smirk to match.

"Because nothing is sexier than a sick woman passing out in her bedroom," I tut. "I suppose I need to thank you again, do I?"

"No, this time you need to hear me tell your little ass off for being so stupid." He turns to face me head-on and with such a serious expression, I cease smiling. "What made you think it was a good idea to walk back in peak-day sun, with no water, and with a proneness to migraines?"

I bite my lip sheepishly because I guess he's right this time. But weirdly, I also kind of like the fact that he seems to be concerned.

"You are not to do that again; do you hear me?" he says assertively. "Never again!"

He takes my glass and places it to his own lips to drink. Now that my eyes have adjusted to the low light, I can see all of his usual gorgeous features - his dark, ruffled hair, ice-blue eyes, full lips, and impossibly firm body.

"Don't try and tell me off, Lucius," I snap, grabbing the glass back, "I'm not a little kid who needs -"

"Spanking?" he whispers with a devilish quirk of his brow.

Once again, he takes the glass from me, only this time, he places it onto the floor beneath the bench. Before I can protest, he places his thumb pads against my cheeks and begins stroking them gently, all the while looking intensely into my eyes. The feeling of his skin on mine is surprisingly relaxing, so I place my hands over his wrists, keeping him there, surprising both of us. His mouth drops open and he looks conflicted, as though he wants to do something, but knows that he probably shouldn't. Then again, I probably shouldn't be waiting for him to press his mouth to mine, but I can't help it; I want him to.

"I have to warn you, Topolina," he whispers as he leans in close, so much so, our lips are almost touching. It's different this time, I'm aching for it. I want it so badly; I find myself squeezing my thighs together. It's unsettling.

"I am not good for any girl, but especially not for you. I will give and I will take, but I will never hold back, even if it breaks you. Do you understand?" I'm not entirely sure what he means, but I find myself nodding, albeit slowly and cautiously. "I want to fucking consume you, Helena!"

I offer him nothing but a look of wanting, even when he closes his eyes and breathes in deeply like an addict trying to resist his next fix. Thinking back to Meri's words at the mall, I decide to take a risk, make the wrong decision, and live with the consequences. At least I'll enjoy the ride.

I slide my hands all the way up his arms until I reach the back of his neck where I begin lacing my fingers through his hair. I explore him for a moment or two, indulging in the feel of him inside of my hands, but then, without opening his eyes, he pulls me over his lap. My body straddles his when he kisses me roughly, primally, fully. His hands run up and down my back while his hips slam against mine through the thin layers of our clothing. He is as hard as steel as he thrusts his groin into me, using my behind as an anchor with his hands. As I gasp for breath, his mouth moves down the column of my neck, nipping and sucking, causing me to moan over the new sensations. The sexual sounds falling from my lips prompt him to lift me up and lie me down along the bench, with him soon crawling on top of me where he begins thrusting.

Loose, Helena, you're behaving like a loose girl; loose girls have bad reputations. What would your family think if they could see you now? What would your daddy say?

With little effort, Lucius moves my hands above my head and locks them in place, pinning me to the wooden slats below.

And God, I want so much more of him, and I know he is ready to take me in anyway he can.

Good girls don't behave like this, Helena, where has my good girl gone?

When he moves his hand down to my soaking wet panties and tries to reach beneath the cotton, I recoil and push him away from me.

"No, please, stop...I can't!" I gasp. "I'm sorry, I can't."

He jumps away from me like my body is made of fire, then whips his hands up in a defensive stance. I immediately sit up, straightening my dress while keeping my eyes shamefully to the ground. When I eventually look up into his eyes, I can't make out if he's hurt or angry. He's pacing with his hands running through his hair in frustrated, rough, and angry movements. It's scaring me so I decide to remain quiet; I'm embarrassed and feeling angry with myself too.

After a few tense moments, he reaches for my glass and launches it across the garden in a fit of rage. His jaw clenches when he sees it smash into smithereens on the path up ahead. The shock brings tears to my eyes and a whimper escapes through my lips without warning. He spins around to face me, and I physically flinch. If looks could kill, I would be six feet under in an instant.

Unable to bear his stern and angry stare, I break our eye contact. He says nothing. Instead, he turns once more to walk away with angry strides against the gravel beneath his feet. I physically shudder when I eventually hear the slam of a door in the distance. It is only then that I allow myself to wrap my arms around my knees and let the tears run over my cheeks in long, unforgiving streams.

I stayed outside until about four in the morning, trying to think about what to do next. What on earth is going on with me? Why am I falling for someone who everyone has warned me not to go near? Do I feel angry about what happened, or do I feel guilty? I know I feel utterly humiliated, not by Lucius, but myself. Fear got the better of me and I couldn't go through with it, but deep down, I know I led him on, only to withdraw at the last minute. The words 'cock tease' spring to mind and I physically cringe over how pathetic I must have looked to someone like Lucius. But he doesn't know what it's like, doesn't understand the pressure I feel to be my father's perfect little girl; to always be the *good* girl. It's been drilled into me for as long as I can remember.

"Girls don't get away with what boys do. Girls who act loose never shake their reputation. Be good, Helena, and you'll be happy."

Time to try and forget it ever happened. Move on and accept the fact that boys like Lucius aren't for girls like me. Except… I have that annoying part of my brain that saves up these sorts of horrible and humiliating memories. Each one to consistently replay in bright technicolor. I'll never be able to forget the look on his face before he stormed away. He'll no doubt avoid me until I leave this place, when he can pretend I don't exist. And stupidly, I feel sad about that.

It takes hours to fall into a restless sleep where I have a series of anxious dreams. Dreams of being trapped or running away, only to find myself wading through glue. I have night sweats on and off until eventually, I wake up and have to shower. As I'm drying myself off, I hear my phone ringing. It hasn't done that since I arrived, so I run to grab it, hitting my ankle on the way over, but continuing to run through the pain so it doesn't ring off.

"Ow, shit, fuck, hello?" I answer, wincing over my foot, which is going to have one huge bruise on it.

"Hey, Hels," Nate beams down the phone to me; I still can't get used to his broken voice. He sounds so manly, but to me, he's my kid brother who has Star Wars toys hidden under his bed, alongside Lego he still builds models with when he thinks no one is watching.

"Haven't interrupted anything, have I?" he asks with a theatrically suggestive tone of voice.

"No, course not," I reply, fake smiling from ear to ear. "How are you? I'm missing everyone."

"I'm good," he says cheerfully, "apart from setting off a girl fight. I bet I'm still having a better time than you though, especially with Lucius Hastings sleeping down the hall."

"Er…yeah," I reply, blushing over the thought of last night's humiliation. "Causing heartbreak and mayhem, are you?"

"Ah, only a now and then," he giggles, bringing out the little boy in him. "But how are you, sis? Are you managing to get out more?"

"No, not really. I'm fine though, can't complain really."

"You're not sleeping with Lucius, are you?"

His words have my heart feeling like it's stopped frozen in time, while all breath seems to have escaped my body at once.

"What? …What? …I mean…What? No!" I barely manage to gasp down the phone at the same time as I hear him slip into another chuckle.

"I'm messing!" he laughs. "Even I'm not stupid enough to

think you'd do that."

As relief hits me, I emit a fake, pitched laugh down the phone. *Lord, I think I just survived my first heart attack…just!*

"Oh, I gotta go," he says, sounding carefree and happy. "I miss you, Hels. See you next month."

"Be good," I call out before he disappears, after which, I sink into a heap on the floor. Now, on top of everything else, I'm incredibly homesick. Things must be bad if I'm missing my annoying kid brother.

Chapter 11

Helena

Walking downstairs, I feel anxious, all the while hoping against hope, that I don't run into Lucius. In fact, if I can stay clear of everyone today, that would be just peachy. It's not long, however, until I hear two deep voices coming from the direction of the living room. Grimacing over my own misfortune, I freeze on the spot, knowing that one of them belongs to Lucius, and from how he's talking, the other one must belong to his father, Paul. He sounds much too respectful and too manly to be one of Lucius' friends.

The voices are calm, but I don't want to disturb whatever it is they're talking about, so I decide to just hang about on the stairs like a stale old cobweb, hoping to remain unnoticed. I'm already in my gardening gear and the door to outside looks awfully tempting, but I know it sticks sometimes. Fate is bound to mess with me and make a noise if I decide to bolt for it.

"Lucius, she would be proud of you, you know that," Paul says, trying to convince Lucius of his words. "*I* am proud of you."

Oh, God! I inwardly cringe over my intrusion on this heart-touching moment, eavesdropping like a common, little thief, a pickpocket of sentimental, private moments between a father and son. Feeling the need to leave as soon as humanly possible, I turn to try and make my way back upstairs. However, my footsteps falter when I hear Lucius breathe out a long, sad sigh that causes my heart to drop. I've never heard him sound so sad, and all from a single sigh.

"What if...?" he begins to say but stops himself for a moment. "I can't...fuck, I wanted..." He sighs again, this time sounding frustrated by his inability to put his thoughts into words.

"You didn't, and besides, what you felt was normal. You won't turn into him, Lucius, believe me!" Paul tries to reassure him.

"I think you're right, this time away is a good idea," Lucius says, sounding determined. "I'll get a bag together ASAP and meet you at the office. It's time I learned the ropes before I go back to college anyway."

"Great," Paul replies, sounding just as certain as Lucius. "I'm looking forward to having the company. See you in about an hour?"

"Sure thing, Dad," he says. There's a pause, but then someone begins to head this way.

Shit! What do I do? They're going to know I've been listening. Think, Helena!

Deciding that going up to my room is too far away, I begin to walk down the rest of the steps to try and look as though I've just descended the staircase. Once I hit the bottom, Lucius enters the room with his brow furrowed and his hand running anxiously through his soft, black hair. Memories of running my hand through that same hair last night causes butterflies to begin flying through my chest. He freezes while staring at me in such a way, I want to wither into nothing. Instead, I stare back at him, chewing on my bottom lip over the awkwardness of the situation. Eventually, I open my mouth to say something, but he moves to grab his jacket from the breakfast bar and turns to walk swiftly out the door. I close my eyes in regret and emptiness. However, I'm not entirely sure which bit of everything I'm regretting more.

I don't see Lucius for a week or two, but Meri informed me he had gone to New York with his father on some business trip. Disappointment floods through me, and in so many ways. I find that I'm missing his little jibes, his white cards and his perfect cursive script, his attempts to kiss me, and his overall presence here. I'm so disappointed with myself for letting things go as far as they did, only to pull away at the last moment. Maybe I'm also disappointed with him. He teased me for being a virgin and yet he seriously thought I'd give it up so easily. Then he got pissed at me for changing my mind. I know his reputation isn't warm and fuzzy with hearts and rainbows, but I kind of thought…I have no idea what I thought.

Just to add to the mix of crap, I've now run out of stuff to do. My little spot in the garden is complete, so apart from weeding and watering, there's not much to do out there. Some shoots have begun to surface, which shocked me. I expected them not to grow because it's me who planted them. And no one needs to point out the link between my garden and my growing feelings toward Lucius, even I realize how blatantly obvious and pathetic it is. If my life were a novel right now, the teacher would be asking her students how the patch of dirt and plants represent my growing feelings toward someone I never had confidence or trust in.

Sadly, I do miss him though, much more than I thought I would. However, his absence is probably a good thing for me, he warned me after all, so I should take this as an opportunity to get over him without having actually ever got under him...Well, unless you count the humiliating encounter that happened on the bench. *Damn that moment on the bench!*

My head feels muffled all the time. I haven't had any full-blown migraines for a while, but there's a warning feeling in my head twenty-four-seven. Like a flashing beacon, it's warning me that if it wants to, it could easily blow into one. I'm careful to drink plenty, stay out of the sun, and basically be more of a recluse than I already am.

Being confined to my room has given me plenty of time to think about my life choices. I know I want to do something creative, and I know I want to travel, so I make a conscious decision to do so next summer. I'll be eighteen and can use the summer vacation to go somewhere new and exciting. I've applied to colleges to study textiles and photography so it will fit in nicely, gaining me some experience as well as building up my confidence. Lord knows I'm seriously lacking in that department. The idea of doing just that begins to make me feel excited, even relishing in the challenges and experiences ahead of me. Perhaps I can take the next year to learn a language, even if it's just a few words with which to get by.

After hitting this epiphany, I jump up to go and talk to Jen and Meri about it. I need some encouragement to try and cement the decisions I've made. However, before I can even reach the door, my phone rings and stops me in my tracks. I look down at the caller ID and it surprises me, but in a great way.

"Hi, Mom" I answer enthusiastically, "how are you guys? Where are you?" My enthusiasm turns to concern as soon as I hear my mother begin to sniff and sob through the phone. "What's wrong? What's happened?"

"Hi, sweetheart," Mom forces out through her tears, "it's bad news, I'm afraid."

"What? Is it Dad? Cam? Nate?" My voice sounds panicked, and I feel a heavy, painful lump forming at the back of my throat.

"It's your nonna, Hels, she passed away yesterday."

As if saying those words makes it all the more real for her, she breaks down into full-on crying. My eyes feel glazy and there's a distinct blurring to everything as they fill with unshed tears.

"Hi, Hels," Dad says as he takes the phone from her, "I'm so sorry, honey. She passed peacefully in her sleep. The doctors said she was just old, and her body had slowly been giving up. There's nothing anyone could have done."

Trying not to let out a yelp akin to a howling dog, I nod my head, even though he can't see. However, my emotions soon get the better of me, forcing me to release a sob of my own, the sound of which forces me to collapse on the bed and bury my head inside of my hands. As if some higher deity knew I needed someone, Meri appears at the door, putting her hand up ready to knock. When she sees me, she stops dead in her tracks. She frowns with indecision before uttering, "I'll go get Mom."

"Honey, you still there?" Dad asks softly.

"Yes, sorry," I reply with a long sigh made through crying. "Do I need to come back now? What about a funeral?"

"Don't worry about all that, we're still in France," he explains. "I'll make the traveling arrangements for you and send the tickets your way. Probably for a couple of weeks' time. We can't get back until next week anyway. We'll pick up Cam and Nate on the way back. You gonna be ok? Is Jen there with you?"

I look up and see my aunt hovering by the door with Meri.

"Yes, she's right here," I say to him.

I instinctively pass the phone over to the adult in the room and half listen while she talks to her brother. Meri, being the sensitive soul that she is, begins to tear up before lunging for me and holding on tightly while I sob against her hair. As soon as Jen finishes on the phone to Dad, she passes it back so he and I can say goodbye.

"Come here, Hels," Jen says before grasping hold of me for a long hug, only so fresh tears can fall into her hair too.

"I feel so bad for Mom," I cry, "I can't imagine losing your mom!" The thought alone has me thinking about Lucius again, but as a poor thirteen-year-old boy, lost in this huge house without his mother. No wonder he is so emotionally distant.

"I know, sweetie," she says calmly, "but it's life, I'm afraid. We are here for you; you know that, right?"

I nod, agreeing with her, but it doesn't feel any better. It's at moments like this when people who tell you they're there for you just sounds like a throwaway comment, because how can they be? How can they feel what you're feeling when they have no emotional attachment to the person you've lost? In fact, a horrible thought passes through me, a thought of envy over their feelings of normalcy. I resent their lack of grief right now. It's cold of me to think like that, but I guess I'm just wishing I could be with my mother right now. I know she has Dad with her, but I feel so helpless being stuck here. She's lost her mother, and her family are all over the place. Two weeks seems like such a long way from now, and without Lucius or my gardening, time seems to be passing by at a snail's pace.

It's been a few days since my nonna passed away, and it's got me thinking about my life. She was such a personality, full of wild and exciting tales of the things she had done over her lifetime. When she was my age, she was quite the beauty and had many male admirers. She used to laugh cheekily when she told me how she liked to play them off against one another. It wasn't until she met my grandpa when he was fighting overseas, that she truly fell in love. She had met him at a local bar in her village when he and a bunch of other soldiers were having a rare night off and had decided to sample the local nightlife. She told me it was love at first sight; no question about it.

Of course, she also told me she had played hard to get, but after a few dances and the odd kiss here and there, she knew he was hers and she was his. I need to have a life like this and break out of this mold I've built around myself. I also need to break free of what my father has had me believing about being a good girl; I need to make mistakes and own them. I need to stop being feared of others and put myself out there. And I need to let the Lucius' of this world know I am here and waiting to be swept up in their intensity and passion. Too bad I've blown my chance with him.

It's Thursday lunchtime and I'm chomping on a rather dull sandwich in the garden, on the very bench Lucius had tried to touch me. I can smell the same herbs from that night, and it makes me feel sad and regretful of lost opportunities.

"Hello, Topolina," a soft, low, and familiar voice says from behind me.

Mid-chew, I turn to see Lucius standing next to the bench, wearing a navy suit, sans tie, and his usual aviators. I have no words to describe how amazing he looks. Butterflies fill my stomach, suddenly seeing him for the man he is, not the boy who's only few years older than me. He moves slowly to come and sit down beside me and, instinctively, I twist my legs so I can face him.

"Hello." My voice sounds gravelly, unused.

"I'm sorry about your grandmother," he says, stroking my cheek with his thumb pad, "I can appreciate what it's like to lose someone special."

He looks so sad, my heart aches for him.

"Thank you, she was special. The funeral is in a couple of weeks, so I'll be going home next weekend," I tell him with a fake smile. "That's something for you to look forward to."

Lucius looks up at me with a serious expression and his thumb pauses on my cheek.

"Where've you been?" I just about manage to whisper while he's looking at me so intensely and as though he's hurting over what I've just said.

"Paul's LA office, helping him with a case he's working on," he mutters, still studying my lips with a frown of torment on his face.

"Sounds…interesting," I utter.

"Not really. A couple of fraudulent bankers," he says with a hint of a laugh that holds no mirth. "Country club types who failed to cover their tracks."

"Oh."

"Yeah, Paul's causing rifts amongst the banking world as well as the golfing community. The name 'Hastings' will be mud for years to come."

"Will that include snubbing you?"

"Undoubtedly," he says, finally bringing his eyes to meet mine. "Comes with the territory."

"But that's—"

"Helena, I have to apologize for my actions the night before I left for New York," he says, to which I must look beyond confused; I thought he was mad at me. "I knew you weren't ready, but I pushed you anyway. You have to believe me when I say I'm not into pushing myself on anyone like that."

"That's not what I thought, Lucius," I tell him as I take hold of his hand. "I led you on and I certainly don't blame you for anything. I wanted to, I just suddenly felt too nervous to do anything. *I'm* sorry."

"Mia topolina," he whispers softly, suddenly looking hurt and fragile. "I'm not ready for you to go, but perhaps it's for the best." It's hard for me to hear him say this and I don't know how to respond without turning into a blubbering mess. "I'm going to tell you something and I trust you more than anyone not to let it go any further. I feel like I owe you an explanation after how I reacted. I want you to know I was not angry with you at all."

"You weren't? But the glass? The way you looked at me? You left?" I sputter it all out at once.

"I know, but I was angry with myself; I was terrified of turning into him," he says with a heavy, sad sigh. I can tell that whatever this thing is, it's difficult for him to talk about.

"*Him?*"

"Paul isn't my biological father," he explains, "my mother was raped when she was very young, younger than I am now." I drop my mouth open in shock before trying to cover it with my hand. I always assumed Paul was his dad by blood as well as by any other means. "She fell pregnant and being Italian and a devout Catholic, she refused to have an abortion. Paul was her boss at the time and had always liked her from afar. He found her crying in the office one night and she let the whole story fall out of her. He helped her, found somewhere for her to live, got her proper healthcare, and even bought her baby stuff. During all of this, they fell in love with each other and that's how they became a couple. They married after I was born and decided to raise me as his."

"I don't know what to say," I reply rather unhelpfully; what do you say? "So, how did you find out?"

"Turns out her rapist didn't live far from here and he found out about her marriage to a multimillionaire." He smiles without an ounce of cheer and begins staring into the distance. "He hounded them both, sent threatening notes as well as other unsavory messages until eventually, he broke her. She killed herself, just after my thirteenth birthday. Hung herself from that tree over there." He points into the distance, but I don't follow his finger, instead, I keep my eyes firmly fixed on him.

"Oh, God, Lucius," I whisper, holding his hand tighter and shuffling closer to his hunched-over body.

"In true thriller movie fashion, the housekeeper found her. Dad and the gardener had to cut her down so I wouldn't see her when I returned home from school. There was a note left for me, but he was scared about what she might have written, so he read it first. He explained everything to me when I turned eighteen. The note was long gone. Apparently, it had been very graphic and incoherent, so Paul had to put the kiddy gloves on for me and tell it in his own way. It still wasn't pretty though."

"What happened to the man who raped her, Lucius?" I don't want to make any reference to him being in any way related to Lucius; it must be so painful for him.

"You really don't need to know those details, Topolina," he says with a clenched jaw and a dark look in his eye. "Just know he won't be hurting anyone again."

"Oh," I utter, sounding a little taken aback. However, I soon shake it off so I can focus on him again. "I'm honored that you would share this with me, Lucius, but what has this got to do with the other night? Surely you don't think…?"

"I am terrified of turning into him," he says angrily, "after all, I am the bastard son of a rapist!"

"Don't you ever say that, Lucius!" I snap, wiping away tears that seem to have appeared from out of nowhere. "You are so much more than that and you must know it. You are Paul's son, no one else. I'm not proud of overhearing what he said to you on the morning you left, but I'm pretty certain he sees you as nothing other than his son and that you make him proud. And as for being a rapist? God, no!"

He stares at me intensely again, all the while I look back at him with conviction. He still needs convincing; I can tell from the look in his eyes.

"The way you reacted tells me you are the last person to force a woman into anything. I'm sure other guys would have tried to pursue it, tried to talk me into it, but you didn't, not at all." I stroke the side of his face as I lean into him. "Please, Lucius, you scare me in some ways but never have I thought you would force yourself onto me. Not since you said so in my bedroom that night."

"You're scared of me?"

"A little," I admit, "when you said I was yours and that you wanted to consume me, it made me feel things which I'm afraid of. Though, what scares me the most is the fact that I…I liked it."

I whisper that last bit, not sure if I want him to know it. But after all the contemplating I've been doing recently, I decided to put on my big girl panties and admit it to him anyway.

Lucius reaches his hand up to cover mine on his cheek and gives me a real, genuine smile that has me falling into him a little more. He then pulls my hand behind his neck before placing his own on my waist. With a gentle pull, he draws me close, and my heart feels as though it is thudding at double its normal speed, but I know I want this more than anything. He presses his lips to mine and brings our chests against one another, igniting a sudden heat between our bodies. I taste his mint gum when his tongue enters my mouth, and I know it will forever remind me of this moment. Our kiss isn't wild and primal this time, it's soft and tender. We take the time to explore each other. When we pull away, he keeps his eyes closed and rests his forehead against mine, as though he's relieved to have gotten everything out in the open without me running away from him.

"So, I have one week with you?" he whispers, to which I sadly nod. "Then I'm taking you out for dinner tonight, tomorrow night, and every other night until you leave. I'll have no arguments, mia topolina."

"I have none to give," I admit as I pull away and offer him a stupid grin.

"But this time, there are no expectations for us to do anything. Do you understand, Helena?"

We look at each other for a few moments before I venture to give him a response.

"But if I want to?" I finally pluck up the courage to ask.

His icy blue eyes study me for a few moments before he pushes a strand of hair behind my ear.

"Then, I'll decide if you're ready for me."

Chapter 12

Helena

My last night at *Hastings Villa* comes around faster than I thought it would. I've spent every night being wined and dined by Lucius, who still has a wicked tongue and his trademark smirk to give him his reputable edge. But, at the same time, he is also tender and caring toward me. We make out frequently but go no further, both of us being too afraid to push the other beyond their limits.

I have steadily fallen for him over the last week and the thought of leaving him brings the sting of tears to my eyes. There has been no mention of trying to continue anything past my stay here, and I don't want to be the one to bring it up and ruin what we have right now. It's ridiculous to have let him in this far because I already know I'm heading for a prolonged period of heartache. I have no idea what this is to Lucius, but I do know, from what Meri has said, it's the longest 'relationship' he's ever had with a girl.

We arrive back at my bedroom door, where he leans into me to kiss me goodnight. We dressed up a little tonight, him in a black shirt rolled up to his elbows and dark denim jeans; me in a borrowed slinky black dress from Meri. I probably looked very uncouth trying to walk around in heels, but he never said a word if I did.

When we do kiss, it's soft and chaste, just a gentle pressure against my lips.

"So, thanks again for dinner tonight," I say, feeling a little disappointed from the vanilla type of kiss he just gave me. "I'm going to have to start running or something after all of these rich meals."

"You're too damn skinny anyway, Topolina." He smirks as he looks me up and down gratuitously. "I like a woman with curves."

The way he subtly licks his lips causes my whole body to throb with a lustful urge I've never experienced this deeply before. He can tell what I'm feeling, I'm sure of it, but he wants me to spell it out. I scan my eyes over his body and bite my lip nervously, knowing what I want to say but finding it too damn hard.

"Well, I guess I should go," he whispers, "I hope you're journey back is pleasant." At that, he turns to leave.

"Wait!" I grab his arm to pull him back to me. He turns with that wicked smile on his face.

"Something you want, Helena?" he asks, purposely being bad at playing dumb.

I shake my head, "No, there's something I need," I whisper and begin to pull him into my room. Invitation enough, he kicks the door closed behind us and places his hands on my hips, looking intensely and lustfully into my eyes.

"What do you need, mia topolina?" he asks, rubbing his hands along the sides of my waist. "Tell me!"

"I need…" I gasp but lose all coherent thought when he begins kissing me up and down my neck. His hands move to slowly unzip my dress so that it falls to the floor in a puddled heap at my feet, along with the logical part of my brain that has been screaming at me to not fall in love with this man. But fuck it; this time, I'm ready and I won't stop him. "I need you."

"Yes?"

"All of you."

"Right now?"

"Right now."

"Willingly?"

"Completely."

"Mine?"

"Always."

There are no words after that, instead, he grabs and pulls me onto his body, kissing me hungrily like I am his very last meal. He places both hands on my ass and lifts me off the ground, carrying me over to the end of the bed where he throws me down. With lightning-fast movements, he pulls away his shirt and throws it to the side before unbuttoning his jeans and pulling them down with his boxers. He stands before me completely naked, and I am almost salivating over how beautiful he is. Pure muscle and tanned skin, the definition of an Italian heartthrob; the epitome of male flawlessness. My focus turns to his manhood and that's when my nerves return in abundance. I have not seen a man's dick in real life, so I'm no expert, but it looks huge. Long, thick, and throbbing between his legs.

It must be obvious where I'm looking because he laughs softly and grabs it inside of his hand, stroking it gently in front of me.

"Don't be nervous," he says, "I'm not here to hurt you."

"Er, I might be a virgin, but I do know that's going to hurt, Lucius," I reply, sounding a little panic-stricken as I point to his erection, which is currently standing to attention up to his stomach muscles.

"It will a little," he says, climbing over me, "it will a lot, but I will help you."

He kisses me gently, then pulls the fabric of my panties away and down my legs. There's not a hint of shame on his face when he spreads my legs wide, making me feel so exposed, I can feel myself blushing. He begins to kiss the inside of my legs while stroking through my untouched pussy with his fingers. I emit a gasp of pleasure when he eventually swipes his tongue through my lips and begins to circle the tip over my clitoris. In fact, I lose hold of everything I've been fearing, and grab hold of his hair between my fingers, just enjoying how good this feels. This I can handle, this is …*so* good.

"I fucking love your taste, Topolina," he growls from between my legs, "you're so wet, so sweet for me."

I should have guessed he'd be a dirty talker in bed. Lucius Hastings is dirty enough when he's not in bed. My thoughts are suddenly interrupted when he inserts a finger inside of me, causing me to wince over the stinging sensation that stabs at me deep inside. He begins pulsing his finger while flicking my clit with his tongue. It begins to feel good again, so much so, my breathing deepens, and I arch my back to meet him more greedily.

"That's it, Topolina, let me fuck you with my fingers, make you ready for me," he whispers, sounding low and on edge. He adds another finger and then another, groaning each time my body accepts him. It feels sore at first, but so good when the shock of it subsides. He soon builds up to a faster pace, curving his fingers inside of me, all the while licking my clit with his wicked tongue. A mountain of sensitive feelings begins to build higher and higher within me.

"Come, mia topolina," he whispers gently, and within moments, I obey, exploding in a flash of lights and ragged breaths.

Coming down from my high, I do not have time to process what just happened before he moves up my body and begins kissing me with so much desire, I'm not sure I'm going to survive him taking what he needs from me. My cheeks heat when I taste myself on his tongue, at the same time as his hands move to my bra, pulling the lace down so he can touch my naked breasts and peaked nipples.

"Fuck me, these are beautiful," he says, using his thumb pads to circle around my hard nubs, which feel tender and sensitive. He leans back, sitting on his knees while he looks down upon my body. The hungry look in his eyes makes me feel sexy, confident, and so lustful, I'm not sure how I've survived without this. Soon after, he bends to suck on my nipple, his hard cock brushing against my opening.

"Hold me, Helena," he whispers in a strained voice, "I need to be inside of you."

I do as he says and reach up to grab his shoulders. Once in place, he grabs a foil packet, and tears it open before slipping it over his erection. The action makes me tense up with nervous anticipation, but as if sensing this, he returns his hands to my face, cupping it as he gently kisses me long, slow, and gentle.

"Shh, open for me, mia topolina," he whispers into my mouth. "Relax for me, let me in."

In but a few moments, he pushes forward and enters me with the tip of his cock, then pauses. This isn't so bad. Then he tenses and drives forward again. It hurts so much, I gasp and release a tear from the burning sting, which quickly rolls down my cheek. He remains still and kisses my neck gently, allowing me to adjust to him, letting me relax for him to move.

"So soft, so beautiful," he whispers, "so mine."

His words help me to release a little of the tension from my muscles, so he begins to rock gently, forwards and back, looking at me the whole time while I grip hold of his neck.

"Does it still hurt?"

"Yes," I whisper, "but I'm fine."

He smiles and begins to rock faster, his eyes closing as he does so. I watch him intensely as his face contorts with pleasure, holding back as he hisses through his clenched teeth.

"You feel so good, I knew you would," he moans, "fuck, I could live inside of you forever."

"Kiss me, Lucius."

I almost weep with how sore I am but the closeness I feel between us is worth the sting. The words he utters helps to turn it little by little into sheer pleasure. I cannot be certain whether they're true or not, but it doesn't matter, because right now, they are. Without question, he obeys and kisses me more passionately than the last time, and as our tongues collide, he ups his movements again. I try to spread my legs wider to let him move the way he wants to, to let him sink deeper inside of me.

"Oh, God!" he groans as a deep throbbing inside of me signals his release, deep, deep inside. Gasping for air, he continues to thrust a few more times before finally stopping. I secretly smile to myself, knowing his reaction to me is genuine and powerful; something I don't think I'll ever forget.

Lucius kisses my forehead gently as he pulls out. The feeling is a mixture of soreness and heat, but also loss when he is separated from me. As soon as he is free of me, he begins to kiss my face, to the point where I start to giggle. He looks into my eyes and smiles.

"Thank you, Helena...*my* Helena."

His gratitude has me feeling a little weird about it all, but soon after, he gets up and goes to the bathroom to dispose of the condom. When he emerges, he has a warm flannel in his hand.

"What's that for?" I ask, sounding confused. He points to between my legs, revealing a stain of blood on either side of my inside thighs. "Oh," I blush and instinctively shut them close. "Oh, shit, Lucius, it's on the sheets; this is so humiliating!"

He immediately walks over and pulls my hands away from my eyes, tutting as he does so.

"Don't you dare be embarrassed, beautiful," he says firmly, "I will deal with it anyway."

He begins to pat the flannel gently between my legs, with my opening still feeling extremely tender. He then throws it onto the floor and lies next to me, stroking my hair as he does so.

"Go to sleep, Helena," he says before kissing at my temple. His body envelopes me from behind and I close my eyes with a feeling of true happiness. "I won't be here with you in the morning."

My eyes dart open again, and it feels as though my heart has just free fallen into a state of panic.

"Why not?" I ask, sounding horrified.

"Because…" he begins, then swallows hard. "Because I can't do goodbyes. Especially after this amazing gift you've given to me." Unable to stop myself, I blink tears down my face, which he wipes away with his hand. "Don't cry," he whispers, "this is not the end for us. And next time will be great for you too."

"Lucius, let's not kid ourselves," I sniff, probably looking like a snotty mess, "we have no idea if we'll ever see each other again. You're back off to college and I'll be back home. I knew this, I did, I just didn't know how brutal it would feel."

"Saying goodbye to someone you…*love* is always hard," he says and kisses me gently on the mouth before holding me closer to him. "But we are here now, together. Sleep with me, Topolina, and enjoy the here and now of us."

I didn't want to fall asleep because then he'd be gone, and I would be alone. However, as if he had just uttered a spell, I black out soon after, my body betraying my desire to stay with him for as long as possible.

Just as he said, Lucius is gone when I wake up. There is no sign he was ever with me, apart from the stained sheet. There's nothing of him, not even one of the notes he was so keen on leaving for me all those times. Feeling empty, I cry quietly so no one will be able to hear me from outside this room; inside, however, it's deafening.

A full hour passes by before I force myself to leave the bed and wash the sex from me. It's sore between my legs and the soap stings when it trickles down there. I can't decide if I want the burn to stay or go, for it reminds me of what I gave to a man who made me feel everything, from love to heartache, all in one night.

I honestly don't know how people do this with perfect strangers, because giving myself to him only to wake up and find my bed empty, feels torturous. I feel dirty, hollow, and bereft. I cry again when I realize how stupid I've been, especially when everyone warned me, even myself. I'm the cliché nerdy protagonist who let someone into her heart, only to have them rip it out and take it with them when they left. I'm pathetic.

After I've washed all the hatred away, and then some, I pull the offending sheet from the bed and bundle it into a bag. I pack my things and leave with nothing but clothes and an empty feeling that refuses to go away. The same tired message whirls around my head on an irritating repeat: *You weren't supposed to fall in love with him, Helena. You were warned, even by him, but you did it anyway. He's right, you are now his, but he doesn't even want you anymore!*

Lucius

Creeping out of Helena's room is one of the shittiest moves I've ever made, and that's saying something. I'm not proud of myself but it was the only way to spare us both from a painful goodbye. I've had enough of those to last me a lifetime. We'd both done the unthinkable and fallen for one another...hard. She was only meant to be a plaything, a bet. To her, I was supposed to be the one man she should have avoided at all costs. So, I guess we both fucked up.

My mood is not helped by a familiar voice now sailing through the air from down below. Eric, the mouthy son-of-a-bitch, whistles up to me as I walk slowly down the staircase and into the small living room where he's stretched out along the sofa like he owns the place.

"I guess you got some virgin pussy last night then?"

He grins at me like an evil Chesire Cat, but I'm in no mood to be down his depraved rabbit hole this morning. I glare at him before making my way out into the yard so at least we won't wake Helena upstairs. She doesn't need to know about our childish little who-can-piss-the-furthest contest, a game we've been playing since we started middle school. As could have been predicted, he falls into walking behind me, quickly followed by him throwing his arm around my shoulders and laughing hysterically over my supposed 'win'.

As soon as we're out of earshot of Helena's room, I shuck him off and glower at him, hoping he won't need actual words to tell him that he needs to fuck off immediately. However, being a brainless cretin, he doesn't get the hint and begins to ask me what it was like, how hard I went on her, and other such crass shit that reasonable people do not even think about discussing. Reasonable people don't make bets about taking a girl's virginity either, but what can I say? I guess I'm an evil motherfucker too.

"Keep your car, Matthews," I utter, "the bet's off and you can go home now."

I smile tightly before continuing forward, nodding at Owen on my way up to Helena's little patch which she spent so long creating.

"Dafuq?" Eric scoffs as I walk onwards. "Dude, you already won! You tapped that little cunt and now you've got a car for your efforts. What the fuck is wrong with you?"

He takes a drag on his cigarette before throwing it into Helena's garden. I don't know if it's that action, or the fact Owen just looked at me like I'm the lowest form of being on the planet, that has me grabbing hold of Eric's shirt and thrusting him up against the fence behind him.

"I said the.Bet.Is.Off! Now fuck off and don't let me catch you here again." I drop him rather ungraciously to the ground, leaving him to rub his hand around where I just had hold of him. "I've outgrown you. Tell every other motherfucker that all parties are canceled. I'm done!"

Eric shakes his head like I've gone criminally insane, which right about now sounds appealing. He cautiously walks away from me until I call out once more.

"Wait! I've changed my mind." I pace up to his scowling face and hold out my hand. "Keys."

The idiot curses under his breath before slamming them down on my palm.

"I always knew you were fucked in the head, Lucius Hastings," he mutters when he's far enough out of reach. "It's a good thing that poor girl is heading home, far away from you, you twisted motherfucker."

I step forward and the asshole runs off across the lawn and out of sight. My attention then returns to Owen, who's still looking at me like a piece of crap that's festering on the ground, tarnishing his otherwise perfect garden. He tuts, shakes his head, then continues to walk away up the path. I follow him down the gravelly strip for a few minutes, knowing he has something to say. I also feel like I need someone to pull me up, to punish me for being a prick. I badger him with my incessant footsteps crumpling upon the gravel beneath my shoes. It's only a matter of time before he flips, I just need to wait for it.

"If you're waiting for me to do something, boy, you'll be waiting a long time," he mumbles with his hint of an Irish accent that stems back from childhood. "I ain't lowering myself just to make you feel better."

Frustratingly, Owen is both street-smart and intelligent. I guess his criminal background and short stint in jail only made him more so.

"Oh, come on, Owen," I poke at him with a thick frosting of arrogance, "you know you want to punch me. Plus, they'll be no comeback because you'll be doing me a favor. Come on, right here on my smug chin!"

He laughs loudly, tipping his head back before spinning around to face me. His fist makes quick contact, but with enough force to knock me backward. It stings like a bitch but feels oh, so good for about five seconds.

"Atta boy," I laugh, gripping hold of my knees to steady myself, all the while he shakes out his fist.

"Feel any better?" he asks with a knowing grin.

"Not one fucking bit." I laugh again, clutching hold of my jaw where he just flattened it. Hopefully, it will bruise, nice and ugly.

"Good, now do you need me to tell you the obvious?" He stands up tall with his beefy arms folded across his chest and looks down at me like the pathetic little rich boy that I play so well. I shake my head, not looking at him for fear of seeing the disappointment written all over his face. "Then I'd say you have about two hours to pull your head out of your ass and go and tell that girl how you feel before she's out of here. Understand?"

"You and I both know that's not going to happen," I sigh as I stand up to meet him face-to-face. "What would be the point? I'm here, she's there. I'm Satan, she's Gabriel…"

"Bullshit!" He spits at the ground like a common thug, looking cold and angry. "The point would be you letting her know she actually meant something to you more than a fucking bet. The point is she won't feel like the cheapest thing alive after giving up something most people feel pretty special about. The point is, Lucius, you aren't that much of a dick, no matter how much you profess to be. The point is Billy looks up to you and I can't let him do that if you don't go and make this right. So, get gone!"

I look up, nodding slowly, because I guess the Irish bastard is right. He turns to walk away from me, so I turn in the opposite direction to go and think about what I want to say to her.

"Hey, Owen?" I call before I've even really thought about it. The hulking figure turns to face me with a frown. "Here!" I throw Eric's damn keys over to him, which being the epitome of a cool, hardened ex-criminal with cat-like reflexes, he catches one-handed. "Enjoy the new ride!"

Helena

Walking into the airport 'Departures' building, I try to perk up by reminding myself that I am going home and will be seeing my family. I've also made plans to revamp my life. I'm going to finish high school, apply to colleges that are a little further afield so I can move out, learn a language, and spend at least one summer abroad. Yes, life is working out and it's all going to be great. My attempts to be positive must be pretty piss poor because both Jen and Meri are giving me a look of severe pity. A look that says, 'tread carefully before she crumbles.'

True to his word, Lucius was nowhere to be seen this morning. By the time I came downstairs, his Maserati was gone and so were his jacket and sunglasses. I read his message loud and clear, the one that said, 'I fucked you like I said I would, so now I'm moving on to the next unsuspecting virgin.' I almost feel sick over my complete naivety and inability to distinguish between genuine feelings and, let's face it, an asshole with the emotional depth of a pile of puke.

Meri, bless her sweet penchant for sniffing out gossip, had tried to probe me about what went down between us, but I just shook it off and put on a practiced fake smile. I've been doing this my entire life. Normally I'm an expert at acting the happy daughter, sister, whatever. However, I could tell Meri wasn't buying it at all. Not only has Lucius taken my heart and my virginity, but he also refuses to let me pretend when it comes to him. I need to get away from him, as in get-on-this-plane-and-fly-hundreds-of-miles-away from him.

When we reach passport control, the swarms of people trying to bottleneck through are overwhelming, so I urge Meri and Jen to go and let me wait it out alone. It's a beautiful day and who wants to be stuck in a busy airport with screaming toddlers and impatient tourists? It doesn't take them long to concede; I'm pretty sure they could sense my wanting to be alone anyway.

Jen hugged me goodbye first, then Meri. She held onto me extra hard and for an extra-long time. I'm going to miss her, but we agreed to speak at least once a week and to compare colleges.

Who knows? We may even choose to go to the same one. The relationship we've built over this summer has perhaps been the one good thing to have come out of this trip. I've never had a close girlfriend before; it only took me seventeen, nearly eighteen years to gain one. Being cousins just makes it even more special; we'll be forced to keep this friendship, to hold on and never let it slip away. I suspect half of her current friends will do this when they spread out across the country to attend college. Though, as my new best friend, she can instantly read me like a book.

"Oh, Hels, I told you to stay clear of him," she whispers inside of my ear. "Are you really going to keep me hanging over what happened between you and Satan?"

"I'm fine, really, it was just a couple of dinners," I lie. "Lucius can do whatever he wants, with whomever he wants."

"Yeah, ok," she mocks me, "I believe you. Millions wouldn't, but I do."

When she finally pulls away, she swipes a rogue tear away from my cheek, tutting as she does so. I wave goodbye before they both turn and walk toward the exit. I watch them go with a sense of relief. I want to have a little pity party for myself, even though all my brain is currently saying is, *"Told you, told you, loser, loser!"* My brain can be the world's biggest bitch sometimes. Let's face it, no one knows how best to hurt you more than yourself.

Pulling up my big girl panties, I stand up straight and head toward the check-in desk, smiling at the woman with far too much makeup, and big, shiny white teeth. I don't listen to even half the crap she's telling me in parrot fashion, so when I eventually pull away and feel a hand grab me from behind, I have an irrational thought that security is accosting me for not listening properly. The hand pulls me back against them but before I can scream, I inhale and smell him, hear him breathing, and feel the outline of his chest as he leans in closer to me. I know it's him, I know Lucius is standing right behind me, placing his forehead against the back of my head.

"Don't turn around, mia topolina," he whispers, "just let me feel you one last time before you go."

Dazed, hurt, and confused, I stand silently, with my eyes closed and my erratic breathing causing a light-headed sensation. His forehead rubs up and down my head in small purposeful movements, like a wild lion nuzzling his mate. His breathing is deep, silent to the masses, but clear as a bell to me. His warm hand squeezes mine with possessiveness, and we stand like this for what feels like hours, though, it is probably more like a fleeting moment. Knowing that it eventually must end, and end soon, is playing on my mind like a black cloud threatening to spill.

When that moment eventually arrives, he slips something into my hand, takes one more breath, then pulls away, leaving me feeling bereft and hollow. My eyes shoot open, and I gasp over the sudden influx of noise re-entering my head like an unwelcome guest. Of course, when I'm brave enough to finally turn around, he's already gone.

The object in my hand is a small white card, one that looks so familiar, it feels like an old friend. I slip it into my jacket and save it for later. I then shake it off and walk toward Passport Control where I begin the long wait to go through. It's not until I'm sitting safely on the plane, taxiing for take-off, that I have to courage to look at it. The blank side stares up at me, and with trepidation, I turn it over, casting my eyes over the one word he's written – ***Mine***!

Part II – The Fallen Angel

"Hell is empty, and all the devils are here."

- William Shakespeare

Chapter 13

Helena, Freshman year, College

"This band is pretty good," I try to shout over the music to my friend and colleague, Jet, a guy who is as beautiful as Henry Golding and has a wicked sense of humor. What makes him lethal, however, besides beauty, brawn, wit, and intelligence, is the fact he has the biggest heart I know. He's constantly surrounded by college girls, with each of them just wishing he might choose them to take out on a rare evening when he's not working here. Meri once asked me if I would consider it if he ever asked me out. I had scoffed and told her not to be so ridiculous, that the guy literally has his pick of whichever girl he lays his eyes on. What I didn't tell her is that he's already asked me out. I had smiled awkwardly before letting him down gently.

Jet had taken it well, theatrically slamming the palm of his hand over where his heart rests beneath his beautifully tanned skin, then we both laughed about it.

"Let me know if you ever change your mind," he had whispered before moving back into the throng of the audience to collect empties.

Truth be told, he reminded me too much of Lucius, perhaps in a more socially acceptable way, but they could easily be mistaken for brothers. And my poor, pathetic heart hasn't got over him enough to look past the similarities. Besides, Jet deserves a girl who will love him without thoughts of the devil lurking around inside her head.

Speaking of which, not once has he tried to contact me, or even mentioned anything to Meri about me. I should know, we share a dorm room thanks to Paul's rather large donation to the university, as well as his ability to pull a few strings in not only this state but also far beyond. I never asked her to tell me about Lucius, being stubborn to try and save the little bit of pride I have left when it comes to him, but she offered up the information anyway. In fact, she offered too much information, including the names of some of the girls he's been rumored to have hooked up with. She was swiftly told to never mention his name to me again. She apologized, I wept a little, we hugged, and that was that.

That was at the beginning of the academic year, but now we're nearing the end. I've survived my first college year living away from home, something both my father and I never expected to happen.

"Yeah, they cover some good songs, and not your modern shit either," Jet says, leaning against the bar and he beginning to dry glasses fresh from the washer. "My dad used to listen to these songs back in the day."

He grins casually my way, making a gaggle of Sophomores

melt into a pool of goo over my shoulder.

"You mind if I head out with my camera? I'll be ten minutes, tops." I grab it from under the bar anyway because I already know he'll say yes. It's a quiet period; the band has just started playing the next set so most of the crowd is already refueled and listening intently to the cover band strumming away on their guitars.

"Why are you even asking?" He rolls his eyes, shaking his head while I grin and make my way through the crowd of excited, engrossed, sweaty bodies. No one even notices when I crouch down in front of the stage to the left-hand side, hidden by the shadow cast out from the old velvet curtains. Their musty smell betrays their age, as well as the fact no one has washed them in all the years they've framed this stage.

I click away on the Leica camera I bought using some of the money left to me by my nonna. The rest I put away into savings for more sensible things, like buying a place of my own one day. I hope she's not cursing me too much up there; she had left the three of us a note telling us to blow it on something fun. To be fair, I'm not the only one who is saving their inheritance for a rainy day. Nate bought a car and Cam is investing his share in his own company, which is something to do with computers. Truthfully, I have no idea what it is because I'm clueless when it comes to technology outside of my camera. He's a frickin' genius though. I always go to him when I want him to do stuff to my photos, and being the kind of the big brother that he is, he's keen to teach me how to do it myself. I can tell it's frustrating for him because I am crap with technology. But we're close, really close; we'd do anything for one another.

To say I'm in love with my new camera is an understatement. The longer I spend using it, the more natural I feel with it. I'm constantly thinking about new ideas and ways to capture different shots; it has become an obsession. Sometimes, I wake up in the middle of the night, just to try out a new technique or frame that's come to me. Tonight, the band is giving me all kinds of inspiration, so I snap away at the guys on stage, their faces etched with all the emotions they're feeling as they play. The lead singer is right there, living and breathing the song while he strums against his electric guitar. It's a beautiful thing to watch, to listen to, and I get to capture it all on my camera.

After the song ends, with the sound of the crowd emitting whoops and whistles, the band decide to play something a little more upbeat and a little less heavy in subject. I slowly straighten up, the whole time snapping away to try and get the perfect shot, when someone comes barreling into me at full force, causing me to collapse onto the floor with a huge, male body landing on top of me. I laugh because I didn't reach out to save myself or protect any of my body parts, instead, I'm gripping my camera close to my chest to make sure it's not harmed in any way.

"Helena?" I immediately open my eyes to see who just said my name, because I don't recognize the voice, even though they obviously know me. "Helena Carter? Is that you?"

When my eyes finally manage to refocus, I look closely at the man on top of me and begin filtering people through my head, trying to work out who he is. It's only when he helps me to my feet and smiles at me with recognition that I see him as the boy who I went to school with.

Evan Stone was in my year at school, but he never spoke to me. I remember him as a popular preppy rich kid who ran around with Mason Spencer. They were usually terrorizing the local female population, not that they complained. I actually know Mason better than Evan because he played football with Cam. In fact, they're still friends, and always catch up with one another in the school break when they both return home from their respective colleges. Fortunately, Evan appears to be charming and polite, which can't be said about Mason.

"Can I get a drink with you? After you finish work?" he asks after we have reacquainted ourselves. His nervous, hopeful expression encourages me to take pity on him, so I agree to finish up with Jet and then meet Evan at a local café on campus, one that stays open during the night instead of the day. I'm not sure I'm ready to go out with a guy, but perhaps it will do me good and set me on the path to moving on from Lucius Hastings.

"Who was that?" Jet asks with concern etched all over his face.

"Oh, some guy I went to school with," I reply with a happy-go-lucky smile. "What a co-winky-dink, huh?"

"Hmm," he says, looking none too impressed by Evan who is now back to chatting and laughing with his own group of friends. "He's a prick."

"Wow, Jet! Don't mince your words, will you?" I laugh, swatting his behind with my cloth. Usually, he joins in with my playfulness, but his eyes are remaining firmly fixed on Evan and his group of beautiful friends, the type he used to hang out with at school.

"He's in one of my classes and he sure does love himself," he says, now openly scowling in Evan's direction.

"Don't worry, I have no interest in dating him," I reassure him as I clap my hands on top of his shoulders. His eyes are still on Evan, who is now staring at the two of us with a strange look on his face. It's at that moment, Jet steps into my arms and presses his lips on top of mine, with his hands gently resting on my waist. It's a nice kiss; a reawakening from the Lucius fog that has clouded my head ever since we slept together. But it's not him. It's not the all-consuming, desperate need that I had for him.

"Nothing, huh?" he says when he steps back from me. I look at the ground with a heavy sigh, not wanting to hurt his feelings, but not able to lie either.

"It was nice though," I admit, wincing with an awkward smile, "and if I wasn't so fucked up from a guy in my past, who looks just like you, I would have been really into it…really into you."

"Yeah, well, he's a prick too," he says in such a way, I know this won't mess up our friendship.

"I won't disagree with you but…well, you know." I drop away from him and pick up the cloth I had dropped on the floor so I can throw it into the washing basket.

"You're still in love with him," he says, and I freeze, realizing that I am, and might always be. God, I feel so pathetically crap right now.

"Oh, come here, Hels," he says as he pulls me into a friendly hug while I break down in tears. Tears of sadness, tears of frustration, but mostly tears of humiliation.

"I don't know how to get over him," I sob, clutching onto this beautiful, funny, lovely man who would probably put everything into trying to make me happy if only I would give him a chance.

"You will…one day," he whispers. "But don't try and do it with that piece of shit over there. I don't trust him, and you are worth a lot more than his kind of arrogance. You'd just be swapping one asshole for another, trust me." I pull away, wipe my eyes with the back of my hand, and nod. "Atta girl," he says, patting my arm before we both fall into work again.

⚸

An hour or so later, I arrive back at my dorm room, worn out and more than ready for bed. Alas, when I unlock the door, I am met with heavy grunting and a vision of naked flesh that will be forever etched inside my mind. This isn't the first time I've walked in on Meri and her boyfriend, David. Yes, *that* David. I've seen his hairy ass more times than I've seen my own. It doesn't stop me from slapping my hands over my eyes, even if technically, the damage has already been done. I begin backing out the door when Meri suddenly calls out for me to stop.

"God, Hels, sorry. Give us…two?...Three then?" She's not even talking to me now; she's bargaining with David over how long it's going to take for them to finish. I almost wish I hadn't canceled on Evan. I could have been sipping tea in a café instead of teetering on the edge of somebody else's orgasm. "Five minutes, Hels!"

I mumble some sort of acknowledgment as I close the door, then slide down the wall to sit on the floor beneath me while they noisily finish their sex session. The girl across the hall walks back from the end of the hallway and gives me a smile and a wave that conveys her sympathy for my current situation. We've met many a time like this, so I smile and wave back, silently telling her, "Yes, David is over for the weekend again."

Less than five minutes later, I hear them finish but make no attempt to move until the coast is crystal clear. Instead, I reach for my phone and give Cam a call. I've been pestering him about not giving up on college because his business might well be starting to take off, but he still needs to have the know-how to run such a venture. It's late, but I know he'll still be up, probably messing about on his computer.

"Hels," he says after two rings, "how is my favorite sister?"

"Waiting for Meri…again!" I listen to his dirty chuckle and suddenly miss him, Nate too. "Mom said you were home this weekend. David's here and I was wondering if I might come and see you guys?"

Plus, it might be good to give Jet a little bit of distance, just so we can start afresh after our impromptu kiss.

"Actually, yeah, I am. Did she tell you they were headed out of town? One of Dad's work things. Anyway, we may or may not be throwing a little social gathering," he says, sounding sly. My parents would flip if they knew that's what they were planning, but more fool them for leaving the place alone with my wayward brothers.

"Oh, ok, don't worry then," I begin as I make to stand, ready to head back inside.

"Come over, Hels, party for once. Be wild and stupid…shock us!" His offer sounds daring but a house full of high schoolers and Cam's old high school crew doesn't exactly make me feel desperate to go.

"Mm, maybe," I mumble, ignoring the long sigh he's emitting over the phone. He's already given up on me going. He's probably right to. "Listen, do you remember Mason's friend, Evan?"

"Yes," he says in a drawn-out way but offers nothing more than that.

"Turns out he goes here," I explain to my less-than-helpful brother. "He asked me for a drink, but one of my friends said he was a bit of an asshole. What are your thoughts?"

"Can't say I really hung out with him." *Again, ever so unhelpful.* "But Mason thinks he's great…actually, maybe that's a good reason **not** to hang out with him." He laughs at the same time as I tut. "I don't know, give it a go. What do you have to lose?"

"I don't know." I begin to chew anxiously on my fingernail. "I'm not sure I really like him in that way, and I don't want to lead him on or anything."

"Jeez, it's a drink, Helena," he laughs, "not a proposal of marriage. Give it a go. Be rebellious, go wild, and stop listening to that inner-Dad voice inside your head."

"Easy for you to say, brother, you and Nate were always allowed to do whatever the hell you wanted…still are. Do you know he asks me every week if I have a boyfriend? Which you know is code for, *'Have you hooked up with anyone?'* Mom won't leave the room when I speak to him on the phone anymore in case he gets even more inappropriate. Oh, and I still get the *'Remember, Helena, a girl's reputation sticks around with her forever'* speech."

"Oh, Jesus," he half sighs, half laughs. "Tell him the fifties want their spokesperson back. Helena, you know the man's a fossil, so think about what you want and just go for it. It's the twenty-first century and you know he's talking out of his old-fashioned ass. Go for the drink or come to the party but do something!"

"I'll think about it. Ok, I'm going to risk it and go back in. Wish me luck!"

"Good luck!" he sings songs. "Oh, and Hels?"

"Yeah?" I reply, freezing my grip on the door handle.

"See you tomorrow!" he laughs.

"We'll see; bye, Cam."

I can't sleep. To be fair, it's virtually impossible for anyone to sleep with Meri's boyfriend sounding like a freight train coming at full speed toward you. I don't know how she does it. I begin to count between his snores, getting momentarily frustrated when he breaks the pattern. I huff, puff, and blow out in exaggerated breaths, contemplating going for a cup of tea down at the café. The last time I did that, Meri lectured me on my personal safety, informing me that the weirdoes are out at this time of night. She also called Jen, who called my dad, who then lectured me every day for a week after. But given my current state of agitation, it might be worth it.

With nothing else to do, I reach inside my bedside cabinet to try and find a book to read, or at least my mp3 player so I can listen to something other than heavy snoring. It might be the only thing that stops me from going over to smother him with my pillow. However, when I reach inside, the very first thing I touch is the small white card that Lucius had left me with at the airport over a year ago. The day my heart shriveled up and died with him stomping all over it.

I can only just make out the black lines and swirls of his handwritten word in the moonlight that is streaming through my bedroom window. I can't sleep in complete blackness, not even with a migraine, it makes me panic. Speaking of which, they've been a nightmare recently. I've been getting at least three a month. Mom made me go to the doctor but we both agreed it was stress induced. Clutching this little reminder of Lucius is tempting another one, but I can't seem to stop staring at it. I wonder if he ever thinks about me, even just a little bit.

"Psst, Helena?" Meri whispers over to me and I laugh.

"Why are you whispering, you nut? Apart from your bear of a boyfriend, everyone is up." She sighs before coming over and crawling into bed next to me. She makes an 'mmm' noise; my bed must seem huge after sharing with David, who is both tall and broad, and often has his limbs flopping all over the place.

"I'm sorry," she says and holds my hand. I don't mind really, she's like the sister I never had. I'm close to both my brothers but I've always felt like they shared a relationship I could never have, simply because I'm a girl and they're very *guy* guys.

"I don't mind," I reply with a giggle. "But I'm going to give you guys some space tomorrow. I'm going to head home and spend some time with Cam and Nate."

"You don't have to, Hels," she says as she turns and brushes my hair out of the way, only so she doesn't choke on it. "Jeez, now I feel like I'm pushing you out of your own place."

"Not at all," I reassure her. "I kind of want to go and see my brothers. I haven't seen them in ages."

She slumps her shoulders, physically relaxing with relief. A moment later, she's scrunching up her eyes, focusing on the card that I'm still stupidly holding up in the moonlight.

"Oh, Hels, is that what I think it is? When are you going to let me burn that thing? It's like your own little weapon of self-torture!"

I quickly stuff it under my pillow and shake my head, feeling embarrassed for keeping it. I *should* let her burn it, but I can't seem to let it go. She's right; it is self-torture.

"I didn't mean to reach for it, it was just a moment of weakness," I try to convince her. "Besides, I met a guy who I used to go to school with today, not to mention Jet and I kissed."

"What?!" She jumps up to lean onto her elbow, eyeing me with a face-splitting grin. "Deets. Now!"

"It was nice, really nice, but…"

Meri groans as she flops back down to the mattress in frustration.

"I can't help it," I huff noisily, "he's taken up residence inside my head and won't fuck off. The squatting bastard!"

"Well, you need to evict Lucius Hastings and go out with the walking, talking orgasm that is Jet. Or at least give the guy from school a go. For your sanity as well as mine. Now, thanks to you, I have to go and pee."

She pulls back the cover and stomps across the floor toward the small bathroom that we're lucky to have all to ourselves.

"How on earth did I make you need to pee?"

"You just did!" she replies before closing the door, leaving me to laugh at her ridiculousness.

"Hey, Helena?" I jump at the sound of David's gruff voice. "Sorry for keeping you up."

"Oh, I'm used to your nightly rhythm, David," I laugh, "don't worry about it. Tomorrow is Saturday."

"Listen, I hope you know what I'm about to say is for your own good. I care about you, Helena, and I know how much you're hurting over Lucius," he says, sounding guilty for mentioning that name to me.

"Okay?" I draw the word out, bracing myself for what he's about to say. David rarely says more than two words to me. He's generally a man of little words and like a big cuddly teddy bear, so if he's got something to say about Lucius, and with that sheepish-looking expression on his face, it can't be good.

"Listen to Meri and take a chance on someone else. Lucius gets more pussy than a rescue center after Christmas. You deserve to move on from someone like that."

"What's going on?" Meri asks as she comes out of the bathroom.

"Nothing." I try to laugh again, even though it has no mirth in it. "David was just apologizing for his snoring. Thanks, David."

He bobs his head before inviting Meri back into bed with him. I watch them snuggle together before turning onto my side and silently sobbing into my pillow, leaving a little wet patch on the white fabric beneath. I fold my body into itself, trying to be as small as possible, then give myself a stern talking to. Lucius Hastings has officially been given his eviction notice.

Chapter 14

Helena

I left before Meri and David woke up. I didn't want to feel their pitying or judgmental eyes on me. To have David give me relationship advice must mean I've sunken pretty low; the guy usually restricts his personal communication technique to grunts and huffs. With that in mind, I've thrown a load of gear into my overnight bag, which I'm currently trying to get into my tiny Ford car without causing too much noise. It's still early and I would imagine most people are trying to sleep in. I'll catch up with sleep when I get home. It will be nice to get into my old bed.

Before I set off, I quickly nip into the all-night café to get a cup of tea and a croissant, if only to keep me going for the journey. It's only going to take a few hours and my music mix should make it pass by more quickly, but I need a bit of a sugar fix to keep me going. It's fairly quiet and I know they'll be closing in about an hour, so I head straight for the till to pay for my sugary treats.

"Hello again." I turn in the direction of the voice and instinctively smile to be polite. "I guess we'll be getting that drink after all. If you're not busy that is?"

Evan's beaming smile and doe eyes, together with Cam's, Meri's, and even David's words of advice, have me agreeing to sit with him while I eat my rather unhealthy breakfast.

"So, what are you up to today?" he asks after taking a sip of his coffee.

"I'm going back home actually," I reply with my annoying nervous laughter. "My parents are away for the weekend and Cam and Nate are having a 'social gathering' as they like to call it."

"Yeah, I heard about that. Mason." He says by way of an explanation. "It's funny how we never got to know one another in high school, given that my best friend is friends with your brother."

"Probably because you were the cool kid running after the cheerleaders and other 'hot' girls, whereas I was a quiet, shy, nerd." I laugh but he looks like I just accused him of being an ass. "Not that I blame you. I preferred my own company. The thought of public speaking or being the center of attention always brings me out in hives. I guess I purposefully made myself unnoticeable."

"You were noticed, Helena," he says quietly with suggestive eyes. I feel myself blush, to which he smiles in such a way, I can suddenly see why all the girls liked him. He's cute, funny, and wholesome, just what my father has always wanted for me. He's the complete antithesis of Lucius. "You just seemed a little standoffish, like you'd tear a guy down before he'd even asked you out."

"To be fair, I probably would have," I reply honestly. "But only because I was terrified of the prospect of boys being interested in me, not because I thought I was above anyone."

"And now?" He tentatively places his hand on top of mine

from across the table, the whole time looking hopeful. "What if I were to ask you out to dinner with me? Like on a real date."

We look at one another for a moment or two, with nervous bile working its way up my throat, threatening to erupt at any moment. I blow out long and slow before I answer him, giving me a few moments to think about it.

"I won't bite."

"I know," I murmur, trying to find the words to explain myself without sounding completely pathetic. An impossible feat it would seem. "I just don't know if it would be fair of me to date anyone at the moment. I kind of trusted my heart to someone, a rather foolish action on my part. It's still recovering from where he stomped all over it."

"I see," he says softly but shows no sign of releasing my hand. "Well, then, can we maybe hang out?"

"Sure, I'd actually like that."

Maybe Evan is the guy to help me get over my obsession with Lucius Hastings. I know what Jet said about him, but he seems genuine and extremely patient. Maybe what Jet has seen is just male bravado in front of his friends.

Making a decision to move forward, I agree to exchange numbers before I make a start to drive back home. I'm pleased. I'm beginning to evict the devil from my head, and I'm doing it at my own pace. So, patting myself on the back, I head home to see my brothers and to try and forget all about Lucius Hastings.

THE DEVIL

Helena

"Helena!" Cam and Nate simultaneously cry out when I let myself into the house.

They're currently lying across the living room couches, playing Xbox and generally making the place look untidy. My big brother's the first to get up and wrap his arms around me; he sure has bulked up over the last six months and Nate isn't far behind. They're both sinfully vain and remind me more and more of Lucius every day. He, too, liked to work out like a weightlifter on steroids and always looked immaculate, albeit in an effortless kind of way. I just hope they don't break hearts in the same way that Lucius broke mine.

Nate hugs me after Cam does, then helps me with my bag. He then invites me to come and sit with them in the living room. It's weird to begin with, like I'm a guest in my own home, but after a few games of Grand Theft Auto, where I gasp and berate them for their choice in games, they soon begin teasing me just like they used to. It finally feels like we're back to being bickering siblings again.

After a while, I tell them that I'm heading up for a nap because after the late night and early morning drive, I'll admit, I am exhausted. I put on my comfy, baggy, saggy PJs and slide into my bed, with its rich smell of home and nostalgia. I make a long 'mmm' sound while wriggling around like I'm trying to absorb all of my bediness in one hit. However, a knock at the door stops me in my make-out sesh with my bed and before I can yell at whoever to come in, Cam opens the door and invites himself in to lie on the bed with me.

"You do realize I could have been in a state of undress?" I utter, to which he laughs while shaking his head. I nudge him with my foot from beneath the covers. "What?"

"I've missed your old-fashioned turn of phrases," he chuckles, "'*state of undress?*' No one your age talks like that. Besides, I already heard you getting into your bed, so I was pretty certain I was safe."

"So," I begin, ignoring his jibe, "how can I help you, big brother? Girls? School? Nate? Parents? Secret alien lifeform manifesting inside of your rectum?"

"Meri called to see if you were ok. So, are you ok?" His expression has turned serious all of a sudden, and I let out an exasperated sigh because he knows exactly why Meri might be worrying about me. "I warned you, didn't I? I told you to stay away from that asshole."

"You did," I concede as I roll over onto my back to stare at the ceiling, if only so I can avoid his penetrating gaze. "And I should have listened. There, is that what you wanted to hear?"

"No, I wanted to hear that you'd forgotten about him and were moving on with your life," he says in his big brotherly tone of voice. "When are you going to forget about Lucius damn Hastings?"

Mmm, never?

"I don't know, soon I guess…I hope," I reply with a smile, though it's completely fake.

"Make sure you try real hard, Hels, I've had enough of seeing how sad he's made you. You deserve happiness, you know that? You're my favorite sister."

"I'm your only sister, doofus," I retort as I nudge him with my foot again.

"Have you met Nate?"

We both laugh at my poor baby brother's expense before he kisses me on my forehead and leaves me to sleep. I decide, there and then, that I'm going to try really hard to let my guard down tonight; to let loose and go a little wild like they want me to. I need to remember I'm single and do not belong to Lucius in any kind of way. In fact, I need to forget he even exists.

Regardless of the little pep talk I had had with Cam earlier on, as soon as the party is in full swing, it's as though I cease to exist. I watch both him and Nate from afar, fascinated by the posse of girls who are all fawning over them and their friends. It amazes me how high school students behave in this way, as though all common sense exits their brain for a few years. Hell, it turns out I was one of them. I, too, saw all the signs of a complete player and I still fell for Lucius. Here, I watch a gaggle of beautiful girls, all fopping over my brother because of how he looks. Each one is hoping he's going to pick just one of them. Please, he's not going to turn down what is being offered to him on a plate, is he.

I also watch Mason, Evan's friend, with a vested interest. I figure, fairly or unfairly, that if he's a dick then so too will Evan be. He's loud and pretty obnoxious, but he seems to be nice enough to both the guys and the girls. However, if someone is monopolizing Cam's attention, I notice he'll sulk like a little kid. He'll then say something inappropriate to grab back Cam's focus. I guess he hasn't outgrown the thinking that bad attention is better than no attention at all. Perhaps he has mommy issues?

My private thoughts have me giggling to myself until I feel

the heat of someone pressing up behind me. I look up at the doorframe I've been leaning against and sure enough, there's a hand hanging over me, a man's hand.

"What are you laughing at?" whoever it is mutters inside of my ear, his breath causing a few loose curls to fly away from my neck. I slowly turn around, recognizing the voice and feeling surprisingly pleased about it being here.

"Just people-watching," I reply. Evan's smirk tells me he's been doing the same, though, I think I'm the one he's been studying. "What are you doing here? You didn't mention coming this morning."

"Well, I kinda thought…" He trails off, trying to think about his answer, all the while staring off into the distance, until eventually, he chuckles at me. "Mason mentioned it a few weeks ago and I wasn't gonna come, but when you said you were, I thought it might be a good place for us to 'hang out'."

"'Hang out'?" I utter in a mock accusatory fashion, folding my arms in front of me but grinning all the same. "Just like we agreed, huh?"

"Exactly," he says, pointing at me as if I've just given him the key to his explanation.

"Ok, then, Evan, let's 'hang out'." We take a moment to smile at one another. "I need to refill anyway. This vodka is going down a little too easily, so I'm counting on you to not let me get into any mischief."

"On my honor," he declares, holding up one hand while placing the other one flat against his chest. "I won't let any harm come to you, m'lady."

When we walk through into the kitchen, there's a strange

smell in the air, a familiar scent that takes me back to Lucius' parties. Huddled around the kitchen table sit Nate and a few of his friends, with a fog of smoke lingering suspiciously around them while they giggle and cheer at one another.

"Nate?!" I gasp in my best Mom voice. "Are you smoking pot?"

"Busted!" His best friend, Max, laughs at him while Nate rather stupidly tries to flap away the smoke surrounding him. He looks sheepishly at me, then back to Max before exploding in a fit of laughter. They high-five one another before returning their gazes to me with half-guilty expressions.

I walk right over to where they're sitting, staring my brother down while the whole room silently watches on with bated breath. I reach down to his hand to take hold of the blunt that's sitting limply between his fingers. Once I take hold of it between my own fingers, I look at it for a moment, then back to him before I bring it to my lips and suck on it. My eyes wince, filling with tears as I begin to cough and splutter. For the life of me, I cannot see what all the fuss is about. The crowd of high schoolers begin laughing while Nate and Max high-five one another.

"Yessss!" they both hiss in unison.

"What the hell?" I sputter before Evan takes the blunt from me and grins over my poor attempt to smoke weed for the first time. He says nothing but places it between his lips and takes a long drag on it before letting out a small cloud of smoke, and without the rather ungracious coughing and spluttering. "How do you do that?"

"When you take out the blunt, inhale deeply so it fills your lungs," he says, handing it back over to me. "You're a newbie though, so you're going to cough."

"Ok," I mutter as I take it from him and try again, but instead of breathing out when I remove the stub, I inhale deeply, taking in a little fresh air with it. He's right; I cough but not nearly as much as before. I feel it traveling down my windpipe and into my lungs. Shortly after, I take another inhale and it feels even better than before. "Ok, good, I'm being 'wild'."

Pretty soon, Nate and I are laughing uncontrollably at each other, even though neither one of us is making a lick of sense. Of course, this is mostly the basis for our laughter. Evan has had a few inhales but appears to be hanging back, much preferring to watch the show that is my little brother and me.

"Hel-, Hel-, Hel-...Helena!" Nate drawls as he slings his arm around me, all the while I laugh at him. "I always thought you were so dull!" He winces before emitting a ridiculous high-pitched laugh. "You never let loose; you know?"

"Nate, you are such a bitch!" I gasp and when his friends erupt into fits of giggles, the sound shocks me, and I literally jump out of my skin. "Fuck! When did all your other bitches get here?!"

"They've been here the whole time!" He sounds ridiculously pitched, so we laugh again. "Anyway, as I was saying, you never let loose. But since you lost the ol' v-card, you have definitely chilled out. It's ok though, we won't tell Dad; he's still a stick in the mud. But not you, Hel-, Hel-, Helaba. High-five, big sister!"

"Is he seriously expecting me to high-five that?!" I ask Evan, staring at Nate's limp hand that's still hovering up above me.

"What the hell, Helena?!"

Cam's angry presence stands before me as he rips the

blunts away from both my hand and the one in Nate's. This time, it's me and my little brother looking up half-guilty at him before bursting into fits of laughter.

"Busted!" I whisper shout to Nate.

"Jesus Christ!" Cam grumbles with exasperation in his voice. "Evan, can you take my sister up to her room before she embarrasses herself! I'll sort my stupid little brother out."

"Sure," he says before smiling at me, adding a wink when Cam isn't looking. "Come on, stoner."

Without warning, he whips me up into his arms like I weigh nothing more than a small child.

"You'll have to show me the way though."

"I'll try," I sing song before lying limp inside of his arms. "You have a really strong chest; did you know that?"

He shakes his head and laughs at me while he carries me up the stairs. Shortly after, though I'm not entirely sure how, I manage to direct Evan to my room. He delivers me onto the bed before closing the door and switching the light on. I took my last inhale about half an hour ago, so the peak of my high is beginning to wear off, but I'm still a bit dizzy and very giggly. Evan comes over to me with a huge smile on his face, obviously finding the whole thing extremely amusing. He tucks me under the cover, then proceeds to lie down next to me.

"Hey, mister, what are you doing on my bed?" I laugh as I turn to face him, weirdly trusting the guy who I only properly met yesterday. "You wouldn't take advantage of me, would you?"

"Nah, I promised, didn't I?" He shuffles down and cups my face with his right hand. "Besides, I don't tend to force myself on women who are high on weed."

"Good to know," I whisper, remaining still all the while he leans down to gently press his lips against mine. I reciprocate the soft movements and eventually open to let him slip his tongue inside my mouth. His hands slide down my body before stopping firmly on my hip. It's a nice kiss, a really nice kiss, and I try really hard to be more into it, but at the end of the day, he's not Lucius.

"I'm going to stop us there, Helena," he murmurs against my lips, "I'm not risking fucking this up because I already know I like you...*a lot*. And as much as I could easily fall straight into you," he begins before pausing to theatrically close his eyes and bite down on his lip, which makes me laugh over his dramatic compliment, "I want to respect your wishes, so I can get to be more than a one-night stand."

I take a moment to study him, realizing he's giving me the complete opposite of what Lucius gave me - a future. So why can't I fall for him as I did for Lucius? Am I that masochistic? The fact that he is offering it to me makes me really want to try though. And I will.

Chapter 15

Helena

A few hours later, I awake to find Evan fully clothed and sleeping beside me. He's not nearly as loud as David and not at all as absent as Lucius. He's already gone up in my estimation, so I take a few moments to look over his handsome face, and his well-built physique, the whole time willing myself to fall for him instead of being hung up on a man who is very much unavailable. After all, a fallen angel can't fall in love, they're far too busy trying to tempt some other poor soul into giving everything to them.

The sound of my phone ringing brings me bolt upright. Anyone calling you at three in the morning can't have good news, right? I glance at the ID and find Meri's name flashing up in front of me. A list of potential names that might have come to harm flashes through my head, all of them meaning a great deal to me.

"What? What's wrong?" I gasp, waking up Evan in the process. He immediately frowns over my worried expression.

"I didn't know whether to call you, but then I thought fuck

it, and did anyway," she sighs. "Lucius has been in a car accident. He's in the hospital. David has already left for New York and I... Well, do you think...?"

"Meri, do you want me to come with you?" I shut my eyes and let a tear run silently down my cheek. And yes, his name had appeared on my list too. Evan sees it and grabs my hand in a supportive way. My eyes move to look directly at where our skin is touching, though he doesn't seem the least bit perturbed by the shock on my face.

"Yes please," she says quietly.

"I'll be a few hours, unless you can meet me there?"

"Yeah, I can get there, see you in about an hour?"

"Sure, and don't worry, Meri," I try to reassure her, "I'm sure Satan will return him if he makes his way down there." We laugh nervously but we're both secretly scared of what we might face when we finally see him. "See you in a bit."

Evan looks at me for some sort of explanation, but at first, I can't find the words with which to speak. Instead, I jump out of bed and begin getting myself fixed up to look more hospital appropriate. As soon as I get out of the bathroom, he's up and pacing, waiting for me to tell him what's going on. I feel so horribly guilty that I close the gap between us to grab hold of his wrists so I can offer him some reassurance.

"Evan, I've gotta go. Meri's cousin is in the hospital, and I need to offer her my support." I see instant disappointment in his eyes, but being the kind of guy that he appears to be, he nods with understanding. "But I really want to thank you for last night. You were beyond great, and I appreciate it, I really do."

"Hey, no worries, it's what any decent guy would have done."

I nod back before picking up my jacket and bag. When I reach the door, something tells me to turn around, so I do, only to see Evan looking sadly at the floor. I sigh over my hesitancy, but then, in a moment of madness, I walk back over to where he's standing and place my hands over his cheeks before pressing my lips over his. His body tenses at first, but soon after, he pulls me into him and kisses me right back.

"I'll see you back at college?" I ask.

"You bet," he replies with a broad smile, after which, I bolt for the door because I really do need to get going.

When I meet Meri at the hospital entrance, a little over an hour and a half later, I can tell she's been crying. She looks marginally worse than I do. I never knew she cared that much about Lucius; they had always fought like cat and dog and held each other in contempt. Still, I give her a hug and tell her not to worry, that we don't know anything yet. On the inside, however, I'm preparing to die a little more if anything has happened to him.

We meet Aunt Jen and Paul on the third floor and collectively sigh in relief when we see them looking calm, happy, and relaxed. They're laughing over something in a magazine. After the initial feeling of relief, I turn to face my cousin so I can give her the stink eye for getting us all worked up over nothing, by the looks of things. She ignores me, and instead, takes hold of my hand and begins marching over to greet them. Aunt Jen is the first to notice us, but given her expression, I feel like I'm intruding on a strictly close family affair.

"Helena? What are you doing here?" she asks as she wraps her long, willowy arms around me. "Not that it's not great to see you and all, but you didn't need to concern yourself."

"You mean Lucius is ok?" Meri cuts in, still sniffing and looking red-eyed.

"Oh, Merial, did you dramatize his little accident into something it wasn't? What am I going to do with you?"

She hugs her daughter who looks at me, wincing while mouthing an apology my way. Part of me thinks I could easily make this into something more dramatic by stabbing my cousin for involving me in this ridiculous charade.

"He's got a nasty cut to his leg and a bang on the head. They've kept him in for concussion, but I think he's going to be released anytime now."

Just at that moment, a pretty blonde nurse comes walking out through a set of doors with a clipboard and a kilowatt smile for each of us.

"Mr Hastings?" she says, prompting Paul to stand and shake her hand. "Your son is fine; he has a few stitches but no concussion. We're just sorting the paperwork and then he can go home. I think my nursing staff will be sorry to see him go, he's quite the charmer."

I'll bet he is!

He thanks her before she turns around to head back through the doors she just came from.

"Well, I'm obviously not needed, thank you, Merial," I announce with sarcasm dripping from every word, to which she winces again. "I'll head back home then."

"Wait, Helena?"

When I turn to face the voice that just called for me, I'm surprised to see that it came from Paul. I barely saw him over that summer and when I did, we kept conversation to a polite minimum.

"Do you think I could talk to you for a moment?"

Meri looks at me, appearing to be just as confused as I am. However, curiosity gets the better of me; that and my need to be polite and obliging at all times. I follow him over to a corner of the waiting room, just out of Jen's and Meri's earshot.

"How can I help you, Paul?" It feels weird using his Christian name out loud, though to be fair, the whole thing seems pretty uncomfortable.

"Lucius confides in me, and I know he confided in you during that summer; at least, to a certain extent?" I blush but nod all the same. "I want you to know he told me about the two of you." *Oh, God, this night just keeps getting better and better!* "And I also want you to know that my son thinks the world of you, even if he doesn't want to admit it. But he knows, and I know, that he must have hurt you. His feelings for you run deep, which shocked me, but also filled me with hope. A hope that he can love someone even after everything with his..." He pauses to clear his throat of what I can only assume is uncomfortable emotion. "His mother."

"Listen, Paul, I really don't think Lucius-"

I don't get to finish that sentence because the devil himself bursts through the double doors, handing a familiar small white card to the same blonde nurse from before. He's eyeing her darkly, lustfully, just as he did with me once upon a summer. My heart cracks and crumbles a little bit more and I instantly feel the threat of tears on my lower lashes.

"I...I have to go. Sorry," I mutter to Paul who looks at me as though he's embarrassed on behalf of his son, especially after what he was just telling me. Unfortunately for him, he got it all wrong. Lucius' feelings for me have never run deeper than surface level. Not wanting to see him flirting with the nurse anymore, I fly for the elevator before he can even notice that I'm here.

Lucius

Winking at the pretty nurse who is melting over my melodic chat-up lines, I glance forward to see the back of someone I will always remember as ***my*** Helena. She slips inside the elevator without looking back, pressing all the buttons with a desperation to get out of here. Her name is on the tip of my tongue to call out, but before I can, she's gone.

Do I go after her? No. I am not worthy of Helena Carter, and she is not damaged enough to even consider ending up with someone like me. She needs to meet her shiny American dream boy who will give her the white picket-fence relationship, along with the promise of a dog and a couple of kids down the line. Just like her daddy has always wanted for her. I can't give her that and I won't pretend to.

So instead, I silently sigh, and wave the nurse off with my business card, with a plan to do what I do with all the other women I end up with. Explain who I am, and what I'm willing to give them. I'll fuck her, and then forget about her, advising her to do the same with me. I'm always the bad boy experience, the little rebellion if you will, just before they find their forever guy. It's never bothered me to have to let them walk away, apart from with her. I dread the day when Meri tells me she's finally found someone worthy of settling down with, someone to whom she can give her all. And yet, I love her too much to take any of that away from her.

I am a little surprised that Paul has brought the wife with him, as well as Merial. I guess that explains why my topolina was here in the first place. Merial, ever the drama queen, looks like she's been crying; I honestly didn't know she gave a shit. Paul, on the other hand, looks positively furious.

"It's not my fault," I laugh while throwing my hands up in the air, surrendering. God knows why because I don't owe anyone here an explanation. "Some idiot ran a red light."

"Jen, Merial, do you think I could talk to Lucius alone?"

His words might be for them, but his cold hard stare is directed right at me. I make a show of checking my watch just to piss him off, to which he rolls his eyes and tuts. Jen and Merial, of course, oblige his request and scuttle off to the elevator. Paul calmly takes a seat and crosses one leg over the other, his patience obviously running thin. My eyes follow the girls as they walk out together before I slump into the chair opposite, giving him my usual nonchalant expression.

"You are one stupid motherfucker, Lucius," he says with a hint of exasperation on his face.

"That I am, but for which reason are you referring to this time?" I show no sign of the anger he's ignited by calling me that; what would be the point?

"She still loves you," he says, then leans forward, as if the motion will drive his message home. "And you love her. And please do not insult my intelligence by denying it. I can't be bothered with fools who try to bluff me."

He reminds me of Shere Kahn from 'The Jungle Book', all power and ruthlessness wrapped up in a neat, debonair presence.

"I'm not going to deny it, Paul, but what exactly are you suggesting here? We both know I am incapable of giving someone like Helena Carter the life she wants."

"How do you know what she wants? You've never given her anything to go on. Lives are not cut and dry, Lucius, you of all people should know that."

My jaw tics whenever he refers to my mother and the details surrounding my conception or her suicide.

"I can't be bothered with this, Paul, I have places to be, people to meet," I huff as I make to stand. What he doesn't know is I have an apartment for one to go home to, with a shower to jack off in. My muse for such a task always being the girl who just ran to the elevator to get the hell away from me.

"You'll regret it, Lucius," he says, looking down at his hands as he delivers this warning, but it doesn't stop me from looking back at him with the same tic in my jaw as before.

"Most definitely, but then at least you can say those four little words you do so love to say to me - I.Told.You.So."

THE DEVIL

Helena

I head straight back to my dorm instead of going home. I'd already packed and brought my bag with me. Besides, the thought of facing my brothers in the morning is too much to think about, so I take the coward's way out and head back to a room for one so I can cry myself to sleep. I text Cam to apologize for not sticking around to help with the clear-up, explaining the fiasco I'd just been made to be a part of with Meri. *What a joke!* I should have just stayed in bed with Evan instead of getting my heart burned in front of me.

I feel bad because I tell a little white lie by swapping Lucius' name for David's. I'm going to be walking on a knife's edge for the next few weeks, hoping I haven't tempted fate into landing poor David in hospital too. However, the alternative was to listen to my big brother lecturing me about Lucius, all the while I melt under the heat of my humiliation. Cam's heart is in the right place, and he's certainly not worried about my reputation like Dad is, he just wants me to be happy. I only wish my heart did too.

As soon as I'm inside, I head straight to the drawer where I keep Lucius's stupid little white card and angrily rip it to pieces before flushing it down the toilet. The imbecile that I am, honestly thought he had only done the little note thing for me, but apparently, it's his trademark trick. A playboy technique he uses for the masses. In fact, the thought of how many women he has used this with, suddenly makes me feel dirty, so I head straight to the shower and take a burning hot one to try and wash away the fury radiating off from me. *Bastard! Asshole! Motherfucking fuckface!*

Of course, halfway through my burning rage, my temper tantrum runs out of adrenaline, and I end up in a sobbing heap on the floor of the shower. It's not until Meri arrives home half an hour later, that she forces me to retreat from the shower and crawl into bed while she whispers apology after apology. She tries to soothe away my pain by stroking my long hair, but it takes some time before it has any affect. I guess we must fall asleep like this because when I do finally open my eyes again, it's sunny and bright.

Meri treats me to breakfast at one of the nicer restaurants in town, even though I look like a sad sack, sulking against the window where all the happy, shiny people go about their daily cheerful lives. Meri stares at me with a concerned expression before handing over my migraine medication. I silently take it from her before knocking a few tablets back with a glass of water.

"Right, that's it!" she snaps, banging the table with the palm of her hand, causing me to jump up and look at her like she's just grown a second head. "We're going to go and get our hair done, have a massage, buy something sinfully frivolous, and then we're sorting out that trip of yours to Spain. And I mean booking it and everything, no arguments. We are getting you over the Lucius funk and casting him out for good. Got it?"

She expects me to argue, so when I do answer in the way that I do, she looks like a modern-day Disney princess with their wide, almost creepy-looking eyes.

"Yes!" I reply, banging the table too. "Let's do it!"

"Well, thank the Lord!" she eventually cries out and we both giggle over our newfound focus for the day, which is definitely not Lucius Hastings.

Meri and I instantly look at one another as soon as we hear a knock on the door. While her eyes are full of glee and excitement, mine are full of deep-rooted anxiety. I must have lost my mind when I decided to ask for pink hair at the salon. Granted, the hairdresser, who was beyond excited to have something off the wall to work with, went for something more of a rose-slash-silvery effect, but still, I look *very* different. Meri took a whole five minutes to stop jumping up and down when my blow-dried waves were finally revealed. My little rebellion to everything Lucius also gave me the courage to book a flight to Spain, precisely one week after we break for the summer, which is just a month away.

We spent the afternoon looking for jobs online, after which, we booked a shared room with a girl named Silver, who I chatted with over Messenger for about two hours. She seemed pretty cool, but now I'm worried she's actually a middle-aged pervert with an unhealthy attraction to pink-haired girls who are still in college. We decided to have my nonna's money in an easily accessible account should I have to make a swift getaway back to the States, or at the very least, stay in a hotel.

I had felt empowered after achieving so much, but now, Evan is here to take me on a date, and I look more like a hippie than the shy, conservative girl he was with just this morning. I can envision him screaming over the sight of me, then bolting for the stairs, which would be horrifying for all involved. A second knock sounds and I begin breathing in deeply through my nose, then blowing out through my mouth, trying to calm myself down. It's not working.

"Helena?" his muffled voice calls through the door and I feel as if I want to be sick.

Before I have a chance to shout out, Meri is already opening the door to Evan, who, to my horror, is dressed up in an expensive navy suit and with a huge bunch of roses in hand. I'm glad I dressed up in a black shift dress and a pair of heels, but with my hair, I may as well have put on a pair of ripped jeans and a concert t-shirt from work.

When he takes in his first glimpse of my pink waves, his mouth drops open and his eyes practically bulge out of his head. I immediately wince over the look on his face, especially when he throws the flowers onto my bed and begins walking around, as though trying to take me all in. Meri and I glance at each other with bated breath, but nobody says a word, and it's about all I can stand.

"Evan, if you don't want to-"

Before I can finish my sentence, he dramatically pulls me in, swings me down toward the floor, and presses his lips against mine. His eyes are firmly shut, but mine remain wide open in shock. Meri is jumping around in the background again, doing all but clapping her hands and singing. When he pulls me back upright, he gives me one of his charming smiles, the type girls used to gossip about at school.

"I love it," he whispers, and I think I just about manage to stop my heart from giving out.

"You never told me how Meri's cousin is?" Evan says as he pours me another glass of wine over dinner. "Is he ok?"

"Oh, that," I scowl, "he's fine." I smile tightly and can't

help thinking *unfortunately*, which is an awful thing to say, but I think I'm beginning to hate Lucius Hastings. "Meri, as per usual, was totally overreacting. He had a cut leg and suspected concussion."

Evan chuckles softly before sipping on his wine with a finesse my parents would be proud of. I can imagine my father being just like him when he was this age, which is a little weird to think about. Though, this is exactly what he wants for me; a man he knows he can trust to look after his only daughter because he's a younger version of him. Cut out the sexual part of the relationship and I can see his logic. Who doesn't want what they consider the best for their child? I just sometimes wish he knew how much I can look after myself, and that *I* also know what's best for me.

"Some girls live on drama," Evan says, snapping me out of my thoughts at the same time as he takes my hand within his own from across the table. I keep telling myself, *'Come on fireworks, come on tingly feelings, come on butterflies,'* but I get nothing.

"Listen, I've got to be honest," I begin, not giving up on the potential of me and Evan, but also knowing he deserves to hear about my plans for the summer. I also need to tell him that until I get back, I don't think it's right to try and define what we are to one another, especially as I'm not overly sure of how I feel about him. It's only fair to both of us. I sense it's going to make quite an uncomfortable conversation, but here goes. "I'm going to Spain for the summer. I leave in a month."

Evan's expression is unreadable but given that he's paused with his forkful of steak floating about in the air, I'm guessing he's a little shocked.

"It's something I've been dreaming about since my nonna

died a couple of years ago. I've been learning Spanish, slowly, and I want to practice my camera skills somewhere new. And I guess I just want to step outside of my comfort zone, you know?"

He slowly places his fork down onto his plate and takes hold of my hand again. He still doesn't give much away, so I'm bracing myself for him to be angry, for leading him on or knocking him back. Who knows?

"I think you're so amazing, Helena. You just keep on surprising me. Sure, I would have liked to have spent some time with you over the summer but I'm also proud of you for following your dreams. You are going to be safe though, aren't you?"

"Oh, yeah, I've got a backup plan and savings behind me, should it all go disastrously wrong. I'll be fine." I shrug it off even though I am anxious as hell about it. But a good anxious, an I'm-actually-going-to-do-this anxious. "Of course, my folks don't know about it yet. I can't wait for that conversation!"

"Yeah," he says in a drawn-out fashion, though with a smile on his face. "I don't envy you that one. Listen, can I be selfish for a moment?" I nod as I twirl my pasta around my fork, if only to keep my fingers busy so I don't end up chewing nervously on my nails. "What are your thoughts about us? I know what I want, but I'm not sure what you want."

Oh, God! Taking in a deep breath, I reach for my wine to try and procrastinate while I think of my answer. *Just be honest, Helena.*

"I really like you, Evan; you're the first person I've dated since the bastard who shall not be named." I smile at him when I see him stifling his laughter. "But I think I need to do this summer abroad alone before I define anything. I want to keep seeing you, but I totally understand if what I'm offering is not enough. I just don't think I can agree to anything official right now, it wouldn't be fair to either of us."

My heart, what's left of it, drops when I see the disappointment swimming around in his eyes, but then he brings my hand to his lips and smiles in such a way, it puts me at ease again.

"I'll take it. Have your summer and then come back to me, ok?"

"Are you sure? I mean, I don't expect you to stay monogamous or anything. I know guys like you have needs," I blurt out, then instantly blush when he offers a cheeky grin over our intertwined hands. "God, this is embarrassing. We haven't even done anything ourselves."

For God's sake, Helena, shut up, you goon!

"Do you not have needs, Helena?" he asks in a low, seductive tone of voice.

"Er…not really, I mean, I don't know." Feeling embarrassed, I lean forward and whisper, "I have no idea what the right answer is to a question like that."

We both laugh, even though I am being deadly serious; I *don't* know what I'm supposed to say to a guy when they ask you that.

"Tell me," he says, tracing an intricate pattern on the back of my hand with his index finger, "do you like sex?"

My cheeks heat up like a gas flame, instantly and intensely.

"Well, from the one time I had it, I'd say yes," I tell him honestly, then look away because this is all too humiliating.

"You've only done it once?!" he gasps, looking at me like I've admitted to homicide. "I thought, you know, when you were hung up on that guy, it was because you had had a long, intimate affair with him."

"It's complicated and I don't really want to talk about him…ever!"

"Fair enough," he says, dropping our hands back onto the table. "Would you be willing to let me show you how great it can be?"

His bluntness shocks me to silence to begin with but then I sit up straight and look right back into his lustful eyes and nod, being nearly convinced of my decision.

"Good, stay at mine tonight then."

Oh, God!

"Ok."

Chapter 16

Helena

Two hours later, and I'm feeling thoroughly disappointed over the fact that I am currently underneath Evan, thinking about what things I'll need to pack for Spain and how I'm going to break it to my parents, all the while he thrusts into me. I know I'm not experienced or anything, but the fact that we stripped down, and kissed for a bit before he fell into missionary, has kind of dampened the excitement of it all. He might not be as well-endowed as Lucius, but he isn't what I would consider 'small' either. The problem is he doesn't seem to have any idea what to do with it. With all the moaning and groaning he's emitting, that and the fact he keeps crying out, '*You're so tight, you're so tight*', I'm guessing he's getting off on it. So that's something I suppose.

"I'm coming!" he suddenly shouts, then sort of shudders before collapsing on top of me, where he stays, all the while trying to get his breath back.

Shortly afterward, he rolls off to the side and smiles before sauntering off to the bathroom. When he gets back into bed, he throws his arm over my waist and grins with a satisfied and contented expression written all over his face. At least one of us is.

"That was amazing, Helena. Did you enjoy yourself?"

I have two choices here; tell him the cold, hard truth, or smile sweetly and feign satisfaction. I don't much feel like going through it all over again, so I go for the latter.

"Yeah, it was great," I lie, so he smiles and pulls me into him before he soon falls asleep, emitting gentle snores every now and then.

I am left to stare at the ceiling, thinking about everything that has come to pass over the last few days. Images of Lucius during that summer and in the hospital last night haunt my mind for what seems like hours, with each one bringing a strange concoction of emotions that begin to make my head hurt. It is only when Evan turns over in his sleep that I manage to break the cycle of heartache and anger over all things Lucius.

Is this a sign? A sign that Evan is the way out of all of my hurt and anguish? If so, why do I feel so lackluster about him? And why was what we just did so…so…so *disappointing*?

Perhaps it was better than I'm giving him credit for, my mind and heart being too wrapped up in Lucius. Perhaps it is unfair of me to judge, particularly as it was only our first time together. No, I need to give this more of a chance to blossom into something that could be a hundred times better than what I had shared with Lucius; a chance to fall for a mortal, wholesome boy who will be everything my father has been trying to sell to me. I need to leave my fallen angel well alone, let him lead the life he so obviously needs to be happy…without me.

When I return home the next day, Meri is on me like a bad case of heat rash, practically salivating and clawing at me to give her the juice.

"Tell me everything! Was it good? Did you come? Ahh! Oh, my God, wait till I tell Lucius!"

"No!" I shout in a panic. "Do *not* mention me at all to your evil stepbrother, promise me!"

She tuts before pulling me over to my bed to make me divulge all of the juicy details, not that there are any to speak of.

"So?" she says in a long, drawn-out way.

"It was…" I must pull a face that portrays my true feelings on the matter because she physically slumps at the same time as her face drops into a frown.

"That bad?" I can't help but laugh over her own disappointment.

"It was ok…ish," I begin before slapping a hand over my face. "It was dull, Meri, really dull. He got off, but I most certainly did not. But you know, sex isn't everything in a relationship, is it?"

She pulls the most horrified look I've ever seen on her. It's so comical, I have to laugh, which I do until tears are streaming down my face. In the end, she's laughing with me.

After we've both managed to calm down, I take a deep breath and pull up my big girl panties, ready to tell my parents about my plans for the summer. It's going to be a long call, so Meri bids me good luck before leaving me to it.

THE DEVIL

Here we go!

The month passes by quickly, and after my parents' initial shock over my plans to go away, my mother managed to calm Dad down to only a mild frenzy. The only way I could talk him out of forcing Cameron to go with me was the promise of bringing Evan home to meet them all. It was supposed to be a farewell dinner but is turning more into the Evan appreciation show. Dad is over-the-top pleased that I have managed to 'bag a Stone' as he likes to put it. Stone Accountancy is well known in our town and the fact that they're one of the wealthiest families in the area only adds to the appeal. I wouldn't be surprised if he's already mentally planned our wedding.

Speaking of Evan, we've had sex a few times now, and apart from giving him a blow job, which he heavily hinted for, it's not been any different from that first rather disappointing time. I haven't climaxed once, and it's beginning to grate on me that he seems content to take what he needs from me but offers nothing but boring missionary sex in return. He obviously doesn't believe in returning oral sex; he's not tried to go down on me once, and I'm far too shy to ask. If it wasn't for Lucius showing me how amazing it feels, I doubt I would have even worried about it, but he did, so I do. Meri is right, I don't want to settle for a relationship that gives me no sexual satisfaction at all; I think I'd rather go without any boyfriend.

It's sad really, because, in all other ways, Evan is virtually perfect. He's sweet, caring, affectionate, and completely spoils me. He's bought me countless phrasebooks and other travel items and has even topped up my phone with extra credit so I can check in with him while I'm over there. Meri thought this was a tad controlling, but I don't think this is his intention, he's just a naturally caring person. He's also incredibly practical; I know he's going to make an excellent accountant when he moves into his father's firm.

Something is still missing though, and it's not just because of the bad sex. There's no spark, no passion, and everything feels so lukewarm. Even Meri has admitted that I might need to consider breaking it off with him. But I'm going to stick to the arrangement and wait until I get back from Spain. Maybe I'll have a clearer head. Besides, it's not like I'm stopping him from pursuing other opportunities.

"I'm kind of nervous," Evan says to me when we pull up outside my folks' place, and it makes me feel bad, knowing that he's seemingly all in while I'm having major doubts.

"Don't be," I tell him truthfully, "they'll love you. It's me who Dad is disappointed with. He doesn't approve of my 'rebellion'. In fact, I think your coming will work in my favor. Come on, let's go."

I use my key to let myself in and call out into the seemingly deserted house. It's Nate who comes out first, looking even taller than the last time I saw him. He gives me one of his lopsided grins, then hugs me before looking all kinds of awkward when he takes hold of Evan's outstretched hand. Cam comes out next and slaps at Evan's hand like he would any of his other friends, which seems to put Evan at ease a little. Though, when my parents come out to greet him, it becomes a little embarrassing.

Dad immediately begins pulling him into the living room, laughing over Evan's polite attempts to be funny, all the while slapping him on the back and offering him glasses of his best whiskey. He's acting as though his long-lost son has returned home to save the family from total ruin; it's borderline cringy.

Nate, Cam, and I look at one another, completely flabbergasted by Dad's sucking up to Evan just because he's wearing a nice suit and is set to have a promising career working for his father. Mom merely shrugs her shoulders before following them into the other room.

By the time we all shuffle inside, Dad and Evan have already fallen into a discussion about the world of finance. Dad is a fraud investigator at one of the biggest banks in the city, so I guess it was bound to happen sooner or later.

After dinner, which is even more uncomfortable with Dad's crushing on my non-official boyfriend, we all return to the living room and have coffee. Nate turns in shortly afterward, obviously bored of the 'grown-up' conversation. To be fair, it's also boring me to tears, much like my sex life. Evan, on the other hand, seems to be lapping it up, so I guess it's ok, even if this is supposed to be *my* farewell dinner.

"So, Evan, what do you think of Helena going away for the summer? None too pleased I bet?" Dad chuckles while I try and resist the urge to get up and slap him. I think living away from Dad has made me see his misogynistic outlook for what it is – extremely outdated and insulting. "Not to mention the hair?!"

"Helena always looks beautiful to me," Evan expertly replies, just as I spy Cam rolling his eyes with silent amusement. "And if she needs the summer to explore herself, then who am I to stand in her way?"

I smile in thanks at him as he takes hold of my hand and delivers a small kiss to it. *God, he's perfect. Too perfect.*

"But surely, as her boyfriend, you must have a more concerned opinion on this?"

Dad's face turns a little stony, clearly not impressed by Evan's answer. I want to say something, to tell him to butt out, but I can't. I've been brought up to never question what he says, to be the good little girl and do as I'm told. I can feel the words I want to say caught at the back of my throat, as well as the frustration of not being able to get them out.

"Well, strictly speaking, I'm not her boyfriend, not officially anyway," Evan says, prompting my father's face to look even more constipated than before.

"What are you then?!" Even Mom and Cam are now looking at me for answers I'd really prefer not to give right now. "What exactly is this between you two?"

"Evan has agreed to wait until I come back from Spain before we label this," I explain, pointing between the two of us.

Cam immediately accepts this explanation with a casual nod of his head. Whereas Mom puts on one of her extremely fake smiles, knowing Dad is not going to be impressed with this.

"Well, I should have known you would be the one holding back, Helena," Dad says with an obvious air of frustration. "And you're happy with this, are you?"

"Well, not exactly *happy*, but I am more than willing to wait for her," he says, bringing my hand up to kiss it again. "I think I've found my person with her."

My father positively beams with happiness, whereas my eyes are no doubt bulging from out of my head. I can't help it; I feel like I could be sick at any moment. Cam is watching me with suspicion. I never could hide my true emotions from him.

"Besides, I've already booked myself a ticket to Spain in July. I was going to surprise her, but I can't help myself. I'm going to come and spend a week with you, baby."

He smiles before leaning in to kiss me, catching me by surprise. And now it's my turn to put on the fake grin. Am I terrible for not wanting him to come over? This is supposed to be about me, only me, and now it feels like he's laying claim to it.

"You're a lucky girl to have found this one, Helena," Dad says smugly, looking at his new best friend like he's won the lottery. "You'll do well to remember that."

I don't even have the words caught in my throat; I am utterly speechless. Even Cam is shaking his head in disbelief, all the while Evan laughs and pulls me in closer against him. Suddenly, I can't wait for Spain to be here now, if only so I can breathe again.

In the middle of the night, I wake up with that tell-tale feeling of a migraine coming on, so I walk downstairs to get some water and find my tablets. I haven't had one of these bad boys all month, but after last night, I'm not overly surprised. It's not helped by Cam scaring the bejesus out of me when he seemingly appears out of nowhere. He's literally been sitting in the dark, so when I switch the kitchen light on, he's suddenly there, scrunching up his eyes and putting his hand up to block out the light.

"Holy shit, Cameron! What the hell are you doing sitting in the dark?" I cry out as I try to catch hold of my breath again.

"I get some of my best ideas in the dark," he says, grinning over the fact that he's scared the crap out of me. "What are you doing up?"

"Migraine coming on," I explain, pointing to my head just to make it extra clear, like an idiot.

He nods in understanding, being more than used to me getting them. After I've grabbed some water, I sit on the chair next to him and take my pills. It's then that I notice him looking at me strangely.

"What?"

"You don't like him, do you?" he says with a small smirk. "You're trying, I'll give you that, but the guy does nothing for you, does he?"

I begin twirling the glass around on the table, unable to meet his eyes, which always manage to see right through me. I guess this is what has always made us close; I can never hide anything from him. He can read me like a book. But I know I can always go to my big brother and he'll have my back. I couldn't ask for anyone better to be my sibling.

"Is it that obvious?" I finally respond.

"Only to me and Mom," he replies with a shrug that tells me he would never judge me for how I feel. He understands. I still nod sadly because I don't want to hurt Evan, and I was hoping he would be the answer to my infatuation with Lucius, but he's not. Cam takes hold of my hand and pulls me around, so I'm forced to face him.

"Don't settle, Helena," he says softly. "I know you still have feelings for Lucius, even if I don't fully understand it, I can see it. But that guy isn't the answer. Don't let him or Dad talk you into being something that you're not."

"God, how do you always know what I'm thinking?" I ask as I wrap my arms around him. "Thanks, Cam. I'm gonna miss you."

"No, you won't," he says with a smile. "You're gonna go and have an amazing time while I'm stuck here being all kinds of jealous of you. Promise me you'll make the most of it."

"I will," I reassure him.

"I also think you should tell Evan not to come for that week," he says, to which I sigh and look sheepishly to the floor. "But if you won't, don't let him ruin it for you. This is for you, Helena, no one else."

"If only I was as brave as you," I tell him, thinking how differently we've been brought up, simply because of our sex.

"Going off to Spain to work by yourself is pretty brave if you ask me," he says. "But now, I'm going to escort you back to your room because I know those tablets will make you all dopey, just like you were when you got high on weed."

"Oh, God, don't remind me," I laugh as he helps me back to my feet. "I was pretty wild though, wasn't I?"

"That you were," he replies with what sounds like pride.

"Some girl is going to be extremely lucky to have you one day, Cameron Carter," I tell him when we reach my door. "You're a good guy."

"And some guy will be lucky to have you," he whispers, knowing Evan is just behind the door. "A guy of *your* choice."

I'm gifted with one more hug before he marches off down the corridor to his bedroom. I take in a deep breath, then return to

THE DEVIL

bed.

Chapter 17

Lucius

Two months later, Spain

It's hotter than hell today, so I've not stepped outside of the shade since dawn. I hit my bed with the air conditioning on full blast and my body spread eagle. Thankfully, even when intoxicated, I knew it would be an awful idea to bring someone back to the boat. My heart's not in it enough to want to suffer the body heat of another person. Pair that with the awkward conversation that comes the following day and I'd rather let my right hand do the job for me. Besides, it matters not if it's another woman or myself, I always picture the same person when I need a sweet release.

Shit, Lucius, get a fucking grip!

Suffice it to say, I began to go stir-crazy hours ago. Even without the blaze of the sun, it's still warm enough to cause profuse sweating and a desire to bathe in a tub of ice. However, my need to get away from this boat that I've rented for two weeks is winning out, so I change into something that isn't saturated in my own body odor and call for the steward. The Spanish sun has been set to burning since I arrived, and if you're stupid enough to not heed its warning, you'll be on a one-way ticket to melanoma and a bad case of sunstroke. I should have known coming over here in August was going to be like visiting the surface of the sun, but you can't help when gaps of time arrive at work.

The trip, so far, has been a well-deserved break, especially after spending the last six months studying and working at the office with Paul. He's worked me hard in preparation for when I one day take over the branch in LA. Whilst it's true I'll be elevated much higher than my college peers, and in a fraction of the time, simply because I'm the son of Paul Hastings, no one can deny how hard I work. For all of my bravado, I have always felt a need to prove myself when it comes to Paul. He took on a child whose own mother didn't even love him.

I came to Spain alone, to get away from the drama of all the people at the office and to also get away from Paul chewing my nuts off about Jen. I don't think they'll last much longer; I was surprised to see her at the hospital after my little accident. She is too boho for him and she...well, she's not my mother. He's been ruined for life and will most likely keep moving on from one wife to the next.

I do not plan to marry at all; I am simply incapable of offering someone that kind of commitment. There may have been one person for me, but we just weren't at the right time or in the right place in our lives. If I'm being honest with myself, she ruined me too. I never contacted Helena after our night together. We knew what it was and what it couldn't be; we were only teenagers. It was never supposed to be anything more than a bet with Eric. But then I went against my own rules, I let her in, just as I had with my mother. We all know how that ended; I will not let Helena meet the same fate. It would destroy me once and for all.

"Mr Hastings, will you be wanting to go ashore tonight?" the steward asks as I sit back in my lounger with a glass of something amber and numbing.

"Yeah, why not," I reply, glancing at my watch, "I'm bored of staring at the ocean."

"Very good, Sir," he says and walks away to let the captain know.

I have the weekend and then it's back to the grind. I can't say I'm looking forward to it, but after a day like today, I'm also getting fidgety. At least when I return, I can give Dan a call to arrange a night of debauchery. Two weeks of no sex has been torturous; my balls are turning blue. Getting myself off is never as appealing when it's just you and a bunch of filthy thoughts. Helena is always the subject of those thoughts, which leaves me feeling severely depressed.

After dinner, we dock and I wander off into the night, dressed quite casually because it's still so damn hot. Besides, I'm not looking to hook up with anyone so who cares what I'm wearing. I walk down the main strip next to the playa and consider my options for which bar to go to. Most of them are rowdy and full of people, probably my age, trying to hook up with one another or get so drunk they can't remember how to get back to their own hotel. It's only when I get to one of the quieter bars at the end that something catches my eye.

Live music is playing, but not club music, it's traditional acoustic guitars playing gentle Spanish melodies. The customer base is made up of older couples and a few boho chicks and surfers with tattoos, facial hair, and fashionable, I'm-not-trying-hard-but-still-wanna-look-on-trend, man buns. Donning board shorts from a day of catching waves on the more secluded beaches, they smoke and vape at the bar, chatting and laughing quietly amongst one another in different international languages. The older couples smile contentedly, watching the musicians expertly move their fingers across the strings of their instruments. This is definitely the place I feel like being in tonight. No bullshit, no drama, and no responsibilities.

Having chosen the place based on its laid-back atmosphere, I step into the bar and walk casually up to the only barman, take up a stool, and flop my wallet and keys onto the wooden surface in front of me. Years of stains and wet glasses mark the dark, polished pine, but it still looks clean enough.

"Digame? (Tell me?)," the rather large Spanish guy says to me with a friendly, albeit fake smile.

"Una cerveza, por favor, (a beer, please)," I reply, so he bends to grab a beer from the fridge, showing me the label as he does so. I nod my acceptance, then pay him. My Spanish isn't great, but I can get by with the essentials.

"Gracias," he says in a low, I've-been-saying-this-all-day, tone of voice.

Waving away the change, I turn to face the musicians and let my mind wander off on a tangent. It's cooler at this end of the strip; there's a gentle breeze blowing in from the water down below. I breathe out a sigh when I start thinking about all the shit I will have to face when I return home next week.

"Bonita! (Beautiful!)" The bartender calls out but gets no response. "Mujer! (Woman!)" he shouts, this time laughing. "No hay cerveza!" (I have no beer).

"Ok!" a young female voice calls back; I guess that's why

he's laughing to himself, knowing full well he'll get attitude for calling her 'mujer'.

Soon after, the woman appears behind the bar with her back to me. She's petite, dressed in denim cut-offs, old flip flops, and a work tank top. Her hair is tied back in a messy bun and it's a pale pink, rosy color that highlights her light caramel tan. Like a sixth sense taking over, it occurs to me that I know this woman. I know her very well.

"Senorita?" I call out in a gruff, unrecognizable growl. She immediately turns around with a frown on her pretty features to see who it is that is calling after her. "Buono sera, mia topolina!"

Helena

"You have got to be kidding me!" I gasp at the figure in front of me, nearly dropping the crate of beer I'm trying to hand over to Eliseo.

Lucius Hastings.

At my words, his trademark smug smirk spreads over his face like a dark shadow taking up your sunlight on the beach. It takes me right back to being seventeen on the doorstep of *Hastings Villa*, when I should have run far away instead of willingly walking inside his lair. He moves his eyes over me, all the way from my feet and up to my head, rubbing the fraction of stubble on his chin and giving a look that tells me he likes what he sees. My traitorous cheeks heat, causing him to laugh softly under his breath.

"Bonita, you ok?" Eliseo asks me, sounding full of concern. He's trying to help me learn the language better, but my sudden verbal outburst must have him worried because he's fallen back into using English.

"I...I'm fine, Eliseo," I finally reply as I turn back to face my Spanish colleague. "I was just getting my things ready to go."

My shift ended a few hours ago, but the rush of people for the live entertainment was too much for the two members of bar staff who were scheduled for tonight. The rich but clueless owners are a couple of idiots that try anything to get out of paying their staff if they can help it.

Eliseo nods with a smile that manages to look both affectionate and concerned. I don't say anything to Lucius, instead, I wave and walk out the back to collect my bag, leaving Eliseo to look suspiciously at the handsome figure sitting at the end of the bar.

Trying to avoid unnecessary drama, I sneak out the back exit and begin jogging up the steps to get the hell out of here. I'm not interested in talking to Lucius, I'm still much too hurt after everything. He never ever contacted me after I gave him my virginity, not even once, not even to check if I got back ok or to see how I was after Nonna's funeral. It took nearly six months of having stress-related migraines every time I thought about him and for me to not want him so badly, I felt sick with it. It then took another year or so to finally begin dating. So, no, I do not want to talk to him, thank you very much.

Thinking I've got away with it, I begin to relax and walk down the strip, ignoring the catcalls from drunk tourists, as well as waving or high-fiving the odd acquaintance I meet along the way. I also pop my head in and out of some of the other bars to see what's going on tonight; not a lot it would seem. It's been a great summer so far and I've had a blast, but I'm looking forward to returning home to see my family in a month's time.

I also need to end things with Evan once and for all. His

week over here was enough to tell me we weren't suited to one another and for me to see a hint of what life would be like with him. He wanted to dine in expensive restaurants, dress up and parade around in front of the wealthier diners, while I wanted to try street food and explore nighttime markets on the beach. During the day, he wanted to laze around on the beach and effectively cook himself in the peak sunshine while eyeing bikini-clad supermodel wannabes. I wanted to go off-track and take random, artistic shots with my Leica. And the sex? My god, I don't think I ever want to do missionary ever again. I even got a cramp the last time because there was no change, no variation, and definitely no orgasm. For me, anyway.

Silver, my roommate, had made fun of my fake orgasm noises and accused us of being one of those cliché couples where the woman is only with the guy for his money and his willingness to marry her. I had started to argue but then realized this is exactly what we look like. Except, it's not me who wants his status or his ring on my finger, it's my father. He made it as clear as day that I should hold onto Evan with all my might.

"Helena, I've always worried about you. You're so quiet, so shy, so vulnerable. I've known for a long time that you need someone to look after you. You're not like your brothers who are confident to look after themselves. But now that you've found Evan, I no longer need to worry. Just so you know, if he ever proposes, you have my blessing."

These were the words he had said to me before I left for Spain. I was literally speechless. What do you say to your father when he's practically admitted that he thinks you're a weak little female who needs a big, strong man to come and look after you? And all at the age of nineteen!

In the end, I told him I'd call when I arrived in Spain and

completely ignored his comments about marrying me off to the first bidder. Both Silver and Meri had reacted in the same way when I told them - their mouths gaping open, appalled expressions, and an immediate offer to crack open a bottle of wine.

Before my mind runs off any further about my unsatisfying unofficial boyfriend and his number one fan, my father, I feel a hand grab hold of mine from behind. As it pulls me back, I instinctively turn and smack the owner of said hand on the chin, before kneeing him in the balls. I owe those self-defense moves to Silver; teaching me how to defend myself was one of the first things she did when I told her about my new bar job. I'd like to think we'll keep in touch, but I know she's the sort of person that never hangs around in one place for long. She's probably met a million mes already.

"Fuck, Helena!" Lucius growls as he doubles over in pain. "When did you become such a thug?"

"Oh, God, I'm sorry," I blurt out and go to reach out to help him, but then stop myself. "Actually, no, I'm not. You totally deserved that, even before you grabbed me just now."

"What do you mean?" The asshole actually looks outraged over the insinuation that he's wronged me.

"Oh, I'm not in the mood for this," I sigh and begin to walk off in the opposite direction.

"Wait, wait," he gasps at the same time as he begins running uncomfortably alongside me. "Maybe you're right; maybe I did deserve it...a little."

"Good, are we done? Can you fuck off and leave me alone?" I continue walking, making him squirm as he hobbles by my side, and with a look of pain satisfyingly written all over his face.

"Wait, Helena...*shit*...please stop walking, I think you killed my dick," he says before bending over to cup his injured appendage with his hands.

Although I'm usually against violence of any kind, I can't help but smile to myself. I've been waiting to do that for a very long time. However, moments pass by and he's still holding onto his nether region, so I roll my eyes and take pity on him.

Placing an arm around his shoulders, I help him hobble over to a nearby bench, where we sit in silence for a moment or two. He tries to breathe through the pain between his legs, whereas I sit with my arms crossed and back ramrod straight, looking as if I have no idea who the weirdo, cupping his balls, is. A couple of guys walk past and laugh at him wincing in pain.

"Are you going to be ok?" I eventually ask. "I didn't actually mean to hurt you personally; I thought someone was attacking me."

"I'll admit, it wasn't a very well thought out move on my part," he replies, and for some reason, we both laugh at each other. "What's with the hair?"

"Oh, yeah, I don't know," I reply while twiddling with a loose strand. "Just thought I might like to stand out for once."

"You always stand out to me," he says with a crooked grin on his face.

"Oh, please!" I scoff, rolling my eyes over his cheesy attempt to charm me. "That won't work anymore, Lucius. You made your bed, with me in it, only to leave it in a mess and then forgot all about it. So don't try and be cute."

He merely shrugs his shoulders but keeps that ridiculous boy smirk on his face. I don't know if I want to smack it again or kiss him like we did the last time we were together.

"Come on, Topolina," he says, "we were hardly in a position to have some grand love affair, were we? You said you understood."

"I get that, Lucius, but you could have at least been a friend. Maybe text me to see how I was, to see how the funeral went or...something!"

"I can't be *friends* with you, Helena," he says, now looking completely serious. "I thought it was for the best. For both of us."

"Well, I'm pleased it was so easy for you to just switch off and forget about me. I'm sure the many women of LA are thankful too."

"Merial?" he asks, wondering who's been spreading rumors about him.

"Amongst others," I reply with a shrug and my best sulky pout.

"Are you jealous?" His ability to turn this into me wanting him makes me want to smack him again. But seeing as I've already caused injury to his cock, I best stop where I am.

"Pfft! No way. In fact, I've started seeing someone recently and we've...well, we've taken it to a more intimate level, and I think-"

"He's shit?"

He grins from ear to ear, loving the fact he has indeed ruined me for anyone else. My mouth drops open over the audacity of this guy. How dare he talk about my unofficial boyfriend who I plan on breaking up with as soon as I get home because he's boring and unsatisfying in bed? *Crap on a stick!*

"Totally shit," I finally admit with a long, sad sigh. The bastard simply laughs, even swinging his head back with self-satisfied glee.

"You've totally ruined my chances of ever conceiving I hope you know," he says, smiling at the same time as attempting to uncup his bits and pieces. "I think you owe me a drink."

"Oh, hell no!" I jump up quickly and begin to walk away again. "I'm going back to my Lucius-free life, which means it's stress and drama-free too."

"To totally unsatisfying sex as well?" he asks, to which I stare at him angrily. He merely holds his hands up in a defensive stance and smiles. "Hey, *your* words were 'totally shit'."

"Whatever, I'm off," I call back with a sigh.

I return home in a month and there's still so much I want to do before I leave. Sitting around arguing with Lucius over the state of my sex life is not something I want to waste time on.

"Enjoy your holiday or whatever this is for you. I'm sure Miss-whoever-it-is-right-now is waiting for you somewhere."

"Nope, totally alone," he calls out after me, so I turn and pout at him, feigning pity, before I continue walking again.

Always one to have the last word, he pulls me back by my hand and presses his mouth against mine. A zap of electricity passes through my body momentarily before I can find the strength to push him away. He's a persistent bastard though, so pulls me back for another kiss, this time swiping his tongue into my mouth for just a second. I angrily jerk my head back, to which he raises his brow, as if asking me why on earth I am trying to stop what I so desperately want.

"Lucius, stop it!"

Only he doesn't stop, instead, he leans in and kisses me again, holding me close to every part of his body. I can't resist any longer, so I find myself wrapping my arms around his neck and kissing him with equal passion and hunger to that of his own.

"One drink, Topolina, what can happen with just one drink?"

He smiles cheekily, knowing exactly what can happen with 'one drink'.

"Ok, fine, but no whiskey and no funny business!" I warn him. "Where are you staying anyway?"

"I have a little boat in the marina," he says coolly.

"But of course you do, no run-of-the-mill, normal hotel for you," I utter sarcastically, and with an added bit of sass to my voice.

"I've missed this feisty little attitude of yours. The pink hair's growing on me too. Got any other surprises?" he asks, now leading the way to the marina.

"I may or may not have gotten a little tattoo," I shrug, recalling a drunken night out with Silver and her surfer friends. "Not that you'll ever see it."

"Oh, now that's sparked my interest. I do love a good challenge; care to place a bet on it?"

Helena

When we arrive at the marina, he shows me the 'little' boat he was referring to and, very uncoolly, I gawk over its luxury and opulence. It is one of the most impressive boats in the entire marina. I have to crane my neck to see the top deck for goodness' sake!

A steward is waiting to welcome Lucius back on board, and I can't help but notice the poor guy looking like a bag of nerves. I can only guess as to what it's like to work for my own little Satan. Lucius is curt with his staff and orders him to bring champagne to the top deck immediately. The steward nods his head frantically before running off to do his master's bidding.

"I see you still have such a warm and fuzzy way with people," I comment dryly as he helps me onboard. "Are they *all* afraid of you?"

"The way I like it," he says arrogantly, "I bet you're the source of much gossip below decks now."

"They probably think I'm some sort of dodgy, low-class escort or something," I mutter. I might not be wearing raunchy clothes, but I am donning pink hair, a skimpy uniform, and a pair of old flip-flops. I don't suppose I look anything like someone Lucius would normally be dating. "You do realize they probably spit in your food."

"Probably," he replies nonchalantly, though I'm not sure which of my statements he's agreeing with.

We walk upstairs and he shows me into the lounge on the top deck. It's softly lit and contains a small bar, dining area, and matching navy couches and cushions. The wooden deck flooring is polished to the point of having a reflection, and a deep red rug lies in the middle of it. There are pictures of the boat hung up around the walls and the decorative touches are expensive, albeit completely impersonal.

"Do you actually own this boat?" I ask.

"Only for this vacation," he answers as he sinks down onto one of the couches.

The Steward brings up an ice bucket with two crystal champagne flutes and a bottle of Moet. He pops the cork and pours two drinks, one for each of us.

"Will there be anything else, Sir?" he asks nervously. I can almost hear him mentally pleading inside his head for there not to be anything else; it sounds much like a tape on constant repeat.

"No thank you, Steven," Lucius answers without even looking at him, his eyes are firmly fixed on me as I walk over to sit on the couch with him. "Please make yourself scarce and tell the others to do the same. We do not want to be disturbed."

"Yes, Sir," he replies with a quick nod of his head. I try and stifle my laughter over how relieved he looks, but then he turns to eye me with suspicion, just before exiting the deck altogether.

"Yep, I'm definitely the prostitute!"

I gulp back a large mouthful of champagne to soften the embarrassment. Lucius laughs wickedly, then shuffles up closer, doing it in such a way, he manages to make it look like I'm trying to get nearer to him instead of the other way around. It must be unusual for Lucius to actually have to make an effort with a woman.

"So, is it serious with this guy who's crap in bed?" he asks, snapping me out of my unpleasant thoughts of him being with other girls.

"I don't know," I answer non-committedly with a sad shrug. I never thought I'd be discussing Evan with Lucius of all people. "He spent last week out here with me, and he seems pretty keen."

"I'm sure he is, Topolina," he says while slurping back on champagne like water, not a bottle that probably costs the same as my weekly pay packet. "I mean it when I say you are very beautiful. He no doubt thinks he's scored one hot fuck!"

"Gracious as always, Lucius," I tut, frowning over his crudeness.

"But tell me, if he is so bad, why are *you* settling?"

I clear my throat, because hearing those words out in the open, blunt and honest, makes it all the harder to stomach.

"*Settling*? What do you mean?" I ask, acting affronted by his accusation, even though it is precisely what I've been doing. Then again, Lucius is somewhat responsible for my lackluster feelings towards Evan.

"Oh, come on, Helena, I can see you have, at best, lukewarm feelings for the guy! Why else would you admit he doesn't get you going between the sheets?"

"Maybe lukewarm is all I'm looking for. Maybe it's easier that way," I reply contemplatively. "It took a lot of painful migraines to get you out of my head."

Way to be cool and distant, Helena, a real fine effort you put in there.

To my surprise, he casts his eyes to the deck floor, almost guiltily, but then quickly lifts them back up to meet mine and smiles tightly. I can't help but wonder what that look means, if anything. I shouldn't care, but I do. However, the moment passes, and neither one of us says a word about what passed between us.

"You deserve more than lukewarm, Topolina," he says quietly, "and that body of yours deserves hot, passionate, scream-into-the-sheets sex. I can at least deliver that to you."

"Well, too bad that's not going to happen," I say determinedly, as tempting as it sounds, "and whether I stick with Evan or not, you can keep your thoughts to yourself."

"*Evan*?! Is that the asshole's name? He sounds like a preppy, boring piece of shit," he says with an unflinching, serious expression. I simply sigh, looking away from his smug expression before I bite. "You do realize he's probably boning everything in a skirt while you're away. Spreading his mediocre sexual talents around other poor, unsuspecting women."

"Sounds like you're the one who is jealous now, Lucius," I tell him with my own smug expression. "Besides, we're not exclusive, so if he is, I have no right to complain. I'm the one who's been holding back from getting serious. Even my parents love him."

"Oh, fuck, it just keeps getting better and better," he laughs, "be a good little girl, Helena, and shack up with the fucktard that Daddy Carter approves of. Your life will lack any kind of spark or passion, but at least you've made a sound choice."

His cocky attitude is beginning to piss me off, so I stand to leave, but no sooner than I have, he runs out in front to stop me. I get no further than the end of the stupid, pretentious rug with golden filigree patterns woven into its border before he's grabbed hold of my wrist. I look at him with a stony glare, even when he cups my face and looks at me with softness in his eyes.

"Stay here with me," he says, stroking my face with the back of his hand. I try really hard not to lean into it, but I'm fast losing the battle, which would only lead to devastation. "Give me the weekend and I will show you what sex should be like. I will worship you, Helena."

I heard that from Evan and it was a complete farce, but something tells me Lucius isn't bigging up mediocre talents. No, Lucius Hastings will be completely mind-blowing between the sheets, and after weeks of totally unsatisfying activity with Evan, I need to know what it can really feel like.

"Not a chance, Lucius," I fire back, but even I can hear the weakness in my voice. With that in mind, I try to appeal to his emotional side, even though I doubt he has one. "I've only just managed to get you out of my head. I'm not going back to that place again."

"This is just sex, Helena, one hurrah before you go back to prep boy for frustrating sexual experiences," he says with a raise of his brow, daring me to just give in. My own wicked little devil. "Live a little, remember?"

I try to pull down his hands to get them away from my face, but they won't budge. Besides his obvious physical advantage over me, I'm much too tempted by his offer to put any real effort into it. Alarm bells are ringing in my head, but I don't want to listen to them. There hasn't been anyone who has heated me from the inside like Lucius, just as he's managing to do now, and with only his words and icy blue eyes. We look at each other, with unapologetic lust; after all, I am not a virgin this time and I want so much more.

Sensing my doubt, he rests his forehead against mine, weakening my resolve completely. I close my eyes if only so I can't see him looking as sexy as sin. Mentally, I want to flick that naughty little devil off my shoulder, but he's very much glued to me, whispering words of temptation to just let go with the man who I have been in love with since that summer at *Hastings Villa*. This is self-annihilation at its best.

"Just say yes, Topolina! I can see it's on the tip of your tongue," he tempts me. "You remember what I can do with my tongue, don't you?"

He begins kissing my cheek with gentle fluttery kisses. He presses his hard cock against my core, making me breathe just that little bit harder.

"Three days of carnal, unadulterated, animal pleasure on every deck, in every room, in any position we feel like."

His tongue darts out and my eyes instantly home in on it. He presses his wet mouth momentarily on top of mine; a little taster of what he has to offer.

"Does *Evan* go down on you?"

I shake my head.

"Does he place his fingers inside of you, bringing you to the brink of pleasure?"

I shake my head.

"Does he suck your pert, hard, pink nipples?"

I shake my head.

"Does his cock feel as good as mine?"

I shake my head.

"Fuck, has he ever made you come?"

I shake my head, wincing over my own betrayal, to which he laughs with pure deviousness.

"Then let me give you what you need, Topolina. I will give it all to you."

Against every fiber of rationality in my body, I let him kiss me. In fact, I give as much as him, equaling the passion and still wanting more.

"Say your answer, Topolina, say it out loud for me," he teases.

"Yes," I breathe out, not fully believing the word is leaving my lips.

"Good girl," he whispers, then drops to the floor, where he undoes the button to my shorts. He yanks them down with my panties, all in one go, grabs my hips, and is on me like a starved animal. He is rougher than last time, more animalistic as he licks me from the inside out.

"Oh, God!" I gasp as a wave of pleasure begins building already. Though I can't blame myself, I've been without for so long. I grab his hair and run my fingers through it as he takes me deeply, all the while circling my clit with his thumb pad. "Oh, God, I'm going to come already…"

"I want you to come, Helena, you've been denied for too long," he says through clenched teeth, "and when my mouth makes you come, I'm going to take you so deep, so hard, you'll come again!"

I climax within an instant, as if my body is desperate for what he's just promised. Bright sparks flash before my eyes, causing me to lose my breath as I come down from the eruption. But before I even have a chance to bring my body back down to normal, he hoists me over his shoulder and carries me into what looks like the master bedroom, where a huge king-size bed takes center stage. He lies me on top of the Egyptian Cotton sheets, then hurriedly and unashamedly strips off in front of me. Has he been waiting for this just as much as I have?

"Take your top and bra off and rub your nipples for me, Topolina," he says, then smiles tightly when he sees the utter horror on my face, as though he's frustrated by my coyness. "If we only have one weekend, we're going to do this properly. There's no room for being shy. Do it!"

I slowly peel my tank top away and unhook my bra, letting my breasts fall out, which feel big and full. He stands fully naked at the foot of the bed and watches me stroke my breasts and pinch my nipples until they are red and standing pert. Lucius wets his lips as he begins to stroke himself in front of me, jaw clenched, eyes dark.

"Open your legs for me, I want to see you wet for me." I do it, feeling completely exposed to him. "So beautiful, Helena."

He rubs himself harder in front of me, so, having already given into the devil on my shoulder, I move my hand down over my abdomen and through my soaking wet lips below. I'm still sensitive from my last orgasm, so I stroke myself slowly, teasingly, all the while looking right back at him, as if we're in competition to see who will look away first. He licks his lips again and groans when I find my clit and begin to circle it, eventually swinging my head back in pleasure.

"Take me, Lucius," I whisper, still touching myself, "I'm not a virgin anymore, you can take me how you want me this time. I'm yours, remember?"

With those last words, he closes the gap between us and flips me over onto my front. My ass is pulled up into the air and is given a swift smack that has me gasping, feeling both excited and nervous at the same time. Thank God he hasn't tried to enter me missionary style, that would have been more disappointing than I could bear. He mounts the bed and smacks my ass cheek again before rubbing his throbbing head against my opening and up to my clit, then back again.

"Is this what you want?" he asks, teasing me with his hardness against my wanting sex. "Answer me, Topolina."

"Yes," I breathe, biting my lip as I wait for him. "Please, Lucius."

He enters me slowly, hissing through his teeth the whole time. I'd forgotten how full he made me feel. Evan is positively small by comparison and has no style or technique to speak of. Dirty talk consists of his own grunts and moans. For some reason, I need Lucius' wicked tongue to get me going, to make me beg for what he has to offer.

At first, Lucius thrusts slowly, using my hips to move in and out the full length of his cock. As I push back for more, we get into a slightly quicker rhythm, enjoying the feeling without the build of an orgasm to end things too quickly. He leans over me and grabs my nipples underneath, pinching and pulling at them.

"Fuck, I don't want to stop, you feel so amazing, like you were made for me," he growls as I clench around him. "Feel how you take me, how you hold me; you will always be mine, Topolina."

When I emit a moan of agreement, he begins to move faster and harder, no longer able to contain his animalistic urges to have me roughly.

"Oh, God, Lucius," I gasp, and he slaps my cheek again. It sparks off the catalyst of another orgasm and I find myself crying out for him to give me all he's got. He growls from the back of his throat as he pummels against me from behind. He adds his finger to my clit, circling it as he fucks me like he owns me, like only he knows how to get me to that euphoric state of pleasure. It's too much and I explode with a scream into the pillow below me. Not having had his fill, he flips me over so that I am on my back, and enters me from above, hooking my leg over his shoulder. He is taking me so intensely, I can't keep up with his movements, so I am shocked when, yet another orgasm begins to surface. Chasing the high, I tilt my hips to meet him more fully. I clench around his cock, causing him to moan out loud before we come together in complete ecstasy.

Lucius' heavy body falls on top of mine, and he holds me close to him for a while. I lie in a kind of fuzzy blur as I come down, hardly believing this is happening. Eventually, he brings himself up onto his forearms and looks into my eyes before kissing me gently on the mouth. Enjoying this side of him, the side that makes this more than just lust and fucking, I stroke his hair and sigh. I should be feeling guilty about Evan, but he hasn't even crossed my mind. Everything right now is Lucius. It always has been.

"Holy fuck, Topolina," he whispers, stroking back my hair, "how have you survived without this for so long?"

He laughs and I can't help but laugh back. It's at this moment, I realize I am right to let Evan go. If I had any deep feelings for him, I wouldn't have done what I just did with Lucius.

It wouldn't have mattered that we're not exclusive, I would never have shared myself if he was someone for whom I had strong feelings. But with Lucius…I have never felt this way about anyone.

And now, Helena, you are royally fucked!

Chapter 18

Helena

I insist on returning to my apartment for the night, if only to remind myself of what this is; a weekend of non-committed sex, nothing more. When I get back, I look at my reflection in the mirror with a little contempt. My just fucked hair taunts me with my betrayal of whatever progress I had made since I left *Hastings Villa*. And then there's Evan. I haven't cheated for I was careful not to label what we were. But he came out here to see me, kept telling me that we were going to end up together, convinced me that no one would care for me like he would. If only I would agree to make things official. But I couldn't commit to that, precisely because of the man I've just slept with. Guilt begins to creep in and I wonder whether I should call Lucius and tell him the weekend's off, even if I am desperate to lie in his arms.

After a few more moments of doubt, self-preservation forces me to consider what Lucius had said about Evan sleeping with any number of girls back home and I smile. I'm almost certain that he has been sleeping around, for his phone was buzzing non-stop when he was here. The smirk on his face after he had read these messages was enough to tell me what I suspected was true. Not that I was angry about it. Even before seeing Lucius, I wanted Evan to understand that he was free to pursue other girls, to maintain some distance between us and not feel trapped. But it works both ways; I never promised him monogamy on my part, so I know I've done nothing wrong. My relief is quickly followed by the realization that I just smiled over the thought of my unofficial boyfriend sleeping with other women. Evan and I are doomed, so I'm going to enjoy this limited time that I have with the man I fell in love with two years ago.

The next morning, I meet Lucius at the bar where I work. Silver is working the morning shift when it begins to fill up with people wanting morning coffees and families who are coming to set up on the beach. She eyes Lucius and me together and high-fives me when his back is turned, silently calling me a 'slut' in the most affectionate way she can. The sun is already warm but it's not yet at its peak, when you're in danger of burning to a crisp. During this time of day, this place usually attracts small children and their parents. They'll stay till lunch then head back to their hotels to avoid the blistering heat.

Chewing on my nails as I study his casual frame, I watch Lucius looking totally relaxed with the situation, beyond peaceful with himself. Shrugging off the feeling that this is just another regular weekend for him, I glance over at a little girl who is clinging to her father's leg while staring at Lucius with nervous curiosity. I smile at her, but she just shoves her little thumb inside her mouth. It takes Lucius a few more seconds to realize he's being stared at. He eyes the girl with the same trepidation as she does with him; I can't help but watch their interaction with keen interest. After a moment or two, he pulls a mean but silly-looking face, and she giggles. To my surprise, he then ever so slightly quirks his lips to give her some semblance of a smile. Contented by this, she then grins at her father who gathers her up inside of his arms before traipsing back down the beach again.

"I saw that," I utter with smirk.

"I know you did, Topolina," he says nonchalantly, "why do you think I didn't tell her to get lost?"

"Oh, so, being nice to a small child was for *my* benefit?" I grab hold of my cup and sip to calm my nervous anticipation for what he has planned for us today. "Is it some sort of seduction technique? Be nice to a little kid and I'll be eating from the palm of your hand?"

"It's only natural you should want a guy who likes children; a woman's urge to procreate is strong, is it not? And choosing a mate who can provide and look after his offspring is of vital importance, is it not? We are but animals after all."

"Wow, how very factual you are about how I choose who I am attracted to. I'm just a little, meek female looking for a potential father to my future children? Trouble is, Lucius, I already know children would be the last thing you would want, so I don't really need to worry about you fathering any potential offspring with me." I raise my brow to show I've won this round. "So, science lesson aside, I would have to conclude you're not as evil as you like to make out."

Lucius throws his head back and chuckles manically before grabbing hold of my hand from across the table and placing it against his soft lips.

"If it makes you feel better to think that about me, then be my guest," he says, shrugging his shoulders and gazing out across the flat calm sea.

"Don't worry, Lucius, I've heard plenty of rumors about

your behavior, both in and out of the office."

He takes his time to turn away from the water to look at me. He then leans forward to brace his forearms on the table, as though I'm going to let him into all of these devious little secrets.

"Go on," he eventually says with devilish amusement written all over his face.

"Well, let's see, there are so many to choose from." I tap my chin with the tip of my index finger, trying to select the best ones from memory. "You fired an intern for referring to Jen as your mother?" He smiles in such a way, I know that must be true. "Ok, you make contracts so water-tight, you can fire employees at will, for little to no reason?"

He leans back and flaps his hands up as though that's a given.

"You bully company directors into deals that are less than favorable to them by finding loopholes and assisting their competitors to devalue their true worth?"

He nods slowly while I look at him like he's some sort of spawning alien.

"Are you even yet fully trained? How do you manage to do all of these dastardly deeds?"

"I've been working with Paul since I was fourteen," he replies. "Trust me, when it comes to business, the guy is just as evil as I am…for now. As you said, I am still training; I have not yet met my true potential."

"Ok, I guess we all need goals, even if they are diabolical. You never sleep with the same woman twice."

"My, my, I really do have to have words with Merial, don't I? However does she have the time to spread such meaningless gossip?"

"Except one," I continue, ignoring his attempts to bypass what I just said. "An intern whom you dated for three months." He remains tight-lipped and leans on the table again. "What happened to her?"

"To begin with, Topolina, I never 'date' anyone, I merely sleep with them. Secondly, I would rather endure a conversation with Merial and her old gal pals than admit to such a thing to you. But, since you asked, yes, I had been sleeping with the same girl for a few months, which is highly unusual for me."

"And what made her different? Did she resemble a supermodel or something?" I ask as I begin anxiously playing with a packet of sugar.

"Please, you insult me, Topolina, to think I would be attracted to such cliché qualities in a woman. Do you take me for someone like Eric?" he tuts, looking genuinely insulted.

"Still not answering the question, Lucius," I huff.

"She looked like you," he replies with a sigh, gazing across the water again to avoid my eye contact.

"Oh," I gasp, feeling an emotion I can't quite put my finger on – shock, sadness, relief?

"She found a picture of you one evening and asked who you were. I told her you were the one girl I had actually developed feelings for."

He looks up at me and smirks at my bulging eyes and gaping mouth. I feel like I might break down at any moment, but instead, I look sheepishly to the floor, as though feeling guilty on his behalf.

"Anyway, she couldn't help noticing the similarities between you and her, so she asked me if I was only with her because she reminded me of you."

"Oh, God, what did you say, Lucius?" I cover my face with my hands, awaiting the answer which I think I already know.

"I told her the truth," he says nonchalantly.

"Christ, Lucius!" I cry out with a groan at the end for the poor girl. "She must have felt awful. Do you have no shame?"

"Please, she was only with me for superficial reasons too," he says, "it was no grand love affair for either of us."

"Still, you need to learn some diplomacy, Lucius. Surely, you must need some of that in your line of work."

"I can bullshit people if I have to, but otherwise, I am what I am; they can accept it or not, it matters little to me. There are very few people who matter to me. In fact, come to think of it, there are only two."

"Paul?" I whisper, fearing who the other one is, for it's only going to break me more than I already am when it comes to him.

"Yes, and…?" he says, taking my hand and bringing it to his lips.

"Me?" I venture, closing my eyes to indulge in the feeling of his contact with my naked skin.

"Always," he whispers.

My eyes open to see his icy blues looking right into mine and with a wicked grin on his lips. Such a simple kiss on my hand, an international gesture of respect and politeness that has been passed down through centuries. Who knew it would symbolize the moment I sold my soul to the devil? For though I can deny it as much as I want, Lucius Hastings will always own my heart, my soul, my body, my everything. And the worst part? He more than knows it.

"S-s-so, what are we going to do today?" I just about manage to ask through the haze of my falling under his hypnotic stare.

He merely raises one of his eyebrows in a devilish fashion that has me tutting over his filthy mind. Though, the sound I emit is enough to break his spell if only for a moment. I suspect he took pity on me and did it purposefully.

"Thought I'd take you out on the boat," he eventually replies.

"Ooh, how the other half live," I tease. "I'm up for that."

Helena

Mere hours later and we're lying on top of the sundeck feeling warm and smug all over. Life onboard a luxury boat is quite something. Whenever I am hungry or thirsty, my every desire is granted. If we fancy stopping to go ashore, all we need do is mention it to the steward and he sorts it. Even the sea is beautiful today with its shimmery reflection hypnotizing me whenever I look overboard.

After lunch, we visit a small island that has a private beach. Unbeknownst to me, Lucius has hired it for the afternoon so we can have it completely to ourselves. Steven, the nervous steward, drives the small motorboat over to the island shore and helps us to unload a few supplies before returning back to the boat, which has been anchored around on the other side of the island. Wildlife and foliage supply our romantic backdrop while azure blue sea spreads out in front of us. The sand isn't white and fine like Caribbean beaches, but it is still soft beneath our feet. If you look close enough, you can see sparkly pebbles and intricate shells scattered amongst the fine grains of sand, which I collect and place inside a small hessian bag to take back with me.

I brought my camera so set to taking shots of the wildlife all around us. Lucius catches my eye while he attempts to arrange mats and umbrellas on the sand. I begin snapping wildly, taking shots without him even realizing. This is my passion, capturing people when they think no one is looking, when they're being completely natural and uninhibited. There's no pretense, not even with Lucius.

My artistry is short-lived, however, because as soon as he's caught me, he tears the camera away from my hands and begins returning the favor by taking multiple shots of me. I try to reach for it, but he grips hold of my arm and continues taking photos. However, he soon turns so the shots are of both of us grinning like a couple of idiots. Well, I am anyway.

Before long, we end up kissing slowly and passionately on top of a rustic mat that provides the only barrier between my back and the blistering hot sand. His hands move up and down the length of my body while I grip hold of his raven black tufts of hair. It feels a little crispy from the salty water and I enjoy softening it between my fingers. When we eventually break for air, I giggle over his devilish grin.

"You know the Spanish word for devil is *'diablo'*?" I

whisper, still with my hands buried inside of his hair. "I think that's what I'll call you this weekend, my 'naughty diablo'."

"I can live with that," he says as he begins moving down my body, sucking and nipping at the same time as looking into my eyes.

"Stop, come back up here to me," I say, gesturing with my hands. "I want you to actually make love to me, Diablo. Can you do that for me?"

He looks at me intensely, contemplating what I've just said to him, before nodding and taking hold of me inside his arms. His kisses begin to come thick and fast. I try to lose myself in this moment, to take his touch for what it is, but no matter how hard I try, something is playing on my mind. Something that threatens to ruin everything we have in the here and now.

"What did you mean when you said I was the only person you would consider having a relationship with?"

"Exactly what I said," he mutters between sucking my flesh into his warm, wet mouth. I'm writhing beneath him, but my mind is still working on overtime. I'm so confused by his need to consume me, but always at arms' length.

"But you won't," I whisper, as if to myself, though I know he heard me, for he immediately stops his oral assault on my stomach.

His eyes move up to look at me from where he is hovering over my abdomen; his tongue is still in contact with the space between my breasts and belly button. He says nothing, which says everything, though I still feel a need to punish myself by probing further.

"Have a relationship with someone. You won't, will you?"

My heart drops when I see his eyes look away from me, the answer to my question is written all over his face. Shaking away my disappointment, I lift his chin to look back at me. "It's ok, Lucius, don't stop."

We slide each other's costumes off and shortly after, he slides inside of me from between my legs, which I use to wrap around him. It's my old friend, the missionary, but somehow, I find it all the more intense with Lucius. No matter what I do, however much it hurts, he will always be *my* person, even if no one can be his.

He moves slowly at first, making me feel loved and needed, as if his body is apologizing for his inability to commit to anything more than what this is between us. He peppers me with gentle kisses along my jaw and down my neck. I tilt my hips to meet him more deeply and he moans over the sensation of me clenching all around him. When I come, I hold myself around his cock so hard that he soon follows with a groan against my hair. We lie still for a while afterward, just feeling content to be in each other's arms.

"I can't fall in love with you again, Lucius," I whisper as he rests his head on top of my chest. "It broke me the last time."

He doesn't reply for a while, and I end up closing my eyes sadly over his silence.

"I think you still love me now, Helena. I can't help but still want you to love me."

He asks me with a fear of doubt in his mind. Lucius needn't doubt my feelings for him, for even I know my feelings have already reignited, and in such a short time. However, this time, he doesn't sound like the smug devil who is forever trying to seduce me. This time, he sounds like the little boy who is desperate to be loved, desperate to be wanted. Leaning up onto his elbows over me, he studies the silent tears falling down my cheek and kisses them away.

"You're messing with my head all over again, Lucius, why would you say that?"

"You said you understood, that you knew what this was, Helena," he says sadly.

But *why* is he sad? If this is nothing but sex, why does he care how I feel? I throw my hands over my face and sigh heavily to ward off the urge to cry. He pulls them away and moves up to look at me more carefully, his eyes holding me captive.

"The devil doesn't get to fall in love, Helena," he says, looking sincere. "If he gets too close, he sends his love to hell. I would rather send myself there alone than condemn you to that kind of life. Even if it means I lose you."

"Why do you think that about yourself, Lucius?" I whisper, placing my hands on his cheeks.

"I was told the truth a long time ago," he says with a smile so sad, it's even more heartbreaking to see than if he had broken down into tears.

Unfortunately, I can't think of any words with which to answer him, so I say nothing. After a few moments of silence, he pulls away and gets to his feet, pulling me up with him.

"Come with me, Topolina. Sometimes the devil can walk amongst mortals without condemnation. This is that time...with you, only you."

His smile is enough to snap me out of my funk, and his words remind me to enjoy the time we have together. So, even though I'm going to regret this come Monday, I smile back and let him lead me into the water.

"Making love on a beach isn't at all as romantic as I thought it would be," I giggle as I brush the sand away from what feels like every crevice on my body.

"Well, there's always the sea," he says as he hauls me over his shoulder and marches us further into the water with my bare ass on show.

Sex with Lucius is beyond euphoric and something I could repeat multiple times on a daily basis. I make up for the fact that I can never have this beyond this weekend by letting him have me on board the boat when we make our way back to the harbor. We go down on one another with greed and lust; I even lose count of the number of orgasms I have. After, when I'm severely sensitive down there, I have a much-needed shower before heading up to have dinner on the top deck.

Chapter 19

Lucius

She'll be waiting for me, I know this, but I'm stuck inside the shower, trying to shake off this feeling of anguish.

The devil doesn't fall in love.

You already have, you piece of shit.

Be that as it may, not even I'm that evil; to force the woman I love to live a life of torment with me.

You're just like him, Lucius, the man who raped me. The man who ultimately drove me to a piece of rope and that tree. You're his spawn, his curse upon me. No one could ever truly love you; I should have had you terminated to save you from a life of horrific loneliness.

But I could be the one to break the curse.

Do you really believe that, Diablo? Do you really think Helena Carter deserves to have a love based on 'could'? She is an angel, and you are fallen; don't bring her down with you, Lucius.

I'm half you too, Mom.

I was an angel too, once, but he dragged me down to hell with him; I took my life and left my son, I am just as fallen as you are. Don't force her to become like me; don't make history repeat itself.

I can be good...

Oh, baby, you were born bad...it's in your DNA.

"M-Mr Hastings?"

A sudden tap on my door, one that seems almost too loud for Steven's nervous disposition, echoes across the room.

"What!" I snap as I wrap a towel around me.

"Erm, well, apologies to disturb you, b-but Miss Carter, she's wondering...that is to say, she's worried about your, er..."

"Fuck's sake," I mutter to myself over this guy's lack of balls.

He's terrified of you, son, he knows you're evil too. Stick to what you're good at – being the heartless devil who keeps everyone at arm's length. Make this your last night with her.

"Get the fuck out of my head!" I growl at myself before slamming the closet door shut. "Steven, tell Miss Carter I'll be five minutes. Now, leave me the fuck alone."

"Y-y-yes, Sir, of course, Sir," he stutters, flapping his feet about on the floor before rushing off, probably trembling as he goes.

Listening to his anxious footsteps pacing away as fast as he can, I sink my ass onto the bed and release a long, frustrated sigh.

"You're right, Mother."

Lucius

She stares at the stars above, but my eyes focus solely on her. She is everything I do and don't want. She's everything I can't have but want more than anything in the world. She's the reason I will never have a relationship past one night. She's the reason I will live an angry and frustrated life; she's the reason I will hate myself for every day I'm not with her.

"Dance with me, Topolina."

I hold out my hand for my wide-eyed girl and give her one of my rare genuine smiles. She cautiously takes it, probably wondering why I'm suggesting we dance when there's no music to dance to. However, I know in about a minute and a half the hotel next to the marina will restart their set and I may or may not have offered the band a few hundred dollars to play the song I wanted for us.

She stands inside my arms, and it has never felt more natural. When the music begins, I point to the sky to make sure she can hear it too and when she does, she pats my shoulder playfully and laughs softly. I smile and pull her in closer so we can sway gently to the melody, the words, and the messages that I cannot tell her myself.

I feel her gently shudder against me as she listens to the words. I knew she'd get it because nothing slips past that brain of hers. Too clever, too sensitive, too perceptive to be able to hide anything from her. And yet, I still can't say what she desperately wants me tell her, to say what I want to say to her too. So, instead,

I hold her close to me and inhale her scent so I can at least take it with me when she leaves. Which she will. She has to.

Helena

Lucius and I make love one more time in the master bedroom before we break apart. For a long while after, we lie completely still with a gulf between us. I stare at him knowing I will never get over my diablo, and yet, I don't want to get over him. I feel too much when it comes to him. As he stares back at me, I wonder if he is thinking the same thing, if he's finally realized what this could be between us.

"I return home on Monday," he eventually whispers, and I feel the space between us widen, even though we haven't physically moved. "When do you go back?"

"Four weeks," I utter, to which he simply nods without words. I'm already losing him again. "Is this where you say it was fun, but see you around?" I laugh but he doesn't smile back. "You mean, this is totally it? You have no intention of seeing me again?"

My surprise at his reaction shocks me. How could I not have seen this happening? How did I manage to convince myself that this might have been more than what it was? I've just set myself back two years.

Forcing tears back, I sigh into the dark space between us and roll over to stare at the ceiling, having never felt so cheap and unwanted in all my life. It takes a long time before either of us speaks; my heart is too busy breaking all over again.

"What were you hoping for from me?" he asks, frowning with ignorance, even though he knows exactly what I was hoping for. I know what we had agreed but I never thought this would be the last time he'd see me. I thought…I thought…I have no idea, but it wasn't this.

"You've ruined me, Lucius," I whisper. "I didn't believe you when you said I'd be yours, but it turns out you were right...sadly." He looks away guiltily and it only confirms that this is the same as last time, a limited experience. I need to shake this off, to save myself from any more torture. "I can't stay, I have to go," I utter as I get out of bed.

"What? Why?" He looks at me with so many emotions, I can't even tell which one is winning. "You gave me the weekend, remember?"

"Because...because..." I can't even say the words and the stupid sting of tears are threatening even harder to fall. "Shit! Why did I ever agree to this? I must have 'masochistic ho' written across my forehead."

With anger winning in my court, I grab my clothes, which are scattered around the bedroom, and living room, and begin to dress myself with jerky, angry movements.

"Helena, what do you want me to say to you?" he says, grabbing my arm. "Tell me, please!"

"You don't want to know, Lucius," I reply bitterly, "you don't really want to know anything about me apart from who I'm fucking and if I'm going to fuck you. That's it for you, isn't it?"

Lucius doesn't answer but he doesn't seem to be letting go of me either. He looks at me with frustration, even though he knows I'm right.

"Tell me what you want from me," he says through clenched teeth.

"Why? So you can drop me all over again? So you can

leave one of your stupid cards in my hand before forgetting me all over again?"

"Please, tell me how you feel about me," he practically begs with what looks like indecision in his eyes.

"You say how you feel about me," I challenge him. "Tell me you want to be with me; to be mine and only mine."

He offers nothing but a pained expression until he stares at the floor and growls in frustration. The sound of his pain shocks me and I jump back, releasing a whimper as I do so. Before I can move away any further, he shoots his gaze right back at me, and pulls me in close, resting his forehead against mine while stroking at a lock of my hair.

"I can't," he says sadly, and my heart feels like it's just been pulled into a tight knot of agony.

"Then neither can I," I tell him truthfully. "I felt so empty last time, and I refuse to feel like that again. So, let me go."

He looks at me one more time with a whole host of unsaid words. I break free of his grip and begin gathering my things again, during which, his emotions shift, until eventually, anger gets the better of him. A rage he feels toward himself but would rather direct at me is coming to the surface.

"You're a coward, Topolina," he says bitterly when I stand before him, fully clothed and ready to walk out of his life, once and for all.

"Well, that makes two of us then," I retort before finally turning to leave.

As I walk out of the marina, wiping my face and trying to remain composed, I hear the sound of a glass smashing to pieces

THE DEVIL

against a hard surface. I guess this time, we broke each other.

Chapter 20

3 months later

Helena

"What?" I ask quietly. "I mean, could you repeat that please?"

"You're pregnant," the young, bubbly physician repeats with the same vomit-inducing grin she had given me the first time she had delivered this gut-wrenching news. She's met with a blank expression and a whole load of silence. "From your periods, I'd say you're a little further on than women usually are when they find out."

My heart feels like it's stopped beating altogether, whereas my head is filled with a high-pitched scream. The doctor's words become nothing more than fuzzy noise in the background, and the world around me blurs into a haze of broken dreams and responsibilities that I'm not sure I'm at all prepared to face. I feel my mom's hand gripping around my shoulders as the shock takes hold of my rationality, or rather, my lack of it.

"Excuse me," I whisper before grabbing hold of the waste basket and begin retching noisily inside of it.

"Oh, my," the doctor gasps, "have you had much sickness, dear?"

"A little," my mother answers for me while I continue throwing up in the middle of her office.

Ever since returning home from Spain, I have been suffering from strange bleeding patterns down below and have not wanted to eat or drink at all. When I assured her I had been careful, that I'd used protection when Evan came over to Spain, my mother began to worry there might be some terrifying, underlying cause, and to be honest, so had I. At first, they thought it was a bug and that my lack of eating was messing up my menstrual cycle. Last week, they ran blood work, the next step would have been a scan, had it not been for the paralyzing truth that came back from my tests.

"It's pretty normal in the first trimester; did you suffer from morning sickness, Mrs Carter?" the doctor rambles on cheerfully.

"Erm, not much," my mother responds politely, for her concern is focused on me and my never-ending vomiting.

When I finally look up at them both, I can see the doctor beaming down at me and my mother smiling awkwardly. She doesn't know how to respond, not that I can blame her. This is so not what I was expecting to hear. With no words of my own, I cover my face with my hands and start to sob uncontrollably.

"This can't be happening!" I eventually cry. I can't even begin to try and cover up my horrified reaction like I've been schooled to do since childhood, not even with the doctor watching my obvious breakdown. "How can this be happening?"

"Oh dear," the doctor responds, looking concerned over the hysterical noises now coming out of my mouth. "This is not happy news then?"

"No, it's not happy damn news!" I snap without meaning to.

"Helena," my mother says gently, "it's not the doctor's fault. Come on now, Hels, it's not that bad."

"I'm sorry," I whimper to the doctor, wiping my nose rather ungraciously across the back of my hand, "but I don't understand. I always made sure we used condoms! I was safe…always!"

"Hmmm, well it would seem you've just been unlucky then," the doctor says sympathetically. "I would estimate you at being about four months gone, though you hide it very well. Baby must be tucked up nice and tightly inside." She laughs but then stops abruptly when she sees the abject horror on my face. "Shall we examine you then?"

Leading me up to a gurney, I cling to my mother's arm like a crutch, not quite believing that this is really happening. My shirt is pushed up high while the waistband of my jeans is pulled down to reveal the top of my pelvis. I try not to look, instead, I stare at a patch of missing paint on the wall next to me, feeling just as tainted. The doctor then measures my uterus with her cold hands, all the while making little 'mmhmm' noises.

"Bang on for three months," she laughs to herself, sounding proud of her earlier estimation at the same time as I crumble that little bit more. "I'm just going to put this gel on; it might be a little cold."

I take in a sharp intake of breath when she squeezes a blob of icy cold gel on top of a tiny bump that I hadn't even noticed before now. A few moments later, she's pressing a doplar machine against my abdomen, which she then begins to move around, presumably searching for signs of life. At the sound of a crackly heartbeat, my eyes burst open, just as Mom's hand leaps up to her mouth in disbelief. This just made it all real and it's absolutely terrifying.

"Oh, God, what the hell am I going to do? What about college? My life is officially fucked!" I rush out in a panic, no longer caring about my colorful language. "Evan and I are still all over the place; we haven't even seen each other properly since Spain. I'm probably going to give him a heart attack when I tell him. His parents hate me and…and…" How do I tell them he wasn't the only guy I slept with four months ago?

"Er…maybe we had better book another appointment for next week," the doctor suggests, now blinking at me uncomfortably. "It will give you time to process all of this."

"That's a good idea, Hels, let's take one step at a time," my mother tries to reassure me. I nod in stunned silence while Mom takes the various information leaflets from the doctor, then helps me to vacate the stifling atmosphere.

With my shirt still untucked, I practically run out the door and take a deep breath of fresh air before finding the nearest bush in which to throw up…*again*. I remain hunched over, even when Mom comes over to rub my back.

"I think we need to get you home and have a chat with your father," she says softly, but I can tell she's disappointed in me. She's yet to hear the best part of this whole tragedy.

"I'm looking forward to it already," I answer dryly, but follow her to the car obediently.

Mom already has her phone in hand and is calling my

father to give him the good news. Ever the businessman, I'm almost certain his next call will be to Evan himself. He'll want to meeting the shit right out of this debacle and have a plan of action by the end of it.

Helena

When we enter the house, Dad is already waiting for us in the living room with a serious look on his face. I walk in tentatively, feeling like the black sheep of the family, disgraced and ashamed. To my surprise, however, when he first lays eyes on me, he stands and takes me into an all-encompassing hug.

"You ok, sweetheart?" he asks with warmth in his voice, and I feel like a little girl again. I nod with a fake smile before taking a seat on the couch opposite. At least Cam and Nate are both at school and college, far away from this humiliating conversation.

I sip a glass of water, bracing myself for the impending conversation. I open my mouth to say something, anything, but am silenced by a knock on the door. It causes me to jump, even though I can already guess as to who it is.

"Hello, Mrs Carter," Evan, the ever-polite boy greets my mother with a cheerful tone to his voice. He soon comes into the living room wearing a suit and a well-rehearsed smile for his number one fan, my father. "Mr Carter, so good to see you."

They shake hands in a manly fashion before he walks over to me wearing a frown, no doubt wondering why the hell he's been summoned in the middle of a Wednesday afternoon. Poor, unsuspecting Evan; a stab of guilt pierces through my heart, but I force myself to smile at him. As always, he plants a chaste kiss on my cheek before sitting next to me.

Things are still undefined between him and I. Between Spain, his internship, a boys' vacation, and my avoidance tactics, we haven't yet sat down to discuss what is going on between us. And yes, I'll admit, I've been a coward and oh, so confused. Deep down, I know I should have broken up with him when I had decided to that night on the boat, but what with the way things went with Lucius, I decided to ignore everything about that weekend, including my decision to end it. Besides, when I tried to voice my feelings with Mom and Dad, my father offered me everything he could to make me stick with it, if only for a little bit longer. I didn't accept any of his offers, but I still caved, like I always do.

We've been on dates, had a few intimate exchanges, but have otherwise had to make do with phone calls and text messages. It might have been the wrong decision, but no one can accuse me of not trying. I really have given my all, working hard to be the perfect girlfriend, even when his mother took one look at my hair and curled her lip with disapproval.

"Thank you for coming, Evan," my father begins the formality of this business meeting. "I think you had better start, Helena."

I breathe out a long, nervous sigh while Evan turns to me with even parts affection and confusion.

"Evan, I'm pregnant," I blurt out, "they think I'm about four months, but will need tests to confirm. We heard the heartbeat today, so whether I like it or not, I will be having a baby."

Believe me, I've thought about the alternative and having a

termination. However, whenever I do think about it, I can't help but consider the little life growing inside of me, being dependent on me, and who has a little heart beating. Besides, my family would never forgive me if I did; Nonna would turn in her grave. It's a hard choice for any woman, a personal one, and I guess this is mine.

At first, Evan's eyes bulge and his mouth gapes open like a fish. Seeing his shocked expression forces me to gulp back more water in the hopes I can prevent bile from churning in my stomach. Evan looks at my father, my mother, and then back at me. I instinctively shrug my shoulders like a clueless child, no longer knowing what to say.

That's when Evan reacts in a way I would never have expected. He breaks into a smile, small at first, but is soon grinning from ear to ear. Before I can respond in any way, he grabs hold of my shoulders and hugs me fiercely. I swallow my mouth full of water and look at my parents with a thoroughly gobsmacked expression. Their initial reaction is a look of equal shock, but then they begin to smile at each other as though they're reassuring one another that the knight in shining armor is cool about knocking up their daughter.

"I'm going to be a daddy?" Evan cries with a sickeningly sweet smile on his face. "I mean, everything is ok, isn't it? How are you feeling? We'll have to get married! Don't worry, baby, I'll get you any ring you like. Oh, God, sorry, Mr Carter, may I have your daughter's hand in marriage?" Evan's diatribe of rambled thoughts has my parents chuckling at one another, all beaming smiles, while I seem to be the only one frozen in utter shock over this man's unexpected and weird reaction.

"Y-you're happy about this?" I ask him, looking at him as though he's taken leave of his senses.

"Baby, I'm over the moon!" He hugs me again and I can't breathe. "I mean, yes, it's a little early in our relationship and I would have liked us to have been married and all, but hell, yes!"

"Well, that settles it then!" my father declares with a beaming smile. "Looks like it's all turned out for the best."

"Wait! What?" I stand and stare at them all with an irrational rage building inside of me. "What do you mean 'that *settles* it'? I haven't even answered or said how I feel or anything."

"Helena, honey," Dad tries to reason, "you're expecting a child with the man, and he wants to marry you. What is there to decide? You love each other, right?"

"Of course, we do; right, baby?" Evan rushes out with his teeth gleaming inside of his smile.

"Your mother and I can help you out with your own place and Evan can adjust his course so he can work more and study in the evenings to complete his degree."

"Dad! For Christ's sake, shut the hell up for five seconds!" I shout, probably louder than they've ever heard me speak before. Silence engulfs the room as they all look at me with horrified expressions. "You don't understand, any of you!"

"What do you mean, darling?" Evan says in that frustratingly sweet, concerned voice of his.

"There is another potential candidate for the father position," I finally utter, shutting my eyes firmly so I don't have to look at any of their disappointed and judgmental faces. My mother gasps and when I finally open my eyes to face Evan, he looks away with pain written all over his features.

"Who?" My father pushes out angrily. "You better tell us, young lady, you owe Evan that much."

"I was in Spain four months ago. Evan and I weren't exclusive and although he did come and see me for a week, there was also someone else, a one-night stand if you like. I'm not proud, but I won't apologize for it either, so stop trying to make me out to be the fallen woman. We weren't exclusive; Evan was seeing other people too."

Evan looks up at me without expression but doesn't deny any of what I just said.

"Do you even know his name?" Mom asks more softly.

"Yes," I reply in a low, broken voice. "It was…I was with…it was Lucius Hastings."

"What?! Paul's boy?" My father shouts furiously and with his face turning dangerously red. "Why on earth would you sleep with someone like that?! The boy's a monster, an asshole who I wouldn't trust with a sandwich, let alone my only daughter. Do you remember what he did to your brother's girlfriend at that wedding? Jesus, I thought you had some sense, Helena, I thought I had brought you up properly!"

He begins frantically pacing up and down until Evan suddenly rises to his feet. For a moment, I think he's going to slap me, but instead, he takes hold of my hands with gentle affection.

"Helena, I still love you very much. I can't pretend it doesn't hurt to know that you might be carrying another man's child, but you're right. We weren't exclusive and I did do my fair share of sleeping around with other women. So, I will be there for you during the pregnancy. When the baby is born, we can have him or her tested, and if… If it is mine, I will marry you and we can put all of this behind us."

"You're a decent man, Evan," my father says arrogantly, "there's not a lot of men who would do the same in your position."

I roll my eyes over the hypocrisy of it all, but keep my lips closed. I don't trust myself to be civilized if I bite back now.

"Now, if you'll excuse me, I need a little bit of time to process all this," Evan says, dropping my hands and walking toward the living room door. "I'll call you later, Helena, look after yourself."

He nods to my parents and marches to the front door where I hear it open and close with a heavy thud.

"Poor guy," my father sighs. "He's a good one, Helena, let's hope it's his."

"And I'm bad? Is that it?" I snap.

"I can't believe you would be so stupid!" he shouts at me. "Lucius fucking Hastings! You have always been the sensible one! The reliable one!"

"You know what, you are being so unfair!" I growl at him. "I *was* sensible; I used protection with both of them. And you heard Evan; he was sleeping around with multiple women at the same time. I had one weekend, one damn weekend with Lucius, and suddenly I'm supposed to be grateful to Evan because if it is his kid, he'll do the decent thing and stick around. He'll even marry me like this is the dark ages! For your information, I don't love Evan at all, not even a little bit."

My father narrows his eyes in my direction before asking, "And you love Lucius? That little shit who has the worst possible reputation and thinks everyone is beneath him?"

My eyes can't hide the answer to that question, and it kills both him and me to admit it.

"Oh, God, Helena, are you that stupid? Do you really think he'll offer you the same as Evan if you tell him? No, he'll leave you high and dry, or at best, throw some money your way to keep quiet about it. From what I've heard, the man isn't capable of love; get your damn head out of the clouds, Helena!"

He softens a little when he sees the tears rolling down my cheeks because I know he's probably right. He then closes the gap between us and takes me into his arms while releasing a long sigh. It's enough to make me cry against him.

"I can't help it, Dad," I whimper, "I wish I didn't, but I do, so much. I wish I could love Evan instead; I really do!"

"Oh, honey," he sighs again, "you can learn to love Evan, especially when you see him with your child, trust me."

"You really think this is a good idea?" I ask as I pull away to look him in the eye, searching for any hint of doubt.

"I think you're a fool if you don't take Evan with full and willing arms, not to mention selfish. This is no longer just about you, Helena, you must think of your child," he says before kissing the top of my head. "And if you don't, you're…you're on your own."

Before his words fully hit me, he walks away and out of the room altogether. When I realize the full weight of what he's just threatened me with, I turn to look at Mom, who is looking just as glassy-eyed as I am.

"Mom?" I sob, and in an instant, she is holding me as tight as if I am a little girl again who has just hurt herself. She doesn't say anything, but holds me, all the while trying to soothe away my tears.

Chapter 21

Helena

"Can you feel it?" Meri asks for perhaps the tenth time already. She's been poking at my growing belly for almost an hour while we lie around in my bedroom. I told the others I was feeling unwell, but in truth, I just didn't feel like celebrating Christmas. Meri is staying with us because David is ill, and Jen and Paul are on vacation. She suspects it's a last-ditch attempt to save their marriage. Unfortunately, she's flighty and he's a workaholic and most likely still suffering from the trauma of losing Lucius' mother in the way that he did.

"No," I reply bluntly. "Will you quit poking me?"

"I still can't believe this is happening to you of all people," she giggles. "I mean, me? Totally. But you? I just can't wrap my head around it."

"I'm getting used to it," I sigh, "me and a little bubba; the two of us against the world."

"And Evan if you don't get your ass over to Lucius and tell

him the situation."

"Well, neither option is appealing," I huff. "I don't love Evan and Lucius will most likely run a hundred miles."

"What is the deal with you and Evan? Are you together or not?" she asks, turning to face me with a frown on her face.

"It's…complicated. We're like a couple but without any of the physical stuff. I guess he wants to keep some distance so if the baby does turn out to be Lucius', he's somewhat protected himself. I can understand that. He's a really good guy, just not *my* guy. Not that I'll have any choice in the matter if the baby is his."

"Your dad is being a real dickbag, if you ask me," she says with a disgusted look on her face. "What kind of father in this day and age threatens to abandon you and his grandchild if you refuse to marry someone? Mom always said he had a stick up his ass, but seriously, even she's shocked by his reaction."

"As is my mom, but honestly? I'm not at all," I reply sadly. "Perhaps shacking up with a man I see more as a brother than a lover is better than staying here with him."

"What do Cam and Nate think about all this?"

"They only know that I'm pregnant and that it's Evan's baby. Dad said it was best, so they wouldn't see me differently."

"Jesus, that's cold," she scowls.

"I've never felt so dirty, so…*wrong*," I whisper, only to end up crying.

"Oh, Hels," she says with sympathy in her voice as she takes me into her arms. I take her comfort for all that I can. "You are far from wrong; you're amazing! You have a beautiful little baby growing inside of you, you're still kicking ass at school, and you're my best friend. I love you."

"It's just so unfair," I tell her between loud sobs, "Cameron is forever hooking up at college, and I know Nate's already had a few girlfriends, but nothing is said about them. I've done everything he's ever told me but the way he looks at me sometimes…such disappointment. And all I ever hear is him telling so and so how proud he is of Cameron and his business venture, or how amazing Nate is on football field. Sometimes, all I want to do is scream, and yet, I hold my tongue and smile, because that's how he's taught me to be."

"There is someone who you don't have to hold your tongue with," she says, and I close my eyes because I know she's talking about Lucius. "Are you going to tell him?"

"Yes," I reply, "after New Year, after the holiday season. Let him enjoy it."

"You know he doesn't enjoy anything unless it's thoroughly wicked or…"

"Or?"

"You."

"Yeah, right," I laugh sadly.

"Deny it all you want, but the boy loves you. Always has, ever since that summer. He's just-"

"Helena?" a familiar voice calls through the door before opening it to reveal its owner. "There you are."

"Hi, Evan," I reply, sitting up and trying to cover my belly with my oversized sweater. "I didn't know you would be coming over."

"Well, your father invited me, and I couldn't resist," he says with a perfect smile.

"Course he did," Meri mumbles, so I nudge her to try and shut her up. None of this is Evan's fault and he doesn't deserve her bitchiness.

"Merry Christmas, Merial," he says with a fake smile. "Do you think I could have a moment alone with Helena?"

"Er, sure," she says with a smile that is just as fake as his. "I'll go and nibble on leftovers I neither need nor want."

Once she's left, Evan walks over to sit beside me on the bed and gives me a kiss on the cheek. He then places a hand over my bump and laughs.

"So weird to think my kid is in there," he says. "Well, I hope so, anyway. Do you?"

"What?" I ask gormlessly.

"Hope it's mine?" he asks, taking hold of my hand and looking into my eyes with intensity. When I don't answer straight away, his hand tightens around mine and I can't tell if he's desperate or angry. "Because from what I hear, this Hastings guy is a real piece of work. Your dad says his family is shifty too, as in mafia ties kind of shifty."

"I have no idea about that, Evan, but I know *he* isn't, so I wouldn't judge him for it anyway."

"No, no, course not," he says, bringing my hand up to kiss the back of it. "I'm just worried about you; I still love you, Helena."

We fall silent and I feel awkward. I have no idea what to say or how to respond to his declaration of love and the longer it goes on, the worse it gets.

"I know you don't love me," he says sadly, "but I'm hoping that when baby is declared mine and we marry, you'll get there with me."

"How can you want to marry me, Evan? This is all such a mess."

"I've always loved the quiet Carter girl," he says with a smile, "even at school when you were so aloof. You're my perfect woman. What's the point in looking for anything else? You, Helena Carter, are perfection."

"I am not perfection, Evan," I tell him truthfully. "I'm carrying a child who could belong to one of two men."

"Yeah, but I forgive you for that," he says and moves into kiss me, but I pull away before he can. "Helena?"

"You *forgive* me?" I ask with both hurt and anger in my voice.

"Well, yeah, of course I do. I love you."

"Right, ok," I mutter to myself, unable to find a voice with which to argue with him. "You should know I plan on letting Lucius know about the baby after New Year."

"Why the hell would you do that?" he snaps, getting to his feet and beginning to pace with angry footsteps. "Are you stupid or something?"

"He deserves to know, Evan," I tell him, trying to sound braver than I am. But I'm arguing nonetheless; I'm arguing for

Lucius and his potential child.

"No!"

"*No*? What do you mean *no*?"

"I forbid it. If I'm that baby's father, I'm not going to let you endanger it by going to tell that piece of shit you slept with a mere week after being with me."

"What's that supposed to mean?" I challenge him.

He opens his mouth to argue, but my father walks in before he can say a single word. I've never been so glad to have him barge in on me.

"Everything ok? We heard raised voices," he says, sounding flustered over his potential son-in-law being upset.

"Jacob, please talk some sense into your daughter," Evan snaps, sounding completely exasperated by me. "She wants to go and tell Lucius Hastings about the baby!"

"Helena, no, you can't," Dad gasps, now looking just as annoyed as Evan. I should have known he'd take his side.

"Dad, wouldn't you want to know if it were you?" I argue, raising my voice ever so slightly, even though it goes against every natural instinct.

"Evan, would you mind giving my daughter and me some time alone so I can talk some sense into her?" Dad asks him over my head.

"Please do!" he growls before stomping out of the room, slamming the door for good measure.

"I would, yes, but we're talking about Lucius damn

Hastings, here!" he shouts me down. I've seen him do this with Cameron in the past, but my brother has always been able to fight back. Even worse, he's usually allowed to; I'm too 'female' to be able to do the same.

"But -"

"Besides, Helena, he's already seeing someone new," he says, delivering the final blow against me.

"Wh-what?" I just about manage to gasp through my lack of breath.

"I spoke to Paul yesterday when I was trying to get hold of Jen," he says, now looking less angry and more sympathetic. "He's been seeing a woman for the past three months; Paul says it's serious, Helena. Even more reason to leave things as they are."

"Three months? As in, the same girl? As in, it's a relationship?" I ask, dropping back down to the bed and feeling suddenly sick.

"Helena, it's best this way," he says as he sits beside me to wrap an arm around my shoulders which are now shuddering against him. "Oh, shh, my baby girl."

"You haven't called me that in a long time, Dad," I sob, and he kisses my head. "I know you're disappointed in me, but I didn't plan any of this."

"I know, sweetheart, and I'm not disappointed...well, maybe at first, but now I know you and Evan are going to make excellent parents. You've got a great life ahead of you, Helena."

"I have?"

"Of course you have," he laughs softly and I begin to

release some of the tension in my muscles.

For the first time since I found out I was pregnant, I feel ok, like I'm still a member of this family. But something is still off, and I know exactly what it is. It's something I can't ignore.

"Dad, you know I have to tell him if the baby is his," I utter against him and I feel him immediately tense up beside me. "Whatever you think of Lucius, it's the right thing to do."

"Will you promise me one thing?" he asks, and I relax, knowing he's still talking calmly. "You wait until we know for sure. What's the point in causing drama with Evan and Lucius' new girlfriend if the baby isn't even his?"

Listening to him say 'Lucius' girlfriend' makes me want to fall into a coma and never wake up, but I can't let him know that, so I simply nod. Call me a coward, but I can't face Evan and Dad's wrath if I don't agree, and I certainly can't face seeing Lucius with another woman. The thought is bad enough, let alone seeing it in the flesh.

"Good girl, you always are," he says with a beaming smile and a desperation to let Evan back in. "Now, make up with your boy."

I don't bother to correct him; I suddenly feel too exhausted. He opens the door to reveal Evan looking both angry and anxious, so rushes to put him at ease again.

"All sorted," Dad says cheerfully, "must be the hormones messing with her brain, ay?"

"Thank goodness," Evan says as he walks in to wrap his arms around me. "And if that's the case, perhaps you should put everything through me," he says, pulling back to deliver a condescending smile. "I've only got your best interests at heart,

Helena, yours and the baby's."

"Hmm," I mumble before falling back to the bed. "I'm really tired. Do you mind if I take a nap?"

"Of course, baby," Evan whispers, "you take all the time you need."

"Goodnight."

"Night, baby."

When he finally leaves, I release a long breath and ready myself to cry until I pass out, which I hope will come sooner rather than later.

Lucius

It's Christmas day and I'm sitting in my uncle's seedy nightclub, aka, his cover for his criminal businesses, including, but not restricted to, money laundering, arms and drugs dealing, prostitution, and smuggling. As a young impressionable teen, Uncle Anthony from my mother's side offered me a position in the family business. It was a rapid and hard pass for me. I was already heading straight to hell; I didn't need to give Satan any other ammunition against me. Besides, rich boy falling into the criminal underbelly of the city was a little too Hollywood for my tastes. I prefer to carry out my somewhat questionable deals in a top-floor office, surrounded by some of the most powerful people in the country, and without the threat of incarceration. It's far more stimulating for me to be somewhat creative with our laws, manipulating them for my own gain.

However, that doesn't mean I won't enlist his services should and when I need them. Had it not been for Anthony's assistance, my rapist father would still be walking around instead of being buried beneath a layer of thick concrete that now has a five-star retirement village on top of it. Well, parts of him at least. Paul had warned me to never deal with Anthony again at the time, that this was a one-time thing, a special exception. I agreed, promising to only see Anthony on a family level. And to this day, he still believes that. Not that I've had anyone murdered since then, but occasionally, he acquires information on my behalf.

Half-naked women and creepy old men are my current company, which is beyond pathetic. However, what with Paul and Jen trying to reconcile a broken marriage, my half-sister staying with the woman I refuse to think about, Anthony was the only person stopping me from falling into a whiskey coma back at my apartment. It's not much of a step up from that, but a step all the same.

"You wanna girl or two out back?" Anthony shouts at me over the music. "Good ol' Uncle Anthony can hook you up like that!" he says with a sleazy grin and a click of his fingers. He's met with one of my usual expressions of nonchalance that more than conveys how much I would not like him to 'hook' me up. I'm then met with one of his unsubtle laughs that manages to carry across the assault already on my ears, aka, the music.

"Oh, nephew, you're too young to be this hung up on one girl. What's her name again? Helena, is it?"

"I warned you to never utter her name," I growl, which shockingly, he heard. I need to forget her. Forget *us*.

"Who have you been sleeping with then?"

I train my eyes forward, clenching my jaw, because I'd

rather get up and shake my ass to the awful music than tell him the truth.

"Ah, shit, man, that's sad. No wonder you're always fucking miserable," he says contemplatively. "A man without sex is a pathetic creature indeed."

"I do not need, nor want, a woman," I utter with disdain in my voice. "I want a relationship even less so."

He merely puts his hands up in surrender while bulging his eyes over my lack of any sort of love life. I then see him open his mouth to say something innocuous, though luckily for me, my phone buzzes to life. I immediately answer it without checking the ID; it's my ticket out of here.

"Hastings," I answer formally, as if anyone in a professional capacity is going to be calling on Christmas day.

"What-up, bro?" Meri trills.

"Merial," I reply, wondering if I would have been better off staying with Anthony in that God-forsaken room. "To what do I owe the pleasure?"

"Happy Christmas, by the way," she chirrups, to which she's met with stony silence. "Ok, Ebeneezer, I'll get straight to it; are you seeing someone?"

"I fail to see how that has anything to do with you," I sigh, "or why you would deem it appropriate to ask me such a thing on a public holiday."

"God, do you ever just reply with a straightforward answer?" she huffs. "Well, you're gonna be particularly awful when I tell you, but for Helena's sake, I'm going in."

My body automatically stiffens at the mention of her name, and I brace myself for what is about to come out of Merial's mouth.

"Hels' father has just told her that you've been seeing someone for the past three months and that it's getting serious. Apparently, this came from Paul, who I would have gone to first, but seeing as he and Mom are away, I thought I'd risk it and ask the devil himself."

For a moment or two, I only have a string of expletives with which to answer my step-sister, but then I begin listening to my more rational train of thought. This is an opportunity to make sure Helena is finally set free from me, ensuring I have no hope of getting to her again. My lack of willpower will be worth nothing if I give Merial the answer that is sure to make Helena keep away from me for good. It will be the final nail in the coffin that is our love for one another.

"Not that it is any of yours or Helena's business, but yes, I am. Now, is that all?"

"Oh, no, there's plenty more, but it's Christmas and I try not to use expletives or threaten people's lives on this sacred day."

"Jesus and I are beyond grateful," I mutter.

"Screw it, you're a piece of shit," she says, "whoops!"

I'm then met with a continuous tone, signaling the end of our phone call. I stare at the screen, never having wanted her to still be on the line more. But it's better this way…for both of us. I sigh before heading home to my whiskey coma.

Chapter 22

Helena

"It's a girl, Miss Carter, and she looks bonny," the Scottish midwife beams at me.

It's been a long, hard labor, and I swore a few times, but otherwise, remained quiet throughout the whole process. Only my mother was with me during the birth, which was my request. I am covered in blood, sweat, and tears, and have vowed never to get pregnant again. But as soon as I hear those words, my only thoughts are for the little girl to whom I have just given birth.

Moments later, they place a floppy little baby, all covered in blood and God knows what, on top of me. I don't care though because she's pink underneath. She's gurgling and wriggling, which means she's alive and she's mine. I barely feel myself deliver the placenta; my only thoughts are of her.

"Will you be breastfeeding?" Sandra asks as she begins cleaning my baby for me.

"I want to, yes," I reply, full of smiles for the first time since the day I found out I was expecting her. Sandra helps to place her on my breast and latch on to my nipple. It takes a few tries but when she begins to suckle, it's a weird feeling, and it makes me giggle at my mother. Mom is a weepy mess, squeezing my hand proudly as she watches me feeding her first and only grandchild.

"Well done, Helena, you did so well," she whimpers with a beaming smile. "I can't believe I'm a nonna. She's so beautiful!"

"The best nonna," I whisper, making her cry even harder.

I am soon cleaned up and offered tea and toast. You'd think you would feel exhausted after childbirth, but strange natural instincts kick in and you're suddenly wide awake. My baby, on the other hand, has finally had her fill of milk, or colostrum, and has fallen asleep. I can't help but stare at her; she truly is a miracle, so tiny and perfect with ten little fingers and ten little toes, which look like tiny pink peas. She has a sprinkling of black hair and slightly darker skin than me. Taking in all these features, I begin to think about whether she looks more like Evan or Lucius.

Evan is fair, so my heart begins to hope she might be Lucius', although I'm not sure why because I know he would be less than happy about her arrival into the world. We left each other on such bad terms, and he has never once hinted at wanting anything other than fun between the sheets. Besides, as far as I know, he's still seeing whoever this woman is. He always said he couldn't be in a relationship, but what he meant was he couldn't be in a relationship with me. Sadly, I know I mean a lot less to him than he does to me. Then there's Evan, who thinks a lot more of me than I think of him.

"What a mess, little one," I whisper to her while she sleeps. "I'm so sorry your mother is a complete screw-up. I really hope you grow up knowing your daddy because you deserve everything. I can't make promises for him, but I can promise, as your mother, I will love you, protect you, and do everything in my power to give you the best upbringing I can. If Evan is your daddy, I will marry him for you, but if Lucius is your daddy, then I will try my very best to convince him to have some part in your life. As for me? I have you now, so that's all that matters."

"Hi," a soft, male voice says after coughing to alert me to his presence. "I hope I'm not disturbing either of you. How are we?"

The reference to 'me' now being a 'we' feels so strange when said out loud, though I guess we do come as a pair now. Evan walks forward with a bunch of flowers and the customary *It's a girl!* balloon. Something that Lucius would no doubt scoff at, together with a roll of his eyes. Still, I can't blame him for not being here, I never told him about the pregnancy. I was too afraid of his reaction, or rather, his non-reaction. Regretfully, I agreed with my father that there was no need to tell him anything unless we had to.

"May I?" Evan gestures to my sleeping daughter. I nod so he walks over to take a peek. "She's beautiful, Helena, just like you." He kisses me on the cheek, then stares down at the sleeping bundle in the cot. "How was it?"

I sit back down on my hospital bed, squeezing my legs tightly together and linking my fingers through one another.

"Well, I'm never having sex again," I joke. He laughs and rubs my leg affectionately as he sits on the edge of the bed next to me. "But it was ok, I guess. In any case, she is more than worth it. What's that you've got there?" I ask, gesturing to a large envelope that he's carrying.

"Er, well, I hope it's not too soon, but it's a genetic testing kit," he says, looking somewhat guilty about it. "I kind of thought it best to get it over and done with. The sooner, the better, right?"

"Of course," I reply quietly, suddenly feeling awkward under the circumstances. "You have a right to know, Evan, of course you do. So does she."

"I just need a swab from inside her mouth," he says, sounding just as uncomfortable as I feel. "My, she has a lot of hair, doesn't she? Mom said I was exactly the same."

This time, my smile is fake, but so is his. After a moment or two of not knowing what else to say, he returns to a serious expression while getting up to collect the sample. My poor girl is so tired she doesn't even notice him sticking the small cotton wool swab inside her mouth. Evan takes the same sample from himself and then fills in the details ready to be sent straight away. He then places the sealed kit on the bed and sits next to me, taking my hand inside of his. It doesn't feel like the hand of my lover, more like the hand of a close friend, but I know he wants it to be more.

"Helena," he says, now looking at the floor, "you know how I feel about you and I want you to know that whatever the outcome, I still want to marry you."

I shuffle uncomfortably as I look away. *I don't want to marry you, Evan, but I will if you are my daughter's father because her happiness is far more important than mine.* If he is not her father, then I will track Lucius down and make him take responsibility for her, even if he hates me for it. Evan nods his head at my silence, then picks up the kit to send away.

"How long does it usually take? The testing?" I call out when he reaches the door.

"Between two to five days. I'll pay the extra to fast-track it and will let you know as soon as I do," he says matter of factly.

"Thank you, Evan, you've been amazing throughout all of this." I smile at him because in all honesty, he has, and I do feel bad for him.

"I hope she's mine, Helena," he says with an air of assertiveness, "because I love you…very much."

Helena

Four days after I gave birth to my baby girl, I finally return home. I'm still calling her 'Baby Girl' because I feel uncomfortable naming her without consulting the father, whoever he is, so I've decided to wait. Cam and Nate are behaving like doting uncles and are currently having an argument over who gets to have the first cuddle with her. Meanwhile, I'm trying to sit down without feeling how sore I am down below. My nipples are cracked, and I've never known exhaustion quite like this. However, all I have to do is look into my little girl's eyes and none of it even matters; just her, she's all I care about.

"What are you going to call her?" Meri asks when the others finally leave me to try and feed her.

"I know what I want to call her, but maybe I should see who her father is first," I reply, now beginning to wince as she sucks on my sore and chapped nipples. I can't help but wonder why nature has to make such a basic thing as feeding your child so damn difficult. Surely, it shouldn't be this painful.

"He may have an opinion on the matter," I eventually add.

"Screw that!" she scoffs. "You're her mother. You carried her, gave birth to her, and are currently trying not to cry while you feed her. You name her, Hels!"

"You haven't told Lucius, have you?" I ask in complete panic. "You promised you wouldn't."

"No, don't worry," she says reassuringly, "you know I've got your back. That being said, I think if you do marry Evan, I'm gonna have to tell him, Hels." She touches my arm sympathetically, and the tears in my eyes tell her everything. "Oh, Hels, why are you two so damn stubborn? Tell him how you feel, please!"

I shake my head at the same time as I try to wipe away my tears one-handed.

"He doesn't share my feelings, Meri, he has never once contacted me outside of hooking up. It's not his thing, falling in love and committing to one person. Well, not with me anyway. Evan is offering me all of that and without the angst that always follows whenever I have any kind of encounter with Lucius."

"But you don't love Evan at all! Are you really going to commit to someone and sleep with them for the rest of your life, knowing that you are in love with somebody else?"

"I will, for her. She is everything to me now," I reply as I look down at her gripping my finger so tightly, her little pink fingers blanch white. "Let's face it, who will be the better father to her?"

"Hey, that's not fair!" she snaps, crossing her arms and making me feel guilty with just her eyes. "How on earth do you know what kind of a father Lucius will be? How do you even know how he will react to the news that he has a child?"

"I know, I'm sorry," I utter guiltily, "I'm just sleep deprived and frustrated by the whole situation."

"I hear what you're saying, Hels, but remember, happy mom, happy baby. Plus, I gotta say, I'm a little suspicious of Evan."

"What do you mean?"

"He's...*shifty*. At least Lucius is open about who he is," she says, wrinkling her nose in disgust. "I just don't trust him."

"Well, he might be my baby's daddy, so watch what you say around baby and him," I warn her, though only being only half-serious about it.

The doorbell rings, but I let Dad open it. I instantly hear Evan's voice, and my heart stops dead. This is it; he has the results. Within moments, my parents and Evan are walking into the living room with papers clasped tightly inside of his hand. I've just put Baby Girl down into her crib, so stand abruptly to await my fate. Meri grabs hold of my hand in support.

"So, I'm guessing you know who the father is?" I ask quietly, even though I'm not quite ready to hear it yet.

"I do," he replies, then breaks into a wide smile.

My heart feels like it's just dropped like a ton of bricks, I can already feel tears beginning to sting my eyes, and a huge, painful lump is now lodged firmly inside of my throat.

"Good news, darling, I'm 99.99% positive for being Baby Girl's father."

I lose breath at the same time as he hands the paper over to my father, who studies it for a few moments before shaking Evan's hand.

"Congratulations!" my father eventually announces, beaming and hugging Evan like one of his very own sons. I swear he's marginally happier than Evan is right now.

"Yes, yes, congratulations," my mother offers Evan, though her concerned eyes remain fixed firmly on me.

Meri grips hold of my hand more tightly and rubs my back while my head becomes dangerously dizzy. I can't help but feel like my life is officially over.

"Hels, you ok?" Meri whispers so quietly, no one else but us can hear.

"Congratulations, Evan," I offer tentatively, ignoring Meri's question, for if I focus on it too much, I'll reveal just how much I'm not ok. "I just need to…er…need to… Please excuse me for a moment."

I run from the room and upstairs to the bathroom where I throw up. I retch so hard, I know I'm at serious risk of setting off a migraine. Tears from straining so much run down my cheeks, while loud sobs escape between each breath.

"Helena?" Meri calls, as if trying to find me, then runs straight to my side when she finally discovers where I am, curled up and shivering on the bathroom floor. "Oh, Hels," she begins crying with me, "please, for the love of God, don't marry him!"

"You know what my dad said, I have to!" I cry out with frustration and sadness, to which she says nothing, for there's nothing she can say. It is what it is; I made my bed and now I have to marry it, for Baby's sake if nothing else. She doesn't deserve to struggle while I try to bring her up alone without any support.

"Besides, what does it matter?" I eventually murmur. "I may as well be dead to Lucius. I have another man's child; he'll never want me now. Not that he wanted me before." Standing up, I clear my face with a splash of water, sniff back my need to sob, scream, and shout, and instead, breathe slowly. "No, I have to do this for Baby Girl, *our* baby girl. Mine and Evan's. Dad's right, I can learn to love him, and he is a good man."

Without looking at her, I march out feeling determined to make things right once and for all. When I reach the staircase, I take hold of the rail and put on a mask, one I will have to learn to perfect if only so I don't look as bad as I feel.

Evan is waiting for me at the bottom of the staircase, along with my father. I feel like I'm walking into some kind of arranged marriage, suffocating by what little choice I have now that everyone officially knows that he is her father.

"Helena, you feeling ok?" Evan asks as soon as I reach him.

"I'm fine. Just letting the stress of the last few days get the better of me."

I smile tightly and stand beside him, showing both men that I am submitting to what I know I must do.

"So, how about it, honey? You gonna put the boy out of his misery and agree to marry him?" my smug father laughs. Evan laughs alongside him and at that moment, I hate them both. In fact, right now, I despise both Evan and my father with everything in me. Which isn't fair on the father of my child, but hormones, exhaustion, and a future that's been decided for me, are all making me feel like I could scream at everyone here.

"If Evan will still have me," I whisper instead. Evan steps

forward and kisses me right in front of my father, Meri, and my mother, who is looking sadly at me from behind Evan's shoulder.

"Nothing would give me greater pleasure," Evan says with a smile that I can't even begin to try and reciprocate. "And sooner rather than later if that's ok with you? Make Baby Girl official and all?"

I want to scream at him, to yell at him and ask him what the hell does that even mean? Is she not official now?

"Of course, whatever you want," I utter. "I'm sure you and my father can arrange something between you. I have to go and see to Baby Girl."

I immediately turn to leave but Evan's voice soon stops me in my tracks.

"I was wondering if we might call her Jessica? After my mother?" he asks, and it feels like another knife stabbing at my heart. I had wanted to call her Elena, after my nonna, but, feeling defeated, all I do is smile and submit.

"Jessica it is then," he sighs with a beaming smile, excited after having gained a baby daughter and a wife-to-be, all in the space of about ten minutes.

My mother follows me into the living room where I break down inside her arms.

This is it; it's done.

Chapter 23

Lucius

"Send her up," I snap into the intercom when my secretary informs me that Merial has arrived. I'm putting a few days in at the office before I return to law school next week. Honestly, school is the last place I want to be when I'm already so involved in the place I'll be heading one day. It all seems so pointless, and yet, I need a damn piece of paper to say I'm qualified.

Being interrupted by my vapid step-sister is the last thing my patience can deal with. What the fuck is so fucking urgent that it can't wait until the weekend? She practically screamed at me when I told her I was busy, so against my better judgment, I decided to relent and meet her just to get her out of my hair. My mood is for want of a better word, shitty, so she best be quick. Ever the drama queen, she walks in looking like a wild woman instead of her usually perfectly coiffed self. It piques my interest a little but not nearly enough to alleviate my dark mood.

"What is so urgent, Merial?" I ask her in a bored tone of voice while fiddling with paperwork on my desk.

"Helena, you fucking idiot!" she barks at me like a rabid toy dog; the type that's carried around in a purse because its legs are too small to handle a walk down the path. However, it's the mention of Helena's name that immediately gets my back up. I've made it clear to everyone around me to never mention the one woman who I can't get out of my head; it's too damn painful to admit to feeling so strongly about her. I can't be with her and having to explain myself to others is just an infuriating waste of time and energy. Case in point, right now.

"What has that name got to do with me?" I growl, showing only a fraction of my irritation.

"Everything, if you were man enough to admit it!" I stop what I'm doing and look at her through narrowed eyes and with my jaw clenched in rage. "Yeah, you heard right, fucktard."

"Careful, Merial," I warn her.

"She's getting married to some guy she doesn't love, doesn't even like, if you ask me," she shouts. "She doesn't love him because she's madly in love with you. God knows why."

"I'm confused," I sigh, rubbing my forehead before I hit something with it. "Why is she marrying him?"

"Because she's just had his baby and thinks you will have nothing to do with her now. She actually said she may as well marry him because her life is basically over now because you don't want her!"

She's openly fuming with me. It's probably fortunate that she can't see what I'm thinking right now. I can assure you, it's not pretty.

"Smart girl," I mutter calmly, acting as though I don't care, when deep inside, I want to find this guy and rip out his vital organs. "I wish her well."

"You don't mean that!" she gasps with shock in her voice. "She is distraught, Lucius. You should see how lost and broken she is. Please don't abandon her, Lucius!"

"I'm not doing anything. Now, if you'll excuse me, I am very busy, and people seem to be bothering me with things that are none of my business."

I look down to pretend to work again, biding my time until she leaves, when I can finally let go.

"Lucius, you love her; I know you do," she says, now practically begging.

I say nothing, just continue to work, paying her no attention at all. Hopefully, when I look up again, she'll be gone.

"You are self-centered, egotistical, and above all, a stupid coward and you don't deserve her!" she shouts, flicking the final switch deep inside of me.

"She made her bed and now she can fucking live in it!" I shout, silencing her once and for all. When I look up, instead of being gone, she's still standing there, though now with tears running down her cheeks. At her decision to remain at my desk, giving me a death stare, I lower my voice but sound no less threatening, when I tell her, "Now get.The.Fuck.Out!"

"Lucius…" she whimpers.

"I said, GET OUT!"

This time she doesn't argue, instead, she turns on her heels and leaves in a flurry of tears, slamming the door on her way.

This is when I let go and destroy the room completely. I

fling the computer against the wall, causing a huge dent, while sending papers to fly everywhere. Every motherfucking glass in that office is thrown across the room so that a cacophony of smashing sounds echoes all around me. I upturn every fucking piece of pretentious furniture before punching the walls with my fists until they bleed.

Fuck you, Helena Carter, I wanted...I wanted... Fuck, you were supposed to be mine!

Helena

Midnight and I'm up for one of Jessica's many feeds; I suspect this is just a comfort feed. Though, sometimes, I crave these moments when it's only me and her. She falls asleep on me with her little mouth still open and her eyes running wildly behind their lids. I wonder what she's dreaming about. Probably my boobs.

"I guess it won't be just you and me soon, bubba," I whisper to her with a sad sigh. Her eyes peek open, looking up to the corner while her mouth mimics sucking, and I laugh.

"Haven't heard you laugh in a while," Cam says as he walks into the living room with a glass of water and his laptop. Usually, a sudden presence would make me jump, but I'm too tired. "Which is odd considering you've just got engaged."

He looks at me with a knowing look. I knew I wouldn't be able to fool him, he called me out on it before I took off to Spain. If only I had told Evan back then that I didn't want him coming out to see me, that the relationship was over, then I wouldn't be having to marry him. That thought makes me want to slap myself, for I would also be without Jess, and I love her so much.

"Don't," I sigh.

"Why are you marrying him, Hels? You don't love him, you never have," he says sadly.

"Isn't it obvious?" I reply, keeping my eyes on my sleeping daughter.

"It's the twenty-first century, Hels, and you know we'd all be there for you if you decided to go it alone."

"Would you?" I ask, thinking back to my father's words. I half-wonder if he'd force my brothers to abandon me too. For all of Cameron's words of support, Jacob Carter is still very much the patriarch in this house, paying for their college education and living expenses. He could easily threaten them too, just as he has with me.

"What? Why would you even ask that? You're my baby sister, of course I would support you," he says, getting up to come and sit closer to us. *Us*. I wouldn't change having her for the world.

"It's for the best," I tell him, "for her, at least. I want to give her what Mom and Dad gave us, a stable environment."

"Mason told me how his mother responded to the news…hag!" he says through clenched teeth. "How dare she look down her nose at you?!"

"I don't know, he's her only son and he wasn't exactly discreet about needing a DNA test. I think the pink hair pushed her over the edge."

"Is that why you dyed it?"

"Helena, darling, you're a mother now, and soon to be my wife, I would prefer it if you sorted your hair out. It was fun before you had responsibilities, but now, it's just inappropriate; please dye it back before the wedding."

"It just seemed like the right thing to do," I murmur.

"Yeah, ok," he scoffs, "you can't fool me, Hels."

"It doesn't really matter either way," I whisper when Jess begins to shuffle about.

"Look, I know I shouldn't say it, but I can't not," he says with indecision still written all over his face. "I don't like him, and I don't think you should marry him. The guy is still going to clubs with Mason, mostly strip joints where they turn a blind eye to certain recreational activities, if you know what I mean."

"Oh," I gasp, shocked to hear this after how much Evan's been on at me to become more responsible, which is code for more like his uptight mother.

"I'm sorry, Helena, but he's not a good guy and you deserve better. Hell, I think you'd even be better off with Hastings."

"Please don't mention his name," I whisper, trying to hold in the ball of emotion inside of my throat. "Don't mention that name ever again; it's too painful."

"Ah, shit, Hels," he says as he moves in to put his arms around me. "Don't cry, you don't have to do this."

"Yes...yes, I do," I whimper. "And I do love him for giving me her, for giving me Jess. Now, can we please just talk about something else, please?!"

"Ok," he says with a heavy sigh. "She is ridiculously cute, you know that, right?"

"Yes," I half-laugh, half-cry, "she really is."

"And when she's old enough for boys, you just call her Uncle Cameron round to warn them all off."

"Idiot," I smile against him. "Love you, bro."

"Love you too, sis," he whispers and kisses my cheek. "Now, you set her up down here with me and go and get some sleep. I'll let you know if she starts searching for food."

"You sure?" I ask, already getting up to do as he's just said because I am exhausted. "You're a lifesaver, thank you."

Just before I climb into bed, I do something which I know is going to hurt like hell; I wander over to my 'Lucius' box. I open up the lid and afford myself two minutes or so to look through the photos we had taken during that weekend in Spain. I touch our faces that look so ridiculously happy, it's enough to bring on more tears of sheer sadness.

*I wanted it to be us; it **should** have been us.*

Chapter 24

Helena

Evan and I were married less than a month after he had confirmed that he was Jessica's father. It was a small, quiet affair that was held in my parents' backyard. Both sets of parents were in attendance, his mother scowling at me the whole time, my father looking like the pompous lord of the manor, while Mom held my hand in support whenever she could. Cameron, Nate, Merial, and Jen, all joined in with the 'celebration', though none of them looked exactly pleased for me. 'Concerned' would be a better word to describe most of the faces on my side of the family. Evan's best man, Mason, just thought everything and anything was funny, even though it clearly wasn't.

As for me, I remained in a daze as I floated through the whole day as if it were all some kind of drug-induced nightmare. It may as well have been my funeral. Every time I felt like bolting, I would look for my little girl to gain back a little bit of strength so I could get through it. I didn't wear a wedding dress and I didn't carry flowers. What I did wear was a mask I am fast perfecting, only so no one would ask me any questions that would mean me having to lie.

Are you excited to be married now?

Are you going to have more children?

Have you and Evan been in love since high school?

Is he your first love?

I kept trying to tell myself to buck up and be thankful that Evan was at least nice, that he seemed to genuinely care for me and wanted us to live happily ever after. Surely, I had very little to complain about. After all, our little girl would have two adults to love and care for her, and isn't that all that matters?

The trouble is I am in love with someone else. All I can think is, I've been railroaded into this situation; it wasn't my choice.

Helena

As night falls in Evan's small townhouse, I prolong Jessie's bedtime, knowing what is to follow. There's no excuse now, I can't turn away his advances as I have been for months. He's been patient, even if his frustration has been coming out more and more, but now I can't say no. This is our wedding night; we're supposed to consummate our union. Surely, he deserves to have my body, especially as I can't give him my heart.

But I don't want to.

It's weird, seeing as we've slept together so many times before. It's never been what I would call pleasurable or for my benefit, however, I never felt this upset over the prospect of sleeping with him. I suppose I never believed it would be this permanent or so much like a duty before. It feels as if giving my body to him tonight sets everything in stone – my fate, my life, my independence, even ownership over my body. I'm his wife, his property, all of me, including my womanhood, and sense of self. I've lost myself to him. And with that, I allow the tears to fall while I sing Jess a song goodnight. I then read story after story until she falls asleep, but even then, I don't leave her. I won't leave until my new husband summons me.

"Helena," he eventually calls, and I close my eyes. "She'll be fine. We need to have a chat."

After a few more moments alone with Jess, I take a deep breath and walk quietly into the main bedroom. I then sit on the bed where I wait for him to come out of the bathroom, all the while feeling completely sick with nerves.

"Ah, good, you're finally here," he says calmly while drying himself after a shower. "Listen, now that we're married and you're my wife, a few things need to change." I nod casually, thinking he might be talking about joint accounts and such. "First of all, I've phoned your college and told them you won't be returning; I explained about Jessie."

"Wait, Evan, I went to college all through pregnancy. I only have one year to go, and they have excellent childcare facilities, not to mention Mom has already offered to -"

"You're her mother, Helena, not the college and not her grandmother."

"But –"

"And my mother is going to take you shopping so you can

dress more appropriately," he continues as he combs his hair in the mirror, not even looking at me.

He sounds eerily assertive, completely contrasting with how he normally talks to me. There's no saccharine sweetness to his tone; it's as if there's no longer any need to be charming, or even friendly. I've officially been downgraded; I am beneath him.

"You can also tell your brother to stop looking at me the way he does, or he can forget seeing either you or Jessica ever again. And I no longer want you to see your cousin. She's associated with the piece of shit with whom you cheated on me."

"What do you mean *cheated*? You agreed we were never exclusive and that you had fucked around with a lot more people than…"

I trail off as I lose sense of everything when my new husband begins slowly walking toward me, making every step determined and purposely thought out. Barely inches away from my face, he grips hold of my chin between his finger and thumb, pinching my skin so I am unable to turn away.

"Don't fight me on this, Helena, I'm your husband and you will do as I say. Do you know how easy it would be for me to paint you as a bad mother? Here, take a look for yourself."

He pulls up his phone so I can clearly see an image of me smoking marijuana with a table full of minors, looking horrifically out of it. I had no idea he had taken a photograph of me that evening.

"Th-that's an old picture," I stutter, pointing at it as if it's something I can destroy with only my finger.

"Is it?" he says with theatrical confusion. "I can see you, very clearly, and I can see a bunch of high schoolers, but I don't see a date."

"Wh-Why?!" I gasp, sounding pitched and on the edge of a meltdown.

"Because," he says, leaning in to kiss me on my cheek, which only makes me feel incredibly nauseated, "believe it or not, I want you; I've always wanted you. Regardless of the extremely questionable picture here, you have perfect wife material written all over you. Socially, financially, and aesthetically, we are a perfect match. Your father has trained you well, keeping you on a tight leash and making you extremely obedient to a man like me; I must thank him for that one day, Helena," he whispers, sounding menacing.

"He looked so proud today, don't you think? I remember meeting him at various business soirees, the famous Mr Carter with the darling Carter children. Of course, he knew about us Stones, knew of our firm and reputation, so he naturally gravitated toward me. It took him all of five minutes before showing me your picture, though I already knew how deliciously beautiful you were from school. But how he gushed about you, how he wanted you to make the perfect match. He sold you to me like a piece of prime real estate. And I was sold, Helena, I really was. And I did everything right; I was Prince fucking Charming to you, but I still didn't compare to the asswipe who fucked you once and threw you away. Not that I was going to let that stop me from getting what I wanted…what I *still* want. Jessica was an added bonus to speed things up and to keep you how I want you. Do you really want to risk losing Jess?"

The look in his eyes terrifies me; they tell me he will make good on any kind of threat he chooses to throw against me. He lifts the corner of his mouth into a wicked smile the moment he sees my fear. Only then does he finally release my chin. He then turns away from me and gets into the bed, looking expectant.

"Now, take off your clothes, and let me consummate our marriage."

I remain frozen, feeling unsure as to what to do next until he suddenly jumps up with his face looking like thunder.

"Fine," he huffs, "I'll do it for you!"

I'm spun around so he can unzip my dress, letting it fall to the floor in a rather undignified heap at my feet. He then rips my panties away and unhooks my bra with aggression.

"I've waited months, Helena, fucking months, and you will learn to behave for me!" he growls through his teeth, so close to my ear, I can feel spittle landing on my skin. I am then pulled to the bed where he pushes me onto the mattress. My whole body turns rigid while my mind is questioning the reality of what is happening and what he is about to do to me.

When he enters me, it feels angry and painful. There is no kissing, no foreplay, no affection, no concern for my pleasure, just cold, hard fucking. My new husband thrusts with venom, all the while I bite the inside of my cheek to stop myself from screaming. Tears roll down my cheeks as I fast come to the realization that life isn't over; the nightmare is only beginning.

"Good morning, Mrs Stone," Evan says as he whips the cover away from my body the day after our wedding. "Time to get up!"

I take a moment to look at the man who has managed to

infiltrate my life under the guise of a totally different person. Then I remember my daughter and the fact that I haven't heard her crying for her early morning feed. My heart feels like it leaps into my throat over the thought of something having happened to her, so I jump off the mattress to try and get to her. However, before I even reach the door, Evan blocks the frame with his giant arm and an expression that is nothing short of menacing, taunting me to try and fight him. I don't though, I step back, and he smiles. He's enjoying the fact that I am already falling into line under his heavy-handedness.

"She's been fed, if that's what you're worried about," he says as he steps toward me. "My mother has her, so we can have some 'alone' time. That's what newlyweds do isn't it? Have 'alone' time."

"They have this magical stuff now, it's called formula," he says with an arrogant shrug of his shoulders, still smirking in my direction. "My mother fed me on formula, and I was one of the healthiest kids at our school. Besides, I don't want my wife getting her tits out in public and I sure as hell don't want you spending any more time than is necessary having to feed a child who can be fed in a fraction of the time using a bottle and formula. Gotta start thinking with that brain of yours, sweetheart," he says while tapping against my temple with his rigid fingers. "Put something formal on, we're going to lunch with some of my dad's clients."

"But I want to breastfeed my child," I demand with my anger beginning to rise. "You should have discussed this with me. How dare you!"

Evan walks slowly toward me with a scowl taking over his face; I'm slapped hard across the cheek with a burn that quickly spreads across my skin. I've never been slapped before, and I was kind of hoping it would be one of those experiences I would be fortunate to live without. However, something tells me the feeling is going to become a familiar one.

"She's *our* child, Helena, so what I say goes. Now get your ass dressed and stop arguing with me!"

"Who the hell are you?" I ask with genuine confusion and shock in my voice. I can no longer hold it in, even if it means I incur more of his wrath. "I don't get it; you're like a totally different person. Do you even *like* me?"

"I love you, baby, how can you ask me that?" he mocks me, theatrically placing his hands over his heart.

"No, you don't. If you loved me, you wouldn't hurt me, you wouldn't be treating me like you're the subject of a country and western song right now."

I stupidly place my hands on my hips as I work myself up, though, this turns out to be an inflammatory action, for seconds later, he's gripping hold of my chin between his finger and thumb. The act is anything but affectionate; it's a promise of what is to come if I dare try to stand up to him again.

"I did love you and I did everything right! I took you out for fancy dinners, I looked after you when you were off your face, I waited, I even came out to damn Spain to be with you, and what did you do? You slept with the cretin who took your virginity and dumped you! You really are a stupid slut because not only did you go back for seconds, but you're also still in love with him! Do you realize how fucking stupid I looked having to tell my friends and family that the kid in my girlfriend's stomach might be the result of someone else's spunk? The woman I had told everyone I was in love with might possibly be carrying someone else's spawn?"

His words are bitter and have me feeling guilty for a few

moments before I realize that I have been nothing but honest with him. He cannot say the same for himself.

"Before I point out the fact that you have been anything but faithful to me, can I just ask why the hell you married me if I've wronged you so much? Or is this all some elaborate revenge against me for not choosing you?" His sinister grin tells me that's exactly why he married me, and it both horrifies and disgusts me. "So, you just plan on keeping us trapped in a lie? In some kind of version of a fake marriage?"

"Oh no, baby, I plan on you being everything a wife should be. We do have a child together, after all, and I doubt either of us wants her growing up in a tempestuous atmosphere. However, my role as a 'husband' might be a little different to what you've grown up with."

"Meaning?" I venture, even though I'm terrified of the answer.

"Meaning I can pretty much do what I want," he chuckles arrogantly, "but you can't. You won't do anything without my say so and, just so we're clear, my say so is the bottom fucking line."

"And if I don't want to be your wife?"

"Then you lose Jess; she will come with me," he snarls before shoving me out of the way so he can get to our closet where he begins pulling out dresses for me to wear. "It wouldn't be that hard, I have the means to make you look like you have a bit of a problem with cannabis, or maybe even stronger. After all, I did enjoy filming you getting high with your underage brother. Then there's the fact I needed to do a paternity test because you were sleeping around with a man like Lucius Hastings, a hell of a dodgy motherfucker with a less than scrupulous background. Word has it, he broke someone's nose at the tender age of thirteen. Not to mention he was the unwanted result of rape. Oh, and if necessary, I might have to tell everyone about my poor girl having a bit of a coke habit. It's not too hard to get hold of if you have the right contacts. In fact, I think it might be a good reason for why you can't even breastfeed our child anymore."

He looks at my horrified expression before throwing back his head with a sadistic laugh.

"S-so you're just going to 'punish' me for the rest of my life? Is that your plan?" I gasp with a horrified expression.

"Pretty much," he replies as he comes in close to stroke a strand of hair behind my ear. "Sorry, babe, your knight in shining armor isn't gonna come for you. You may as well be dead to that asshole. Now get fucking dressed, you look God awful!"

God awful. Yes, my life was to become God awful.

Part III – The Devil Comes

"When a devil falls in love, it's the most hauntingly beautiful thing ever. And you should be terrified, for he will go to the depths of hell for her."

-UNKNOWN

Chapter 25

Lucius

11 years later

Nathaniel Carter has certainly grown up since the last time I saw him. Of course, he was a pimply teenage boy full of hormones back then. Now, he looks confident, professional, and self-assured, even if he is doing a bad job of concealing his puppy dog eyes for his PA. I can't blame him, she is very attractive, but she isn't the woman who has sparked my interest. Standing next to them is a woman I haven't seen in eleven years; a woman who should have been mine. She makes me stop dead in my tracks, but then I remember I am in work mode. I need to always maintain a hardened exterior, to make sure no one thinks I am anything but the asshole everyone knows me as.

She is still as stunning as the day I last saw her all those years ago. Her hair has returned to its natural chocolate brown color, but otherwise, she looks virtually the same as she did when she had stormed out of my life in Spain. Helena Carter will always be the most beautiful woman I have ever laid eyes on. Seeing her unchanged, a piercing pain runs through me, one made up of equal parts hurt and regret.

Helena is the first to see me walking toward the reception

desk, and from the way she just dropped her glass, I know she must have instantly recognized me. It's not hard, I am pretty much a broader version of the man whom she made love to eleven years ago. Coming up close, I notice her beautiful wide eyes, which once sparkled with a feistiness reserved only for me, but are now vacant of any kind of life. She looks lost, empty, and beaten down. I can't help but glance at her left hand; she's not wearing any rings.

Nate's PA is the next to look my way and has the reaction that most people do when I walk into a room - unnerved but with a hint of curiosity. Finally, the youngest Carter notices me, though he has the expected reaction of a person in his elevated position. There's a hint of contempt behind his fake smile and confident gaze. Though I suppose groping one of his brother's girlfriends at my father's wedding didn't exactly go down well in the Carter household.

We greet formally with professional smiles and handshakes, exchanging pleasantries and other meaningless chitchat, even though I'm desperate to bypass him and talk to Helena instead. After longer than I'd like, I eventually get the opportunity to turn and face his older sister, the only person in the room, on the planet even, who I really want to talk to.

"Helena," I say with confidence, shielding my inner insecurities from everyone, "it's been a while."

"Yes," is all she manages to whisper.

"How is the family? A husband and a daughter, isn't it?"

After Merial came to tell me of her intended marriage all those years ago, I made her promise not to ever mention Helena's name to me again. It was the only way I managed to survive living in a world where my topolina was married to someone else.

My Helena opens her mouth to answer, making a small 'o' shape that I am well familiar with, having spent years picturing those lips in the dead of night.

"Thankfully, Hels got rid of her ass of a husband, didn't you, Hels?" Nate replies for her, to which she looks at her brother through narrowed eyes, though she doesn't say anything. She just looks to the floor while her pink cheeks turn a deep crimson.

"Really?" I reply, barely able to conceal my utter delight. "That's...*interesting*."

"Nate," Helena pushes out quickly, sounding desperate, "is it ok if I take my lunch now?"

Her younger brother frowns over her sudden change in demeanor but eventually nods his head in response.

"Of course, you don't need to ask if you have it covered. She is my big sister, after all."

He laughs while looking at me, but I watch her nod politely before scurrying out back to get her bag. As she escapes through the revolving doors at the entrance, Nate continues to ask me up to his office, talking about something to do with his brother. However, I'm not really listening; my eyes are already tracking Helena's back as she rushes out of the building.

"Of course, but can I meet you in a moment? I just wanted to ask your sister something about Merial. I haven't heard from her in a while and thought she might know what's going on with that cousin of yours."

I'm not really asking for permission, there's not a chance in hell of letting Helena go without talking to her first. In fact, before he's even replied, I'm already racing out the door, the whole time scanning the area for where she is. When I finally spot her, I almost have to run to catch up.

I reach for her hand and spin her around to face me. The last time I did this to her, I ended up with a smacked chin and a knee in my groin. However, this time, my little mouse shrivels, looking terrified. In fact, she physically withers and braces herself, as though she is expecting me to hurt her. Her breathing is erratic, and her hands are trembling.

"Hey, hey, it's me," I try to reassure her, taking her hands gently inside of mine. "Mia topolina, what's wrong?"

She gently pulls away and steps back, ensuring there is a safe distance between us.

"S-sorry, I didn't know who you were," she stutters, looking to the ground as if ashamed. Her tone of voice is almost alien to the girl I once knew, it's as if she's lost herself.

"Helena, what the hell happened to you?" I ask bluntly, ignoring my inner cautious voice.

She slowly looks up at me and we search one another's eyes for a few moments, just as we did many a time in the throws of passion, only this time, her eyes appear dull.

"Life happened to me, Lucius," she says quietly. "Please let me go."

"Why? You're not with him, are you? Your brother said-"

"I know, but I'm not the same girl you once knew," she says, swallowing back a lump as a stray tear runs down her face. "She died a long time ago. I am just a shell...a hollow shell."

She turns and walks away so quickly, she's almost jogging, leaving me to wonder, *what the fuck happened to my girl?*

THE DEVIL

Helena

Flashing lights, my old friends, sparkle and dance on the surface of my eyes. Granted, they've been absent from my life since the divorce, but I always knew that one day they would return to get me. Today, I almost welcome them; I want to feel the pain, I want to feel...*something*. My past came back to haunt me today and I almost broke. Who am I kidding? I broke a long time ago when I was forced into marrying a monster. If it wasn't for Jess, I can honestly say I would have made a swift exit from life a long time ago.

Lucius is still as handsome as he was all those years ago. The beautiful fallen angel who took a liking to a mere mortal. Still intimidating, still ruthless in business, still as blunt as rock, but I am anything but the girl I was when he pursued me back at *Hastings Villa*. After years of being chained to my husband, I have been left with no self-esteem, no dreams, and no purpose other than to work and look after my wonderful daughter.

Jess is growing up amazingly, but she is starting to need me less and less. She leaves for summer camp at the weekend, and I will have a full month without her. Unlike me, she embraces kids her own age and jumped at the chance to join her best friend at a wilderness camp that is miles away. Remembering how restricted my life was made by an overbearing parent, I want to do all that I can to make sure she is given every opportunity to be everything I wasn't. Besides, I guess I can carry on with my photography while she's away. I always loved taking pictures of people in their daily lives, but my heart's not really in it like it used to be. It hurts to take pictures of people who can feel and show genuine happiness.

My father and brothers only see the timid sister and

daughter I once was, before Lucius, but my mother and Meri can see the true me. A broken shell; a vacant, hollow husk of a woman, drowning in her own depression. I am nothing anymore and I don't want Lucius to know this new version of me. I want him to remember the girl who once had pink hair, a feisty tongue, and a fiery attitude when it came to him. The girl who took chances, who had the ability to comfort him when he confided in her, who walked home in the sun, even though it made her ill, who traveled to Spain to work the Summer, and who had hopes and dreams. I am none of those things anymore.

Bea, Nate's PA, found me on the bench outside first. I had thrown up in the bin twice and ended up huddling on the bench. I wasn't sure how I was going to get home being that my vision was already too cloudy to see straight, and my head felt like something was stabbing at it repeatedly. Thankfully, she went back inside and got Nate; he's now putting me to bed in my house. He reassures me that he will take care of everything, and between him and my parents, they will make sure Jess is not left on her own.

Cam and Nate never did find out about the fact that Jess could have been Lucius' child; they were only ever told that I fell pregnant with Evan. They also never knew about Evan's abuse toward me, and neither, on my insistence, did my father. Mom noticed soon after the wedding and had to watch on whenever I came around with fresh bruises, tears, and a general decline in my mental health. Although I initially adhered to Evan's order for me not to see Meri anymore, Mom was able to sneak her into their house whenever I came to visit.

"Baby, what has he done to you this time? Oh, God, is that a cigarette burn?" Meri cries as she studies the circular scar on the palm of my hand. "Why are you staying with him?"

"He's threatened to take Jess, that's why!" I sob into my

hands. *"It's not so bad, he's sleeping around with other people for most of the week. I barely see him really."*

"And when he returns to you, he beats the shit out of you?" she practically screams, sounding completely exasperated with me. "Are you still sleeping with him?" she asks with fear in her voice. I say nothing. Instead, I burst into fits of tears. "Oh, God, why, Hels?"

"I don't exactly have a lot of choice in the matter," I sob, feeling full of shame.

"You mean he's forcing you?" She jumps up in horror and disgust. It makes me feel all kinds of dirty and degenerate, as though I am the one committing the abuse.

"I don't know anymore," I murmur with a sad shrug. "It's just expected and if I put up any kind of argument, I guess he just takes it anyway."

"Oh God, oh God, oh God!"

She holds me tight, bursting into tears alongside me. Mom's already weeping in the background, having heard it all before. I know I'm making it hard for her, and I know how much she wants to tell someone, but I still refuse to tell my brothers and father about it; I will not risk losing my daughter. Evan has made it abundantly clear that even if he couldn't obtain Jess legally, he would take her anyway. I have no doubt that he could. Ironically, Lucius has always been seen as the 'devil', but my father's golden boy is turning out to be more evil than anyone I know. He's a monster and I'm married to him.

That happened before I lost Cameron, and with him, Nate, to a certain extent. Jess was about a year old when we were all staying at my parents' place for Christmas. Cam had brought his first ever girlfriend back and seemed happy with her. Perhaps not head-over-heels happy, but content, nonetheless. Evan took to flirting with her without any kind of subtlety, though my father seemed to not notice. Either that, or he refused to. Unfortunately, she lapped up the attention and they ended up on the living room couch in the middle of the night, feeling one another up and whatever else they could do. Cam, being a forever night owl, caught them in the act. He, understandably, went ballistic and wanted to get Dad up to prove what a piece of shit my husband is. Little did he realize that Evan had pulled me aside to remind me of the photos he had of me with Nate and a joint in my hand. A silent threat to pull me and my brother into submission. I begged Cameron to let it go, for Jess' sake, which he did, though I paid the price of his silence by losing our close relationship. We've barely spoken since.

Thankfully, Evan got sloppy. He had gambling debts, and involvement with drugs, and was frequenting strip clubs and other shady places. When I saw it was having an effect on Jess, I found the courage to throw him out, and finally, divorce him. After all, she was the only reason I was married to him in the first place. He could no longer prove he was the more stable parent. I did nothing but visit my mother and take care of Jess; there was nothing he could prove. As for taking her, I no longer believed he cared enough to do that. However, by then, it was too late; he'd already succeeded in breaking me.

Lucius

"Merial, get your ass over to my office now!" I bark down the phone. "I need answers and I need them now."

"Evening, Lucius, always nice to be ordered around by you," she says sarcastically, "to what are you referring to exactly?"

"Helena!"

"Oh," she says, sounding suddenly more alert.

"Yes, *oh*! I saw her today." I clench my teeth over the memory of her words, her ghostly expression, and her fear. "I need to know what on earth happened to her."

"Ok, ok, I'll be about half an hour, but Lucius?"

"What?" I snap, my impatience beginning to get the better of me.

"You're not going to like it."

Forty-five minutes later and I'm still pacing around my office. My fingers are twitching, and I've already yelled at four assistants in the last two hours. When I'm about ready to wreck my office again, Merial bursts through my door, panting heavily, sounding like she's just run from one end of the city to the other. A normal person would offer her a drink, ask after her family, or perhaps give her five minutes to get her breath back, but I don't have the reputation I have for being a 'normal' person.

"Evening," she says in greeting, but I merely glare at her. "Ok, then," she says to herself before taking a seat in front of my mahogany desk.

"Talk," I order with a scowl.

"First of all, I'm only here for her sake, you can crawl back to hell as far as I'm concerned; you don't scare me, Hastings. Secondly, you told me not to ever mention her name in your presence, so I only did what you demanded. And finally, I begged you to save her before it was too late and I believe your exact words were, *'She made her bed, now she can fucking live in it'.*"

"I am well aware of what I said." I speak low and slow, trying really hard not to lose my shit. "What the hell happened to her?"

"You abandoned her, Lucius," she says plainly, looking right at me. "Evan turned out to be the real monster. He was the bad guy, the bully, and the abuser. I've had to watch her wither and die over years of abuse from that man. I won't go into details; it's not my story to tell, but you can imagine."

I sit back slowly in my chair, with my hand clasped over my mouth, feeling ready to kill. Merial, thankfully, heeds my mood and remains silent. Ever so slowly, I get up and walk over to the wall of windows and lean against the coolness of the glass. Anger, like no other I've ever experienced, is swirling deep inside of me, ready to surface in a spectacular way. When it does, it will be a destructive force for anyone who comes in its path.

"Did her family know?" I ask as calmly as I can.

"Apart from her mother, no," she replies. "He threatened to take Jess away, so she only confided in me and her mother. It was only when he became heavily involved in drink, women, and gambling, that she believed she could safely end the marriage without fear of losing her."

I remain silent for a while, trying to calm my thoughts, process this information, and stop myself from tearing up my office again. I feel Merial's eyes on me, taunting me with her accusatory body language.

"I want her address," I demand.

She smirks while staring at me but remains silent. She

doesn't attempt to speak until she sees me getting ready to lose my shit with her.

"Lucius, I'm not giving you Jack unless you promise me you won't fuck around with her this time. She's damaged now; do you really think you can handle that?"

"Give.Me.Her.Address!" I demand a second time, ignoring the pain of my teeth clenching together. Merial studies me for a few moments, assessing whether she can trust me.

"Give me that pen," she says, jutting her chin out toward the biro in front of me. I hand it to her and watch as she writes it down, but before she parts with the small piece of paper, she pauses. "You have to tread carefully, Lucius. For instance, I would wait until Saturday afternoon to go and see her."

"Why the fuck would I want to do that?" I'm planning on going straight to her after Merial leaves.

"Because she has an eleven-year-old daughter! You can't go barging in on Helena with Jess there to witness it all; that poor little girl has already had to go through so much, they both have. Helena won't appreciate it; Jess is the only person she really comes alive for, and you have to respect that."

"So, what do you suggest?" I growl impatiently.

"Jess leaves for camp after lunch on Saturday," she informs me, "I think Helena's more likely to accept you if Jess isn't there."

I open my mouth to argue before realizing that she's right. I've waited this long, what're a few more days? Given the information I've just received, it feels like a fucking lifetime. However, for my topolina, I'll wait.

THE DEVIL

Chapter 26

Helena

"Hey, Hels," Nate utters as he tentatively wanders into my room. I guess the banging and crashing I just heard was real, not just my mind playing tricks on me while under the influence of migraine medication. There had been shouting too, but I was still a little out of it, so I wasn't entirely convinced I hadn't dreamed it. Given his concerned, apologetic expression, I'm guessing there really were raised voices. I'm also guessing my little brother was the source of whatever explosion just happened in my very own house.

"It's ok, Jess is fine," he rushes out when he sees my fear. "It's just me who's fucked up."

As he gets closer, I can see him almost hobbling a little bit, so I move over to let him climb in next to me, just like he used to when we were really young. Nate used to be afraid of thunderstorms and would always come into my room because Cam would instantly kick him out if he tried to get in with him. Thankfully, Cam is a little more caring toward Nate, now that he's grown up, even if you have to wade through his brash swearing to see it. It's just me he's not so keen on. I miss him, I really do.

"What have you done now, little brother?" I ask as I lay my head on his lap. He begins brushing my hair with his hand, soothing the lingering headache that's still preventing me from getting up.

"I, er, kind of went mental at Bea again." He laughs softly, but I can tell he's not at all happy about it. "The truth is, Hels," he begins, then releases a long, sad sigh before continuing. "A few years back, she had a one-night stand, and it turns out it was with Evan. From what her big brother just yelled at me, it wasn't what I'd call consensual; the bastard took advantage."

"Oh, God!" I groan, shutting my eyes with the residual pain leftover from my migraine.

"Yeah, it turns out she was going through some shit at the time and came to one of my high school parties. She'd drunk far too much; he took her under his sleazy wing and she ended up coming to with him on top of her. Her brother just told me she tried to kill herself afterward."

"Holy shit!" I bounce up in shock but quickly fall back onto his lap again with the pain in my head pulsing through me.

I'm well aware of how evil my ex-husband can be, but I never thought he took it out on anyone else but me.

The night of Nate's party
11 years ago

Helena

"You're a useless mother and an even worse wife, Helena," Evan grinds through his teeth in between slurps of his beer.

I ignore his temper and begin to pick up pieces of broken plate and coq au vin off the floor. My Mom had shown me how to make it because apparently, I wasn't feeding my husband properly, or so said his mother. He took great pleasure in telling me how awful his mother thought I was and how I could stand to lose a little weight. A year is plenty of time to lose excess baby weight and I was just being lazy, he had yelled at me. I didn't bother telling him that I now weighed less than I did before Jess, what was the point? I was fat and unattractive according to both him and his mother.

"Don't fucking ignore me!" he suddenly yells and pulls me up by my ponytail. It rips at the back of my head but as much as I want to yelp, I hold it in because experience has taught me to keep quiet for an easier life. However, this plan doesn't always work, tonight being such an occasion, because I am backhanded for not responding to him in the way he wanted me to. "Now look what you made me do!"

"Please, Evan, please just leave me alone," I whisper without any emotion behind my words. In my head, I've gone somewhere else, somewhere he can't get me.

"Oh, you'd like that, wouldn't you?" he sneers. "Then you can play the martyr, the victim. I've tried everything to get you to love me; I always come home, don't I? Not that you want me here."

"Evan, you're hurting me," I tell him, for he's still pulling my hair, not to mention I can feel my cheek burning under the sting of his handprint.

"Yeah? Well, now you know what it feels like to have someone you love hurt you in the most brutal way. Your bruises will heal, darling, your betrayal won't!"

"I never betrayed you, Evan," I try to argue, though it comes out weak, as though I can't be bothered to convince him otherwise. I **don't** care anymore.

"Then why the fuck did I have to do a DNA test to prove our daughter is mine?"

His voice has risen to the point that I brace myself for another attack. However, when I make no effort to answer him, he simply pushes me and storms off, slamming the door as he does so. Jess begins crying so I wipe away my tears and rush upstairs to try and soothe her back to sleep.

"Oh, baby, baby," I coo as soon as I walk in. She's sitting up in her cot bed, looking red in the face from crying so hard. My poor girl; this isn't the life I wanted for you, but now I'm stuck.

As I scoop her up inside my arms, I begin bobbing her up and down while whispering soft words of comfort. Sniffing her downy hair and feeling her settle on my chest, all of the pain from Evan's hands melt away. Jess is my rock, even if she has no idea about it, she is what gets me through the day.

As soon as she falls back to sleep, I carefully lay her back down and pull up her cover. I deliver a kiss to her soft skin, then tiptoe back downstairs. The mess of the dinner I had spent hours cooking is still all over the floor, and the walls, so I make my way *to the sink to begin running hot soapy water. I need to keep busy, to focus on anything other than the fact my life is a complete mess.*

My phone begins buzzing on the countertop, it's Mom calling to see how I am, like she does at least five times a day. Seeing her name shine up at me instantly brings a lump to my throat.

"Hey," I murmur, trying to hide the emotion in my voice.

*"Helena, everything ok?" she asks, even though she can already tell everything is **not** ok. "It isn't, is it?"*

"No," I admit on a whimper as that lump suddenly releases without me meaning it to.

"Tell me, I'm alone," she says, sounding ready to hash this out. "Is he there?"

"No, he left," I cry, "after he threw my dinner across the room."

"Do you need me to come over?" she asks, even though I can hear crowds of people in the background of one of their soirees. I want her more than anything else in the world, however, I can't tell her that. Besides ruining her evening, Dad would become suspicious, and he's the last person I want to come over, spouting his arrogant, misogynistic crap about a situation he knows nothing about. In fact, I rarely want to see him anymore; I hold him in part responsible for the life I now lead.

"No, honestly, I'll be fine," I lie, and I know she'll be able to hear the deception in my voice. "He's gone, so I'm going to clear up and go to bed."

"Helena, I don't like this," she says, sounding beyond concerned for me.

"Mom, if you come and he finds you here, it will only make things worse for me," I argue before hitting her with the winning statement. "You know I can't risk him taking Jess, it would kill me."

"Ok, but your father and I will come by in the morning, so you make sure he knows that, Helena," she says with conviction in her voice.

"Ok," I sigh, "have a good night."

"You call me if you need me, Helena," she says like it's an order.

"I will," I reply sadly. "Goodnight, Mom."

"Goodnight, my baby girl," she says sadly, "I love you and I'm proud of you...always."

"Ok," I whimper, "I gotta go, Mom, I just gotta... Goodnight."

As I put the phone down, and wipe my eyes while breathing out long and slow, I turn to see the faucet has been running all this time and water is now flowing all over the floor.

"Shit!" I gasp as I rush over to turn off the water. "Great, just what I need."

As I move in robotic motions, trying to not think about the real problems in my life, I walk over to get the mop, only to end up slipping on the remnants of the dinner I had spent hours preparing and making for my husband. As I land on the floor with a thud, my vision turns hazy, until eventually, I see nothing but darkness.

"Helena, wake up!"

"Cameron? Are you still here?" I mumble. Cameron had shown up after I had managed to knock myself out. I don't remember much but I know he sent me to bed and told me Jess was safe and sound. The memory of which allows me to slump with relief. As long as she's ok, everything is ok.

"Cameron? Why the fuck would your shithead brother be here?"

I release a long sigh, realizing who the voice belongs to. Usually when he returns after an epic temper tantrum, he passes out without a word. The following morning is a guessing game; will he pretend nothing happened? Or will he continue trying to make me feel like the villain?

"Where've you been?" I ask with a yawn, my head still trying to make a decision as to whether it's going to have a full-blown migraine or not.

"Out," he snaps as he slides into bed next to me, smelling like a brewery and smoke. Enough smoke to make my eyes water. What's worse is he's now trying to climb on top of me. I'm pretty sure he's taken something stronger; his eyes are literally spinning.

"I need to fuck off the bad sex I just had."

"Wait, what?" I gasp. Did he really just say what I think he just said?

"You heard," he mutters angrily, "open your legs."

"Are you fucking kidding me? Get away from me!" I snap, trying hard not to raise my voice for Jess' sake. I've had suspicions that my husband sleeps with other women, but he's never said it so bluntly before, and certainly not when trying to *have sex with me.*

"Hold still!" he shouts, trying to force my legs to open. When he looks at me, I know he's not in his right mind; not that his right mind is much better, but now he's high on something, and that can only spell bad news for me. He fumbles at his fly before ripping his pants and boxers off. I ready myself for him and as soon as he comes at me, I try to kick him off, shoving him with my hands.

"No! No!" I scream angrily at him. "I don't want your diseased cock anywhere near me! You don't get to come at me after you've been inside someone else tonight. Fuck off!"

A slap and a knee to my ribs have me clutching my stomach in pain, giving him a momentary weakness that he uses to his advantage. His hand pins mine above my head, while the other rips at my clothes. As he rapes me, as is his right according to him, I don't cry, I don't show any emotion, I just stare back at him with utter contempt. As soon as he finishes, which thankfully, is not long at all, I push him roughly onto the floor where he writhes around with his semi-hard cock flapping all over the place. Only then, do I run to the bathroom to throw up and cry. Most people consider this kind of sexual assault shocking, but it's just my Friday night.

The next morning, he's sitting at the kitchen table, waiting for me to cook his breakfast as if all is normal and peaceful in the world. He plays with pop-up toys on Jess' table, laughing when she jumps with surprise.

As I serve his eggs and bacon, Mom and Dad come into the kitchen with beaming smiles and kisses on the cheek for Jess and me. Dad shakes Evan's hand proudly while my husband plays the perfect son-in-law.

"Wow, my daughter's treating you well, I see," Dad says as he eyes the food sitting in front of Evan.

"That she is," Evan says as gets up to theatrically spin me around on the spot, then throws us back so he can kiss me. Jess giggles over the show, as does my father, looking very much like the smug, 'I told you he was the one' and, 'Aren't you glad you listened to me?' bastard that I've come to think of him.

"Hey, darling, why don't you cook something up for your dad?" Evan suggests, patting my ass before moving back to his place at the table.

Only my mother notices the remains of dinner splashed up against the wall. She peers over at my reflection in the window where I stand cutting up mushrooms to fry. We look at each other in the pane of glass and she knows.

"How was the coq au vin Helena made you last night, Evan?" she asks, her little way of confronting him. "She worked ever so hard on it. She knows your mother thinks she should make more of an effort."

"The coq au vin?" He frowns; he doesn't even remember the dinner I spent hours over, the same dinner he had thrown against the wall. "Oh yeah, the coq au vin! It was delicious, thank you. My mother needs to learn to keep her opinions to herself; right, babe?"

I feel his eyes on me, telling me I better play along or they'll be a matching cracked rib to the one he gave me last night.

"Mmhmm," is about all I can muster for him.

"She's trying, aren't you, sweetheart?" My father pipes in. "And the garden looks amazing!"

"Helena, sweetheart, do you think you could show me that dress you were telling me about?" This is Mom's code for 'I want to know exactly what happened'. "I think it will be perfect for my dinner with the Johnsons."

I nod at the same time as I give Dad his plate of food, then kiss Jess on the head before I take Mom upstairs.

As soon as we're in the bedroom, alone, she looks at me with an expression only a mother can give their child when they know something awful has happened to them. Unfortunately, this is only one awful thing of many, so we no longer dance around the issue.

"Show me," she whispers.

I pull up my shirt to reveal an angry red and purple bruise where he kneed me in the ribs last night. She looks away with her eyes closed and her hand clasped to her mouth. When she eventually regains her composure, she turns back to ask, "And did he?" To which I nod once. She cries because she can never get used to the things I admit to her.

Present

Helena

Back in the here and now, still huddled on my brother's lap, I listen as he tries to explain himself. My mind is still on that awful night, the same one that likes to enter my nightmares every now and then, when I'm feeling down, weak, and like I've failed everyone, including myself. Perhaps I should have let my mother intervene and tell someone, but Evan had convinced me that if I told a single soul, he would take Jess and I would never see her again. My mother, on the other hand, had both of us to lose, and she also didn't want to risk me not having anyone to turn to.

"He didn't tell her he was married until afterward," Nate continues to explain. "With all the other stuff that she was going through at home, I guess it kind of tipped her over the edge."

I begin to cry, though I'm not entirely sure why, for there are too many reasons to pinpoint the exact one. Is it for Bea? For me? For the incredible guilt that I now feel for letting Evan get away with his abuse, just so he could attack Lily and get at girls when they're at their most vulnerable? Or is it for my poor daughter who has a monster for a father?

"Hey, hey, Hels," Nate tries to soothe me, "please don't cry, she didn't know…I mean, he's just bad-"

"I'm so sorry, Nate," I whimper, "I didn't know he did that. Please don't hate me."

"Why would I hate you? Oh, Helena." He pulls me in tightly and gives me a moment to let me have my little breakdown on his lap. "God, I'm not equipped to deal with all you emotional women."

He laughs softly and the sound of his boyish laughter clears my conscience to a certain degree, enough to let me laugh with him, if only for a bit.

"Go and get her, you big idiot," I eventually say to him with a nudge of my foot, but make no real attempt to get off his lap. We've not shared a moment like this since before I went to stay at *Hastings Villa*, since before Evan.

"I will, but first I'm going to stay here with you," he says before kissing my head again. "I think my big sister could use a little comfort right now, couldn't you?" I nod my head against him, so he continues stroking my hair. "I love you, Hels."

"You do?" I ask in complete shock. "I always thought Cameron hated me and that you thought nothing of me."

"You're my big sister; of course I think a lot of you, you idiot!" He laughs as he throws my own insult back at me. "Cam does too, you know. He just found it so hard when you chose to stay with Evan; he convinced himself that it meant you had chosen Evan over him. He felt betrayed, Hels."

I'm about to argue with him, to yell and scream that I never chose Evan over my big brother. But in the end, I don't say anything. My strength is fading and it's only a matter of time before I fall unconscious again, and into blissful darkness.

Chapter 27

Helena

When I wake, sunshine is streaming through the window, and I am alone. Lonely is better than being with a man who you cannot bear to have touch you. Lonely is better than scared.

Remembering that Jess is going away today, I jump out of bed, which is rather foolish considering such an action may well provoke another migraine. However, I only have a few hours before I have to wave my baby girl off to camp for an entire month. I have no idea what I'm going to do to keep my emotions at bay, but I will try my best, for her sake. I know how excited she is to be going and I don't want to take that away from her.

When I finally find her, she's already throwing clothes inside her suitcase. I'm glad my recent migraine hasn't made her anxious about going; she usually worries when I've been knocked out for a long time, though I'm sure Nate would have done his best to reassure her.

She jumps in shock when she sees me standing in her doorway, but then smiles when I wander over and begin to help her pack. We chat about Nate's drama from last night and gossip over his ridiculousness when it comes to girls. I help her sort her toiletries while trying to maintain an upbeat attitude, even if I feel like I'm dying on the inside. My life is all about Jess, nothing else. It's the way it's been since I found out who her father was.

"Mom?" she says, snapping me out of my thoughts. "When Nate was having his drama with Bea last night, I kind of got mad with him, so I came to hang out with you in your room. I was snooping and I found this." She holds out a shoebox full of old photos, sketchbooks, and a few notes - my 'Lucius' box. "I hope you don't mind?"

I look through some of the stuff and find myself genuinely smiling, something I don't often do these days.

"I forgot I had all this stuff," I tell her. "I had to hide it from your..." I stop myself and clear my throat, shaking my head over my thoughtless slip of the tongue. "Never mind."

"You mean Dad?" She looks deadpan at me, embracing the pre-teen side of her. "You don't need to hide stuff from me anymore. I know about what happened with Aunty Lily, I know what he was like to you, and I also know he was released from prison last week."

I snap my head up with a feeling of extreme anxiety rushing around my body.

"How?" I eventually ask, sounding small and sad.

This is the last thing I wanted Jess to know about. He's already sent a threatening letter, demanding I let him see her, but I've stuck my head in the sand like an ostrich, hoping it will just go away.

"Grandma," she replies bluntly, meaning Evan's witch of a

mother. "He's been staying with her and when I went over for lunch on Sunday, all his stuff was there."

"Shit," I blurt out before I can stop myself. "Sorry," I utter when she grins over yet another slip of my tongue. "Did you see him?"

"No, but only because I told her I never want to see him again. Course, that didn't stop her from trying to explain away what he did. That's why I haven't visited her since."

I don't try and talk her around or attempt to convince her to not give up on his family. I don't remind her that he's still her father and that she shouldn't shut him out, because that would make me a hypocrite. I don't want her to see him.

To begin with, I tried to hide the fact that he had been arrested for attacking Lily. However, his mother, in her desperation to defend and twist the fact for her precious son, ended up being the one who broke it to Jess. She thought I had already laid everything bare for Jess so I could turn her against him. Little did she realize, it was the final straw that broke the camel's back for Jess. He was a horrible father, and I can't even begin to explain away how he treated not only Lily, but also Jess herself.

"Anyway," she says with a smile, holding up a photograph of me in Spain, "when did you have pink hair?"

I laugh at the photograph she's holding of me and Silver, my old roommate, pulling silly faces for the camera. However, before I can answer, the sound of a car horn silences both of us.

"That's your lift, Baby Girl," I sigh, trying my best not to turn into a blubbering mess, even though she's already seen me wipe my tears away. She rolls her eyes over my dramatic reaction to her leaving but is still crossing the room to wrap her skinny arms around me. "I promise I will go through all of this when you get back."

"You better had," she says. When she pulls away, she looks small, like my little girl again. "Walk me down?"

"Of course." I get up to follow her, but walk slowly, trying to prolong the moment when she will finally have to leave. When we reach the door, I grab hold of her so tightly, I'm sure I'm cutting off her air supply. I kiss her all over until she eventually groans at me.

"Mom!" She rolls her eyes again, a habit I've seen her repeating more and more as the years go by. "You're embarrassing me, and Billy's in the car!"

"Sorry," I tell her, offering a wince. "To be fair, it's every mother's right to humiliate her child. It's promised to you after you squeeze said child out during childbirth."

"Eww, gross!" She wrinkles her nose and looks so unbelievably cute, I have to kiss her one more time, to which she tuts. "I'll text you when I get there, I promise. Love you, Mom."

She then kisses me on the cheek and bolts for the car before I can embarrass her any further.

"Bye, Baby Girl," I call out as I wave, "I love you."

She waves back but within a blink of an eye, she's gone. I remember this same empty feeling I used to have every time Lucius left me. It's still crippling.

Rubbing my empty arms, I lift my face to the gentle breeze, trying to stop myself from crying, because if I start, I might not stop until she's back home. So, I take a deep inhale, but when I breathe out and open my eyes, I see...*him.*

THE DEVIL

Helena's Thirtieth Birthday

Helena

"Happy birthday, darling," Mom cries at the same time as she throws her arms around my shoulders. "How does it feel turning thirty?"

I hug her back, even though celebrating my thirtieth is pretty low on the agenda right now.

"Much like it did when I was twenty-nine," I reply, smiling tightly before giving in and giggling with her.

She walks us both inside my cottage and I'm about to close the door when Dad shocks me by coming in with her. We haven't exactly spoken much since Evan and I parted over a year ago, merely weeks before Evan attacked Lily. We eye each other cautiously. When I first told my parents we were parting, he went crazy, telling me how irresponsible and selfish I was being and how Jess needed her parents together. I tried to reason with him, but he wouldn't hear any of it. He even told me how Evan had been on the phone with him, giving him his whole sob story of how I had kicked him out with nothing but the shirt on his back. Laughably, he even told my father how much he had tried to love me the best way he knew how, but I had refused to listen. If you believed the lies Evan fed him, which of course, he did, I had 'diva' and 'spoiled brat' written all over me.

Of course, a few weeks later, he attacked Lily and in doing so, revealed his true colors. But Dad never said a single word to me, not even to apologize or eat humble pie. He buried his head in the sand and pretended as if nothing had happened; he hadn't threatened me all those years ago; he hadn't forced me into a marriage I didn't want; he hadn't ignored the misery I had been living in for the past nine years. Mom was livid, but I told her to let it go. I had had enough drama for two lifetimes, and I was done now. I just wanted to live with my gorgeous girl and live a normal, not quite happy, but content life with her. I haven't even considered my life when she will no longer rely on me, but for now, she is all I need.

"Helena," Dad says before kissing me on the cheek, which I accept to keep the peace and because I know Jess is running up behind me. Her giggle is like her own little beacon calling out to me. It still amazes me that in a room full of children, you can always pick out your child's cry, laugh, and voice.

"Grandpa!" she cries as she leaps into his arms. "I didn't know you were coming. Come on, we're having cream teas. Even Cameron and Lily are here."

Things are still weird between my brothers and me, but Cameron had to come because Jess and Lily had made a point of asking him in front of Mom.

I watch as Jess pulls my father out into the backyard where Meri, Jen, and my family are sitting around a table of delicious food, all lovingly prepared by my mother and Jess. To the side, there is a small table with beautifully wrapped presents and handwritten cards for me. Meri sees me standing awkwardly by the door so comes to pull me down into a chair next to her.

For a while, I smile politely and join in with the chit-chat going on around the table. Nate is trying to goad Lily and Cameron into telling us when they plan to get married. Jen is *telling us about a new boyfriend she's seeing, an artist from Milan, while Meri is complaining about David's snoring. The poor guy is sitting quietly eating cake and smiling affectionately at his new wife. My sole focus is on Jess, who is sitting with my parents under the apple tree, showing them her recent school report. She's a swot, just like her mother, but she's also a lot more confident than I ever was. She has tons of friends and enjoys drama club as well as playing tennis after school. I am beyond proud of her, which I make sure I tell her every day.*

A little while later, Jess makes me open my gifts and cards. I always hate this part because I've never wanted to be the center of attention. I'd rather do it quietly and make over-the-top thank-you cards, but Jess is super excited, and I can't bear to say no to her.

"Oh, wow," I say to Meri after unwrapping something that looks like a watch but also something that should be on an episode of 'Star Trek'. "What is it?" I whisper and everyone laughs, including Meri who nudges my arm.

"It's a Fitbit," she explains, "it monitors how many steps you've done and your heart rate and all other kinds of crazy stuff."

"Oh, wow," I repeat again, this time trying to sound more convincing. "I always wanted to know how many steps I've walked."

"Bitch!" she says with a grin as I wrap my arms around my very best friend. As we laugh at one another, Jess shoves another present under my nose, informing me that it's from her. I quickly open it, being a little theatrical just to make her giggle. It's a frame, and inside of it is a black and white print of her hand placed on top of mine. It's artistic, personal, and looks professional, but above all, it's beautiful. Tears prick at my eyes

while everyone else gasps.

"Don't you like it?" She suddenly looks worried, so I quickly nod my head while wiping away at my eyes, not able to get the words out of my mouth fast enough. "I took it when you were asleep. Nonna helped me get it printed and then we got the frame together."

"Jess, it's so beyond words. Come here, I love it!" She runs over and throws her arms around my shoulders where she holds on tightly. I pick her up and place her on my lap, even though she's getting too big for it. "You are my most perfect gift ever, Baby Girl!"

"Love you, Mom," she whispers and when we let go of one another, we're not the only ones with wet eyes. I swipe her tears away and giggle when she does the same back to me.

An hour later, I'm in the kitchen with Mom, Lily, and Meri. I'm washing, Mom's drying, and Lily is wrapping leftovers while we all gossip about this and that. However, my attention is on my father, who is currently standing in the backyard with my brothers. They're laughing and joking and patting one another on the back. I notice Dad's expression whenever he looks at them – momentous pride for his sons. All of a sudden, at this moment, on my birthday, I can't face it anymore.

"Excuse me," I murmur, throwing the washcloth into the sink before rushing upstairs. I even ignore Lily when I hear her asking whether she should come after me. Meri tells her not to worry, that she'll come and see how I am. So, when she arrives in my room about five minutes later, I'm not surprised. I simply look at her without words as she walks in and sits on the bed next to me.

We sit together for a few moments, her with her arm wrapped around my shoulders, me sulking against it. She lets me sigh and quietly rage before she even tries to say anything; I love her for it.

"Feel any better?" she eventually asks. Like a little kid, I stubbornly shrug my shoulders, but say nothing. "Look, I didn't know whether to give this to you or not, but here," she says, reaching into her back pocket and retrieving the smallest card in the world. When I turn it over, I see a perfect cursive script with expert formation over each letter of my name. When we look at one another again, she winces, awaiting my volcanic eruption. This is **his** writing.

"Do you think…? Would you mind if I…?"

She nods before I even have a chance to finally spit the words out. Meri shuffles off my bed and walks over to the door, momentarily glancing back at me before she closes it behind her.

Like a teenage girl obsessing over her recent crush, I turn the card over and over in my hand before inhaling it against my nose. I draw the process out so that I can savor everything it has to offer. When there is nothing left to do but open it, I force myself to remember that Lucius won't be in there. The paper tears to reveal what's inside, a small white card. It looks like the same card he used to use to write his messages all those years ago. I smile because I should have known Lucius wouldn't have sent a normal birthday card, he would have considered it beneath him. But this is better, this is much more personal.

Taking in a deep breath, I turn it over and finally read the message - **Happy Birthday, Topolina. L x**

For the next five minutes or so, I obsess over what to take from it. Should I be happy, sad, disappointed, or elated? What is he trying to tell me? Is he trying to tell me anything?

THE DEVIL

In the end, I decide that it means nothing more than what it is; a short, meaningless, generic happy birthday message to a girl who no longer exists.

Chapter 28

Lucius

Mia topolina.

I've waited for two hours on the road near her house, just watching. I watched Nathaniel leave; I watched a car arrive for her daughter; I watched her cry as her daughter said goodbye and left, and now, I'm watching her, watching me. I couldn't make out too much from this distance, but her daughter is almost a carbon copy of her. Same hair, same build, and same infectious laugh. But now, it's just Helena.

We stare at each other for what feels like an age before she eventually turns around and walks slowly inside. My heart feels like it's freezing on the inside, but then she offers me a lifeline by leaving the door wide open; a silent invitation for me to come and save her. I don't need words this time, so I walk over as quickly as I can before she has the chance to change her mind.

I cautiously walk into the little cottage that has Helena written all over it, being full of old-fashioned touches and a fairy-tale type of garden. There are pictures of Jess everywhere, but I don't really take the time to look at them properly. My sole mission is to find Helena.

When I eventually find her, she is standing adjacent to the door to the backyard in her little ordered kitchen. She's looking out the window with her back to me, sighing like this is a past-time she often wastes her day doing. Years spent in front of a window, begging to be saved, but having no one to come for her.

"Topolina?" I utter quietly, my vibrations disturbing the air between us with my low voice.

For a moment, she doesn't move, just remains staring out the window. I'm about to speak again, but ever so slowly, she turns to face me with her sad, vacant eyes staring right back into mine. I walk tentatively toward her, frightened that the slightest move will spook her. She looks much like a frightened animal who still needs convincing that you are here to help, not hurt them.

After what feels like much too long, I get close enough to take her hand with the gentlest of touches, something I am not known for. As soon as I make contact, my patience instantly dissipates, and I grab hold tightly and bring her into me. She crumbles against my chest, crying with every ounce of energy she has. Her pain-filled sobs kill me and at this moment, holding her so tightly, I especially fucking hate myself for abandoning her all those years ago.

"Shh, I got you, Topolina," I whisper, trying to comfort her while she clings onto me for dear life, a life she has suffered through because we were both too stubborn to tell each other how we truly felt. "I've got you, baby girl, I'm not going anywhere."

I kiss her over and over, relishing her smell, her touch, her essence, her everything. I realize, beyond all doubt, what I've been denying myself since I met her when she was seventeen -

fourteen damn years ago!

We hold on to each other for a long time, even after she has stopped crying, needing to cling together in silence, in this small kitchen that barely houses my height.

"Why have you come here, Lucius?" She breaks the silence with her small, croaky, broken voice. There's no spark, no feeling, and no fight left in it.

"Your cousin came and laid everything bare for me," I reply with a heavy sigh. "I made her tell me everything, and I mean *everything*!"

My Helena pulls away and walks over to the table where she sits down in a defeated heap. Her cardigan drapes over her tiny frame, covering any hint of her womanly shape. I can see how much she is trying to hide behind her oversized clothes and her lifeless hair, but I still see her; I've always seen her.

"So?" she says, hitching up her shoulder, trying to act tough. She can't though; any fight she once had has been beaten out of her. The thought of which has me clenching my fists with intense emotions – rage, sorrow, guilt – all the ugly ones.

"Why should that bring you my way?" she asks, forcing me to focus on her, not on how this is affecting me.

I walk over to where she is sitting and kneel before her, taking her hands inside one of mine before I lift her chin with my finger, silently begging her to look at me.

"I'm here to make you whole again," I vow. "I'm here because I was a fucking idiot and I'm so sorry, Helena." She begins to cry softly, so I place my forehead to hers and whisper, "*My* Helena."

"You can't, Lucius, she's gone," she whimpers, "you're more likely to win the lottery than bring me back to life. Why would you want to even try? Look at me for Christ's sake; I'm a thirty-two-year-old divorcee with a near teenager. I have zero self-worth and hang-ups about men because her husband used to beat and rape her."

I close my eyes when she voices it out loud, feeling sick to my stomach. I always feared I would be the one to destroy her, that I would take her to hell with me, but in doing so, I pushed her away and into the arms of a real monster.

"For years, Lucius, *years*! You can't fix that. Please, you must have a whole harem of women clawing at you for your time; just leave me to drift along quietly."

"Don't fucking talk like this, Helena!" My anger begins to simmer, even though I shouldn't be letting it, not with her right now. She's so fragile, so vulnerable, and I need to be building her back up, not losing my temper over all that has happened to her. My beautiful, strong, little mouse.

"You, you're everything I was too scared to admit I wanted!"

"Why though? I never understood why," she sighs. "Why did you come after me? Just…why?

"Because damn it, Helena, I love you!" I shout, only to then sigh through exasperation over my own temper. "I love you, mia topolina, and because you're mine for always, you told me that once."

My outburst freezes her, causing tears to fill her eyes before she spills them with a flutter of her lashes. I brush them away with my thumbs but remain silent to let her take in my words, to swallow and digest them. I owe her that much patience.

My broken girl slowly takes hold of my face and looks deep inside of me. She really studies me, trying to see if I really am saying what she's been waiting so long to hear from me. People often say I have an intense look about me, but the way she is staring at me right now, is far more intimidating than anything I could ever deliver. My heart is pounding, and I feel like I've lost all breath from my body.

I only breathe again when she eventually gives me life by placing a gentle kiss on my lips. She then rests her forehead against mine, with her eyes still closed and her tears silently falling.

"I've waited fourteen years to hear you say that, Lucius," she whimpers. "Please don't hurt me again. I love you so much that if you ever left me again..." she says before having to stop so she can release a sigh to try and stop her voice from breaking. "If I lost you again, I don't know what I'd do."

I scoop her up inside my arms and speak just loud enough for her to be able to hear my words, my conviction, my promise, my vow.

"This is it for us, Helena, no more dicking around, and no more being a coward. I will never let anyone hurt you ever again, even me. You are mine and I am yours, I swear."

Even though I am desperate to, I don't push contact beyond this; she's been through enough. Merial was right, I need to take this slow with her, but I'll be fucked if I'm not going to show her how much she means to me.

THE DEVIL

Chapter 29

Lucius

Helena is flitting around the garden, and after a few minutes of watching her, it suddenly dawns on me that she's still nervous...of *me*. Or maybe everyone, but whatever the reason, I've decided it's time to put an end to it.

Her home is a world away from mine in her calm, secluded, cozy cottage, and yet, I feel totally at peace; she is my home, wherever she is. For a moment, I envy her daughter for the life her mother gives her, for the childhood that was ripped away from me when I was even younger than she is now. I also envy her for all the years she's had with my Helena while I was without her, the years I denied both of us because I was too emotionally stunted to do anything but wallow in my own anger, fears, and frustration.

Pushing my sunglasses on, because the sunlight is blinding today, I step quietly toward her. I am right behind her when I eventually say her name, causing her to jump before hanging her bird feeder back on the tree. When she turns, I take her in, all five foot four of her tiny frame. She doesn't eat much, I can tell, but she still carries the chest of a mother who breastfed her child. Her jeans hang from her hip bones while her oversized cardigan wraps around her tiny waist without doing it any justice. Chocolate shades of hair blow around her neck as the wind picks up in velocity.

Remaining by the small fruit tree, she waits for me like an obedient dog. She's been trained to only speak when she's been spoken to. The pain of seeing her like this, especially after having known her before, is almost unbearable. But I can be her strength, as well as the man who should have been responsible for her safety and happiness. So, I decide to do what I do best; I don't give into her desperation to have me speak first, I force her into breaking out of her comfort zone. She waits, but I wait longer, maintaining a fixed gaze on her searching, lost eyes. I even raise my brow to let her know it is me who is waiting for her, pushing her to lay some of that old sass on me, the way she used to do when we were unknowingly flirting with one another.

"W-what?" she finally whispers. Her stuttering breaks my heart a little more, as well as causes me to tighten my clenched fists inside of my pockets.

"I was wondering when you were going to stop being scared of me," I reply bluntly, "to lay some of that feisty attitude on me."

"I warned you, Lucius," she murmurs, "I told you I wasn't who you remember. And I don't blame you if you want to take back what you said."

"Come sit with me, Topolina," I tell her, nodding my head over at the table on the patio, complete with a stripy parasol and matching deckchair cushions. As expected, she dutifully follows behind so I take hold of her hand and link it through my arm, meaning she has to walk side by side with me. Being a gentleman, because her ex-husband sure as hell wasn't, I pull out one of the chairs for her to sit on before I kneel in front of her hunched over body. I then clasp hold of her hands and stare at her in such a way, she is unable to look anywhere other than into my eyes.

"Talk to me, Helena," I say softly, "tell me what's going on in that big brain of yours. I know you; you're always thinking. So, share with me."

"I can't," she says, looking down at her fingers which are fidgeting with nerves. "I learned to keep quiet, to hold my tongue, and to do as I'm told."

"Fuck, what era did he have you living in?" She winces over my words, and I feel guilty for my cheap insult, because truth be told, there are no words to describe what he did to her. "Sorry."

"No, please, don't be," she sighs. "You are being you, the man I fell in love with. So, even if I have, please don't change who you are. You, you're everything; you always have been to me, and I wouldn't want you any other way. I love you, even the asshole you," she says, smiling for the first time today, which relieves some of my tension. "Besides, we both know asshole you is only a part of you."

"Fuck, Helena, don't let the whole world know that!"

She laughs and I can't resist the urge to place my lips on top of hers. She kisses back and cautiously places her fingertips on my cheek, as though she is desperate to keep me from pulling away. I don't want to pull away either. Everything she's just said is the polar opposite of what my mother had told Paul when I was only a child. This woman validates me, and I love her for it.

"Don't be scared of me," I whisper against her ear. "Love me and don't be scared of me...*please*?"

"Loving you is easy," she replies, "being scared is a conditioned mindset I am trying to work through. I just need time...and you."

She shocks me when she wraps her arms tightly around my shoulders so I can pull her in against me, silently telling her I can give her anything she wants, as long as she lets me have her.

Lying Helena down inside her bed, I tuck her up and leave her to sleep while I go and make some phone calls downstairs. The first is to Paul. I want to know every single piece of information on her ex-husband, and I want the dirt to come in thick and fast. The second is to my PA, Sara, who thinks I'm a piece of shit, but loves me all the same. I ask her to have a set of clothes delivered to Helena's cottage and to make sure my penthouse is secure while I'm away. The third and final call is to Merial, asking her to go through every minute little detail she knows about the years I have been apart from my topolina.

After several hours of Merial going off on many long-winded and unnecessary tangents, I pour myself a glass of some shitty wine I found in Helena's cupboard. I almost spit up when I hear the door unlock and someone letting themselves in. Not sure who the fuck it is, Evan for all I know, I grab a poker from the fireplace and position myself so I can attack the intruder from behind the door. As they walk through, I hear a gentle sigh before grabbing them by the shoulder with the poker being held high up in the air.

"Ahh! Oh, Jesus Christ!"

As my senses adjust to the shock of seeing the face of this intruder, I realize she looks familiar. I haven't seen this woman since Paul and Jen's wedding, but I have seen many photos of her all over Helena's walls, and I do see my topolina in her terrified, and now ashen-colored face. Standing a little over five feet, I let the tiny woman go and lower the poker. Hopefully, my actions will show Helena's mother that I mean no harm.

"My apologies," I utter when she clutches at her chest. For a moment, I fear she's about to have a heart attack, but when she eventually looks up, she smiles and starts waving a hand in front of me.

"Lucius, Lucius Has-" I begin, holding out my hand, but she stops me before I can finish.

"I know who you are, Lucius," she says rather confidently, especially for someone I was about to beat around the head with an iron rod. "You're the man my daughter has been in love with ever since she came to stay with you in San Francisco. You're the man who broke my Helena's heart."

Shit, this can only go badly, particularly now that she's walking up to me while eyeing me intently. She looks as though she's readying herself to slap me around the face.

"But you're also the man who's going to bring her back to life again, aren't you?"

I can't tell if she is begging me, ordering me, or threatening me, maybe all three. But all I can do is nod at the terrifying woman who is currently having to crane her neck to look up at me.

Helena

My mind is a fog of questions when I finally wake, it now being dark outside when I only remember it being light. It takes a few minutes to remember Lucius coming into my house, telling me everything I've waited for years to hear him say, and yet, here I am alone. Stepping out of bed, I wrap my robe around me, not even considering how old and frumpy it looks; after all, I've not had to think of such things in years.

It's not until I get to the top of the staircase that I hear two voices chatting amicably from the direction of my living room. Two smiling faces look up at me from my living room chairs, though Lucius' is more of a smirk as he studies me looking like a crumpled mess. My mother looks relaxed in his company; she's always been good at seeing beyond the façade and getting to the true person beneath. She never liked Evan for she couldn't ever see the real person beneath the charm.

Seeing Lucius, who still looks breathtaking, I try and rub my hair back into some kind of order, and surreptitiously slip off my raggedy old robe. He gets to his feet to reach for me, but as soon as his back is turned, I mouth over to Mom, asking if I look ok. She grins and nods her head with a flap of her hand. I guess she's never seen me act this way over a man before.

"Better?" Lucius asks before kissing me gently on the cheek.

Unable to speak, I smile and nod before he leads me over to the couch to sit with him. An uncomfortable silence engulfs us as the surrealness of the situation hits the room. Apart from Lucius, who would be comfortable in the middle of a crowded court case while on trial and completely naked.

"So, Lucius and I have spoken," Mom upsets the air between us with her softly spoken words, "and I'm confident that he's going to look after you while Jess is away. With that in mind, I'm going to bid you two farewell and get back home to your father…I probably won't mention this to him yet."

She places down her cup, then stands, getting ready to go.

"You don't have to-" I begin, but she cuts me off with one of her all-encompassing Mom hugs that are both a source of comfort and a means to cut off your air supply.

"It's been fourteen years in the making, Helena, I think I do." She grins over my shoulder before releasing me to head toward the door. "Don't let anyone hold you back, least of all yourselves. Goodnight, Lucius."

He nods and bids her goodnight before she leaves, but I don't come back inside until I see her driving safely off down the road. After which, I find Lucius leaning against the wooden sideboard in the kitchen. His presence makes the room appear even smaller and I'm tempted to laugh over how ridiculous he looks in my teeny, tiny cottage. But when he turns around, I see he's holding a bunch of unopened, handwritten letters with an angry expression on his face. I know what they are, the most recent one was sent only a few days ago. The scariest part is it was hand delivered; the lack of stamp and postmark is obvious to all who can see.

From the thunderous look on his face, Lucius has guessed as to who they're from too. I haven't opened them because I've been too afraid and too angry with the situation they represent, as well as the monster who is responsible for them. Perhaps, for Jess' sake, I should have been braver, but I'm not, so I haven't.

"Explain."

His one-word instructions never fail to make me shudder. I would hate to face him in a court of law, he'd most likely stare you down until you admitted to every misdemeanor in your life, as well as a few you have never committed.

"They're from him, but then, you already know that, Lucius," I sigh as I go to switch the kettle on, if only so I can shift my eyes away from his penetrating gaze. "I'm too afraid to open them."

I hear a rip of paper as he attacks one of the envelopes. I should have known he would have dived straight in, but I'm still shocked he didn't ask for my permission. Within seconds, I step up to him and pull the offending item away from his hands, with repressed anger spreading all through my body from years of being ordered around by men. His face changes to one of surprise, but I let him have it all the same.

"Lucius, I didn't divorce one asshole man who controlled my every movement, just to be ordered around by another. You don't get to come into my house and open my mail. I'll open those when I'm good and ready, but until then, back.The.Fuck.Off!"

We remain at an impasse, staring at one another with equal fury, ready to give the other one hell, if necessary. This is what we do, after all, for with him, I have never felt scared to have my say. In fact, I know he wants the reciprocation. He's always called me his little mouse, but he knows I'm not with him, I never have been. It is one of the reasons we love one another so passionately; my ability to spar with him and nobody else is what he deems incredibly romantic. The devil craves fire, and I give it only to him.

I stare back at him as he leans in toward me, with his intimidating size and couldn't-give-a-shit attitude. I wait for his scathing words, but instead, he kisses me gently on my lips before pulling back with his trademark smirk, the one I've kept locked up tightly inside of my memory for all these years. I frown with a look of utter confusion.

"You lied, Topolina," he says smugly, "you told me that girl I once knew wasn't there anymore, but I've just seen her. She's still there."

I try to keep my stony expression but can't help grinning when he pulls me in tighter against his chest.

"Asshole!"

Helena

Hours later, and I've just read aloud the most recent letter from Evan, demanding that he see both me and Jess at a location of my choosing. He says I can bring my mother with me, seeing as he will be bringing his to look after Jess while we try to talk things out. To, *'at the very least'*, make arrangements for him to see Jess on a regular basis. He'd rather we didn't involve lawyers because *'they will only suck up all our money'* when *'we can easily sort this out ourselves.'* Being in prison has apparently made him consider his treatment of me and how much he still cares about me. He wants us to reconcile and to *'try again'* for Jess' sake, as well as *'for the love we once shared.'* The whole thing makes me feel sick and want to hide under the covers, but instead, I snuggle into the wall of muscle next to me. The thought of being with Evan again, even in the same room, makes my heart thump at a rapid pace, so much so, it hurts.

"Over my dead body!" Lucius says with an eerie tone of voice, and with every muscle tensing under the strain of his rage.

"Jess doesn't want to see him anyway," I add, "but I know

Evan, he's not going to let it drop."

"You don't need to worry about that anymore, baby girl," he says, stroking my hair as I cuddle into his chest. "He'll be lucky if he lives that long."

I laugh over his threat, but it quickly dies out when I see the expression on his face; I'm not entirely convinced he's joking.

"That's the first time I've heard you laugh again," he whispers, "I've missed it."

"Me too," I reply, "and I've missed lying with someone who cares about me."

"Helena, do your father and brothers know about what happened? Merial told me your mother knows, but what about them?" he asks and I sigh because I know he won't like the answer.

"No, what's the point?" He holds my hand and begins to study it as if in deep contemplation, his way of telling me to elaborate without using actual words. "Things between me and them haven't been the same since I found out I was pregnant. I am the black sheep who brought Lily's attacker into their lives. I'm the one who chose a raping monster over my brother. I'm the one who got herself pregnant and disappointed my father all those years ago. I've made my peace with it and convinced my mother not to say anything because perhaps I haven't forgiven them for not believing in me. Only Lily could see what was happening to me without me having to tell her. To them, I was just a mousey wife who followed her husband obediently, no matter what he did." I laugh to myself over my own words. "I guess that's what I was, in the end. But it was never my choice to be with him."

"Hmm," he says, and I know he's brooding over this,

which probably means this won't end well at some point in the future. "I contacted Cameron shortly after our weekend in Spain, did he tell you?"

I spin around to face him, shocked over this new piece of information.

"No, he never said a word," I utter as his expression turns thunderous.

"I told him that I needed to contact you," he says tightly, "that I needed to see you."

"What did he say?" I ask with anger simmering deep inside of me; this could have changed everything.

He sighs as though it was a recent, hurtful memory still whirling around inside his head.

"He said you were officially with Evan and that you were happy," he says, swallowing hard, "that if I really cared for you, I'd leave you alone. So, I did."

"Lucius, I was never happy with Evan, *never*!"

I draw back a long breath, ready to tell him everything that led to my marriage to such a monster. It might be a huge mistake to explain that I didn't tell him about the pregnancy when I didn't know who the father was, but I feel I owe it to him. I open my mouth to begin, but he stops me by placing his index finger to my lips.

"Not now, Helena," he whispers with a soft smile. "I don't want to feel angry when I've only just got you back. I shouldn't have mentioned it. We have forever to talk about such things."

Perhaps I'm being a coward, but I give in and lie back

against his chest, holding him close so he can't get away from me ever again. My empty shell is not yet full, but it is no longer completely hollow either. I know why Cameron did what he did, but I can't understand why he didn't tell me. Perhaps he was angry with me for even associating with Lucius in the first place, or maybe my father told him my entire predicament about not knowing who the father was. Perhaps they both decided Evan was the best choice between them.

I continue to ponder on this when I feel Lucius twisting around and fumbling with something on my bedside table.

"Is this Jess?" he asks quietly, clutching hold of a picture of us both when she turned eleven. I look up and smile at my daughter with pride.

"Yep, that's her."

"She's beautiful," he says, still studying it, "just like her mother. In fact, I can't see anyone but you in her. Believe me, that's a good thing. Well, up until she starts meeting boys that is."

"She started falling in love with boys from about ten years old," I tell him with a sigh. "She must have both her uncles in her. I didn't notice boys until I met some cocky bastard in San Francisco."

"Oh, really? He must have been quite something," he says, playing along, "must have been extremely attractive."

"Yeah, pity he was an asshole," I tease.

"Bet he was good in bed," he continues, "bet he knew all the moves."

"Well, he was ok, very attentive, good with his fingers and tongue, but…" I begin but then pause for dramatic effect. "He turned out to have one of those micro penises. Imagine my shock and horror!" I laugh as he grabs hold of me and spins me underneath him in a playful manner.

"Now, we both know that's not true," he says, grinning darkly, but then pulls back, realizing he's just made things sexual between us. But before he's out of reach, I pull his arms back to me and hold his eye contact with mine. He stares at me, searching my face for what to do next.

"Kiss me properly, Lucius," I ask, hoping he doesn't turn me away. "Kiss me, and touch me, *please*. I haven't had anything like this since the last time I saw you, back when we were in Spain. I haven't had anyone touch me lovingly in all those years, Lucius."

"I don't want to push you, Helena," he says, still looking conflicted. "I don't ever want to be like him or my bastard father."

"And you're not, you never could be," I reassure him. "I know that if I say stop, you will stop. Kiss me!" I whisper as I pull on his arms.

He cups my face with one hand while he leans on his other elbow to steady himself. Lucius is a big man, and I am tiny by comparison, so I reach up to wrap my arms around his neck as he leans in to kiss me. We move softly at first, but it's not long before we let each other in and our mouths collide more urgently, more passionately as he wraps his arms behind my back and our chests press together. He slips between my thighs, still wearing his sweatpants, and me in my pajama shorts. I feel his hardness against my sex and moan with a need for him. He freezes before looking at me nervously.

"I'm sorry," he says, frustrated with either himself or with the situation, I'm not sure. I giggle because he has no idea how different he feels to Evan. I literally winced under any touch from

Evan, but with Lucius, I have only ever felt excitement at the mere thought of him touching me.

"Lucius," I whisper before kissing him on his lips, "I'm in my thirties and I thought all of this was it for me. I thought my sex life was over when I threw Evan out. But now?" I take a moment, needing to release a long breath of nervous anticipation. "You've given me a reason to bring that side of me to life again."

"You were going to give up sex in your twenties?" His eyes widen, as if horrified over such a notion, which has me laughing.

"Shocking, huh?" I mock his surprised face and he laughs at me. "I want you right here, right now, all of it."

"Willingly?" He grins as he raises an eyebrow. I laugh at the sound of his familiar words; they're like old friends you'll never forget.

"Completely," I reply.

"Mine?" he continues, reaching down to kiss my neck. I close my eyes at his touch, biting my lip when his hand reaches under my shorts and moves my black cotton panties to one side, so he can gently swipe his fingers through my sex. He's so tender; I had forgotten what consensual sex and foreplay felt like.

"Always," I whisper into his ear. He pulls back and helps me take off my tank top so that my naked breasts fall in front of him. He grins cheekily over how much bigger they are after having had a baby.

"Fuck!" he says, taking them into his hands. "Your tits are phenomenal!"

"Kind of went up two cup sizes after Jess," I explain before nervously biting on my finger. "I don't like them but…"

"Why the fuck not?" He looks at me, seemingly shocked over my not being in love with them as much as he is. "You are still the most beautiful woman I have ever laid eyes on, Topolina, so stop putting yourself down before you even start."

He tears his shirt off to reveal that same tanned, muscular body that I know so well.

"Jeez, you don't look any different, Lucius!"

Fortunately, I had Jess young enough to avoid stretch marks, but my abs aren't as tight, and my general body self-confidence has declined dramatically over the years. Not helped by Evan of course, whose constant cheating and consistent bullying frequently brought me down.

"Yeah, but I'll let you in on a little secret," he whispers, so I lean in theatrically to listen. "I have to work a damn sight harder than I used to."

"Your efforts are appreciated," I laugh, stroking my hands down his huge biceps and over his rock-hard chest. "Take those sweatpants off so I can see the whole package."

It feels good to take charge over a man again. I lost all control when I found out I was pregnant with Jess and my father practically forced my arm into taking Evan up on his offer of marriage. Lucius smirks deviously while he obeys my command so that he is soon on top of me, fully naked and looking at me with lust.

"May I remove your panties, Miss Carter?" I make a show of thinking about his question before grinning and nodding. He whips them down within seconds then leans back to take in my naked form. I wince as he looks over my post-baby body.

"Fuck, I've missed this," he says before licking his lips.

I giggle, pushing him back off and nudging him so that he is lying on his back, naked and with his erection facing up to the ceiling. Smiling at him, I shuffle down the bed and begin to apply gentle little kisses around his thighs, his testicles, and his erection. He laughs softly at my touch.

"Teasing, Miss Carter?" he murmurs. "I'm enjoying it."

"I'm actually a little nervous," I admit, "I haven't done this in a long time. I remember when I did this to you for the first time on that boat. You helped show me how to do it back then. Are you going to help me now?"

My confidence is growing by the minute with Lucius, especially with the way he is letting me control everything; this is so empowering.

"Whatever the lady wants, the lady shall have," he says with one of those intense smiles on his face.

I look back down at his long, thick, dark cock, which is smooth to the very tip. I lick from the base to the very top where a few drops of precum have escaped. I lick it around the tip, swirling my tongue around the most sensitive part while he hisses slowly between his teeth. I suck the top before reaching a hand around the base to pump him slowly. With each suck, I take more of him into my mouth until I can't take anymore. It's not long before he is thrusting into me to help me take him how he likes it. I kind of like the way he isn't treating me with the kiddy gloves anymore. Now, he's letting me have it, the whole time cursing under his breath. Eventually, he groans, and my throat is filled with the taste of him.

"Fuck, Helena," he gasps, "I did not plan on doing that, I'm sorry, baby-"

"You've got to stop fucking apologizing or I'm kicking you out!" I declare with a half-serious expression.

"There's that feisty mouth of yours," he laughs as he pulls me up to flip me back onto my back. "I knew she wasn't dead," he whispers.

He moves down my body, kissing me as he does so, then sucking each nipple with a strong but delicious suction. When he reaches my clit, he almost becomes wild, giving me everything I haven't experienced in over a decade. His fingers enter me at the same time as he feasts on me. I'm writhing beneath him, arching my back to meet his touch with greed. I try my best to stop the oncoming onslaught of my orgasm, but I've not had this in so long, and his touch is too good for me to keep it at bay. When it comes, I am momentarily blinded by a flash of light before me. My scream is almost silent, but it's there, nonetheless. He doesn't stop until I come back down to Earth, looking crimson from both my climax and my reaction to it.

We make love after that, gentle and slow. His first thrust stings a little; it's been at least six years since someone has even come near me, so it's bound to smart a little. But his touch is like electricity; he has never had to do much more than this to get me to climax. From Spain, I know he is used to a more vigorous sexual experience, but he still comes almost violently, which makes me happy. *Stupidly* happy. I then realize I've not been happy in years. I have my Jess, but outside of being a mother, I haven't had a lot to be happy about. After we finish, it's not long before I have a restful night's sleep, feeling contented and safe for the first time in years.

Chapter 30

Helena

"Yoohoo! Sister-in-law?"

A chirpy voice sings songs from outside, waking me with disorientation and a desperate need for water. After I realize where I am and the fact that it's now morning, said voice bangs on the door a few times and I realize who it is. Cameron and his wife, Lily, must have come back from honeymoon and she's here to get my ass out of bed. I groan against the huge solid mass next to me, hoping she'll take the hint and give up.

"Hels, get your butt out of bed!" she yells up and I find myself grinning over her persistence.

BANG, BANG, BANG!

"Who the fuck is that, Topolina?" Lucius asks calmly, without batting an eyelid. I giggle over his cool persona and morning wood, which is currently tenting up the bed cover.

"That's Lily, my sister-in-law," I whisper, "apparently they're back from honeymoon."

"Will she take the hint?" he mutters.

"Probably not," I reply. "I best go and answer her or she'll start singing motivational songs; she's a kindergarten teacher, so she's been trained to keep going until she gets results."

I begin to get up, but I'm grabbed back by his strong arm and serious expression.

"Helena?" he whispers. "How are you, Topolina?"

"I'm going to have to pretend the great stony Lucius Hastings isn't being a pussy, but other than that, I'm good," I reply cheekily, to which he smacks me gently on my ass.

"Fucking pussy, my ass," he mumbles at the same time as turning over to go back to sleep.

I shove on my jeans, bra, and a random tank top before checking myself out in the mirror, only to make sure I don't look like I've been having sex with the love of my life all night. When I finally get downstairs, I pull the door open to find Lily singing at the top of her voice. I gift her with an exasperated expression, to which she grins. I end up laughing at her before pulling her in for a cuddle, feeling genuinely pleased to see her.

"Singing? Really? It's Sunday morning and we haven't all been in Hawaii for the last week," I giggle as I lead her inside to the kitchen. I know her, she'll be gasping for a cup of tea.

"Yes, but I know Jess went away to camp yesterday, and Nate told us about your migraine, so I felt it was my job, as your sister-in-law, to come and make sure you were at least pretending to function."

"Tea?" I ask over my shoulder.

"Need you ask," she replies casually. She's a well-known British teapot who drinks at least six cups a day. "But I'm sure

Cam will join you with a cup of black coffee."

"Wait! Cameron's here?" I ask, suddenly feeling panicked. He's going to come face-to face-with Lucius and will no doubt guess as to what we've been up to.

"Yeah, why?" she asks, now looking curious over my reaction.

Cameron and I are much better than we were when I was married to Evan, but we're still not the brother and sister duo we once were, not by a long shot. Lily has tried exceptionally hard, with Jess's help, to pull us back together, but it's been a slow process. Him, because he's stubborn, and me, because I've been hollow and indifferent to human emotions. However, after last night's admission from Lucius, I can't help but feel a pang of anger and resentment toward him.

"No reason," I lie. "So, where is he?

"On the phone to Nate, talking over some business thingy or something," she says while waving her hand about in the air. "He's also probably checking Nate and Bea haven't killed each other. I take it you heard all about that?"

She's referring to Nate being totally head over heels in love with his PA, Bea Summers, but deciding to treat her like a total idiot for the last year and a half. I smile and nod, deciding not to voice how totally ridiculous Nate has acted. Apparently, the male side of my family has no logic when it comes to the opposite sex, my father especially.

"So, how are you doing, chickadee? Missing Jess already?" She leans onto the table where she's sitting but looks up abruptly when a half-naked Lucius appears in the doorway. He rests against its frame, practically filling it with his gorgeously tanned and muscular figure. "Or maybe not?"

She then turns to me with a ridiculously shocked grin on her face.

"Morning," Lucius says huskily as he walks over to where I am to kiss me on the cheek. I stand frozen on the spot, finding it half-funny from Lily's reaction, but also feeling half-terrified of Cameron walking in.

"Morning," Lily trills happily his way before getting up to introduce herself. "I'm Lily, Hels' sister-in-law."

"Lucius Hastings," he responds as they shake hands. "I think you can guess as to what I was to Helena last night."

I blush and roll my eyes over his usual bluntness, though Lily finds it hilarious.

"Well, good for her," she says conspiratorially in my direction. "Of course, her brother will be dropping in shortly, so I'm going to say well done to both of you now, and then go and sit over there, where I shall lock my lips."

Lucius says nothing but looks at me with a dark grin forming across his face. He's going to enjoy the impending confrontation with my big brother; he looks positively wicked over the mere anticipation of it.

As Lily turns around to sit down, said big brother walks into my kitchen to find Lucius wrapped around my body and his wife looking up at the ceiling as though she hasn't seen anything. I bite my cheek to stop myself from laughing over her pretending to count the beams that are crisscrossing above her, even theatrically pointing to each one as she mouths each number.

"Morn..." Cameron begins, but then stops and frowns

when he spies Lucius enveloping me like a snake. Lucius merely stares back at him with no hint of moving. For a moment or two, Cameron doesn't appear to be sure of what to do first. I can't tell what he's thinking other than his questioning what his very own eyes are showing him.

"Lucius Hastings?" he asks, sounding completely dumbfounded over his being here in the flesh, right inside of his little sister's kitchen.

"Cameron Carter," Lucius replies formally, releasing me for a moment before holding his hand out to shake Cameron's, looking totally unfazed by my brother's presence. He is quick to resume his protective hold, as if silently telling me he is not going to let anyone give me trouble over this. If they do, he'll be ready for them. Thankfully, Cameron shakes his hand before walking over to Lily and kissing the top of her head.

"No need to worry, dear," he says to her quietly, "you can stop pretending this isn't awkward."

"Oh, thank God, cos it totally is, isn't it?" she says bluntly, though she does manage to break the tension. "So, how do you two know each other? We know our lovely Hels doesn't frequent places for random hookups…which is totally fine if you do, by the way."

"Oh, Helena and I go *way* back," Lucius answers for us, "don't we, Topolina?"

I simply nod nervously before continuing to make drinks for everyone.

"Sure, sure," Lily mutters to herself. "Gives me little to no information at all, but I like the nickname and all."

She makes me giggle and I even see Lucius crack a smile.

Lily is hard not to like, or love, especially in my brother's case. He's usually all over her, but at the moment, he still appears to be in shock.

"So, when did this all happen?" Cameron gestures over to us and I feel Lucius tightening his grip all over me again.

"About fourteen years ago," Lucius answers firmly. "Unfortunately, a few people got in the way of us. But then, you know that more than anyone."

"Ourselves included," I interject to try and dissipate the tension that is beginning to form between these two alpha males. Lily looks confused but decides to remain silent. "Actually, I was wondering if Cameron and I could have a quick chat alone?"

Everyone looks at me in surprise over my new-found confidence, but Lily soon stands.

"Sure," she answers cheerfully. "Mr Tall, Dark, and Brooding can come with me and chinwag about neutral topics while you two have a heart-to-heart chat."

She walks toward the living room with a cup of tea that I hand her, not even waiting for Lucius to respond. Lucius looks at me for a few moments, as if questioning my request, but when I eye him back to show that I'm fine, that I am strong enough to face my brother, he kisses me on the lips before giving Cameron a predatory glance. He then walks over to join Lily in the other room.

When he's safely exited the kitchen, I close the door on them, feeling a little bad for Lily having to try and chit-chat with Lucius. He's most likely going to put up his hard, chilling exterior, knowing that I'm about to confront my brother without him.

THE DEVIL

Lucius

As soon as I leave the kitchen, I make my way upstairs to put on some decent clothes so I can look a little more presentable for Cameron's new wife. I think I've made my point; I no longer need to sit half-naked in front of anyone who isn't Helena. When I finally return to the living room, she motions toward my coffee which is still sitting on the small wooden table in the middle of the room. Smiling politely, I sit back with the cup in hand, but make no attempt to converse. She seems nice enough, but I'm on edge over Helena deciding to have this conversation with her brother without me. I am more than aware of her strength, but after everything, I am no longer sure that she is.

It's not long, however, before I feel Lily's eyes on me. Never one to ignore confrontation, I glance up to meet them. At first, she jumps, which isn't an unusual reaction to one of my frosty glares. It happens frequently.

"Sorry, but I'm sure I've heard of your name before?" she says to me over the rim of her cup.

"Is that a question or a statement?" I ask with a sigh.

She smiles and flaps her hand, silently telling me to forget about it, which only makes me feel like a complete asshole. Normally, this doesn't bother me, but she was there for my Topolina when I wasn't. For that alone, she has earned my respect.

"I'm quite well known in your husband's line of work," I offer. "I'm a lawyer and I'm currently doing some deals with his company."

"No…" she says, thinking about it, "no, that's not it. I work in education so have nothing to do with his line of work. Between you and me, my mind switches off whenever he and Nate begin talking shop."

I smile tightly but I like her. She's very open, if not a little too chatty and perky. I also know she was the one who finally gave Helena the push to leave Evan.

"Weren't you Meri's sort of stepbrother for a few years?" she asks. "Specifically, when Helena went to stay with her?" My facial expression confirms her suspicions. "You're the guy who pissed Cam off at that wedding, aren't you?"

"What can I say? I've always been a bit of an asshole," I reply with a smile. "He's not still going on about that is he?"

"I hope not," she laughs, "that would be one hell of a grudge to bear after all these years. I don't do sulking; he knows that all too well."

"Sounds like you're good for him," I murmur before sipping at my drink slowly. "Not what I'd imagined for someone like him, but definitely a step up."

"Thank you?" she questions my compliment. "But I'm guessing you've never been on friendly terms with Cam?"

"To be honest, I've not had a lot to do with him or any of Helena's close family. However, I am with Helena now and I have no intention of leaving her. If anyone has a problem with that, then I shall let them know how little I care about their opinion."

She studies me for a moment, but I can't read her expression. I don't question it, just leave her to let her take in what I've just said.

"Good," she finally announces. She stares right back at me with a serious expression when I gift her with a questioning frown. "I'll be straight with you because I always am with people. Helena has been through a really shitty time, as you may well be aware. I'm pretty sure she had given up on life outside of Jess, but if you are as committed as I hope you are, I'm glad."

"I'm impressed, Mrs Carter," I tell her with a hint of a smile, for she's managed to make me like her, if only a little. "Most people find me intimidating, but you don't seem to be afraid to say anything to me."

"Oh, you are definitely intimidating, but I've come across many intimidating types in my life. My husband being one of them."

"And Evan?" I hold her gaze and begin to wonder if I've overstepped the mark by bringing up his name after what he did to her. "*You* were responsible for that piece of shit being put away, were you not?"

"Partly," she replies before swallowing hard.

"I apologize if that was too personal," I reply with genuine remorse. "I didn't mean to-"

"It's ok," she sighs, "hell, I think I was lucky. There's no denying Helena had the worst deal out of all this, not that she's ever said anything to me, or the men in her family, but her mother and Meri have hinted at such. Plus..." She trails off before holding up her hand to reveal what looks like an old cigarette burn. "I think we have matching scars."

I stare at the offending mark on her otherwise unmarred skin, which is slightly tanned but not by much. My jaw clenches when I think about the asshole branding her. It gives me an uneasy feeling that makes me think of where I came from; of the man who had destroyed my mother at the same time as creating me. My hands have balled into fists, but I try and remain calm in front of Lily. She's been a fighter and doesn't deserve to see me losing my shit.

Helena

As I pace back and forth across my small kitchen, my brother remains still. He simply continues to watch me in silence, but with concern written all over his face. I've never tried to confront him before, nor have I asked to speak with him alone since he decided I was all but dead to him. However, after last night, the time has come to start fighting back.

"What do you want to say to me, Helena?" he finally asks, sounding calm, but with a hint of anxiety in his voice. He hasn't seen me this animated in years, not since we were barely adults.

"Eleven or so years ago, Lucius contacted you about me, did he not?" I finally stand still to ask him this, wanting to look him straight in the eye for the truth. He looks to the floor and sighs with defeat, knowing I won't like the answer.

"He did," he admits. "I told him to back off because I thought that's what was best at the time. Had I known what Evan would turn out to be, I would not have been so hasty."

"But you never approved of my marrying Evan, so why would you tell Lucius otherwise?" I ask with my brow furrowed in confusion.

"He seemed the lesser of two evils, Hels," he admits with a

shameful expression. "You gotta understand, you had just come back from Spain, seemingly happy with Evan. I thought you'd reconciled while he was out there with you. I didn't realize it was all an act to try and convince yourself that he meant more to you than he did. When Lucius called, I thought you'd finally gotten over him, that Evan was the one who had made you happy again."

"I appreciate that, Cameron, but I don't appreciate the fact that you *never* told me about it," I say boldly. "I am your sister and whether you like me or not, you cannot seriously believe you have the right to speak for me."

"What do you mean, *'If I like you or not'*?" He jumps to his feet defensively before walking over to me. "Helena, I have been angry with you, but I have always loved you."

Tears well in my eyes as I shake my head at him, unable to absorb all the emotion that his statement just evoked from me.

"You've been punishing me for years, Cameron, how can I possibly think that you love me? We were so close, and then you…you just pretended like I didn't exist, that I was the enemy!"

"You're right, we were close, so close, and we went through everything with Dad and Mom, so when you let that guy get away with what he did to you and me, I felt like I didn't know who you were anymore. By the time I began to get over it, you'd gone, Helena; the girl who was my little sister was gone. I have mourned the loss of my little sister every day since the moment we found that scumbag feeling up Amanda on our childhood couch."

"Then why didn't you fight to find me again?" I whimper. I've been holding this in for years and now I can't stop.

"What do you want me to say, Helena? That I'm an awful person? The worst big brother in the world?"

"I wanted you to *see* me, to rescue me," I shout through my tears. "You have always galloped in to rescue people, even though half the time they didn't want you to, but the one person who was desperate for you to rescue her, you turned your back on."

"Helena," he whispers, now with tears in his eyes too. A few moments pass before he lunges for me so we can hold onto one another for support. "I am so sorry, I just…I fucked up! I should have fought harder to stop you from marrying him, I should have stepped in when I saw how lost you were, and I should have gotten over myself when he betrayed both of us. Helena, I.Am.Sorry."

Just as I have been waiting years for Lucius to finally admit his love for me, I have also been waiting years for my big brother, my once-upon-a-time best friend, to recognize how unfair he was on me. To admit that he condemned me when he should have been trying to save me. And now I have a choice - do I hold onto my anger? Or do I forgive and forget?

"I hope you know that I never sided with anyone over you, Cameron," I sigh while hidden inside of his arms. "I had to do what I thought was best for Jess. Evan is the father of my child and at the time, I thought she would need him. It was never about taking sides for me."

He pulls back and takes hold of my hands with an expression of extreme sorrow and guilt. His apology is genuine, albeit a little late.

"I mean it, I'm so sorry, Helena," he says quietly, "and I understand if you can never forgive me. Though, I wish you would. Seeing you as the woman you used to be, I'd give anything to have you back in my life. Even if I'm the one who has been stubbornly pushing you away."

"I'm willing to forgive you, Cameron, but it will take a while to trust that you'll be there for me no matter what."

To be honest, had he known the full story and still treated me as he did, there would be no forgiveness. But he's not the only stubborn Carter in the family; I have, and still do, refuse to air everything out in the open. I just want to forget and move on. Evan has been *my* pain, *my* experience, so it's my choice to leave him in the past.

"I understand, but know I am going to fight to earn back that trust," he says, "fight as I should have from the very beginning."

We pull back and smile uncomfortably at one another. The door creaks open, and Lucius is standing there, waiting for me. I smile, knowing that I should be thankful for the privacy he did manage to give me. Backing off must have taken a lot of willpower on his part.

"We good here?" he asks, looking directly at me.

"That depends," Cameron says, smiling at me with reassurance before turning to face Lucius head-on. "Are you serious about my sister?"

"I have always been serious about your sister," he says with determination in his voice before looking at me with a shy smile. "I was just a little young and stupid before."

He walks over to claim me back by putting his arm around my shoulders in a protective manner, making me feel safe.

"Glad to see you have some clothes on," Cameron says. "Where's my wife? Haven't scared her off have you, Hastings?"

"I'm not sure the Hun army could scare that one off; I'm

impressed, Carter. Your taste in women is infinitely more sophisticated than it once was."

For a moment, it almost looks like they smile at one another, which stupidly makes me feel warm on the inside.

"Think we better leave them to it," Lily says when she suddenly appears from out of nowhere and wiggles her eyebrows at me. "Come on, lover!" she calls over to Cameron and he practically starts salivating before following her out like a little puppy.

When they leave, Lucius looks at me in such a way, I tense up and brace myself for what he's about to say.

"I want to see," he says, "I want to see all the places he has marked you."

"Why?" I utter with sadness and humiliation. "What possible good will that do apart from reminding you that I am damaged goods?"

"Don't you fucking dare say that!" he snaps. "I want to know what I'm up against because when I meet that motherfucker, he's going to pay for every time he hurt you."

"Lucius, please, don't try and seek retribution," I beg. "I don't want anything to happen to you; I've only just got you back."

"Topolina," he sighs, pushing a strand of hair behind my ear, "I have a reputation for more than just being a good lawyer. You don't have to worry about me in that department."

He kisses me gently on my forehead and I worry about what he has planned. Though, perhaps it's best if I don't know.

Chapter 31

Helena

It's Wednesday night and I've been staying at Lucius' apartment all week. He needs to be closer to his office and refuses to let me stay in the house alone. I had shown him the cigarette burns, six in total, as well as how my left little finger isn't straight anymore. The years of cuts and bruises have thankfully healed over the years. The scars on the inside, however, will never completely disappear. Though, I'm hoping Lucius will help me try to make them as small as they can be. For that reason, I have decided not to put off the conversation about my pregnancy a moment longer. Sitting at the dining room table after a delicious meal, I brace myself for the talk I'm about to have with him.

"Speak," Lucius says as I shuffle around in my seat. I smile over his ability to read me like a book.

"Hmm...Evan wasn't the only possibility of being Jess' father when I found out I was pregnant," I blurt without even looking at him. When I eventually do, his expression is unchanged, but he leans slowly back into his chair, readying himself for what's to come.

"Go on," he says calmly.

"It was a couple of months after I came back from Spain when I found out." I look up at him to see if he's realized what I'm trying to say. I can see from his clenched jaw and tight lips, he has. He hisses his wine through his teeth, and I know that's not a good sign. "I had used protection with both of you, so I couldn't be sure who the father was."

"What are you trying to say, Helena?" he asks with an undercurrent of rage running through his voice.

"My mother was with me when I found out about Jess, and she rang Dad who then rang Evan, naturally assuming it was his," I explain. "They were both there when I got home. Evan was thrilled and said he would marry me, but I told them there and then, Lucius, I told them that you might also be the father. Evan said as soon as Jess was born, they would test her DNA and if she belonged to him, he would marry me. Dad said if I didn't marry him, I would be on my own."

I look up to see Lucius gripping onto his glass a little too tightly for comfort, his face remaining clenched, dark, and ominous.

"Did it ever occur to you to speak to me?" he asks, sounding almost too calm.

"I was going to," I tell him, swallowing a lump of emotion when I think back to that day.

"But?" he growls impatiently.

"But he told me you had met someone, that it was serious, and I shouldn't upset things until I knew for certain. Lucius, I would never have told Evan if it had been up to me," I rush out, "my whole life had been turned upside down and I had been given minutes to think about it before people started making decisions for me. I was confused, heartbroken, and being coerced into marrying someone I didn't love."

"Did you love me?" he asks, and I nod slowly with tears now running down my face. "Yet you decided to keep me in the dark?"

"I know and I'm sorry. I was young and in love with someone who had seemingly moved on after breaking my heart for the second time. I didn't know how to tell you. Do you think I would still make the same choices now?" He merely shrugs his shoulders, frustrating me beyond words. "Jesus, Lucius, it's *why* I am telling you now!"

"I take it the DNA test showed Evan to be the biological father?" he asks.

"Yes, Evan brought the letter around to show us; I think I still have it in Jess' baby things," I tell him with a sad sigh.

"Good," he says; the one word feeling akin to a knife being inserted directly through my heart. "I think it might be best if you stay in the guest bedroom tonight."

I stare at him, feeling completely gutted by his reaction, but he merely gets up and turns to walk back into his room. He then slams the door, the sound making me jump in my seat. With nothing else to do other than sit here and cry with disappointment, I begin to clear up robotically, trying to ignore the stupid tears gushing down my cheeks. My shell has become a little emptier again.

In the morning, I begin to pack up my bag and then check

the time to see if it is too early to call Cameron so I can tell him I'll be a little late for work today. I need to go home. I've already spent years in a toxic environment full of hate; I can't do it anymore.

When I walk out into the living room, Lucius is already dressed for work and putting on his coat. He notices me and my packed bag and laughs.

"Where are you going, Topolina?" he asks with a familiar smug expression. "You running out on me again?"

"I'm not running anywhere, Lucius," I reply with confidence and formality. "I'm merely going home."

"Did you not expect me to react the way that I did? Did you not expect me to be angry with the woman who claimed to love me, yet didn't trust me enough to tell me about a potential baby?" he says as he begins walking toward me. He lifts my chin to look into his eyes, but I pull away. "You knew I would be upset," he whispers.

"I knew you would have been angry back then too," I explain, "it's part of the reason I didn't tell you. You wouldn't have wanted a child; you made that clear last night."

"That wasn't your choice to make," he says firmly, "you should have told me and let me decide."

"I couldn't have taken it if I had told you and you had pushed me and your unborn child away," I argue. "But I swore to Jess, when she was born, that if you were her father, I was going to track you down and make you have some part in her life. She is the most important thing to me, Lucius, and if you can't accept that, then this is one huge mistake."

"You never gave me the option to push you away, you took

that away when you decided to keep quiet about it," he says, and I can see the hurt and anger swimming in his eyes.

I sigh and begin to walk toward the door, but just before I reach the handle, he takes hold of my hand and pulls me back, placing his forehead against mine.

"You fucking kill me, woman," he pushes out through clenched teeth, "why couldn't you have just told me how you felt on that boat?"

"Because you were *the* Lucius Hastings, the cold-hearted asshole who placed bets on taking away a girl's virginity." He looks at me, not realizing I knew that's why his whole chase began. Merial had received a text from Eric not long after I had returned home; he'd sounded bitter. I guess they didn't stay friends after that. "I thought I was just a game to you; I was never meant to fall for you."

He kisses me softly on the lips and pulls me into a hug that feels warm and tender.

"Please don't let me go, Lucius," I beg, "I fucked up eleven years ago, but it doesn't mean I don't love you now."

He soothes me while I cry against his huge frame, kissing my head from time to time. I lose track of how long we stand like this, but I really don't care. Cameron was right when he said I appreciate the things other people take for granted; being able to hug your soulmate is one of those things. He wipes away my tears with his thumbs, then looks at me with a smile; a smile that tells me I'm off the hook, and my heart can begin beating again.

"Topolina," he sighs, "if Jess is anything like you, I will love her just as much. You're in my blood now, I can't get rid of you."

"Gee, thanks," I cry and laugh at the same time. "Just what a girl wants to hear from the man she's in love with."

"Do you wanna go and put your little packed bag in my room?" he teases with a mock pout, to which I nod my head. "Wanna tell your brother you'll be late for work?"

He smiles seductively and I nod slowly, already walking into his room and positioning myself on the bed for him.

"Take off your clothes," he orders, jutting out his chin toward me. He takes great delight in me slowly stripping before him. I'm not trying to be seductive, but the authority in his voice has me feeling a little nervous, but excited too. He grabs a chair from beneath the window and pulls it noisily to the foot of the bed before sitting on it. Meanwhile, I sit completely naked on his bed, awaiting his next instruction. He smiles approvingly and begins to unbuckle his belt.

"Open your legs for me, Helena," he utters. I do as he says, feeling totally exposed and vulnerable, but I trust him completely. "Now stroke those beautiful breasts of yours," he orders as he unzips himself to release his erection.

I begin to gently stroke my fingertips over my skin and then pinch at my nipples. By this point, he is also stroking himself, slowly but with enough force to make his cock look as though it's pulsing.

When he can no longer stand just watching, he grabs hold of my legs and pulls me to the edge of the bed. He begins to lap between my sex, using the tip of his tongue to play with me, to tease me to the point where I'm close to releasing. However, he then pulls away, leaving me to feel beyond frustrated.

"You'll come when I want you to come, Topolina," he

whispers against my opening.

"Are you ever going to let me?" I moan.

"The answer to that question is pending." He laughs wickedly before returning to his kind of torture.

After bringing me to the brink several times, only to withdraw when he knows I could easily let go, he stands above me and rubs his cock hard and slow for a good few minutes, watching me play with my nipples so they are red and erect.

"Lie back," he says quietly, and as soon as I do as he commands, he thrusts himself into me, feeling hard but so deliciously pleasurable too. He lifts my hips to meet him, then begins to pull in and out of me slowly but still with force. As I bite my lip to tease him, he smirks and picks up the pace of his movements, using his thumb to rub over my clit. My orgasm is building but he can sense it, so pulls his thumb away to leave me wanting.

"Not yet," he says through his teeth, "I want you to earn it."

He pulls me up and wraps me around his waist so he can sit on the end of the bed while I straddle him. Now, I'm writhing on top of him while he uses my hips to control the speed of our movements. He's deep within me and I no longer need his thumb to build me up. Our breathing is fast and noisy, and my fingernails are digging deep into his shoulders to the point of breaking his skin. He takes a nipple into his mouth and bites hard, making me gasp, before sucking and nipping. His movements soon become jerky, so I know he is close.

"Now," he orders, and I finally let myself explode over him, all the while moaning into the crook of his neck. I feel him throb inside and he curses as he reaches his own pinnacle, after which, we sit, holding onto each other for what feels like a wonderfully long time.

"Do you love me?"

"You know I do, Lucius, I always have," I reply without hesitation, wiping away the sweat from his brow. "I love you."

He doesn't say it back, but smiles at me, looking genuinely happy with my answer.

Helena

Time seems to pass by quickly, living in our own little bubble of bliss. In public, Lucius maintains a protective but cold exterior, clutching onto his emotionless and ruthless reputation. When he comes to meetings at Medina, he is formal, polite, and indifferent, even to me. However, he always leaves a note on my desk that simply says, *Mine*.

Behind closed doors, he is passionate, intense, and belongs to me completely. We make love as well as fuck on virtually a daily basis, always with foreplay and always for mutual satisfaction. He has well and truly removed the kiddy gloves, and no longer treats me like a fragile doll. He is rough, powerful, and primal when it comes to sex, but at the same time, I know I am completely safe with him.

We have spoken very little about Jess, but now she is due home in less than a week, and I know we need to have a conversation about what our living arrangements are going to be like once she returns. I can't stay at his apartment, and he can't stay at the house during the week, and according to him, only seeing me at the weekend is not a viable option.

"So, what do you suggest, Lucius?" I sigh as we sit at the outside table together. "She has to come first for me, you know this."

"Can she stay with your parents once a week?" he suggests, and I can't help but smile over his childlike behavior.

"Maybe now and then, but not every week, no," I explain with an air of exasperation. "She's mine and I miss her. Look, maybe you should get to know her before we discuss living arrangements anyway. I can't just turn her life upside down as soon as she gets back. She doesn't even know you yet. Besides, she's already had to deal with a lot."

I look away guiltily, which he must notice, for I soon feel his hand reaching for mine, giving it a reassuring squeeze before leaning in closer.

"Ok, Topolina, you win," he says, then swallows hard, not really liking the outcome but accepting it anyway. "But remember, so have you. You deserve happiness too."

"I know. I'm sure you two will get along fine," I reply in a pitched voice and a slightly maniacal smile.

"Really?" he asks, having picked up on the fact that I don't exactly sound convincing.

"Honestly? I don't know. You two are a lot alike."

"Amazing, intelligent, and witty?"

"More like stubborn, volatile, and brooding," I correct him.

"That's it, we're doing it in the playhouse," he says with a devilish grin and begins walking over to the old Wendy house which I put together years ago. "Come, Topolina."

THE DEVIL

He's already whipped off his t-shirt. Thank God I don't have any neighbors for a good few miles.

Chapter 32

Helena

"Stop pacing, Topolina," Lucius sighs over my anxiety, which is coming out in spades all the while I wait for Jess to come home. "And stop chewing your nails."

"Sorry," I mumble, not really meaning it. "This is kind of a big thing to me."

"Really?" he says sarcastically while sitting back casually in one of my armchairs that is far too girly for his massive, masculine frame. "You're hiding it so well!"

He's gifted with a fake smile and a narrowing of my eyes. This is a *huge* deal! The love of my life is about to meet my daughter; what if they really hate each other?

"Mom!" I hear Jess yell from the front door, and I freeze on the spot.

Initially, I look at Lucius, who merely raises an eyebrow, but then I run through the house like an excited kid to greet my girl. When I finally lay my eyes on her beautiful little face, with her hair tied up in a French braid, looking so much older than I remember her being, I grab hold of her as tight as I can.

"Mom, I can't breathe!" she mumbles against my chest, so I reluctantly let go.

"Sorry, Baby Girl, but I've missed you so much!" I kiss her face all over while the sting of tears attacks my eyes. She groans over my over-the-top reaction to her homecoming, but I ignore it. This is every mom's right and I'm not wasting a moment of it.

Before I'm done hugging my munchkin to the point of her pushing me away, I hear the sound of Lucius clearing his throat dramatically from behind me, causing Jess to step back and frown at me.

"Sorry, I thought the poor girl needed a swift rescue," he says with a shy smile on his face. She cranes her neck to look at him more closely, her brow still scrunched up with confusion as to who this strange new man is.

"I'm Lucius," he says as he offers his hand out to Jess. She slowly accepts it before they shake.

"Jess," she returns confidently. An awkward silence follows before both sets of eyes fall on me for an explanation.

"Er...Jess, this is Lucius. We've known each other a long time and recently...well, recently..." I trail off at the same time as I begin scratching my head uncomfortably. *God, I should have rehearsed this beforehand!*

"Your mother is trying to explain, very badly I might add, that we are seeing each other," he cuts in.

Jess looks stunned for a moment, so I hold my breath in anticipation of her impending reaction. She says nothing for a moment or two. Instead, she drops her things on the floor and walks over to where he is standing so she can study him more closely. She shows no sign of intimidation or fear while he stands before her, confidently and with his hands in his pockets. She narrows her eyes, and he almost immediately returns the action, making her smile with her teeth on show.

"Ok," is all she eventually says, to which I drop my mouth open and flap my arms up in the air.

"*Ok*?! Is that it?" I ask, sounding completely gobsmacked.

"*Ok*, as in, I'm *Ok* with that. It's about time you started seeing somebody else, and if he treats us better than Dad did, then I'm *Ok* with it."

"Oh, my God, child! I've been chewing my fingers off worrying about how to tell you about it and you just say '*Ok*'? Oh, my life!"

"Don't chew your nails, Mom," she says before heading into the kitchen, "it's a filthy habit."

Lucius smirks at my cheeky little pre-teen before mouthing 'Told you'. We then follow her into the kitchen where I find her already raiding the cupboards for snacks.

"Well, I'm glad you approve, munchkin," I tell her with relief at the same time as messing up her hair. "You got a couple of letters while you were away; mostly junk mail, I'm afraid." I hand her the three letters that she's already gotten at the tender age of eleven. "What did you do at camp then?"

She looks at each letter in detail but it's the final one that catches her eye.

"Oh, nothing much," she utters, completely disinterested in anything that isn't the letter she's holding. "I'm just going to the bathroom," she says, taking it with her.

THE DEVIL

"She's gone for a month and apparently, she's done nothing?" I huff to Lucius as soon as she's wandered out of the room.

"I thought that was a kid's standard response to everything? It's pretty much all you would have got from me at that age," he says as I get up to walk over to where he's leaning against the sink. "She seems cool though. Better yet, she says she's fine with us," he says cheekily as he begins to cage me between his arms. He raises his brow suggestively before leaning in to kiss me, which I am more than ready to give in to, now that I've finally calmed down. However, the sound of Jess running ungracefully down the stairs prompts him to instantly push back.

"Jess?" I ask, sounding worried because her eyes are now wet and she's wearing a huge scowl on her face. "What's wrong, baby girl? You look like someone just ran over your puppy?"

"Yeah, something's wrong!" she screams at me. I glance at Lucius who looks equally confused. "I knew it! I damn well knew it!" she cries, letting tears finally fall and stream down her cheeks.

"Jess, whatever it is, we can sort it. Tell me what's wrong so I can help you," I beg with my heart thumping at double speed for fear of what has caused her to look so angry and upset. What the hell was in that letter?

"You can help me by telling me who my father is!"

She slams a piece of paper down onto the counter in front of me. Lucius and I both tentatively look down, desperate to know what could possibly be written on it to have ignited such a reaction from her. After casting my eyes over the printed words, I realize it's a DNA test result, much like the one Evan had brought to my family home all those years ago. However, this one says something else entirely; it clearly states that Evan Michael Stone cannot possibly be the biological father of Jessica Elena Stone.

"W-what is this, Jess?" I stutter, with the feeling of bile climbing up my throat, getting ready to be expelled from my body in a dramatic fashion.

"Ever since I found out what D... I mean whoever he is, did to Aunt Lily, I thought to myself he can't be my dad; he just can't be. I don't want him to be. He's never liked me, never been nice to me; I'm just an inconvenience!"

Even though there are bigger things at stake here, I still can't help feeling a stab of pain and guilt over how he made her feel; what I failed to protect her from. I have given everything to Jess, even my life, but I still didn't protect her as a mother should.

"Billy and I talked about it and he showed me this website for DNA testing. At first, I thought it was stupid, but when I went to Grandma's before camp, I saw his stuff and thought, why the hell not?" she says, snapping me back to the here and now. "I took some hair from his comb, as well as his toothbrush, anything that might have some form of DNA on it, and sent them all off to be tested. I even used my birthday money to pay for it, and this...*this*," she says slapping the piece of the paper with venom, "is the result! You're a liar!"

I have no words, nothing to articulate the sheer magnitude of this situation or my feelings over it. Instead, I end up covering my mouth with my hands and shaking my head while I try to take it all in. Shock is an understatement, and before I know it, I'm retching into the sink, causing tears to blur my vision. When I stand to face her again, I try to reach for her hand, but she instantly pulls back.

"Don't touch me! Tell me who he is, Helena!"

She spits out my Christian name with such disgust, it has me feeling just as dirty as I did when I first found out I was expecting. I try to take deep breaths to steady my nerves, but I can't control it, and my head soon starts to feel dizzy. I reach back to steady myself, but my hand collides with a wall of muscle. Lucius is standing right behind me, so I slowly turn around to face him. We both know there is only one answer to my little girl's question, but when our eyes meet, he looks at me in such a way, I know he's holding back a rage that is begging to be let loose. His knuckles have blanched white from where he is gripping the kitchen worktop, and his eyes have turned a darker shade of blue.

"Please tell me you know who he is, Mother. You can't have been that much of a slut!"

Her words are like a slap to the face, but I know she is hurting, so I decide to let her venomous words slide. I have to be her mom and deal with one crisis at a time. The trouble is, I have no idea how to deal with this crisis; I don't even know where to start!

"I know," I eventually murmur, but then I look at Lucius again, and he shakes his head at me. I open my mouth to go on, but he storms out of the house, grabbing his keys as he does so.

"Jess, I swear to you, I know who he is, but I need to talk to him first," I try to reassure her, my words rushing out because I know I need to try and stop Lucius before he shuts me out of his life...*again*. "Believe me, baby girl, this is just as big a shock for me as it is for you."

She says nothing, just looks at me like I'm a monster before storming upstairs. Though it's hard to know she's hating me, I breathe a little easier, knowing that at least she is contained and I'm not at risk of her disappearing, unlike the angry hulk of a man who's just headed out the front door. With that in mind, I run outside to try and catch Lucius, only to see him opening up his car door so he can make a quick getaway. I shout for him, and he stops, looks at me, then slams the door closed again.

"You fucking lied to me, Helena," he growls at the same time as stomping up to me, with each footstep sounding angrier than the last. "You lied to me about my own child! What the fuck is that?"

"Please, Lucius, I didn't know! I had a letter saying Evan was ninety-nine point whatever it was, her father. My dad saw it too. Do you really think I would have chosen a life with him over you if I knew this was the truth?"

He looks at me intensely for a moment or two, and I begin to believe that he is seeing sense and listening to me. But then the shutters come down, right there inside of his eyes, and I know I've lost him. He proves as much when he turns around and begins storming away from me.

"I don't fucking care," he shouts over his shoulder. "Stay the fuck away from me!"

When he throws himself into his car, he revs the engine a few times before wheel-spinning off down the gravel road. I hear the screech of his brakes when he hits the end of the road and then speeds off again.

I've lost him.

"Fuck!" I whisper shout to myself, gasping for breath as an uncomfortable, panic-induced heat spreads all over me. "This can't be happening!"

As much as I want to run after him, I need to see to my Jess first; she is my main priority. I gallop back inside and leap up the stairs, two at a time, but when I burst into her room, it's empty. *Shit!* In a blind panic, I check all the rooms of the house, shouting out her name as I go along. It's only when I get outside that I notice her bike is missing. She's gone too.

She must have cycled down the river path, which means I can't track her down in my car. Besides, I know where she's going, so, reluctantly, I concede to the fact that I'm going to have to wait until they eventually call me.

Helena

I'm sitting alone in the garden when I finally get the phone call from my sister-in-law, still sobbing into an undrunk glass of wine.

"Hello," I sniff into the phone, "please tell me she's alright."

"She's fine, Hels," Lily says quietly, as though Jess is close by. "She's very angry, but she's safe. What the hell happened? Did you guys fight or something?"

I shake my head silently as the sobs cause my shoulders to shudder.

"Evan's not..." I begin but can't manage to get the words out.

"Evan?! What's he done now? He's not there with you, is he?" Lily asks in a panic-stricken voice. At her outcry, a more masculine voice suddenly takes over, with his voice full of fear and anger.

"Where the hell is Evan? Helena, you tell me right now or

so help me-"

"For fuck's sake, Evan isn't here!" I cry, cutting Cameron off before he can go on any more about the man who caused all of this. "Hopefully, he's dead in a ditch somewhere." I've never meant those words more, after everything he's said and done, this is the final thing that would push me to homicide. "Evan isn't Jess' father; she did a DNA test without me knowing and now she's demanding to find out who he is."

"Fuck!" Cameron eventually gasps down the phone. "I'm coming over."

When Cameron finally turns up, I end up blurting everything out. Every detail between Spain, the pregnancy, not knowing who the father was, DNA tests, right up to Lucius storming out of here. The only thing I leave out is just how bad my marriage was. That's not important right now; Jess is the crucial thing in all of this, and I need everyone to remember that.

Cameron has remained quiet and pensive throughout, all while holding my hand in a comforting and reassuring way. If nothing else, I finally have my brother again.

"Helena, we will fix this," he says determinedly. "I'm not going to let that fucker screw up anything else. Do you still have the DNA results that Evan gave to you when Jess was a baby?"

"Of course, I kept it with all her baby things."

"Good," he declares, sounding like his role as CEO of Medina Technologies. "You're going to get it and take it over to Lucius right now... Actually, maybe give him half an hour or so."

"Why the hell should I?" I cry in outrage, suddenly feeling anger surging up from the very depths of my being; how dare Lucius sit on his pedestal of judgment?! "Whatever he thinks of me, he's pretty much just rejected Jess and accused me of being a completely heinous bitch. How could he think I would do this on purpose?"

"Hels, I-" Cam says, putting his hands up in a defensive stance, but I'm on a roll.

"I'm so fed up with everyone accusing me of being some kind of slut, even my own daughter! I did the right thing, I used protection, I agreed to a DNA test, and I married who I thought was her father. I gave up my life, my happiness, and I'm still the damn villain!"

"Calm down-"

"No! Did anyone think less of you or Nate when you two slept about? No! Because you're men and that's what men are supposed to do. Us mere little women are supposed to wear chastity rings and save ourselves for our husbands so we can be good little wives."

"Woah!" Cameron cries, grabbing hold of my shoulders to stop my angry pacing and ranting. "Where the hell is all this coming from, Hels? I just meant that perhaps you need to see it from his point of view…if only for a moment. As much as I think the guy's still a cocky little fucker, he has just found out he is a father. Not only that, but he's also the father of a near-on adolescent."

His words finally manage to make me take a moment to breathe. Standing still, I try to do as he says and think about it, even though I am physically shaking with rage. Unfortunately, I'm still breathing fiercely, as if I'm a bull in a fighter's ring, getting ready to go to war, so Cam tries again.

"He has just been told that everything to do with his child

was taken away from him, without him even knowing about it," Cameron says gently, placing his hands affectionately on each of my shivering arms. "This is not your fault, but at the moment, he doesn't know that. He can only see the shit storm before him."

"Damn it," I whisper begrudgingly, "don't come over here being all reasonable about him now."

He simply smiles and gives me one of those brotherly hugs I've been missing for all these years.

"Don't worry," he says as he holds onto me, "you can get back at me soon when I'm sleep deprived and going all goo goo over *my* baby."

"What?!" I gasp with a huge smile on my face. "You mean Lily's…?"

He nods, looking beyond smitten over the news.

"Don't mention it to anyone, even Lily. She's still worried about how much alcohol she consumed at our wedding," he laughs.

"Oh, God, congratulations, you big idiot!" I've started crying again, but at least they're happy tears. "Great, I'm going to look like an even bigger shitty mother to Dad now. You've gone and done it the *conventional* way."

"Oh, Hels, stop! I always thought you were so amazing at looking after Jess as well as you have, especially under such difficult circumstances. She's a great kid and that's all on you, no one else. Not Evan, not Lucius, you!"

"I guess," I grumble with a sullen shrug. "I just wish I could make this all go away. Seriously, it's been going on for years."

"Trust me," he says with confidence, "when Lily and I are run ragged, chasing a toddler around, you and Jess will be looking on smugly, with or without Lucius Hastings. Now, go and get that letter so you can prove to the bastard that you were just as deceived as he was."

Lucius

Hours after storming away from Helena's house that sits in the middle of nowhere, I find myself slumping in front of my living room window that overlooks the city, brooding over the motherfucker of a situation I've just found myself in. The only thing stopping me from ripping my apartment to shit is the burn of liquor I'm currently pouring down my throat. I'm trying to feel the buzz of the alcohol, but I'm so mad, I can't get past it. The lights flicker during rush hour traffic, and I wonder what my Topolina is doing right now. I don't know who I'm angrier with at this moment in time; all I can see is red-hot rage in front of me.

I never wanted children; they seem like too much responsibility for too little reward from what I have witnessed over the years. Every parent is flawed but somehow needs to show they are infallible to their light and joy, otherwise, they fuck them up. But to know that some asshole took my Helena away from me by taking my child at the same time is a major kick in the teeth. To add insult to injury, she never even trusted me to tell me about any of it, she just assumed Evan was the lesser of two evils. Showed what she fucking knew. I'm better off out of it. I've never pretended to be anything other than a self-centered asshole, so why let anyone think otherwise.

"Why are you here?" I growl from my position in front of

the window. "And how the fuck did you get in?"

I know it's her without even turning around to face the figure lingering by the door. I've always been able to sense when she is near, we're much too connected to not know when the other is within touching distance.

"You gave me a key when I stayed here, remember?" she says quietly, though she also sounds determined, resolute, and justified, not the apologetic, quivering mess I thought she'd be when she finally spoke to me. I smile into my glass, feeling a little proud of the fiery attitude I've encouraged her to bring back.

"Just one of the many mistakes I've made over the last few weeks," I reply cruelly.

"If you want to hate me and make me the cause of all your misery, I'm fine with that," she says with a voice that sounds ready to strike. "But like it or not, you have a daughter, and she is distraught right now. I've only dragged my ass over here for her sake. It takes two to make a baby, Lucius."

"She'll soon realize that life is full of disappointment," I reply coldly as I lift my glass to my lips, polishing off the last drops of liquor. "Just keeping it real for her."

"Your ability to not give a shit no-matter-what never fails to disappoint, Lucius," she says bitterly.

She takes a few steps forward before finally turning to face me. I look at her, she's still beautiful, even with her puffy red eyes, messy hair, and an expression of pure rage. She reminds me of her former self, and it fucking kills me.

"Here," she says, slapping a piece of paper on the table in front of me, "this is the paper copy of the results Evan gave to me when Jess was a newborn. It's dated, so you can see I haven't made it up or created it for your benefit. I was lied to, Lucius, just like you." She doesn't take her eyes away from my steely ones, instead, she stands tall and proud. "But unlike you, I had to live through abusive shit for years while I took care of our daughter. I was robbed of those years too, but I don't blame *you* for any of it. At least you got to live instead of just existing."

I take a glance at the paper but refuse to look at it properly; maybe I don't want to be proven wrong. I don't say anything, and I don't move, prompting her to narrow her eyes in disgust. She lets out a long sigh, looks to the ceiling in frustration, and begins to walk away.

"Where is she now?" I ask with a much softer voice. *Do I care?*

"She's with Lily and Cameron, so she's safe." She pauses for a response that never comes. "I'm going to leave her there until tomorrow evening; give her some space." Still, I stubbornly say nothing, which only exasperates her even more. "Look at the paper or not. I'm done explaining myself to self-important men who think they can look down their noses at me. Thanks for everything, Lucius, but especially for giving me Jess."

The only movement I make after that is a flinch of my tired muscles when she slams the door shut. Gone…again.

Helena

I take a deep breath as I walk into Lily and Cameron's house. It's late and Jess is already in bed, apparently exhausted from camp. However, I know it's more to do with the fact that she doesn't want to see me yet. I guess I need to make my peace with that for the moment. If I need to be the baddie for her, the one to blame, I can be that for now. But even so, I feel like the fallen woman walking into the pit of judgment all over again. Fortunately, however, when I enter their kitchen, it's just Mom, Lily, and Meri, three women who are on my side at least.

"Helena," Mom calls to me before grabbing me in a hug only a mom can give you. "Well, here we are again. You know you are stronger now; you can handle this, baby."

"I know, Mom-" I begin but she takes hold of my hands and cuts me off.

"No, wait, Helena, let me finish, please?" she says with her eyes becoming glazy, which only causes mine to do the same. "I've kept quiet for far too long. I tried to convince myself that it was to keep you safe and respect your wishes, but deep down, I knew it was cowardice. I've been so afraid of losing you, Helena, you and Jess."

"Mom, you've had your own heartache," I try to soothe her; I can never bear it when I see my mother cry, not since the day she was broken by my father's infidelity.

"I know, but I'm your mother," she says sadly, "and when I held you in my arms for the first time, I promised to protect you no matter what. I haven't kept that promise, Helena, and for that, I'm so sorry."

"Mom," I sigh to try and ward off a whimper that's caught in my throat. "We've both made mistakes as mothers, all of us do without meaning to. But knowing you're always here for me is enough, Mom, it's always been enough."

"You want to fight this alone, don't you, my brave girl?" she says with a proud smile.

"Y-yes, I think I do. I want to stand up for me and my daughter; to show Dad I don't need anyone else, least of all him. I can do this on my own…I *have* been doing this on my own. For far longer than he thinks."

"Then, I will hold my tongue, but know that I am on your side one hundred percent."

"Thanks, Mom," I whisper just before I wrap my arms around her shoulders and hold on tight.

"We're here for you too, Hels," Meri says as she stands to hug me after I've finally managed to force myself away from my mother.

"I'm trying so hard not to throw up right now; I know he told you," Lily whispers when she hugs me, and I laugh. "Remember to keep your head held high; you are not the bad guy here."

"So, who's waiting for me in the lion's den?" I ask with my nerves suddenly attacking me.

"Cam, Nate, and your father," my mom answers and I feel a sinking feeling inside of me, knowing my father has called upon the men of the family to try and kick me into submission once again. The man is delusional, but this time, I don't need his support or his approval. I've survived more than he knows; I can survive this.

"Helena? Is that you?" My father's voice travels through the house, and I brace myself. But this time, I am a grown woman, so I take a deep breath and walk in.

When I enter Cam's study, it feels like testosterone overload. The three men I grew up with are all sitting around looking like rulers of the world. I'm not really intimidated by Cam or Nate anymore, but my father is a different kettle of fish. He's always managed to make me feel small.

"So, we have quite the predicament here," Dad says to me with a look of pity, or perhaps disappointment; whatever it is, it's an attempt to shame me all over again. "What are we going to do about your daughter, Helena? She can't stay here forever."

"Cam, is it ok for Jess to stay over here tonight?" I ask, completely overriding my father.

"Sure, it's no problem at all," he says casually, looking quite confused as to why we're all gathered here to discuss Jess' lodgings for the night.

"There you are, Dad," I tell him confidently, "Jess will stay here tonight, and I will come and collect her in the morning. Good, are we done?"

"Dad, why did you call us all here?" Nate asks with a shrug of his shoulders when he turns to look at me.

"Now, hold on a minute," Dad says, holding up his hand as a signal for us all to stop and listen to him assert his authority over us 'kids', his favorite pastime. "This is a family matter, and it needs to be sorted. Perhaps we better tell everyone the whole story, Helena."

"Why? This is an issue for me and Jess to work through. It's of no one else's concern, apart from Lucius', maybe," I say matter of factly. "Cam already knows what happened, as do you and Mom, so I'm not entirely sure why we all need to gather around to discuss my sordid past."

"Lucius?" Nate pipes up, sounding utterly confused. "As in, Lucius *Hastings*?"

Cam tries to shake his head discreetly toward my little brother, but I merely release a sigh and decide to just go for it. After all, it's only Nate. Besides, I'm hoping my confidence and refusal to be sorry for anything gives Dad the message that I won't be manipulated again.

"When I found out I was pregnant, it wasn't just Evan who could have been the potential father, Lucius had also been a possibility. I had used protection with both, but obviously, one of them hadn't worked. Evan and I were not exclusive, but Dad seemed to think he was the better candidate. Therefore, when Mom told Dad I was pregnant, he went above me and called Evan."

"Fuck, you called him without Helena knowing?" Nate scoffs but instantly looks away again when Dad glares at him.

"Evan said he would marry me, but when I informed him of Lucius, he said he would do a DNA test when Jess was born. If she was his, he would marry me. When I brought her home, he produced a letter to confirm he was her biological father. Evan and Dad were over the moon, and I was threatened with being cast out if I didn't marry him. That sound about right, Dad?"

The whole room looks over at my father who begins shuffling uncomfortably on the spot; this is not going the way he had envisioned.

Lucius

I wasn't expecting to see Merial when I knocked on Cameron and Lily's door, but her disgusted face tells me she knows everything and is not impressed with me at all. I can't blame her, she's right to be ashamed of me, but I'm not going to bow down and tell her that.

"Well, well, well, public enemy number one has arrived!" She scowls while crossing her arms and leaning against the door frame. "What do you say, Lily? Do you really want slime in your house?" she calls over to Cameron's wife, who has just got up to invite me in.

"Careful, Merial," I warn, "bitch is such an ugly color on you." I walk in and nod politely at Lily, who I notice is looking a little green. "I apologize for barging in, Lily, but I believe my daughter is staying here and I'm hoping my girlfriend is here too."

I haven't called her that before now, but I'm hoping she's still going to be up for having the title.

"Are you sure that's what she is to you right now?" Lily asks with a non-judgmental smile. "They're both here, but Jess is sleeping. I think she's going to stay one more night. As for Helena, she's in Cameron's office with the rest of the family."

She gestures toward the door, behind which, I can hear a range of raised voices. I walk slowly to the door but do not attempt to knock or open it. I want to hear what's being said before I make an appearance. So, instead, I stand for a few minutes, eavesdropping on the conversation.

"You can go in, you know," Merial pipes up.

I do not bother to face her; I merely turn my head to the side and hold up my index finger to silence her. Fortunately, she heeds my warning and remains quiet.

Helena

"I thought Helena marrying the father of her child was for the best, yes," Dad says, lifting his chin in defiance. "At the time, I thought he was a more appropriate match for Helena, and marrying him would be better than letting her raise a baby by herself at the age of twenty."

"Whatever," I huff, "it turns out Evan was lying. Christ knows how he did it, but the letter he gave me must have been fake because Jess recently did her own DNA test, and guess what? Evan cannot be her biological father, which means…"

"Lucius Hastings is?" Nate bursts out. "I didn't even realize you guys were ever a thing. When did that happen?"

"I'm not sure Jess should know that, Helena," Dad butts in. "I mean the poor girl grew up with Evan and now she has to come to terms with being the offspring of someone like Lucius Hastings. The man's not known as 'The Devil' for nothing, his reputation is beyond shady. His uncle is believed to be the head of some criminal outfit in the city. I think it's best that you tell her you don't know who he is."

"Are you freaking kidding me, Dad?" Cam looks at my father like he's finally lost his marbles. "You can't keep that from her, or him; what if that was me or Nate?"

"It's not your decision though, is it, Dad?" I finally manage to push out through my lips with angry tears. "Just like it wasn't really up to you to tell Evan or push me into marrying him."

"I thought you loved him," he lies. God forbid he loses the respect of his precious sons. "It seemed like the perfect solution. How was I to know he would one day attack Lily?"

Cam tenses up at this point, but this is my battle. I don't need anyone to fight it for me.

"How can you say that? I told you at the time that I never loved him. I was deeply in love with Lucius and my decision to not tell him I was pregnant is the biggest regret of my life. Maybe if I had, this would have all been different, but that's my role in this whole shitshow."

"Helena, sweetheart-" he tries to say, but I'm not letting him have any of it.

"Knowing what he was capable of, have you never once wondered what it was like for me to be shacked up with Evan? A guy I didn't want to be with in the slightest. Can you understand what it was like to sign my life away when I was in love with Lucius? You saw how I reacted when he told me the results, you saw me run, you heard me throwing up, and yet you gave me no option but to marry him."

By this point, my father has turned silent, Mom is weeping, and Cam and Nate look a cross between angry and sad. But I'm not finished.

"Well, Daddy dearest, who was so smart, so looking out for me, so in my corner, on the night of our wedding he revealed his true colors. I was told in no uncertain terms that I was to behave the way he wanted me to, to accept his affairs, including turning a blind eye when Cam and I witnessed him groping Amanda on the family couch." All eyes move to look at Cam at this point and he sadly nods his confirmation. "And then…then…" I close my eyes as my voice becomes pitchy and I relive those awful nights in my head. "Then, I wasn't as lucky as Lily to get away." When I open my eyes, they are all looking at me with horrified expressions, except Mom, who already knew. "I wasn't lucky a lot of times during my marriage," I add quietly. "I have six cigarette scars; my finger is fucked and I have been beaten countless times over the years. But nothing, *nothing* was more soul destroying than knowing the man you were supposed to be with, is out there, not being with you."

"Helena…" Dad says in barely more than a whisper and

with tears beginning to fall.

"Enough!" a growl of a voice comes from the direction of the now open door.

"Lucius?" I gasp in surprise when I see him filling the door frame, dressed in his signature black suit. He's heard all of it now - every, last, sordid detail. The question is, is he here for me? Or against me?

The whole room stares at the intense-looking man and his intimidating glare. He walks slowly toward me, and I find myself staring down at the floor, feeling too afraid to meet his gaze. He crosses the room and cups my face, lifting my eyes to his, only so he can gently press his forehead against mine.

"I'm sorry," he whispers, "you don't ever have to look ashamed in front of me."

I cover his hands with mine as we stand together while he kisses me and holds onto me so tight, I finally feel like he will never let me go. Eventually, he pulls back to face the rest of my family while holding up the original DNA results for all to see.

"This is a fabricated document, plain as day to the trained eye," he says matter of factly. "Tell me, Mr Carter," he addresses my father, "were you, or were you not, a fraud investigator for the bank you worked for?"

My father turns a ghostly shade of pale and I begin to feel violently sick as the realization of what Lucius is suggesting sinks in.

"Seems to me, someone with your experience could have seen this was a fake a mile away," he says theatrically as he walks up close to him. "So, either you were pathetically piss poor at your job, or you totally fucked over your daughter, your granddaughter, and…" he pauses before leaning in extra close to my father with a menacing expression on his face, "…*me*."

"Lucius," Cam begins in an anxious tone of voice, but Lucius backs away, and instead, looks at me to make sure I've fully understood the full extent of what my father actually did all those years ago.

"You knew?" I gasp in disbelief. "You knew it was fake and went along with it? How could you do that to me?"

"Dad, what the fuck?!" Nate snaps.

"I-I sincerely thought it was in everyone's best interests," he stutters. "Y-you know you have a reputation, Lucius, you wouldn't have wanted a child. Evan was offering marriage, a stable home, a family environment with a bright future. What I did was out of concern for you, Helena! Cameron, you understand, after what he did with your girlfriend at Jen's wedding, surely?"

"Though it also served you, did it not? After all, what would your friends and business colleagues think about your daughter being knocked up by a Hastings? You see, Helena, when I left for a few weeks during that summer you stayed with us, I was privy to a case that led to the conviction of a number of your father's inner circle. Fraud, very sloppily done too. Do you remember?"

"I remember," I whisper. I remember everything about that summer, right down to the smell of Lucius' cologne, the brand of tea Owen drank, even the pattern of the crystal glasses in which Lucius had poured our drinks.

"Your father never mentioned it, no doubt because of Jen, but Paul caused a lot of ripples amongst your father's peers. And I was just as tainted and probably always will be. Having a grandchild associated with my name would not have gone down at all well at the country club. He couldn't risk such a scandal, could he? No, best sacrifice his daughter's entire happiness instead."

"N-no, that's not…" my father flusters, though when I look directly at him, he loses his argument. He'd like to believe what Lucius just said hadn't played a role in his decision-making, but I can see that it did, if only a little bit.

"You gave me and your granddaughter to a monster," I utter my thoughts out loud with the feeling of my heart breaking in the most brutal way possible. "You took my life from me! I will never forgive you for this…you are nothing to me!" I shout as angry tears stream down my face.

I'm so full of rage, I lunge toward him, hoping to hit him so I can cause at least a fraction of the pain he forced upon me, but Lucius holds me back, so I have no choice but to thrash against him instead.

"Shh," he comforts me as I finally break down inside his arms. "I won't let anyone come between us again, Topolina, it will finally be as it should have been - you, me, and our daughter."

"I-I can't…" I lose the ability to talk so I don't. I've said my piece, and I owe my father nothing. My fight has left me, and I can finally let someone else take the burden.

"This is what's going to happen," Lucius begins as he turns us to face my family, "I am going to take Helena home. We will discuss how to move forward with *our* lives, and *our* daughter. Tomorrow we will both come to collect Jess." He looks at Cam who simply nods, then points his finger at my father. "And as for you, you will have no fucking say in any of it ever again!"

"How could he do this to me? How could he do this to

us?" I whimper as he carries me from the room.

"Shh, my topolina," he says, holding me close, "I am here now, for always. I will never leave you again, I swear."

Chapter 33

Lily

As Lucius carries a hysterical Helena out the front door, I run into Cam's office to see what the hell is going on. For a moment, Cam, Nate, and his mother all stare at the floor while his father covers his face with both hands. His mother's shoulders are shuddering fiercely, and she eventually turns to sob inside of Nate's arms. Nate holds her close before turning to sneer at his father. Cam, however, looks ready to let out a fury I haven't seen since the night Evan attacked me.

"Get.The.Fuck.Out!" he growls at his father, sounding low and ready to burst.

"Cameron, you've got to understand-" his father tries to plead with him.

"I said get.The.Fuck.Out of my house!" Again, he sounds quiet and composed but then suddenly shouts, "NOW!"

"Cameron, please?" his father begs with more tears falling from his red-rimmed eyes. It's almost too much to watch.

When he refuses to go, Cam grabs hold of him by the shoulders, almost carrying him over to the door, all the while his mother cries and his father continues to beg. Instincts left over from childhood have me trying to follow, to try and diffuse the situation, but Nate holds me back with a touch of his hand on my arm. With great restraint, I heed his caution and instead, listen to Cam throwing his father out the front door. When the sound of wood slamming hits my ears, I rush into the hallway to try and calm my husband.

He stands, all six foot three of him, with a shuddering anger taking all over his body. I have had to calm this anger before, but only whenever he was around Evan, never the man whom he has admired above all others.

I walk tentatively over to him as though approaching a frightened animal before stepping into view. His eyes are screwed shut and he has tears running down his face. My poor little lost boy, a boy who idolized his father, is now breaking in front of me. I gently reach for his hand and pull him toward me, where he grips hold tightly and sobs onto my shoulder. I don't say anything, just hold him for as long as he needs me. Sometimes, words aren't needed when your family is falling apart.

*

Helena

I wake up feeling hollow, empty, and dehydrated, the perfect recipe for a killer migraine. I've cried a lot over the years but not as much as last night. Betrayal is an ugly word and it's sitting in my stomach, festering. I spent nearly ten years of my life living with a monster for nothing. I wouldn't expect anything less of Evan but being deceived by my father hurts beyond words. He even suggested I tell my daughter I didn't know the name of her father.

"Helena?" Lucius whispers from behind me, stroking my arm in soothing motions. "Talk to me." But I can't right now, I'm too lost. I don't even know if I've forgiven him for giving up on me, for thinking I could have betrayed him like that. "Are you still angry with me?"

He reaches his naked arm around to pull me against his chest. I don't fight it; I don't have the strength right now. I merely nod to answer his question.

"I'm angry with the world right now," I eventually whisper in a cracked voice.

"I told Lily you were my girlfriend last night," he says to me, "I'm hoping I'm right to call you that."

I almost laugh at Lucius for using the term 'girlfriend'; it seems too alien for him, too beneath him to have such a thing.

"So, the next time a giant bomb is dropped on me, you can turn on me again?" I reply bitterly. I am beyond bitter at the moment, it feels like it could quite easily consume me right now.

"I've kind of had a few bombs dropped on me too, Helena," he says sheepishly. "I just haven't handled them as well as you."

He begins to kiss my shoulder, still holding me tight as if he thinks I'm going to make a run for it. I haven't decided if I am yet.

"Jess," I eventually announce. "She is the most important thing to me right now, so that's where I'm going. You can come or not, I'm not going to force you, Lucius."

"Then I will come," he says with determination. "Everything is in your court right now. The way it should have always been."

We arrive at Cam and Lily's house about forty minutes later. My nerves are shot but I am trying to put on a brave face. I hope to God my father isn't here. Lord only knows what happened after I left last night. Lucius is wearing casual clothing, which are surprisingly, not all black. I think he's trying to look less intimidating, though I also know this is a nerve-racking experience for him too. I glance over to see his face betray his coolness, and for the first time this morning, I feel bad for him. Cam's words echo in my head, and I realize he is also a victim in all of this. Course, I'm not going to go into that now. There's an eleven-year-old girl in there who needs me more.

Cam opens the door before we even knock. His eyes are dark, and he looks pale. I'm guessing he didn't sleep too well last night. Well, that makes three of us. Before I say anything, he holds onto me, and we hug while Lucius stands uncomfortably to one side.

"I'm so sorry, Hels," Cam whispers, "I should have seen it, should have been there for you."

I smile but I know it doesn't reach my eyes, but hopefully, it tells him it's all ok between him and me.

"Dad's not here, is he?" I hear Lucius scoff in the background but feel panic begin to surface over the thought of having to face him this morning. All I want to do, all I *need* to do, is talk with my girl.

"No," he says, placing his hands inside of his pockets. "I made it clear he wasn't welcome here last night." I wince, thinking about all the mess that's been caused by my past. "Come in," he says, standing aside to let us through, "Jess is in the garden with Lily."

We follow him into the living room, where I can see my beautiful, brave girl sitting cross-legged in the yard with Lily. At least she's smiling with her.

"Did she sleep well?" I ask my brother, not able to take my eyes away from her for fear she'll disappear again.

"Better than the night before," Cam replies, "but I think she's missing you."

I nod while I continue to watch them chatting and laughing.

"Lucius?" I ask without taking my eyes away from Jess.

"Yes?" He walks over to join me, holding the small shoebox Jess had found in my bedroom.

"Do you mind if I...?"

"I think it would be best if you approach her first if that's what you're trying to ask," he says, putting his hand on the small of my back. "You say the word if and when you want me. Anyway, I have something to discuss with your brother." I instantly look around at him, frowning over his last sentence, but I can already tell he's not going to give me anything. "Business stuff, you know."

As predicted, I know he's lying, but I'm going to let it go. Instead, I take a deep breath and walk out into the backyard, armed with my box.

Lily sees me first and waves, which prompts Jess to turn around and look at me. I offer her a smile and she quirks her lips with a sheepish expression. I am filled with a little bit of hope.

"Morning, Hels," Lily says cheerfully, "we've been expecting you. I think Jess is missing her mom, aren't you, baby?" I could almost cry again when Jess nods. "I'm going to go and see how Cam's doing. I'll catch you ladies in a minute."

She pats my shoulder in support, then walks inside, leaving Jess and me alone to talk. I take a seat where Lily had just been and place the box on the grass between her and me.

"What's that?" Jess points to the box.

"Do you not remember finding it before you went to camp?" I ask at the same time as I take off the lid.

Once open, I reach inside to take out some old photographs of me in Spain. A lot of them are of Lucius and me, with my rebellious pink hair and boho clothing. We look young and stupid, but so happy in them. We're quite often looking at each other, making me wonder why I ever questioned our love for one another; it's right here in these pictures. Jess studies each one carefully, smiling at some of the more ridiculous poses.

"You look happy here, Mom," she observes, "I don't think I've ever seen you look this happy before." I nod in agreement with a smile. "Is this him? Is this my father?"

"Yes," I reply without hesitation. "Lucius Hastings is your father and he's here, over in the kitchen."

She glances up to try and see him, but the sun's reflection blocks our view of the inside.

"Uncle Cam explained about the DNA test and how you were lied to," she says, swallowing hard and with unshed tears waiting to fall at any moment. "I'm so sorry I called you a slut, Mom, I didn't mean it!" Her voice cracks and those tears finally begin to fall. "I can't believe you had to marry that...that..."

"Shh," I try to soothe her. "Don't even think about that anymore; I'm happy now, honestly. I have you and that's all that matters."

"And Lucius?" she asks. "You've been like Romeo and Juliet."

Her comparison has me laughing over how romantic she already is.

"Well, we'll see. I hope we don't share the same fate though."

"You better not!"

"So?" I pause. "Do you want to meet him properly? It's totally up to you, baby girl."

She nods with a confidence I'm not sure I've ever had.

"But I want my mom with me; you'll stay, won't you?"

"Sure," I reply, trying to sound casual, even though on the inside, my heart is swelling.

Lucius

"What can I do for you, Lucius?" Cameron comes right out and asks me.

"Actually, it's what I can do for you," I throw back at him while keeping my eyes on the girls in the backyard. "How would you feel if I told you I know where Evan is?"

For a moment or two, he says nothing, simply looks at me, and ponders on what I've just said. His shocked expression soon turns into a conflicted one, most likely because he already knows as to what I'm suggesting. Paul finally came back to me with some rather interesting and fortunate information on the guy who no longer has much time to live. Turns out he's pissed off a group of people you really don't want to piss off.

"What are you suggesting, Hastings?"

"You don't seriously think I am willing to let this all go, do you? He took my daughter, raped and beat your sister, not to mention what he did to your wife, and probably countless other women. Do you think a few years in prison is enough for that piece of shit?"

"I promised Lily, a long time ago, I would let it go," he says, but I can tell I've sparked his interest. "I won't do anything that will risk me being taken away from her."

"You needn't worry about that," I reply without pause. "If I can promise you that no risk will come to your family, would you be interested in a little...*retribution*?"

"And what about you, Lucius? Are you going to cause more heartbreak for my sister when they cart you away?"

He turns to face me, looking and sounding accusatory, knowing there is still an element of the devil-like persona that lurks within me. Not with Helena though, never will I risk losing her again.

"Oh, I have enough pull in this city to not let anything happen to me," I reply with a smile which he no doubt pictures smacking away, even after all this time. "No one's going to miss a piece of shit like Evan Stone. Besides, this isn't my first time delivering my own form of justice."

After a moment of confusion, he turns away and sighs.

"And what about my father? You gonna pull something on him too?"

There's a little fear in his voice, but I can also see he's battling his own anger and resentment toward the man.

"Don't think I haven't thought about it, especially when I looked at that forged document," I answer truthfully. "But no. I think that would well and truly destroy your sister and me. Plus, he *would* be noticeable if he went missing. More importantly, however, is the fact that he's screwed himself all on his own. I don't need to do anything to him. What you all decide to do about your father is firmly in your hands, not mine." He nods, seemingly placated with my answer. "So, what's it to be?"

"If you're talking about roughing him up, then I'm in, for sure," he says decidedly. "Anything beyond that, I'll leave to you. If Lily ever found out, it would destroy us, and I'm not prepared to risk losing her."

"I'll be in touch," I utter as I watch Helena get up from where she's been sitting with Jess.

Helena

When I stand up to go and get Lucius, I notice he and my brother in deep conversation about something, something shifty, but I decide to play ignorant. Right now, Jess is all I can think about, and I need to be the buffer between her and Lucius. He only needs to look at me to know it's time, so he nods at Cam, then walks over to grab hold of my hand. My diablo may look like coolness personified, but his sweaty palm tells me otherwise. I squeeze it tight and plant a kiss on his cheek, hoping to bring him some reassurance. He straightens, then confidently looks at me before jutting out his chin toward Jess. She remains sitting on the grass, perhaps because it's less intimidating than the table and chairs. Lucius takes a seat where I've just been, so I sit down behind her.

"Hey," he utters quietly.

"Hey," she says back, sounding a little quieter than she normally would. "So, you're my dad?"

She laughs nervously, but I'm impressed by her confidence. He laughs softly back but then shakes his head; my heart feels like it's stuck inside my throat the entire time.

"No, I'm your biology," he replies, "I haven't had a chance to earn the right to be called your dad." She looks away and I'm not sure if she's disappointed, confused, or just angry. "But I'm kind of hoping to get to know you more, see if I might one day be more than just DNA to you?"

She looks up and smiles a little, a smile that's a start, but also needs more convincing.

"Mom? Can you give us a minute?" she asks all of a sudden, shocking both of us. Lucius looks as if he's going to throw up and quickly glances at me, silently begging me to stay. However, I place my hands on Jess's shoulders, smile supportively, and nod my head.

"Sure, I'll just be inside," I murmur, then give him that old trademark smirk of his when I see his eyes bulging in abject fear over an eleven-year-old. What can I do though? I guess he's on his own.

Lucius

As I watch Helena walking away into her brother's house, I have to desperately fight the urge to bolt after her and beg her to come back with me. I'm one of the most intimidating figures in

LA and yet, here I am, shitting my pants over being left alone with an eleven-year-old girl, *my* eleven-year-old girl. Christ, that thought just can't sink into my head.

When I eventually brave it to look back at Jess, she's watching her mother too, but as soon as the door closes behind her, she snaps her head right back to me.

"You know, my last dad was pretty horrible to me and Mom," she says with a confidence that reminds me of her mother when we first met. "How do I know you won't be the same?"

"Besides the fact this is scary as hell for me right now?" She laughs over my honesty, so I decide honesty is the best way to go. She's smart like her mom, so there'll be no bullshitting her. "I'll level with you, Jess," *fuck, even uttering her name feels weird*, "I'm not known for being a warm and fuzzy kind of guy. In fact, in my everyday life, I often come off as an asshole."

Her eyes almost double in size over my use of the word 'asshole' and I immediately screw my eyes tightly shut for dropping profanity in front of her.

"Shit, sorry. Oh, damn it!"

I cover my face with both hands to try and stop myself from cursing in front of her every two seconds. Her infectious giggle, just like Helena's, eventually causes me to smile and laugh too.

"Don't worry, Lucius," she laughs, "Evan would have thrown me in my room by now, so I already like you better."

I throw my hands up in defeat and we laugh with each other. This girl's going to be the death of my steely reputation, both her and her mother.

"What I was trying to say is, with your mother, it's always been different. I can't promise you we won't piss each other off, but I would never hurt her like...like that other guy. And as for you?" I pause, taking a moment or two to study her face that screams Helena, but also with a part of me. "I don't know you yet, but if you are anything like her, we'll get along fine."

She blushes but smiles at the same time, and damn it if the sight doesn't melt something inside of me. Years after hearing my mother declare I was nothing but a monster who should have been aborted, here sits something that proves I was always meant to be here. I managed to make something pure and beautiful with the woman I was destined to be with.

"You know, now that I look at you, I can see you have the same eye color as my mother, your grandmother," I sigh, looking at her deep, ice-blue eyes. Helena and I have made one beautiful kid.

We talk for a little bit, keeping to neutral subjects like films and sports, friends at school, and such. Apparently, she's part of the 'geeky' group at school and makes no apologies for it. Some boy is sniffing around her, but I haven't yet earned the right to give her grief about that one, so I'll store it for later. It's not until Helena walks out that we realize we've been out here for nearly an hour. Helena looks like she's going to shed tears again, but thankfully, she manages to rein them in.

"So, how are my two favorite peeps getting on?" she asks casually, even though the smile on her face is beyond words.

"He swears a lot, Mom," Jess giggles, prompting Helena to drop her mouth open in feigned horror.

"You ratted me out? Christ!" I gasp, to which she giggles.

"I know, right?" Helena teases. "Doesn't mean you can, little miss."

"Why don't we head out for some lunch?" I suggest. "Cameron and Lily can come too if they want."

"Er… Lils is currently throwing up in the bathroom, so I'm gonna guess they won't be joining us," Helena explains. "Ready to go, Jess?"

She nods before getting to her feet. I follow, but when nobody's looking, I let out a long breath that must have been storing itself up during the entire conversation.

Shit, this is intense!

Chapter 34

Lucius

Almost six weeks pass by before I manage to put my plan for Evan into motion. The bastard has been sending new letters every week, always asking to see Jess and Helena, but I have kept up my cool, calm exterior for both their sakes. He even had his attorney write to Helena, demanding to have access to his daughter. I told her not to worry, that I would sort this one out, being that it falls into my line of work. Jess has made it clear that she would be happy to never see him again, so I decide to speak on behalf of both of them when I call Evan's attorney, a man I happen to know quite well.

My afternoon is quiet, so I decide to pay Abe McManus a face-to-face visit, for old times' sake, and for some old-fashioned theatrics. Given the situation, I feel it needs a personal touch. As I saunter into the high-rise building, I whip off my aviators and straighten my suit jacket, a custom-made effort that probably costs more than half the cars parked out front. The secretary eyes me up and down before placing on one of her professional fake smiles.

"Afternoon," I begin with enough charm to fill a stadium. I flash my teeth at the same time as placing my hands along the countertop, which gives her a good view of my Rolex.

"Good afternoon, Sir," she replies, batting her eyelashes and pushing a strand of hair behind her ear. "How can I help you?"

"I would like to see Abe McManus," I reply confidently and without room for argument.

"I'm afraid Mr McManus is not taking any calls right now," she says before leaning in closer. She places a hand beside her mouth before whispering, "He's not in a very good mood."

I pull back and pretend to look all kinds of concerned, and she giggles over my teasing.

"Oh, that's a real shame," I continue, shaking my head for added effect. "Tell you what, why don't you tell him that Lucius Hastings from PH Law is waiting for him downstairs. See if that cheers him up a bit."

We stare at one another for a moment, wondering who's going to back down first. Lucky for her, she picks up the phone and begins to dial up to the man himself.

"Hello, Sir?" She winces when the old guy begins shouting and cursing down the phone at her. I have to bite my lips together to stop myself from laughing; he really is a punchy old bastard. "Yes, but I have Lucius Hastings…yes, *the* Lucius Hastings…" She looks at me with a smile and I raise my brow, showing her that I'm impressed that she knows who I am. "You can go up, Mr Hastings." I smile in thanks as she gestures toward the elevators. "Top floor."

"Thank you, I know where he is."

I wink at her because she did just get an earful on my behalf. She blushes and looks away quickly, suddenly embarrassed by the attention.

As soon as I saunter into Abe's over-the-top old-fashioned office, he is up on his feet and marching over to shake my hand, all the while offering me any drink of my choosing. Being the gentleman that I am, I thank him, then sit in the chair opposite, all the while declining his grand offers. I can see the perspiration beginning to coat his forehead below his bald head and ridiculous comb-over.

Abe flusters with papers over his desk before finally coming to a standstill, then leans forward and links his fingers together, looking at me for an explanation as to why I'm here. I take my time to answer his questioning expression because I'm enjoying his performance a little too much. I also know that the most intimidating thing you can do to a person is remain silent for as long as possible. It makes what you say all the more powerful when you eventually decide to put them out of their misery. So, I wait for him to give in first.

"W-what can I do for you, Mr Hastings?" he finally asks and I smirk to myself, imagining Helena giving me a gentle slap for my deplorable behavior.

"Well, now," I begin calmly, "I was having breakfast with my daughter and her mother the other day-"

"You have a daughter?!" he gasps, looking and sounding quite stunned. I have to admit, it's still strange to call her that, but also good.

"Yes, information I have only just been made privy to." I

smile over the memory of Helena and I having that talk with her on the lawn outside Cameron's place. "Anyway, we were sharing a family moment, one of many, I hope, when low and behold, we receive a letter in the post from..." I pause as I feign confusion, then point at him, "...you."

The old man points to himself, looking deathly pale, most likely trying to think why on earth he would have sent a letter to my family.

"Are you sure? I mean...I don't..." He trails off, scratches his head, and pulls such an expression that even I feel like I owe him a little more information.

"Does the name *Evan Stone* mean anything to you?"

"Ah, yes. He's trying to get access to his daughter," he begins to explain but when he sees my pointed expression, he realizes that 'Evan's daughter' must be the same daughter to whom I was referring. Knowing he understands what I'm saying, I throw down the DNA results Jess had received about a month ago, followed by another set that we had done to prove that I am, indeed, her father. Not that I doubted Helena for a moment, but we all agreed it was for the best, if only to put her mind at rest. After all, she had been duped for years because of a set of fake DNA results. He picks them up, looking at me for permission before he does so.

"Oh," he flusters, switching his attention between the letter me. "I see."

"I would appreciate it if you desist sending Helena such threatening letters, seeing as my daughter would rather cut off her own arm than see your filthy client again."

"Of course, my sincerest apologies, Lucius," he says, so I

nod with thanks.

"Do me a favor," I say as I make to stand, "keep this information to yourself. Tell Evan you no longer want to represent him, but please do not mention my name."

"Of course," he replies with an over-the-top smile, then hurries to show me out of his office.

Lucius

With a smile of self-satisfaction, I tick Abe off my list and head straight for the second name on it, Anthony Parisi. He owns one of the fancier clubs in town, which doubles up as a place of business for less than legal activities, including drugs, gambling, and women. One of his guys searches me before I'm allowed inside his office, even though I know Parisi both personally and professionally.

"Lucius," Parisi says as he saunters over and kisses me on each cheek before offering me the chair next to him. It's a squeaky, white leather affair, without enough support for anyone larger than an eight-year-old child. Perhaps that's the intention; to make you feel and look ridiculous in it.

"Uncle," I utter. Anthony is my mother's older brother. We only really got together properly when I turned eighteen. Paul was not keen on me seeing the family business until I was an adult, by which point, my future had already been mapped out for me.

"To what do I owe the pleasure, nephew?" I'm offered a drink of top-shelf brandy and a bikini-clad body to hold onto. I dismiss the latter for there is only one warm body I want to feel and it's because of her that I'm here.

"I believe you and I have a common enemy; one we might be able to help each other with. A nuisance as it were."

I take a mouthful of brandy and marvel at the warm, nostalgic taste that instantly fills my mouth.

"I see," he says, looking interested. He begins scratching at his unshaven chin; the rough stubble makes a noise that has me wanting to shave it all off. "Who would that be, Lucius? I have many enemies."

"Evan Stone," I reply without pause. I know he's rather small fry for someone like my uncle, but once I explain what the circumstances, I know he'll be more than happy to help me out.

He shrugs and makes a noise between his teeth, pretty much summing up how he feels about Evan and how unimportant he is to Anthony's business. So, before he can shoot me down, I tell him everything.

"Will you help me?"

"You have a daughter?" he asks with a combination of shock and glee spreading across his hard features. "Congratulations, nephew!" He gets up to embrace me, which I reciprocate, only because it gives me an excuse to get out of this ridiculous chair. "For you, anything!"

"Thank you, uncle." I hand him a small white card with an address, time, and date handwritten on one side. "This is where we will be. Helena's brother and I would like to have a little fun with Evan before you finish the job; you understand."

"Of course," he laughs as he studies the details on the card. "You gonna marry her?"

"Too much, uncle, too much." I redo the button on my jacket, readying myself to go before this gets all warm and fuzzy.

"Fair enough, Lucius," he laughs as he pats my back, "I do so love the asshole in you."

"Goodbye, uncle," I reply before kissing him on both cheeks and departing for my third point of call. A jewelers. Because of course I'm going to marry her.

Lucius

It's early evening when I pull up in front of the abandoned warehouse where I told Cameron to meet me. My guy did good with this place, it looks like something from a low-cost horror movie - small, dusty, abandoned, and with no one around for miles. If he's done what I asked him to do, our guy, Evan, will be tied to a chair and gagged with a filthy piece of rope. It's not original as such, but it's all the motherfucker deserves.

Twenty minutes after I arrive, a black SUV pulls up the desert road, spraying sand and shit everywhere. It's not exactly discreet, but seeing as we're secluded out here, it's not really an issue. I've had to stop myself from going in to see the fucker by myself, but from the glance I got between the wooden slats, there's definitely someone tied to a chair in there. I can't imagine it could be anyone else. His head is slumped forward, obviously still out cold.

The SUV eventually comes to a stop, and I see two sets of eyes through the windscreen.

"I don't remember asking you to bring a plus one," I growl

at Cameron, sounding beyond annoyed over his need to bring his little brother along to everything. "Can you not take a piss without him either?"

"Watch your mouth, Lucius," he snaps, sounding equally pissed with me. Like I give a shit. "You're sleeping with my sister, remember?" He earns himself a don't-fucking-start-with-me look for that one. "Listen, Nate has just as much of a right to show this asshole what he thinks of him, so let's just play nicely together shall we?"

I choose to ignore him and begin walking toward the warehouse, all the while listening to the two pricks walking up behind me.

On my way over, I grab a black bag from the trunk of my car, which contains a few little toys to make the experience more enjoyable. The Carter brothers give me a questioning look when they see it, but I merely gift them with a flick of my brow in return. Once inside, Cameron and Nathaniel move around in front of Evan, while I kneel behind him and grab a scruff of the asshole's hair, lifting his face for them to confirm we have the right guy. I've only seen his face in photographs from when he was much younger, so I'm glad they're here to make sure it's him. The alternative would have been most unfortunate.

I rummage around in the bag to find a bottle of water, then carry it over to where our guest is still unconscious. I unscrew the lid and pour the contents over his head. He begins to stir slowly at first, so I tip his head upward and pour the stuff over his nose. He coughs and splutters as he comes to. It takes him a moment to take in his situation, glaring around the warehouse before setting eyes on Cameron and Nathaniel in front of him. I've chosen to keep my presence secret for a bit longer, so remain behind him. I pull my penknife out of my back pocket and use it to cut the rope that is currently wrapped around his mouth. He spits onto the floor like the miscreant he is.

"Where the fuck am I?" he shouts like a common thug. "What the fuck are you trying to pull?"

Cameron smiles with self-satisfaction, realizing he has the asshole who attacked his wife right where he wants him. He walks over to my little bag of tricks, then looks at me as if to obtain permission. I nod, so he begins to look through it. When he finally pulls something out, I have to smile over his weapon of choice. It's a predictable option, but I can't say I blame him. He swings the long, wooden baseball bat around in his hands, swiping it from side to side like he's about to play at the World Series.

Evan, the sick fucking piece of shit, begins laughing hysterically, throwing back his head and taunting Cameron with his couldn't-give-a-flying-shit attitude. I kind of guessed the fucker would react in this way but from the look on Cameron's face, so did he. He smiles back at him, almost manically. He nods to me and tells me to untie the asshole. He was no doubt a strong guy before his body was abused by drink and whatever drugs he's been shoving into his system. Now, he's no match for any one of us here, but it's more fun to let him think he has a fair chance.

Cameron lets him have a free hit to the face, which he takes unashamedly, smashing the side of his jaw. The impact splits Cameron's lip but doesn't do any lasting damage. Cameron recovers quickly, then grabs hold of Evan's shoulder before gutting him in the stomach. Once he doubles over in pain, Cameron wastes no time in punching his jaw.

"Motherfucker," Evan spits out when his nose starts to bleed. "This won't change anything; I still fucked your girlfriend," he says while smiling sadistically in Nathaniel's direction. He then

THE DEVIL

returns his attention to his older brother and spits out some blood. "And I got a good feel of your wife, Carter. How does that brand look on her wrist? Does it remind her of me? Does she get wet the instant she looks at it?"

This time, Cameron uses the baseball bat to swing at his legs, taking him out so he lands on the floor beneath. I gotta give it to Evan, he's still laughing; the drugs and alcohol must have damaged all his nerve endings over the years because Cameron has done a pretty good job of beating the shit out of him.

"No one could get wet over a piece of shit like you," Cameron says before spitting in his face and beating him on the back with the bat. "If I'd been there, you would be dead already!"

He begins to hit him over and over again, losing control through hate and anger. It's not until Nathaniel steps in to hold him back that he finally pauses, though with the bat still clutched firmly within his hands.

"Cameron!" Nathaniel shouts as he tries to hold him back. "You have a pregnant wife at home, don't get put in jail for this stupid fucker."

"Pregnant?" Evan laughs. "You sure it's yours? I'd have that bastard DNA tested the moment it's born!"

As soon as the final word has left his mouth, Cameron kicks the asshole right in the area that will hurt most. I doubt he'd ever be able to conceive again, even if he was going to live past tonight. As he winces in agony, I decide it's my turn. The Carter boys have had their fun, but now it's my turn, before Parisi's guys come to end Evan once and for all.

"Enough," I utter as I come out from my little hiding place, so Evan can get a good look at me. "I hope you've enjoyed yourselves, boys, but it's time to leave."

Cameron and Nathaniel both look at me, frowning over my order to get the hell out of here.

"Who's this asshole?" Evan spits up more crimson saliva, but I don't make eye contact with him yet. They are still firmly fixed on Cameron and Nathaniel, silently telling them to get gone.

"What happens next isn't going to be pretty and while I have friends in high places, I cannot assure you of my ability to get you two off, so it's best you leave now and get your alibis straight."

I begin to roll up my sleeves, getting ready for the kind of justice I'm about to serve Evan.

"What the hell are you planning on doing to him?" Nathaniel asks. I don't give him anything specific, instead, I just look at him with an expression that confirms his suspicions.

"Is someone going to fucking answer me?" Evan shouts, and that's when I see it; the worry in his eyes, the fear that this is not going to end well for him. I've seen it before, in the eyes of my biological, raping father.

Both Cameron and Nathaniel nod and turn to leave, but not before they look at Evan like the piece of shit that he is. Cameron throws the bat at him, making him tense up once again from the impact of it against his stomach. I wait for them to drive away before I finally turn to face the motherfucker. His mind is working on overdrive to try and figure out who the hell I am. Meanwhile, I pick him up from the ground, not being the least bit careful with his injuries, and slam him back onto the chair. I tie him up tightly, then stand before him, smiling over the horrified look on his face.

"Good evening, Evan," I say formally, "we've not met

before, but I am sure you have heard of me. My name is Lucius Hastings."

For a moment, he looks confused, but then it dawns on him who I am. Apart from my relationship with Helena, he must have heard of me through my reputation as a lawyer and will no doubt know what a bastard I am. There's no forgiveness, no patience, and no emotion when it comes to me in the business world. He should now know he is completely fucked.

"Hey, man," he smiles manically, "I was fucked over just as much as you were by Helena."

"That's not exactly how I've heard it, but let's say for argument's sake, you were. It doesn't exactly make up for the fact that you took away my child from me, does it?"

"I think I did you a favor, she's just as much a pain in the ass as her mother," he says, grinning with what must be his last drop of courage.

"Wrong answer, Mr Stone," I reply calmly as I walk over to my bag to retrieve a small box. "You see, I don't want to kill you myself; I've promised that pleasure to some friends you've managed to upset. However, they aren't due to be here for another…" I make a theatrical gesture of checking my watch, "…half an hour or so. I figure I can have a little fun of my own until they arrive."

"And how the hell are you going to get away with it, asshole?" he grits through his clenched teeth.

"Well, for starters, I happen to have a few powerful clients; the Chief of Police being one of them." I glance at him to see the look of dread wash over his pasty face. "He owes me a favor, so he's agreed to be my alibi for tonight. We're currently cruising around on my personal yacht right now. Secondly, I have all sorts of interesting information on you and your dealings with a few unscrupulous figures around LA, so I know who you've been pissing off. Coincidentally, they're the guests we're waiting for, so I guess there's no need to suspect me in all this...*unpleasantness*. They have so many bodies mount up; I doubt they will question yours. Thirdly, this isn't my first time dealing with worthless cretins like you. Cowards who like to rape and beat women because their dicks are so small and flaccid, they have to pick on people who are more vulnerable than they are. So, I know what I'm doing and how to get away with it. Let's face it, Evan, who the hell is going to miss you?"

"What do you want?" he asks, sounding a little more contrite, and with his face turning a ghostly shade of pale.

"Haven't you been paying attention, Evan?" I smile my most wolfish grin. "I want to destroy you the way you destroyed Helena. I want to make you pay for every depraved crime you ever committed against her. And then? I want to make sure you never get to hurt anyone ever again. Do you understand?"

"Please, man!" He begins to cry while begging with ugly bubbles of spit exploding from his mouth and nose. "I'll do whatever you want, just let me go. Please, I didn't mean to...look, please..."

I begin to laugh as I open the small box that contains a collection of long, sharp needles. I lift one up in front of him, playing with it while enjoying his scared, albeit confused expression. When he opens his mouth to question what it is, I grab one of his fingers from behind his back and carefully insert the tip beneath the nail, pushing it in slowly while he screams and curses. Some people may be put off by this sort of violence and gore, but in my mind, I only think of him hurting Helena, and of taking my daughter away from me. As far as I'm concerned, Evan doesn't deserve anything less.

Anthony and a few of his men arrive a little under an hour later, by which point, Evan is a quivering wreck who has managed to piss himself, as well as making a snotty, bloody mess on the floor. Anthony saunters up beside me where he proceeds to laugh over the pathetic creature before him. Another man soon joins us, a tall motherfucker who looks like he's about ready to blow a fuse when he sees Evan on the ground.

"Lucius, Marcus; Marcus, Lucius," Anthony offers by way of introductions, flapping his hand about lazily with a lit cigar hanging between his fingers. I look at Marcus but his eyes remain firmly fixed on Evan.

"Hey, asshole," Anthony shouts down at Evan. As soon as Evan spies both Anthony and Marcus, he whimpers and begins crying for mercy all over again. Anthony laughs softly, tauntingly, before turning back to face me. He places his arm around my shoulders while seeing me to the door; this is my cue to go without actually being told to. As long as he deals with Evan for good, I'm happy to leave; I got my vengeance.

"Turns out, this dirty bastard slept with Marcus' daughter, then threw her out the hotel room before she could even finish dressing. I am a gentleman, so I'm going to let Marcus deal with him, for all of us."

I look at Marcus' furious expression, and instantly know the motherfucker is dead; no ifs or buts, the guy is done, finished.

"Fair enough."

I hold out my hand toward Anthony who takes it, then shakes just as I hear Evan screaming out in agony.

THE DEVIL

"Pleasure doing business with you, Anthony."

He removes his hand before delivering a shit-eating grin. I then turn and leave before things get really ugly.

Chapter 35

One year later

Lucius

"What?!" I snap at Nate, who is standing beside me while I battle with heart palpitations. Jesus, I've never been nervous like this; my hands are sweaty, and I can hear the thud, thud, thudding of my heart beating between my ears.

"Nothing," he smiles smugly, "just never thought I'd see the day Lucius Hastings being this nervous over…well, over anything!"

"You wait," I gasp as I try to breathe in and out slowly, "it won't be long until you're in this position and I'm going to revel in it!" The bastard just laughs even harder. "I mean, where the fuck are they anyway?"

As soon as I say those words, the music begins, and I hear everyone getting to their feet. It's finally happening and I'm a dripping mess. Maybe I'm not supposed to look but screw it, I have to see her; it's the only thing that will calm my damn nerves.

THE DEVIL

I walk to the top of the aisle where I turn to face her. Jess is out in front, looking beautiful in a navy floor-length dress. As soon as she sees me, she rolls her eyes over my need to go against formalities. When she eventually reaches me, she leans up on her tiptoes to kiss me on the cheek. The crowd gushes over the sight of my little girl giving her old man some affection.

"Gross!" she whispers. "You're all sweaty, Dad."

Jess calling me that still sends butterflies around my chest. It took a good eight months before she felt ready, so it's still fairly new for both of us.

When she moves to the side to stand opposite her youngest uncle, I look ahead to see Cameron leading Helena down the aisle in a simple ivory gown. She immediately takes my breath away. I am clearly doing a piss poor job of hiding my awe, seeing as she's now giggling into the top of her bouquet.

It seems to take an age for her to reach me, but when she does, I grab hold and wrap her up in my arms for as long as possible. The minister coughs rather loudly, but even then, I ignore him and cling to her all the more tightly. I don't hear the congregation laughing or Cameron tutting, I only hear her breathing softly against my ear.

"Lucius," she whispers, "can I finally marry you now?"

I release her and take her hand in mine before practically running up the remaining aisle so I can make that happen. At last, she really is all mine.

Helena

THE DEVIL

Being married for real hasn't really sunk in yet. This time around is obviously a very different affair to that of the first wedding I had. This one is full of happiness and love, whereas my first marriage was full of complete sadness, regret, and hopelessness. I vow to never make Jess feel like I did when I found out things had taken an abrupt turn in my life. I will be there for her no matter what. She will never have to think she has to do anything to please me, ever.

Evan's body was recovered from an old burned-down barn in the middle of nowhere. They told me it was most likely gang related; he had managed to piss off a lot of people in a well-known drug-ring. He had unpaid debts, and the state of his body was in keeping with others they had murdered in the past. I want to say that I felt bad, but I didn't, not even a little bit. He deserved what he got, and I promised myself to not think about him ever again. In the end, we both got the endings we deserved.

As for my father, he is slowly getting back into my mother's good graces, but I know they almost didn't make it. They also don't share a room any longer. Their relationship is none of my business, much like my relationships should never have been any of his.

I didn't want him to walk me down the aisle. He did it so proudly when I married Evan, I couldn't bear the thought of him repeating it, knowing that he did his best to keep Lucius and me apart. He also lost the right to do that when he lied to me and my daughter about who her true father is. We speak civilly now, but I don't think we will ever have the same relationship we once had; the same goes for him and his sons.

"Lucius, Helena?" a small voice says to us when we find five minutes away from the crowd of wedding guests. "May I have a moment of your time?"

Lucius looks at me for the answer, though his lips have grown into a tight, thin line. After a moment's thought, I gently take hold of his hand, then give my father a nod.

"I know I'm not exactly at the top of your list of favorite people," he says, prompting my new husband to scoff over the understatement of the century, "but I really did think I was doing the right thing for everyone at the time. It seems a ridiculous thing to think now, especially given everything we know." At my silence, he pauses, then looks to the ground while shuffling his feet about uncomfortably. "I have always loved you, Helena, you were such a quiet, thoughtful, little girl, and in my ignorance, I thought you still needed protecting, even if it was from yourself."

"There's no excuse for what you did, Dad," I finally say. "Even if Evan had been the best candidate for me at the time, even if I had been madly in love with him, you kept a man from knowing he had a child. Moreover, you lied to that child for years."

"I know and I owe Lucius a lot. I am so sorry for my arrogance, Lucius," he says, now facing my new husband. "It wasn't for me to judge you and to make that decision for Helena and Jess. I will never get involved again; I swear."

"You won't ever have the chance to," Lucius begins, sounding cold and unforgiving, but when he looks at me, he seems to relent a little. "But I appreciate the apology."

"Thank you," he utters.

"Dad, Jess was never told anything about your involvement in all of this; you are her grandfather. However, I don't know if I will ever see you as my father, not in the way I once did. This is going to take me some time, I'm sorry."

He nods his head sadly, before smiling and walking away. I feel horribly guilty, but it was the only answer I had for him.

"Was that really callous of me?" I ask Lucius quietly.

"No, just the truth." He kisses the top of my head before Cam and Lily come walking up to us, holding their new addition. Lily had a baby boy, Matthew, and looks thoroughly exhausted, but so happy. Cameron is positively gushing over his son.

"So, you guys going to give Jess a brother or a sister?" Lily asks rather bluntly.

Lucius and I look at each other, never having spoken about it. To be honest, I have already reconciled the fact that Jess will be my only baby.

"That is totally up to my new wife," Lucius smiles at me, "I'm happy with whatever she wants to do."

"Hmmm…well, I guess I'm happy with my life as it is at the moment," I say to him with a smile, which he mirrors. "We've only just found each other so bringing someone else into the mix is just a whole something else to tip the scales. But who knows?"

Right now, I don't need to have my whole life planned out for me like it once was. As long as I have Lucius and Jess, I'll always be happy.

Epilogue

Five years married

Lucius

"Jess?" I murmur over my newspaper. The girl is wearing a belt with a vest top and a pair of health hazards, or as she tries to convince me, shoes.

"Yes, Daddy?" she says with a batter of her eyelashes. 'Daddy' is a new one she tries to use when she knows I'm going to shit all over her plans to look like an easy date. I'm not sure what she's trying to achieve because calling me that immediately raises my suspicions.

"Turn around, change, and try again," I say without even looking up from my paper.

She stamps her foot, turns around, and wanders upstairs, all the while muttering obscenities under her breath. Helena walks in moments after, carrying her photography gear and a water bottle. She's huffing and puffing while trying to balance everything inside of her arms.

"You two arguing over her wardrobe again?" she asks as she heaves everything onto the kitchen table.

"Mmhmm," I reply, looking up at her for the first time. I smile seductively her way as she begins sorting through all her equipment. "I can't understand why she doesn't take a leaf out of her mother's book. I mean, look at you." I stand to slowly walk up to her before grabbing hold of her waist. "An old pair of jeans, a tank top, sneakers, and..." I pause to pick a leaf out of her hair. "Where the hell have you been?"

"Engagement photo set in the place they first met," she giggles. "So, basically, you're saying I look like a scruff?"

"A very sexy scruff!" I kiss her while wrapping my hands around her back, moving one down to squeeze her ass so she releases a pitched gasp. "When you have it, you don't need to flaunt it for everyone to see." I squeeze her again and she releases a moan from the back of her throat. My cock responds instantly, agreeing with me when I decide I need her here and now.

"Eww, gross!" Our daughter winces from behind us. "You guys are such hypocrites, moaning about my attire when you are dry-humping in the kitchen for everyone to see."

"I know, it sucks, doesn't it?" Helena teases.

I look Jess up and down and decide her change of outfit is more appropriate for daytime wear. A good thing too seeing as someone has just knocked on the front door.

"Is this the 'hot' date you were telling me about?" Helena asks nonchalantly.

Jess instantly looks at me as though anticipating my next move. A silent communication passes between us before she bolts for the door. Unfortunately, my massive frame blocks her at every turn, and when I reach for the handle to open the door, I find a tall, blond guy wearing a football sports jacket. The smile is wiped from his face when he sees me staring down at him, making me grin on the inside.

"Er...erm... hi, Mr Hastings," he flusters as he offers me his hand to shake, which I ignore for a moment before finally accepting it. Still wearing a frown, I retrieve my hand and look at him as if demanding him to give me more information. "I'm Mark, I'm here to pick up Jess...if that's ok with you, Sir?"

"Oh, come on, Mark, don't mind him," Jess grumbles at the same time as she barges past me. "We'll be back by curfew!"

"Wait!" I snap so loudly, they freeze and about turn. For a minute, I think Mark is going to piss his pants. "There will be no funny business, no tardiness, and definitely no third-base action."

I then slowly walk over to them, keeping my eyes focused on Mark's terrified ones.

"I've made people disappear; understand?"

He shakes his head, then nods, not knowing which answer to give before tripping over himself to get away. I smile rather wickedly at Jess at the same time as she scowls in my direction. She points at me with clenched teeth and narrowed eyes while I throw my hands up in surrender and silently laugh at her.

Before she can get away, I crook my finger at my beautiful daughter. Being a good girl, at the end of the day, she comes to me, and we throw our arms around one another. It's a tender moment that makes up for all the years of not seeing her grow up.

"No drinking games," I whisper into her ear, "it's how I got your mom pregnant."

It's not strictly true but I've made my point.

"Eww," she groans as she pulls back. "See you later, Dad."

A peck on the cheek and a waggle of her fingers later, she goes off to the movies with Mark, who is still trying to stop himself from soiling his pants.

"You know, I seem to remember someone taking my virginity when I was her age," Helena says when I close the door. "You *are* being a little bit of a hypocrite."

"Hey," I say, grabbing her hand, "I've never pretended to be anything other than the asshole that I am. Come on!"

"Where are we going?" she asks as I pull her up the staircase.

"You've reminded me," I declare before kissing her with animalistic urges, all tongue and aggression. "I've been meaning to re-enact that night for a while now."

Helena

As Lucius slides between my legs, kissing and nipping at my neck, I place my hands softly on his cheeks and make him look at me. *Really* look at me. He moves inside of me, and I gasp; I always do with him because I still can't believe we're here, together.

"I love this part," I whisper.

"Tell me why," he smirks; a smirk that now belongs to me because I married that trademark.

"Because it reminds me that my little diablo got his topolina," I tell him, then kiss his lips with a softness that tells him how much I love him.

THE DEVIL

"Mine?" he murmurs against my lips.

"Always!"

Let's connect!

Facebook Taylor K Scott | Facebook

Instagram: Taylor K Scott (@taylorkscott.author) • Instagram photos and videos

Website (including my blog) www.taylorkscottauthor.com

Author Dashboard | Goodreads

Sign up to my monthly newsletter through my author website or through the link below:

Taylor K Scott Author (list-manage.com)

Other works by Taylor K. Scott:

Learning Italian

A romantic, enemies to lovers, comedy

The Darkness Within

An enemies to lovers romantic suspense.

Claire's Lobster

An age-gap, romantic comedy novella

My Best Friend

A Friends-to-Lovers contemporary romance

Mayfield Trilogy

A dark, suspense romance.

A Marriage of His Convenience

A historical romance

Coming this year:

Willows and Waterlilies (The Gentleman)

Ellie's story from the 'Carter' series and in connection with the Wild Bloom's Series.

The Knight

Cameron's Story

Coming later this year:

The Devil

Helena's Story

A Marriage of His Choosing

Elsie's Story from my historical romance series (see A Marriage of His Convenience)

Stoking the Fire Series

Due to popular demand, I will be embarking on a spin-off series based on Callie (*The Knight* and *The Fool*) and her family, called 'Stoking the Fire'. Here is an excerpt from her book:

Callie

I hate to do this, ladies, but it must be said. We are living in a world of double standards, and I am here to call it out. From one woman who enjoys sex more than chocolate (yes, I said it), I feel it is a travesty that girls like me aren't celebrated for our sexual liberation. If I was a man, no one would bat an eyelid over the fact that I bed at least four different guys a month. As a woman, I am judged, questioned, even frowned upon. He's a hero, I am dirty and tainted by having a coochie that's invited many a dick inside of her. But I will tell you this, my vagina always delivers top notch hospitality, even when the guest doesn't deliver on his side of the bargain. She simply doesn't invite him back in for a second stay.

Do you know what's really sad? It's not just guys who take issue with my 'promiscuity'; mothers, sisters, friends, Mrs Purple Rince down the road, they all like to weigh in on my personal life:

Callie, why don't you settle down? So, it's ok to have lots of sex, so long as it's only with one guy. That's acceptable, folks.

What happened to that nice boy you were seeing the other month? He was boring, next!

Nothing happened to you, did it, Callie? You weren't abused in some way, were you? Besides being made to sit through 'Twilight', nope.

THE DEVIL

Case in point, right now, Daryl, a guy I met at our sister company, is trying to convince me to enter into a monogamous relationship with him. It's just my luck I would meet the one guy in advertising who wants more than casual sex. And before you say anything, I know I shouldn't have got involved with someone connected to where I work, but the guy is a rugby player…a rugby player from the UK! He tossed me round my room like a rubber ball. Good times.

"I can't stop thinking about you, Callie," he says, now looking more giant teddy bear than rugby God. "I think we should make a go of things, be a real couple."

"Daryl," I sigh, "I told you from the beginning that relationships aren't my bag."

"Yeah, but surely you didn't mean that. Especially after what we shared together."

"It's precisely what I meant. And as for what we shared together, I shared the same thing with two other guys last week." Poor Daryl looks like I just ran over his dog, so I take hold of his hand and give him my best sympathetic smile. "You are a great guy with a great bod; I bet there're tons of girls out there who would love to do the whole relationship thing with you."

"Baby, what happened in your past to make you so afraid of commitment?" he says while cupping my face with his meaty hand. Those calloused bad boys were orgasmic on my back, but not so crash hot on the old coochie lips. I swear, at one point, I saw smoke signals coming from down there.

"Nothing, absolutely nothing."

"Come on, Callie, you can be honest with me," he says with a whole heap of condescension behind his words, causing me to sigh again. "I'll spend our lives trying to undo all that has been done to you."

"You mean the multiple orgasms I've been gifted by all the great guys I've dated in the past? Yeah, no thanks, I'm good."

"What the fuck is wrong with you?" he says, suddenly changing tactics and looking aghast. Fortunately, I'm no stranger to this sort of reaction; it's akin to a little boy not getting his own way. "Are you seriously just that much of a slut?"

"Not the word I would use, D, but if you wanna use it, then yeah, I guess I am." I lift my glass up in a cheers gesture before sipping back the last mouthful or so. I feel a swift exit coming up, as well as begging my boss to not send me to our other office for a long, long time.

"I gave you everything, the best of me, and you want more dick?" he snarls.

"Daryl, we slept together…twice?" I wince, asking for clarification; it was two weeks ago.

"Four times, Callie!" he snaps, slamming his glass on the table.

"Sorry, four times then, but the point is, you're making out like we dated for months, years even. It was a few nights!"

"I can't believe what a bitch you are," he declares very loudly. I'd feel bad, I really would, but I was very clear from the outset what this was.

"If calling me a bitch makes you feel better, then you go ahead and call me that. I've been called worse."

He sits there, scowling at me while I continue smiling.

THE DEVIL

Sometimes, I wish I could give a shit, but I don't, I really don't. Not in high school, not through college, nor during my years of working for MK Marketing Solutions in the city. I just don't care what guys like Daryl think of me. What's worse is I am simply unable to hide this fact from him.

"Well, you're gonna have to quit," he says, flapping his hand up in the air like a petulant kid. "And seeing as I put my heart on the line and you stomped all over it, I think it should be you."

"Yeah, that's not going to happen, big D," I huff. "Or should I say, average D."

"Excuse me?" he gasps with a look of pure horror on his face. "I know the big boss; we play squash every now and then. Plus, he's a guy. He'll side with me over some whore who likes to spread her legs for every man she meets."

"Woah! And I'm the bitch?" I laugh. "Talk about getting your panties in a twist, D."

"Just being real, sweetheart," he says with a grimace and a weak attempt to be intimidating.

"How do you know I haven't spread my legs for the big boss?" I counter. I'm not going to lie; I'm starting to enjoy myself.

"Cos he's married! To a beautiful woman who knows her place and doesn't try to crush a man when he lays his heart on the line. She knows a good thing when she sees it."

"Christ," I mutter at the same time as shaking my head. "Daryl, we're entering the realms of ridiculousness here. We work in separate offices, we both had a few good nights, let's just leave it at that and move on like adults."

"No!" he says, thumping the table, prompting a few other patrons to turn this way.

"And I'm out," I declare as a I get to my feet, leaving a note behind to pay the bill with a healthy tip. "I wish you well in your future endeavors."

"Callie, get back here," he shouts as I begin walking away from the table. "I'm not done talking to you."

"Yeah, but I'm done talking to you, Daryl," I call back without turning.

"Expect to get fired, you lousy lay!" he yells across the entire bar, which is followed by a round of gasps from both the staff and customers.

I stop dead in my tracks, look to the ceiling as if trying to talk myself down, only to realize Daryl needs a good dose of some Callie reality. I turn around, walk back up to his smug looking face, pick up his wine glass and pour the contents all over his head. His mouth drops open in shock, which pleases me a little, but I'm not yet finished.

"Oh, Daryl, Daryl, plain old Daryl," I begin with a smile on my face, "you can call me a bitch, a slut, a whore, whatever, but you must never, ever, question my ability to bring a man to sheer ecstasy in the bedroom. Must I remind you of your own words?" I theatrically clear my throat before mocking his deep voice. *"Oh, Callie, baby, you're so good, so the best I've ever had... Oh, my, God, I'm sorry...I'm gonna... Oh..."* A few snickers sound off in the background while Daryl turns a deep shade of red. "And I timed it, Daryl, you lasted less than two minutes!"

"You're going to pay for this," he mutters through clenched teeth.

"Tut, tut, Daryl," I reply so everyone can hear. After all, did he not just do the same to me? "Take it like a man. Now, I'm going to leave, and I won't be turning around again. You can move on, or you can continue to sulk about it, but it's no longer my concern. I tried to be nice, but like a giant kid, you can't accept being told no. And saying no doesn't make me a bitch, Daryl, it simply makes me a woman who has the right to say so. Goodbye, Daryl."

I even lean down to kiss him on the cheek, feeling the heat emanating from the surface of his skin before I turn and walk away. I receive the odd cheer and clap, but as far as I'm concerned, the Daryl chapter is done.

Like I said, people, I'm here to call out the double standards.

―――

The trouble with hurt egos is they tend to hold a grudge and cause one to act rather rashly, or to put it bluntly, stupidly. Daryl was in possession of a very hurt ego, and it was causing him to question his masculinity; therefore, he felt I should be punished in the most humiliating way possible. Such a thing isn't an easy feat, and while he didn't achieve humiliation, he did set in motion a series of events that would lead to my downfall.

THE DEVIL

Printed in Great Britain
by Amazon